I0597835

Also by Robin Eddy:

The Mayfly
Only Children
A Kind of Heaven
Nothing Untoward
A Mating Dance
A Risk Too Far

The Diverging Lines
Lost in Nomansland
Mrs Klusak's Progress

A Dragon Roused

———

Robin Eddy

Tarnhelm Books (UK)

A Dragon Roused

first published by Tarnhelm Books (UK)

in June 2007

2nd edition September 2009
3rd edition May 2010
4th edition December 2016

ISBN 978-0-9565289-2-6

PROLOGUE

The ringing of the telephone started him up out of a half-slumber. Apart from the miserable blueness seeping through the tall windows from the garden, his huge study was dark and, at first, he was quite disorientated. He had been dreaming, but could not properly recall what it had been about: a vague figure walking along a shore, that was all.

He reached out, switched on the desk-lamp and let the cone of warm light combat the winter afternoon outside, and the strange uncertainty within him. This was normally his quiet time, when the work which he had allotted himself was done, when he could read, listen to music or write an occasional letter. And now his peace was rudely shattered.

He lifted the receiver.

'Is that Mr Roland Millan, please?' An English voice, young, male, hesitant.

'Yes, here.' He had almost lost the trick of using English on the phone.

'I don't know if you'll remember me. It's - ' The voice tailed off.

'Pardon? I didn't quite catch that.'

'Piers.'

The specialist had given him encouraging news last week. Heart, lungs, blood-pressure all in order. No cause for alarm if he had occasional palpitations. Put them down to stress.

No, he was not hearing things. 'Piers?'

'That's right. Piers Moriston. I used to sing at Wharnley Minster...'

Across the dried-up bed of five barren years, memories, both rich and disturbing, came flooding back. His mouth took over, filling gaps, leaving brain and feelings far behind. 'Oh yes, of course. Well, this *is* a surprise...'

'It was seeing you on that French arts programme just recently, which made me think of trying to contact you again,' said the youthful voice, so clear, so elbow-close, 'after all this time.'

His room was unexpectedly being invaded by shadows, so anonymous and wraithlike that one could hardly tell if they were friendly or not. He heard himself take a deep breath, poised to leap into a void. 'Where are you, now?'

'Studying at Cambridge.'

'Oh?' It was really unchivalrous of him to be so monosyllabic, when the boy was paying for the call.

'St Neville's. Doing French and German. I thought that might amuse you.'

'Of course, nice to hear from you. And well done about Cambridge.' Keep hitting the ball back. Make *him* the initiator of whatever it is he is trying to say.

Eagerness was replaced by a new urgency in the young man's voice now. 'Would it be possible for us to meet sometime? Do you come over to England at all?'

What to do? Stall? Refuse? I have taken great care to keep the past carefully sealed up, but how could he possibly realise that? He's knocked me off balance. 'Well, in fact, I shall be making a visit to London a little later on.' I'm amazed at myself for having invented a commitment, just like that.

'Any chance you might pop up to Cambridge, then? There's a good train service. We aren't allowed to leave the town, you see.'

There is such enthusiasm in his voice. What does he *want*, with me, after so long a time? You are trying to unlock a door, young man, and here I am, playing along with it. But caution kicks in. 'I'll have to check my diary to see exactly what I'm doing. It's not to hand at the moment. I can't call you back, I suppose?'

'Tricky. Tell you what: write to me c/o St Neville's College, Cambridge, and it'll find me. Then we could finalise the details.'

'All right.' He was sounding brisker now, wanting to find something warming to finish off the exchange, but still unable to.

'Bye, then.'

'Bye.' He put the receiver down, shaking his head and whistling softly. Could this Piers, who had now sought and found him, be the same boy whose voice had once been in the last stages of treble? But why, *why?* Finalise the details? Full of unease, he went down to the kitchen to make some coffee. Five years had been an eternity. Was this some Second Coming, then? His hands had begun to shake.

I.

By the time his taxi pulled up outside the college, the Spring rain had set in with a vengeance.

'You'll find the Porters' Lodge just inside the arch, sir.'

Behind the street-lights and their glittering reflections, the dark façades of old buildings made a forbidding gauntlet to be run. Here and there, though, a window was illuminated, making him wonder which might be Piers'.

He allowed the porter to show him through a series of dimly-lit quadrangles to staircase "R" and a heavy oak door bearing the title "Mr P.J. Moriston".

'Just give it a good thump, sir.'

He had broken a rule, gone past a point of no return, torn himself away from the security of his home in France. He was vulnerable, like a dragon roused from its slumber in a safe, dark place, and exposed now to the hostile glare of the sun... On the verge of panic, he tapped on the door, and, within seconds, it was flung open by a youth in jeans and a navy-blue roll-neck sweater: exactly how he was dressed when I once collected him and smuggled him out of Wharnley.

'Hullo, Roland.' A tension between them, as they shook hands. He is taller, of course, his face has evolved from sweet to handsome, and he has gelled his hair. But the grey eyes are just the same.

Piers wanted him to come in, take off his coat, sit down for tea and a chat, but the taxi was still waiting, to take him on to Trumpington. Somewhere outside in the wet, a miserable bell was ringing.

'Oh, but you'll need the keys. James - he's my tutor - was supposed to get Bursar to leave them at the Lodge.' They went down again, back along drenched paths, through the Screens and the front court. No, the porter didn't have the keys to Dr Scadder's flat, but he would ring around. Piers was unmistakeably annoyed, and Roland was beginning to weary of it all.

As if the porter saw his growing distress, he said, easily, 'I'll fetch in your luggage and keep it here, Mr Millan. If you don't mind staying in College till I can contact one of these gentlemen. We'll soon locate the keys, and then I'll get you another taxi. You don't need to keep this one waiting, with his clock ticking away.'

Roland gave him a five-pound note, and it was done. 'Resourceful men, college porters.'

'Deadly enemies, if you cross them!' said Piers in a stage whisper. 'Let's go back up and see about that tea.'

A makeshift welcome, but I am in no doubt that it is sincere. For the moment, it is the only comfort I can find in this place. Piers solemnly raises his mug, as if to toast his new guest. Outside, the tinny bell repeats its cynical comment. 'How was your journey?'

I give a silent nod. This breaking of English ice is painful, but to survive I play polite, verbal tennis, just as in those days when we first met. 'And how is life here?'

He pulls a face. 'You'll find that out. This place is very much bound up in itself, like a lost civilisation on a plateau, waiting to be discovered.'

'Are you in a choir?' What a silly, obvious question!

'Three, actually. I'm a counter-tenor now. The musical side's pretty good, but a lot of the rest of it gets up my nose. Still, you don't want to hear all that. We've so much to... By the way, James thinks you're doing art research.'

He was going to say *So much to catch up on.* 'Will that mean submersing myself in the Fitzwilliam or whatever?'

'Why not? When you meet my worthy beak, he'll probably quiz you a bit, you know, in typical fashion, without apparently asking questions. They're rather good at that. His speciality is Logic, you see.'

'Sounds as if I'm being lined up for some kind of oral exam!' An unspoken conspiracy is growing between us already.

Piers gives me an intent look. 'You must do exactly as you please. After all...'

One of those pauses fuller than words can ever be. His eyes are more focussed now, more penetrating. He has already told his tutor a fib about my purpose in being here. *But what do you see as my true purpose, Piers?* Is there any hope at all that we shall somehow pick up where we left off, on a different planet, all that time ago? If you start the trying-to-remember game, you'll find you are standing outside a cave which has been sealed up for too long.

A welcome knock on the oak. The porter had the keys at last. 'Now, do you know where the flat is, Mr Moriston? Will you be showing the gentleman out to Trumpington? I have another cab at the door.'

It was agreed that Piers would accompany Roland, but he insisted he would jog back, rain or no rain. 'Just a mo.' He went into the room next door and reappeared shortly after in a clinging grey cotton track-suit.

'You'll get soaked, in that.'

'I do it all the time. Good training! I've been on my bike to suss the place. From the outside, anyhow.'

The driver's bitter cigarette smoke blows back at us, and I am trapped here next to this oddly attired young man, agonised by the silence. Just as it was when we were in my car together at Wharnley, strings of orange lights guide us out of town. But this is different. There is none of the old, illicit excitement. I feel like an ambassador sent to a strange land.

The drive was mercifully short. Piers went on ahead with the keys, opened up the flat and switched lights on, drawing the curtains in the lounge. Roland paid the driver, and came in with his case and bag.

'There you are, the kitchen's through here...'

Modern. Not that I shall be in here much. Double bedroom. A note to say where the spare linen is. All the signs of an owner gone away, but still politely welcoming one who might lodge here in his absence. Piers bustles about, making the bed up, boiling a kettle for the hot water bottle, while I unpack my few things.

'By the way, I brought you this. Just a small memento from Geneva. So you need never be late for a lecture.' I give him the little packet, and watch his face. There was another occasion, long ago, when we exchanged gifts...

'Roland, it's fantastic! Gosh, it's got hands *and* digits.' He takes off his own watch and puts mine on. 'You really shouldn't...'

'Yes I should. You have very kindly allowed me to disrupt the serenity of your routine here.'

He throws back his head and laughs at this, but not unkindly. 'Serenity! That's good. I like that.'

Now comes another hiatus, requiring a polite formula. 'I mustn't hold you up, Piers. I expect you'll be dining at college?'

'Yup, better scoot off. But what about you?'

'I've brought some stuff to tide me over. Shan't stir out of doors again tonight. Thank you very much for seeing me in and so on. I'm sure I shall be comfortable here.'

'Fine. I... usually make a latish start on a Sunday.'

'Suppose I take you out for lunch?'

'Smashing.'

'Can you recommend somewhere?'

'There's a reasonable little place opposite Fitzbilly.'

'Could you book a table?'

'When for?'

'Say one o clock?'

'Right. If you come to my rooms any time after eleven, I'll show you round the place.' Piers padded away through the wet, turned under a street-lamp, waved and was gone.

Roland went back into the lounge, as if on another planet. He has altered, of course. Five years is a long time in an adolescent's life, long enough to change him from boy to man. Will we find a common language again, I wonder? Perhaps he's forgotten what we were to each other in those days, or has he immersed those things discreetly at the bottom of his psyche, just as I tried to do, and failed? Was he embarrassed by the watch? It was cuff-links last time, to celebrate his becoming a teenager.

So, what am I doing here, and how on earth did it come about? All I know is that he was the power behind it, he found me again. But why? Does he understand what the attraction was, for me, in those far-off days? Boys are so impermanent, the moment of delight for the observer is so quickly past. If only BOY were like a piece of chewing gum, which could be pulled out to infinity.

I can recall with amazing clarity that afternoon (just a few weeks ago), when a magic cord was pulled and the unaccustomed sound of the telephone cut across my dreaming. Piers... The miserable wintry blueness seeping in through the windows of my study was as if softened by that youthful voice, as it tried to fill in some pieces of the jigsaw, to help it make some sense. He naturally wouldn't have known what pains I had taken to disconnect almost all contact with the world that had robbed me of him.

Hard for me to face up to such an innocent-sounding suggestion, having been for so long like the dragon crouched in his lair, not dreaming that a hero could arrive and despatch me with his sword. A period locked up in ice, with all emotion leached out, all humour lost, all hope washed away in the waves that once licked up an English beach... But this unexpected development was enough to send me scurrying over to my special place on the lakeshore, to seek the calm of a steady and immutable world. I had always looked for solace near water. Anthy sur Léman: the lake was a sullen sheet, and, on that day, its brooding tranquillity was powerless to soothe the chaotic emotions working away inside me.

How strange, that it could all start up again, just like that, without time to prepare. A phone call, a young English voice, and there it all was: a glimpse of the old excitement and, with it, (as the realisation began to dawn), the old pain, a bursting of the soul's stitches, new raw blood to soak into the sere resignation of years, as though Judgment Day had arrived early and unannounced, after a long, long time in Purgatory. Piers had gone to the expense and trouble of finding me out and phoning up, but why? And who *was* this young man, anyway, who appeared so eager to renew the acquaintance with me? Acquaintance? Ye gods. Scars never heal, and acquaintances do not make scars.

He ran the bath before getting to bed. With the water swirling around his legs, he was put in mind of a moment, on the lakeshore, when the surface began to stir, as though some unseen hand were acting in sympathy, sweeping about beneath. In sympathy with what? After building barriers of caution, I could never let fragments of all that return again - the suspicion that I might have ruined him. A thought to make one tremble. But no - *I destroyed myself, not him.* That's the truth of it.

While I sat there, letting it all churn about within me, clouds came up from the direction of Mont Blanc: a flurry of flakes, as the short day went into decline. That was why the water had stirred. Piers... What else could I have done or said, but agree to come and visit you? A kind of sale-or-return arrangement, for I was in dread that all my hard-won resolve and resourcefulness might be swept away.

As I drove home through the darkness, with the snow thickening, cohorts of flakes darted at me, picked out by the headlights. The road had become a narrow blur between invisible hills, and I was already in a labyrinth, exactly what I had sought to avoid by living out here. My mind wrestled with all kinds of let-out. I needed time to hesitate, to change my mind, draw back into the cave. And yet - even as I reached home, a new and unaccustomed light was strengthening slowly within me, its luminosity holding the distant figure of a boy, now in quiescent repose, now galloping through shallows on horseback. Piers, like a bright bell-note. Piers, Piers, Piers - summoning, beckoning, gathering me in.

*

He sat in his room, unable to take anything in - too amazed by what he had set up. *Created* might be a better word for it. Just like that time when, as a senior chorister, he had passed his eye along the members of the congregation up in the canons' stalls opposite - and, one day, found Roland. From that moment, it had gelled.

Now, after losing touch, I've got him back. No, that's wrong: he seems as bemused as I am, as if we're two bodies recovering from concussion. We were lovers once, in several senses of the word, but now that cannot be, not any more. It was curiosity which made me go to him then and, though the whole thing has changed, it's still curiosity (about what we've both become) that has driven me to do this. The maddening thing is that, just as at Wharnley, I have no-one in the world to discuss it all with, except Roland himself, - but there the shutters are tightly closed. That is my paradox. If only he weren't so withdrawn, like a mental case cut off from the outside world.

How old will he be now? He was born in thirty-six, so he's forty, by God. His fair hair's thinning a little on top, but his face is still quite striking, with that expressive mouth. There are dark shadows round the eyes now, and more wrinkles. I guess he's been through some bad times recently. Is he ill? He used to get very emotional at times, and he once said he'd had some sort of a breakdown. On that TV programme, he was talking French like a native, but so unsmiling, so coldly correct. Only his eyes betrayed something profounder. And when we sat face to face in here, swigging tea and trying to keep the conversation going, that expression was back again, as if he needed help, like a man right out of his depth. *Was that the reason why I wanted to find him again?*

But all his strength seems to be sucked out, like a puppet that's lost its filling. Now that he's in Cambridge, does he hope that we might somehow..? If so, I shall put it to him that the physical side between us died that night at Wharnley, when I got out of his car for the last time and walked straight into the trap at school, realising only later that he'd *hoped* I'd get caught. For all his strangeness, I guess he's still the charismatic and yet vulnerable man I used to know - except that I couldn't have expressed it like that, then. I think I've grown up a bit, in between, but he seems to have gone into his shell in a bad way…

*

'The river's just down there. They hire out punts in season.' Piers pointed across the gardens glistening in the sun. He had dutifully conducted his visitor round the college, court by court, made him peer into the Hall from the Screens, and taken him up the spiral staircase to the library where, even on a Sunday morning, students sat at tables, working. Roland had been impressed by that, but, whenever another student came past, he pretended to study some archway or bush, praying that he would not be introduced. Returning through the gardens, they came across Piers' tutor, from whom there was no escape.

He pumped Roland's hand. 'Oliver James. Capital to see you, Mr Millan. Are you comfortably installed? Do forgive the mix-up over the key.'

So this slight, sandy-haired man is the perhaps unwitting accessory to our coming back together? I know that that phone call must have come from his rooms. *What confidences might he have heard about me?*

'Look, I insist on inviting you both up for sherry.'

He took them to his sitting-room, which was noticeably better furnished than Piers'. It had some hand-coloured prints of Cambridge on the walls and some very nice items of antique furniture. 'Do plonk yourselves down? Sweet or dry? I know you haven't long. A table booked for lunch, I believe? Well, *santé*. It's really very nice to meet you.' He had a twinkle in his eye that looked anything but menacing.

Roland found his voice. 'I must thank you - and Piers, of course - for having arranged such pleasant accommodation.'

'I'm sorry we couldn't put you up here at College, but it panned out well enough, with Scadder away, digging up the Sudan... Now, I'm mightily intrigued by what Piers has told me about your work, especially the stage-designing for operas - though I'm sure you'd rather talk about that when we have more time.'

James is so incredibly adept at small talk. Just hope he doesn't start his usual *spiel* on the potted history of St. Nev's, and its hopes for the next ten years, because it'll lead to an attempt to screw Roland for a benefaction - the Millan Scholarship.

His tutor caught his eye, stopped mid-flow, looked at his watch, wished them 'bon appétit', and escorted them out. 'Millan, I hope you will come and dine with me in Hall one evening - that is, if this man will kindly relinquish his guest for such a purpose.'

*

When they were ensconced at their table in the *bistro*, Piers leaned forward with some amusement in his expression. 'Well?'

'I beg your pardon?'

'What d'you think of James, then?'

Shades of the boy I once knew! Quite unable to match his bright-eyed eagerness, I toss back a neutral remark, hoping to mask how overawed I am by this place, how upstaged by Mr James, and how depressed by everything and everyone that isn't Piers. 'Visitor' may be my official title, but *whose* visitor? James looks set to take me on one side, which may make Piers resentful. He fortunately seems oblivious to my discomfiture, chattering, with a kind of brittle nervousness, about all manner of things. Despite their brilliance, they are surely quite unaware that I am a man just awakened from a long, deep slumber in the ice, shielded by darkness from the world and its unwelcome truths? In allowing myself to be plucked out, I reap the harvest of my folly. The classical heaviness of the Fitzwilliam casts its shadow across the street. In fact this town bears down on me like a coffin-lid. I spear a piece of chicken on my fork, as if incapable of doing the simplest thing in a normal way.

We sit over our wine like a couple of dummies. I would love to throw a string of coded questions at him, to see if he really is still the Piers I once knew and loved, but the defences are up, all around us. Polite English reserve... Desperate to lighten the atmosphere I get him to talk about how he'd managed to find me after all this time, and his face relaxes, even becomes animated and recognisable again

'We get foreign TV programmes relayed to the Languages Department, and I chanced to see that French arts programme where you were being interviewed. You once said you had a place out there, so I got on to International Inquiries, and they dug up your number. I have to admit I was very jittery about contacting you like that, out of the blue.'

Jittery, why? You don't have the monopoly of the jitters. I get them myself, all the time at present. I would like to congratulate you on finding me again, but couldn't do it without touching on the potentially alarming consequences.

Now he drops an unexpected one: when his father died, his mother moved him from his boarding school in Dorset to a state school in Guildford. There had been an unfortunate accident in Turkey. 'While they were cleaning up some grubby old frescoes, he fell from a scaffolding platform and fractured his skull. It meant we were suddenly not as well off…'

Said in a dispassionate kind of way. Did you ever talk to him about me, I wonder? I would have paid your school fees without blinking, if you'd still been part of my scene. But seals have been placed on certain things which so occupied both our lives five years ago, and there is a whole world which I do not think we shall ever share again, unless, maybe, you will reveal your true reason for wanting to recall me from your past.

He's working hard to keep the conversation flowing, bless him, and now he drops something akin to a shot across my bows. 'What's Geneva like, Roland?'

The new Piers sitting opposite me might be a comely young man with a delightful touch of naiveté, but his expression at this moment is just as when he peered out at me from behind the metal scroll-work of his stall, in those heady days before we exchanged mere looks for words. 'It's a rather dull Swiss town. My place is just over the border into France.'

'And did *you* call your house "Orphéon"?' His eyes are intently searching my face. 'There's a male voice choir at St. Julien, then?'

'Not that I know of.' He's fishing, I think.

'So "Orphéon" is a sort of memento of Wharnley?'

'You could put it like that.'

He escaped at last, with the lame excuse of being tired after yesterday's journey. It sounded ungrateful, but there was something like relief on Piers' face. A taxi conveyed him back to Trumpington, and bed, where he took a couple of the tablets his doctor had prescribed 'against the rigours of the English scene.' Perhaps that's the root of my dilemma: I am not at home over here, and never could be.

The cue to talk about Wharnley was never followed up. It would have led inevitably to reminiscing about what we were to each other at that time, and how we both felt when finally torn apart. I had a faint impression that he wanted to get on to the big things, but could not find the way in, any more than I could. He must have found me very unresponsive. As a boy, he had often taken the initiative. Now, as if to mock me, the images came rushing back: the gift shop in the square beneath the carved west front of the Minster, a boy in a blue blazer, a boy from the choir. So fresh, so young, a treasure beyond compare... and it marked the beginning of something marvellous but also very dangerous. A smile can devastate the beholder, can it not? How much of all that does he remember? How much has he, like me, tried to suppress?

Here, at his *alma mater*, we are so far on a tolerably safe footing. The pretence is that I'm over on some kind of research, but I'm sure his tutor isn't hoodwinked. I am keen to hear from Piers just where the land lies, but this means working out the right questions.

Recognising, in his frustration, that he had just come up against another of the many ingeniously constructed blank walls inside his mind, he fell asleep in his chair.

*

There was a pure note inside his head, like the unearthly singing of telephone wires in a wind. When did I last hear that? Am I about to have one of my funny heads? Now comes an image that was presumed lost, along with everything else: the sun blazing in through the great west window of the Minster, during that final evening - a moment near the end of the *Symphony of Psalms*, when Piers' treble detached itself for a second from the others, sweet, pure, haunting, a signal to me that he too was living in the anguish of our enforced separation. "I shan't forget you. I'll come and find you again." And, caught in the great bars of coloured light, I fled sobbing from the building.

Looking at his watch, and surprised to find that it was well into the afternoon, he was taken by a rare and urgent need to witness his musing translated into reality. He had once leapt into his car and rushed the twenty-odd miles from his cottage to the Minster, just to see and hear Piers in action. A spring, which he had long since considered to have dried up, seemed to be miraculously flowing again. He lifted Dr Scadder's phone and dialled for a taxi.

Seated beneath the flamboyant Gothic roof of the Chapel, it comes home to me how much I have missed all this, for isn't it as close to paradise as one might get to be, on earth? My life is full of things that were never meant to happen. One warm afternoon, when the Minster stood on its hill like a great ship of stone, I casually entered its cool interior, quite ignorant of what was to follow, even allowing myself to be placed in a canon's stall above the choir. And the place accepted me, the alien, as if aware that I would become an actor on its stage.

Now the Evensong is replayed: the boys come filing in, then the men and priests - a theatrical ballet *à la* Wharnley. During the responses I play the old game of taking a long and searching look at the front row opposite, disappointed to find that not one of these sanitised and asexual choristers, (however pure his voice, however sweet his face might be) comes anywhere near the young Piers in promise. I once panned amongst the silt and found the grain of gold. No mere mortal could ever hope for a repetition of that.

In my frenzy (for that is exactly how it was), I would loiter in aisle or cloister as they were marched to and from the school, my increasingly bold efforts being finally rewarded on that special day when he managed to absent himself from the others after the service, and came alone. Smooth brown hair falling to just above the eyes, milky skin, a picture of innocence. I wrestled with myself and, as always, lost. In the narrow passage he almost brushed me, a light from the east windows of the chapel fell across his features - pale, like a cherub's. He looked up, and our eyes met.

We never talked about our early beginnings at Wharnley: there was no need, where actions spoke instead. Now, when it's a case of recommencing the ancient business of feeling the way forward, I am sorely tempted to abandon caution, and ask Piers how much he can recollect. But to quiz him about how he had *felt*, during those tentative but crucial gambits, (not to speak of the glorious times that followed) - that would be a daring one, resurrected from the lockers of my mind. Besides, I acknowledge that his new *persona* awes me somewhat.

Young boys are supposed to have only a primitive range of emotions, and so I must have assumed that he too would lack the delicacy necessary to convey the thrill he must be feeling - that is, if it was anything like my own. But then, in the narrow passage between the

Minster church and the cloisters, he suddenly said it all quite naturally, with that devastating smile which wiped out, at a stroke, all my previous resolve to terminate the dangerous conversation of eyes we'd been playing at in church. Tadzio reincarnated...

We're treading on eggshells now, Piers, perhaps even more than in those early days when our words were clumsy, but so rich in coded meaning. You're still here, and so am I, and for that, at least, one must be grateful.

The choir was singing a psalm, and his attention was caught by the third verse: *"My tears have been my meat day and night."* How well that summed up the past few years...

Some prayers, a hymn, and it was over, the choir and clergy making their mechanical departure to a Bach voluntary from the organ loft, followed by the sparse congregation.

Then, as if his thoughts had been realised in some magic way, a face from the past was offered to him, one which he knew but could not give a name to. Walking out among the rest of the congregation was a young man, fair-haired and with arresting eyes. A student, to be sure, and here to listen critically to the music, for, as he threw his beautiful head round to catch the last notes of the postlude, his lip had a superior curl to it.

They emerged from beneath the organ screen, and the young man stopped. He was displaying a very familiar public school tie.

'Pardon me,' said Roland, drawing level, 'but you must allow me the small liberty of saluting a fellow Old Sallowburnian.'

The blond-headed youth turned his dark eyes on him, and the expression was sardonic. '*Grace*,' he said, ' dismissed that thing in G as, quote "early Weimar", unquote, and a load of tosh, yet it gets played in here.' The voice was deep, but with more than a hint of effeminate nuance.

Pieces of jigsaw began to fit together in Roland's brain. 'I think we either met before, or I saw you somewhere. My name is Millan.'

The youth put out a limp, moist hand. 'Keith Fillingham. It'd be Wharnley, I expect. Yes? In fact I do remember you. You used to come to services, didn't you, and - '

They stepped out into the Great Court with its neat lawns in the grey light of evening, and the earlier picture was revived: Keith Fillingham had been Piers' opposite number in the choir. A splinter of memory drove into the soft yielding underbelly of his consciousness, leaving a painful little wound: Piers had warned him off, told him that the boy known as Filly was not nice to know, was jealous of him, even.

He stood there in indecision and, because the youth made no move to go, apologised. 'I'm staying out at Trumpington, so I don't really have the chance to invite you for a coffee - and an Old Sallowburnian chat.'

Seeing the dark eyes open up at the word 'coffee', he had judged it wise to repeat the public school connection.

'Oh well, look, there's a rather ducky tea-room just over the road. We could go there, if you've the time, Mr Millan. And the inclination, of course.' The word 'inclination' was given just the suggestion of emphasis, which did not go unremarked.

On the special afternoon in question, I approached your young colleague with the formula, 'Is an admirer of the choir allowed to invite one of its senior boys out to tea?' Now, the boot is firmly on the other foot. I seem fated to take tea with delightful young men.

Despite my efforts to fight it off, our past history comes pouring back with a clarity that shocks me to the core, so long has it remained hidden in the dark. Early summer: in the square to the west of Wharnley Minster, among the swarming tourists, I had espied a couple of boys in the uniform of the Choir School, set free for a short while after Evensong, staring in at the gift-shop window. I could not hear their voices above the bustle all around. In anticipation, I closed my eyes. A cool breeze began to blow about me and, when I opened them again, a cloud had come across the sun and the square was in gloom; no other people nearby, just a solitary boy, who all too obviously had adopted my habit of loitering - and I understood that he had engineered the other boy away for my benefit. If the boy Piers was sufficiently knowing to place himself outside the gift-shop, ensuring that we would meet, then the young man that he has become must have good reason for engineering us together again this time. *Why? I must know!*

'Mr Millan!' I jerk back to reality, to find Fillingham gripping me by the elbow, on the pavement in King's Parade. 'Are you all right?'

'Yes, of course, sorry. Miles away as usual, I'm afraid.'

Within moments, I am steered into a tea-room and over to a small table in a corner. The waitress brings a pot of tea and a plate of chocolate digestive biscuits. 'D'you eat these things? Some people reckon they're fattening. There used to be fig rolls with our choir drink on Sundays. Did you like Wharnley?'

This quickfire stuff takes me aback. Piers, at the tea-table, was always more self-effacing and ready to listen. 'The town itself was rather nondescript...'

'But the Minster?' the charming youth asks, his mouth full of biscuit. 'Was it the architecture that took your fancy, then?'

Took my fancy? Ah, so he devined that I wasn't there just out of polite interest. I notice that, with the light from the lamp above in his hair, he reminds me so strongly of a ravishing boy in a fresco by Raphael. 'Aspects of it, yes.' I only arrived here yesterday, and ever since people have been peppering me with questions. Those beguiling eyes are on me, humorous, searching for reactions.

'Talking of which, I assume that you're up here to see Piers Moriston, right? Thought so. Have you seen him yet, then? And his tutor man - whatsisname - Johns?'

'James. Yes, I have.' I need not tell him that I am here by invitation.

'And now me, eh? You can call me Keith, by the way. I don't mind at all. How long are you up for?'

Ascanius, that was the lad's name - the young son of Aeneas. And they were fleeing from burning Troy. 'Just till Wednesday. Do you get to see Piers at all?'

'Very rarely, these days. Though I did go to a recital he gave at St Nev's, a couple of months ago. You really should hear his new voice!'

I intend to! 'Do you keep the musical side going?' I am really out of my depth here.

'Not singing any more, but I help out on our Chapel organ. I occasionally pop in to Evensong at Kingies, in case I might meet someone interesting.'

Is he flattering me? No, I'm sure he means someone who might find *him* interesting.

'What are you studying here?' Get on to safe ground!

'European History, actually. For my sins I'm supposed to be doing a thing on Cathérine de Médicis, François Premier and all that poisonous crew, - which will probably mean visiting the Loire valley, if I can get round to it.'

'What made you choose a school in the far north?'

'They put me down for Oundle, but I made a mess of my Common Entrance Maths, and Sallowburn was my second choice.'

The young man's frankness is rather disarming, when it isn't verging on the outrageous. 'Did you enjoy it?'

He pulls a face. 'Awful climate, wasn't it? The only place I know of where every sport got rained *on,* but sadly never got rained *off.*'

'Were you sporty, then?' I am beginning to find this young man much easier to talk to than Piers. Is it because he has about him a dangerous fascination mixed with a touch of menace?

'Not Pygmalion likely. Didn't have any time for those beefy hunks with no brain, who only got in because they were good ball men!'

Perhaps, in his mind, he sees himself on a higher plane - among the sensitive, artistic ones. I too have trodden that path and been punished for it. 'Going back to Wharnley Minster, I was there really to hear the music. The standard of the singing was pretty high, wasn't it? And is that where you learnt to play the organ?' Oh God, he'll take that as a *double-entendre.*

The blonde boy looks at me with a trace of amusement. 'The singing came and went a bit. A choir's always changing, and it takes a long time to train the little sprogs. Yes, I started learning organ with Hutters - he was the Deputy - but he was silly enough to get caught *trousers down* with one of the kids. You... used to hang around in the cloisters, didn't you? On the lookout for Piers.'

How does he know all this? Was I so blatant about it? And now he is virtually bracketing me with that seedy little man, whom I last saw in the tea-shop. I always suspected that Dr Hutley, having espied me together with Piers, shopped us to the school. How the hell do I explain to this young man that there was nothing furtive or degrading between Piers and me? No-one else in the world would ever understand that it was possible for it to be beautiful, and touch our souls.

'How did I know it was about him?' he goes on implacably, as if reading my thoughts. 'Oh, not that he told me - he never spoke to anyone about *personal* matters. No, after the Whit half-term hol, when we all arrived back, I saw him get out of your car with his bag. You've got a Merc, haven't you? Foreign?'

Christ, this young man is too canny by half.

'Sorry if I've blown your cover!' (His tone suggests that he isn't in the least sorry.) 'But don't worry, old Wharnleians stick together, just like Old Sallowburnians.'

All this gives me the fidgets. If I don't get out now, I shall end up in deep trouble. I begin to get up.

'Oh, but you can't go yet, Mr Millan. I mean, there's so much you haven't told me, such as whether or not you enjoyed some favours with him then, and whether you're here for some more! After all, he was hardly very *ready* in those days, was he?'

Even in my distress, I recognise that his face and posture are saying, quite unmistakeably: 'It's different now, and, if you're so inclined, *I'm* more than ready to show you what a fresh and potent young lad of eighteen has to offer in *that* department!'

I play the coward, lamely insist that I must be getting along, and offer to see to the bill. 'Oh, and... should you meet Piers, I'd be grateful if you didn't mention we'd had this talk.'

There was a tinge of scorn in the boy's expression now, but, allowing his voice to drop into a very camp timbre, he suggested they meet again. 'There are one or two other things…'

He escaped, as it were, with his life, got a cab back to Trumpington and spent a frantic evening going over it all. There were topics he now very much needed to talk about with Piers, but he had no idea where to start. Or would it be better to cut his losses and depart first thing tomorrow?

*

He awoke with his heart thumping, fiddled with his radio, and found the familiarity of a French waveband. It's no good - I just can't fit into this alien land and I'm too wayward to be right for him. The dragon had emerged but was already poised to take a wrong turning.

'*Il est quatre heures.*' God, that's 3 a.m. here. Although the French voice failed to soothe him, a comforting idea was already forming in his mind: a return invitation, *that* might have possibilities. For the moment, there was still business left undone here, for Piers and him. A formula was needed for staking out the ground between them, and re-establishing their parts in the drama. But how could the circle be squared, now that a dangerously attractive blonde youth had shown up, who looked poised to assume the mantle of blackmailer?

He managed to find a bus which deposited him much too early on the edge of Parker's Piece, where he was enchanted by the universal sight of small boys doing sport, the sun gilding their bare legs, a fitting prelude to the Greek and Roman statues which he and Piers would soon be viewing. From a window in his mansion, he could look out across his wooded park and glimpse them playing, in summertime, down in the *stade*: youngsters in brilliantly coloured nylon shorts, dots of energy, life, young beauty - other people's children. What were they to him?

We were never parent and child at Wharnley. *We got to know each other closely, without witnesses.* It was love, for *possession* of a boy would have been all wrong. Love was all right. But the world is incapable of making such a fine distinction. We thought we had as our sole ally a God of love, light and life, not a vindictive or punitive being. Yet, at the end of six blissful weeks, Nemesis cornered us.

This triggers another Proustian moment of recall: the cool cloister, where, one day, I was surprised by the sudden irruption from the Chapter House of a flock of boys in white singlets and shorts, each carrying a chair to be placed out on the field for their sports event - flitting white forms, echoing voices, bare pink arms and legs. And, when *he* arrived (we had not yet officially met), he looked straight at me, yet did not stare. In his eyes, though, there was an intensity, a sweet knowingness that went far beyond his years. Moments later, while I perched on an ancient stone coffin, the parallel hit me like a dart: Aschenbach and Tadzio... Except that, later on, Piers and I walked together much further than they did, down the forbidden path... *Yet still he wants me...*

Needing one of his tablets, he dropped into a coffee bar, sat in the window and, over a cracked mug set down on a chipped formica table, dreamed of another café, far away, with a view of the familiar quays, the immaculate white boats moored up in the frost. Geneva could be amazingly quiet without tourists, and conference delegates were rarely seen down there.

That brief phone call, just a few weeks ago, but seeming like centuries, had knocked him sideways, turned the key in a lock which was supposed to be rusted up. Piers. He'd practically forgotten the name, had consigned it with everything else to a dark, disused time-plane deep inside, during those pointless years in which he had struggled to efface self and become a virtual hermit. Shutting himself away in "Orphéon" had only increased the sense of vulnerability, the hyper-consciousness of every little pain, both physical and spiritual. He'd been in and out of clinics, attended by a costly succession of specialists, probing his body and trying in vain to dissect his mind. The only telling thing which his present man, Le Gaillard, had said to him on the subject was: 'You display the symptoms of one desperate to father a child.' That, at least, had brought a smile from him.

For five years, the only contacts, apart from his part-time housekeeper, had been the unavoidable business and fashion contacts, operatic directors, musicians, magazine editors - people to take coffee with, but that was all. Noting his dislike of mixing with other people, they viewed him with the suspicion one accords an outsider. But he knew his worth as a designer, as did the opera house managements who were so keen to hire him, and for his part he ignored the palace gossip behind his back, and got on with the job.

If I have a *confidant* at all, he is a very unsatisfactory one, and I amaze myself that I ever let him cross my threshold. Perhaps Guy Bannerot calls on me to flatter my vanity, or seeks to flatter himself by cultivating me. How much have I ever let out to him? I suppose he admires my work, without ever saying it in so many words, - while I go to his concerts, just to lose myself in the music.

I tried to perfect the art of living in a cocoon, nursing my wounds and eschewing personal happiness which, for me, was always bound to go hand-in-hand with personal pain. There came the point when one could stand the pain no longer, but, if I tried to explain this, would anyone understand? Would Piers? If I now suggest he comes to Geneva, he may not want to, and the little episode will be over before it has begun.

A bus rumbled noisily past, making him start. A group of undergrads came into the coffee bar, talking in that loud, rapid patter which all young people affected these days. Am I becoming such an old man, that my remoter memories break in on me with such clarity? Why am I here? Is it a sign of weakness to put everything in the hands of Fate, to open one's hands metaphorically and await what each morning brings?

When he reached the Fitzwilliam, Piers was already hanging about on the steps. His face is bright, flushed and still bearing a touch of the old innocence, unlike his young contemporary up the road, in whom the iron has already entered the soul. As we go in, he kicks off by asking me where I studied Art, for we both know we are playing a game today.

'The Slade, then Paris. Rather long ago, you see.' In my nervousness, I cannot help evoking the age-gap thing.

'But what did you actually do?'

In his eagerness, he puts me on a level with himself, just as it always was. 'Well, the Slade taught me how to draw, but it was Paris that really showed me how to paint. I tried to put some boring letters after my name.'

'I'm trying to get a few boring letters after mine, too.'

'By the way, when are you going to let me hear this famous new voice of yours? I gather you gave a recital - '

'How did you hear about that?'

The sharp tone betrays that he's keeping tabs on me here - which shows he still cares... 'I must have seen an announcement somewhere.'

As we stand before the Pashley sarcophagus, my eye instinctively follows the contour of the buttocks of the stone man walking behind the stone elephant, and of the child sitting up on his shoulders. Does he see it that way, too? Surely not.

'I don't think I'd better start singing to you in here. How about grabbing a sandwich at the Mill after this lot? Then we could go back to St Nev's. There's a practice room on the next staircase to mine. Do you play the piano?'

'I must say sight-reading never was my strong point.'

They spent some more time viewing the exhibits, - 'just so that you can truthfully tell James you've started your "research" in here' - but there was a new fire in Roland's breast which refused to be quelled. The consciousness of what he was doing in this city had begun to filter through like fingers of light penetrating a dense mist. He was finding erotic symbols everywhere, as though the academic side was but a thin crust through which one could fall at any moment, to find oneself in a delectable hell peopled by satyrs. His period of abstinence had not, after all, purged him of his old malady. Piers might be his reason for having come here, but the boy Fillingham was carefree and quite evidently available. Taking tea with him was a very different matter from sharing a table with Piers, because any number of sinister undertones came up.

As they ate sandwiches and drank beer, in a pub crowded with undergraduates, he was afraid that Fillingham might turn up and see them together. Or do I secretly wish it, so that I might play off the one against the other? I risk resembling the besotted Aschenbach, loitering in the disease-ridden streets of La Serenissima and hoping (ever more desperately as the clock ticked on) for what he hardly dared to desire.

Piers' choice of music was very Italian, very ornamented, and rather fiendish. Roland got through it on the piano as best he could, but his ear was all for the new vocal register. He usually could not abide counter-tenors, but, even in a rehearsal room setting, this one was intriguing: a creamy-rich timbre, which stopped just short of sounding feminine.

'I know male alto isn't everyone's *tasse de thé*,' said Piers, when they paused, 'but I want you to be frank about how it sounds to you.'

'Can't claim to be a *connoisseur*, but your voice is very smooth and sweet. There's nothing forced nor metallic about it.' I detect a quality that could move and thrill the listener.

He grins. 'You make it sound like a wine.'

'You'll always be in demand with an instrument like that.' Can these small details add up, Piers? Could each day bring us closer, to melt a little more of the polar cap? Do I really deserve that? 'When your voice broke, did you have to give up singing?'

'For a bit. But there was a very good music man in Guildford who knew an ex-opera singer in London and arranged for me to see him. And Denis (that's my coach) tried me out in various registers and decided I had a pure falsetto. He made me do all sorts of exercises and things, then he gradually began to train me. I use the odd fee I get to pay for lessons. He's been ever so good, and sometimes doesn't charge anything.'

'That treble voice is gone for ever, then?' A stupid remark, but he'll understand what I mean. Male development, a new body and fresh desires.

'I'm afraid it's preserved for posterity on a ghastly cassette - one of the songs of the Auvergne.'

'Wouldn't mind hearing it. Are you aiming to be a future Alfred Deller?'

'Something like that, but there isn't too much work around for free-lance counter-tenors. They're mostly in choirs.'

He's in a madrigal choir here, which must include women. I'm intrigued to know whether he has a girl friend yet. Perhaps he'll tell me, later on. If he introduces me to her, I'll pack my bags and be gone!

After they had done some more music-making and returned to his rooms, Piers put the kettle on. 'It seems ages since we spent time together like this. You haven't changed at all, really...'

I know exactly what you mean: I am odder, insecure, so terribly defenceless. If this is a bait, I shall not rise to it.

Over tea, he allows me two treats: while the cassette-player produces a boy's pure treble, singing *Bailero* to piano accompani-ment, he gives me a photo of himself, taken at a school dress rehearsal: Piers as Ariel, clad only in the briefest of loin-cloths, his arm raised, his face full of anticipation, ready to dash off round the earth. The light caught him at an angle, moulded his naked torso, made his thighs three-dimensional. I am both fascinated and shocked. This is not the boy I knew before, but something developed, wilder, a creature with its own identity, to be admired only at a distance. My heart pounding, I look up to catch a flicker of amusement in his eyes.

'You can keep it.' (I was going to add 'for your collection,' but I don't know if you've still got those other photos you took, when you had me to stay at the cottage. Does "Orphéon" have its lumber-room of memories, too?)

'How old were you here?'

'About fifteen. Tell you what, I'll inscribe it for you.' He found a biro, wrote on the back and passed it over.

He's written "For Roland, with love from Piers". My hand has begun to shake.

'It *is* all right to put that? I mean, people just do, nowadays.' Oh God, I've flummoxed him, given him false hopes. We share a mutual embarrassment, as if both of us have overstepped the mark.

Now I am all too conscious of two things that cannot be reconciled: his questioning look, and the rendezvous with Keith Fillingham planned for tomorrow. 'It's fine, Piers.' I wish I could find the courage to ask him, straight out, why he has called me back again, like a spirit from the deep, but I dare not. It's early days, yet. When you were twelve, I had to learn the art of treading slowly and gently…

Piers was looking at his watch. 'By the way, aren't you supposed to be dining at High Table tonight? D'you want to hang around here till then?'

'No, I must go back to get changed. Thanks, all the same.'

'Just think of me down there with all the other plebs. I hope they serve you something better than the pigswill we get. And best of luck with my tutor!'

*

Duly washed and changed, he presented himself at Mr James's door. Cambridge, unlike the Arabs, kept strict time.

'Hullo, Millan, good to see you. Dry, wasn't it?' He poured a glass of sherry, and handed it over. 'Did you see young Moriston today? I'm quite anxious to have a word with you about him, if you have no objection? Do have a seat.'

I am suddenly on my guard, not having expected the attack so soon.

'One can't always be *au fait* with the plans of one's *protégés*, but it wouldn't surprise me if he were to read music next year. He could still keep one of his languages going.'

Safe stuff so far! 'He *is* very musical.'

'You've heard him sing, hm?'

Ah, here it comes... 'Some time ago, when he was a treble at Wharnley.' This man's perceptiveness is legendary, but even if he got wind of our session in the practice room, at least the secret is safe of the cassette and photo which I bore away like trophies.

'I see. Just a wee lad.'

Rather big for his age, but I shall not say that.

'Did you have connections with the choir, then? Sing yourself?'

'No, I just went along to services.' I can see very well where this is heading, but I'm damned if I'll gloss it over.

'Would that have given one the opportunity to hear him sing solo?'

'Only occasionally, in public. He sang sometimes when we were together.' James studies my face in silence, and now I am sweating. 'You see, I had a cottage, over on the coast, and he came to stay, one Whitsun.' Put so baldly, it sounds tame and hazardous at once.

'Oh, to make house music?'

'That sort of thing.' (What a lie, as you must very well know!)

'And so you kept in touch, over the years?'

'Not exactly. In fact, we went our separate ways.'

'But now your paths cross once more.'

'Yes, you might say that Piers found me again.'

'You know, do you, that he lost his father a few years ago? Sad business. I get the impression that it hit him more than he's prepared to admit. He's trying to find himself - not unusual, at this age.'

'As far as I can judge, he seems well adjusted, despite... I mean, he isn't a child any more.' I once told Piers as much, when he was twelve, going on thirteen. He never was a child, with me...

'Ah, he's talked to you, has he? About the big things? Pardon me, Millan, if I sound rather earnest. The welfare of my charges means a good deal to me.'

'We have always been able to talk.' Until now... The walking-on-eggshells game. Of course we talked about the big things, in those precious days.

But his eyes are on me again. 'He sometimes throws up barriers, don't you think?'

'I suppose that goes with the age.' For the umpteenth time since I arrived, I am out of my depth.

'They can be so reticent about themselves,' he says, with a sigh, 'but then so full of youth's idealism, as yet untempered by the wisdom of the wider view.'

The only response to such a display of donnishness is to take a swig from one's glass. He clearly isn't done, yet. 'Look, Millan, I can't be his guardian. I've a dozen others as well. I do what I can, of course, but I'm just another beak to him. You and he have a rather special affinity, hm? He seems to have taken a shine to you. Of course, you live abroad, but I should be so grateful if you could sort of *godfather* him for a while. Please forgive this inelegant presumption on my part.'

Now I feel like a man granted a precious bequest. At last, someone who understands! Stupid of me, to have been in such awe of the place, when it is evidently a welcoming powerhouse inhabited by people who genuinely and intelligently care about others.

They went down to the Senior Combination Room. He was glad he had put on a dark suit, for James immediately began introducing him to some of his gowned colleagues.

Mercifully, the bell for Hall was already ringing, and they all trooped in to High Table. The undergraduates were lined up at their long tables, Grace was spoken in Latin, and everyone sat down, beneath the watchful eyes of the portraits.

'I sense that young Moriston was miffed when I purloined you tonight,' said James.

If you think you have 'purloined' me from Piers' company, you just don't know the half of it. How can I sit down among this august collection of dons, when I shall be seeing his former fellow chorister before I depart?

Some waiters began to serve the meal, and conversation became fragmented, as the gathering fell upon the food and wine. The students were too numerous and dimly lit for Roland to be able to single out Piers. A strange feeling was coming over him, that something was about to happen, but he had no idea what it might be.

'What's new, then, out there in Switzerland, Mr Millan?' The Master himself, but two chairs away.

'There is never anything new in Switzerland, Master.' Something is wrong with me. I never crack jokes.

'Then it must be like Cambridge, but with mountains!' cackled another voice, from somewhere, causing a ripple of amusement.

Ignoring this, the Master began to preach about the pros and cons of political and economic neutrality, which fortunately exempted anyone else from needing to speak until the main course arrived.

'Sorry about that!' murmured James, on Roland's left. 'We seem to have struck one of the less stimulating nights.'

A Fine Arts man, opposite, managed to buttonhole the new guest. Had he seen the Fitzwilliam yet? Was he an artist, himself?

Sensing a modest reluctance to answer, James weighed in. 'Much more than that. He designs operas. He did *Death in Venice* for Geneva - is that not so, Mr Millan?'

He shrugged. 'That was a while ago, now.'

'Is this your first time in Cambridge?' asked another. 'What kind of an impression does it make on the outsider, if I may be permitted to place you in that category?'

This was too much. The impressions were already far too many and varied to be paraded here. Were these academics plotting together to seek out his Achilles' heel? Later on, he tried to ascribe what happened next partly to the effect of the alcohol reacting with his medicine: moving purposefully from the main part of the Hall towards the High Table was an androgynous figure in shirt and crumpled jeans. As it stepped on to the dais, however, the light caught the face, the eyes, of his ex-wife. There was a roaring in his ears, voices were suddenly distant, and then he passed out.

When he came to himself, two waiters were hovering.

'Are you unwell?' James had taken his arm.

'I'm sorry. Excuse me, Master.' He found himself being propelled towards the door.

James sat him down in the empty Combination Room. 'Now don't worry. Its our strange *milieu*, perhaps. Do you wish me to get a doctor?'

But he shook his head, loosened his tie, undid a button. His mind, like a snowstorm in a glass globe, was slowly settling again. *Fiona*, dressed like a youth? Good God!

A few minutes later, he insisted upon going outside into the street, with an ever-solicitous James still at his side. Then Piers arrived. 'What is it, Roland? What's the matter?'

He passed it off as a silly attack of claustrophobia which affected him now and again, thanked James for his hospitality and declared his resolution to walk back to Trumpington.

James looked at Piers. 'Are you sure?'

'It's all right. I'll go with him.'

'Good man.'

The air was cool, the streets dark and empty. He felt better at once.

'What exactly happened? Did you faint?'

I cannot divulge to him that a ghost came walking in from my past, a *female*, served up from some dark corner of my psyche, though I once told him about my short-term wife. How could I expect to cope, at my age, in this undergrad world? At Wharnley I was thirty-five and he turning thirteen, and yet it didn't seem to matter then. It was a union of souls, crossing all the barriers. Now, it threatens to turn to ashes for us. 'Bless you, anyway, for coming back with me.'

During our walk, he seizes the initiative. 'Tomorrow's your last day, Roland. Where would you like to go?'

He really will be glad to get shot of me now! I shrug. 'What would you suggest?'

'I was wondering about Ely. It's not far by train. One of those *vaut le détour* places. Cathedral, and all that. James doesn't mind if I leave town when I'm showing you around.' Hope my embarrass-ment didn't show, just now. Christ, all the other men were agog when I got up from the table and rushed out. He needs taking in hand a bit.

Ah, so it's a *fait accompli* then, a conspiracy to whisk me away from this town, where we're likely to be recognised together. Keith – oh my God…

'Are you sure you're OK?' asked Piers, at the door of the flat.

I would like to invite him in for a nice long sober talk, but I do not think he would want that. 'Thanks, Piers. Don't worry about me.' How would Fillingham have handled that one?

*

Back in his rooms, Piers flopped down in his chair, trying to remember if Roland ever had a do like that at Wharnley. He was always a bit peculiar in things he said or did - but *this!* What will James think? What will he say to me about my unruly guest? Maybe it was a mistake, putting all that time and effort into contacting Roland. It would have been kinder to leave him alone out there with his memories.

Face to face, he's all screwed up, inward-looking, and no longer the warm, close man he was, a few years back. Come to think of it, he looked so sad on that TV programme. Now, when we're together, there's hunger in his eyes. I once thought I knew so much about him. There were all those things in the lumber room at the cottage, from his past - before I came on the scene. Photos of his parents, his ex-wife... Strange, how we discovered each other, like two magnets coming together. He always made me feel much older than I really was. But the one thing that hasn't changed at all is the twenty-two years between us. Perhaps it seems smaller, as you get older.

His devotion to me verged on obsession, he came to every service, sitting in the same canon's stall and always looking across at me. He wore a suit that wasn't quite English: there was a foreign air about what he said and did, as if he was living to a completely different code of ethics. With him, I could see horizons opening up. It wasn't one-sided, because I was smitten too.

My problem now is that there's no-one else I can share him with, nobody here who would understand. And at home I could let out only a bit of it. I was going to tell Father everything - we had begun to get that close - but it wasn't to be. And a woman just wouldn't understand at all.

*

He sat over breakfast in unusual gloom, unsure whether this was caused by Millan's collapse yesterday, his own colleagues' catty remarks afterwards, or his concern about his student. Perhaps a combination of the three.

One did not need to apply logic to this case. The very flavour of the Millan-Moriston thing was overpowering. Whatever happened in the past, they seemed to be on good enough terms now. But, oh God, he had sent Piers back with him to Trumpington and Scadder's flat last night. Might Millan's sudden infirmity be nothing more than an elaborate piece of trickery, to get them together out there?

Should he approach Millan, Moriston, or both? He could write one of his cheery little notes to the former, or even ring him up in his French home, for there were still some things he felt he needed to know and say. Or buttonhole the boy (not so easy - he could be quite prickly if he chose), and do a bit of in-depth work, to find out if Millan was an appropriate companion for an undergrad, and a sensitive one at that. Surely one did not have to take up references on everybody in this day and age?

*

A tap at the front door; he put on his dressing-gown and opened it.

'Hope I didn't wake you, Roland. Just cycling this way, anyhow. I have to drop an essay into the beak before nine, or I'm for it. Thought I'd look in to see if you're...' Piers face was shining with perspiration, his hair tousled. The same figure-hugging track-suit.

'Come on in. Have you breakfasted yet?' His heart had leapt when he saw who it was, but plummeted when he recalled his stupid fit in Hall.

'No, I was just going back for some.'

Roland made them some filter coffee and toast. He felt dirty and unshaven, but immensely glad to see Piers. 'I'm so sorry about that unfortunate incident last night.'

'Think nothing of it. Hope I haven't been tiring you out.'

'No, I'm all right now. What's your essay about, then?'

He produced some tightly-folded sheets from the pocket on the front of his tracksuit top.   'Just some rubbish about Molière.'

Out of courtesy, he put down his cup and took the proffered manuscript. The handwriting has matured, of course, since that boyish scrawl which once said *"I am grateful to you for our friendship, despite everything, and I will come and see you again some time."*   He *has* come back – that's no illusion.

'Tartuffe,' Piers was saying. 'We were supposed to write something sticking up for him. Well, how can anyone defend that hypocrite? Singing hymns one minute and having it off with Madame the next.'

Roland looked at him, but it was meant harmlessly. He pretended to read a page or two. 'What time did you finish it?'

'About three!'

'And here you are at just gone eight?'

'I can survive. So are you still game for Ely?'

It is on the tip of my tongue to be frank with you, as we once were, aeons ago before the ice-age set in. I should admit my qualms about returning to an English cathedral city so soon, and with you of all people. I should confess that I have met your former chorister colleague, that *our* special relationship is known to this third person, and that he has invited me to his college for drinks this evening. Everything seems stacked against me, I fear I may cause an ugly situation which would lose you to me for ever, and destroy me yet again.

But there's something akin to apprehension in his eyes. Perhaps he's worked out that I've spoken to Keith. There's an unnervingly efficient grape-vine in this place.

'Roland, since you arrived here, I've been thinking quite a lot about… well… then and now, and - '

'And what?' Even in my relief I jump down his throat, because at last it looks as if he's going right to the very heart of the matter which I'm so anxious to discuss.

'It just can't be the same for us any more, that's all.' Studying my face, he is quick to add, 'I mean. We can still be good friends, can't we?' So, there it is. He has set out his stall, gone on the defensive, pointed out that we're different now. I came here hoping, and he's disappointed me. Friends… As if a heavy lid has just dropped down on my head. The ball is in my court now, but I cannot find the right words. 'Yes, of course, Piers, if that is how you see it.' I have just suffered a rejection as cruel as any could be. He does not want me any more, *in that way,* and it must be showing in my face. *There are two little questions which still remain unanswered: why did you seek me out again, and what am I in Cambridge for?*

'Let me try to explain a bit.'

'Don't bother.' You have said enough. It's as bad as if you had a girl in tow.

'No, give me a chance. I've recently been taking a fresh look at myself. As far as I can judge - because most men don't discuss it anyway - life's about being mostly either hetero or nothing at all, not yet anyway. That's why I'm grateful to you, for - '

Ah, is this to be the great revelation?

' - for once telling me I ought to get married later on.'

This is a clumsy attempt on your part to externalise what was once between us. Like the politician toeing the party line, you have also acquired skills in repressing ideas, suppressing, erasing them, to order. For you, the glittering mountain (so bright again now in my mind in its every detail) has dwindled down to a mere pimple in the landscape. The flame that has begun to flare up again, deep inside me, may have lost its lustre for you. Other things have moved up and blotted out the view. And yet you have called me back. Surely that says something? It isn't mere curiosity on your part (morbid or otherwise), or some mercenary motive? I have good reason to know your warmth, your unspoilt nature. Like me, you find the Cambridge atmosphere austere, even a touch brutish. In some ways, you have become harder, but I'd guess that all this is just a façade, part of your need to survive, here.

Do you really *believe* the defensive statement you have just been making? You used the expression 'mostly hetero'. That speaks volumes for me. I doubt very much if there is a girl in your life, nor that there will be, however much you go on about marriage. My role takes on some definition, Piers. I have to test you out, just as you seem to want to test me, to measure the strength of our ancient love for each other. I cannot believe that that love ever guttered out, deep down, however much pain it may have given us both. Otherwise you would not have come in search of me, like the boy Siegfried. And I still keep that ring, as proof of what we once were to each other. The testing will happen not here, in this very short space of time, but at "Orphéon", where you shall come and stay for as long as you like and, in the process, I will help you to find your true self.

*

As we settle down in the train, I wonder how the conversation will go, given that the most important area for me has been savagely blocked off.

'Didn't you once tell me you went to boarding school somewhere up north, Roland?'

One avoids the more painful episodes of one's past life, and that includes the beginnings of one's sexuality. 'Yes. Sallowburn.' Is he asking because he knows that Keith Fillingham went there too?

'How was it?'

'Like a white Zulu enclave, if you can imagine such a thing. Full of aggressive little men, and so on.' And the occasional attractive one. I had quite a reputation for godly looks, myself...

'We'd like to see all public schools and prep schools abolished.'

'Sorry, who would?'

Piers looks at me, shaking his head. 'You don't go along with Socialism, then?'

'Oh, I see..'. This is a new side to him. Of course students get themselves politically engaged, but I'm too much of a foreigner now, to be able to judge these things. It comes of not having properly lived over here for some years. 'I don't really keep up with politics. Hardly ever read an English paper. So why do you want to get rid of private schools?'

'They only reproduce themselves, don't they? Look at the sort of person they turn out. Cambridge is awash with public school drunks who are only there because Daddy went too.'

'But these persons have to run the country, Piers. Who else would you get to do that?'

'Bloody hell, Roland, they'd all be in the State system, as I was. It didn't do me any harm. I still got *here*, didn't I?'

'You must forgive me if my ideas are out of tune. I don't really want to sound prejudiced.' By now, he will be thinking we've hit an all-time doctrinaire low, and the rest of the way to Ely promises to be an entertaining *exposé* of his political beliefs and aspirations for Britain.

But no - he is weighing into his mother now. 'I don't think she even wants to understand me. She loves me, in her way, but we're poles apart, really. She looks after me as best she can in the material sense, of course. She's not rich, but she's very snobbish, true Blue to the roots of her hair. When I got my place here, it was the greatest event in her whole life, but we really don't have anything to be snobbish about.'

Ely cathedral, when they first caught sight of it, thrust its towers into a pure blue sky. Walking in from the station, they found a café and ordered coffee.

'By the way, Roland, how did you get on with James? Did he subject you to the third degree?'

'Not exactly. As you said, he was more subtle.'

'Did I come into it?'

'He said you might be going to do music next year.' I make it sound as casual as I can, but it's obviously a *faux pas*: Piers doesn't like being talked about behind his back.

'Don't know where he got that from. And what else did the two of you discuss, *à sujet de moi*?'

The way he spits out the last phrase, I daren't mention what was said about godfathering. 'He raised the subject of Wharnley. Wanted to know how we'd met. I stonewalled as best I could.'

'Ah,' said Piers, colouring, 'that's a topic I've never aired with anyone else, least of all him. Best left under the wraps, as far as others are concerned, don't you think?'

This spiky tone of his is new to me. Whatever my role is to be, it isn't adviser, any more than it's father or uncle. As we wander into the cathedral, all manner of spirits are astir inside me.

'Not quite as impressive as Wharnley,' said Piers.

Feeling both triumphant and expectant of what lay ahead, we used to drive out across open country to the cottage, leaving the dark towers of the Minster behind. It was on that holy occasion, soon after we had properly met, when we went to a spot on the river bank and you made the first move - that very special kiss - , that I realised you were no ordinary boy of nearly thirteen. If there was any fault, it was not all mine.

The choir stalls bring me up short, for here the similarity is so unexpected. Dropping one of the misericord seats, I sit down above a carved owl, though I do not possess wisdom. As if taking that as a cue, Piers strides, with all his old dignity and assurance, into the middle of the Choir, bows to the high altar and takes up his position in the front row of the stalls, exactly where he used to stand at Wharnley. Turning round with a self-conscious smile, he says 'Remember?'

Oh yes, the memory came back with a suddenness that knocked him off balance. From his high position in the cavernous Choir of the Minster, he gazed across at the boy in his black cloak, a white ruff at his neck. The place was alive with people, priests in rich vestments, and superb singing from the men and boys. Even before the anthem was quite finished, he stood up, descended the steps to the stone pavement and crossed it. A priest began to say a prayer. Roland stood at the end of the file of trebles and said 'Piers,' in a low voice, but the name was somehow picked up by the acoustic, and plucked into the vault where, almost like a scream, it reverberated: 'Piers -iers -iers -iers!' He put a protective arm round the boy's shoulder. All faces, including that of a fair-haired chorister opposite, stared at them, and his boy was looking up at him with terror in his eyes. Even the ancient stones seemed permeated with the humiliation of it.

Seeing tears on his face, Piers hurried over and grasped him by the arm. He'd seen this before, light-years ago - and then there was that odd business last night. 'Hey, come on, what's the matter?' Luckily, there was no-one else about.

'Sorry, it just came over me... Seeing you there, like that.' Hallucinating again. What will you think? That I was suddenly overcome by shame? Perhaps that's just what it was. Old-fashioned shame, guilt and all the burdens of the past...

They found a pub offering bar food. Piers had scampi, Roland fiddled about with a rather tough steak.

'I bet you'd never have dreamt in a million years that I'd be treating you to a pint, one day!'

Nor that I would even meet you again in this life. But today is full of things that must either remain unuttered or postponed until the right moment presents itself. Stay out of the quicksands.

After the meal, they wandered down to the Ouse, where narrow boats and pleasure cruisers were moored up for the winter, the sun reflecting in a thousand eddies from the surface of the river.

'Do you row, on the Cam?'

'Not likely. That's for the bully boys.'

Echoes of Fillingham. And do you take some stick from the bully boys because you sing counter-tenor?

Piers decided to exploit the easier atmosphere. 'There's something that amazes me about you, Roland.' Don't pause, don't give him time to react. 'You're a designer, but you aren't arty or trendy. You know what I mean?' When did I last see Roland throw back his head and laugh like that? Perhaps when we were splashing about in the shallows near the cottage, or when he took that ciné film of me on the horse, cantering over the sands...

I shall take that as a compliment! 'There are enough brassy, exhibitionistic types around, to be sure, but all their posturing doesn't add one jot to art. If our stuff is really worth anything at all, it can stand up for itself.'

'Do you have to work with these people, then?'

'Sometimes, not much.'

'When it's an opera?'

'Well, all the designing's finished by the time the curtain rises, so there isn't much left to do with the others on stage.'

'Was it a success, your opera?'

'Correction, Britten's opera. He sent me a nice letter afterwards.' When he asked Piers if he'd read *Der Tod in Venedig* (he said Venny-dig), he got a scowl.

'It's on the reading list. Pretty hard going. There are so many subtle strands to it. Didn't get to the opera, I'm afraid, but I saw the film. Oh, they mucked about and oversimplified it. All the important classical stuff had gone. Bogarde was OK as Aschenbach, but that *boy*. I mean, he was so insipid, and much too old. All he did was keep looking on in that awful simpering sort of way. They never got anywhere, did they? Tadzio needs to have something diabolical about him, lascivious, even.' He stopped, in confusion.

Touché, Piers! Is that how you see yourself, as you were at thirteen, or is that how I wanted you to be? You weren't a pale, two-dimensional phenomenon. You worked through the entire gamut of BOY when we were together: uproariously funny, vulnerable, assertive, close. Very much the rounded figure, but always, for me, the essence of sweetness.

By the time their train reached Cambridge, the sky had clouded over and the first drops of a mean and miserable drizzle were already falling. This place will be the death of me. I wish I had the courage to tell Piers how warmly I still feel towards him. Will there ever be an opportunity for that? He's just made it clear he's happier if we remain good friends, instead of tearing down the barriers which separate us. I am sure that we can never be properly close, as long as we are in England...

We part company outside the station, I in a taxi and he walking into town. It wrenches my heart to see him, so independent now, so grown-up. Can we have any sort of future together?

*

Pountney Hall, strident and functional, at least had the grace to occupy a discreet site on the edge of town. Keith Fillingham's room was on the fourth floor, and the lift was not working.

'Hallo, Mr Millan! What sort of a day have you had?' Just as a tutor would have greeted me. Except that my host is turned out very differently, the blond hair fluffed up, the T-shirt bearing the legend "Come on in, its great!" and the denim shorts reaching just below the knee. The boy's legs and feet are bare, and he has been using an exotic scent. 'Let's have that brolly - and that wet coat of yours!'

Having come here with every intention of ensuring we spend a scrupulously correct evening, I shall start by ignoring the slogan on his front.

He solemnly accepts the bottle I have brought, reading the label: '"Crozes-Hermitage". Sounds as if it's been made by naughty monks! Has it?'

'That would be telling!' I trust that, as I take off my raincoat, he will not notice the trembling of my hands.

'I'll just pop your things into my bedroom.' Said with a wicked look.

He returns and finds a corkscrew and two glasses. 'Do have the armchair... What have you been up to today, then, Mr Millan?' Again, that naughty nuance!

'My friends call me "Roland". Please feel free to do the same.' I am already fidgeting in my seat.

'Right ho, Roland!'

'Well, I made the acquaintance of Ely cathedral.' Neutral territory...

'Ah ha! You're a collector of cathedrals, then. What took you to Wharnley in the first place?'

'My work.' I am playing the minimalist answer game, to see how much I can tease out of you.

'What *is* your work, Roland? Are you some kind of a teacher?'

'Lord no. I'm an artist. I chiefly design operas.'

'In *Wharnley*?' Keith has finished his glass.

I take the bottle and replenish it. 'I was redesigning the interior of a mansion which had burnt out.'

'Right. Hey, this stuff's pretty good, and it does help to oil the wheels, wouldn't you say?' He swallows a mouthful as if it were water, the little vulgarian. Maybe he'll pass out and I'll be able to slip away. The trouble is that it's affecting me too. My God, he does have beautiful eyes...

But then his host quite unexpectedly became serious. 'I said there was something else to tell you about Piers. Did you know he had something like a breakdown in his last weeks there?'

A breakdown. Oh Christ, no. He has just given focus to a notion that bothered me much, in those days after I lost Piers. I have been along that miserable road myself, and I wouldn't wish it on anyone, least of all him. Was it my fault?

'He was always bursting into tears, and they more or less locked him away, apart from the practices and services. We were told nothing, and he said nothing, but word went round that he'd been copped coming back in, illegally. It must have been a bad time for him. I say, are you all right? You're shaking like a leaf.'

Of course I knew he got caught, stealing back into school after seeing me, but I didn't know that he'd flipped. Oh God. And then there was that final morning at the end of the Summer Term, when he came out of school and got into a taxi, with me planted over the road, still hoping that he would come across, and everything would be all right. But he was taken out of my life - for ever, as it seemed. 'I'd got it worked it out already, of course. There was something between you, wasn't there? Is that what shattered him?'

'I'd rather not talk about that'. I see now that coming here has opened up a can of worms.

'If it affected him like that, how did it affect you?'

What would be the point of revealing to you where I have been, emotionally, for the last five years?

'But now you're together again. How did that happen? Did you put an ad in the *Times*, or something?'

How do you explain a miracle like this? 'I was sitting at home, the phone rang, and there he was again.'

'So Piers came in pursuit of you and not the other way round? Interesting... Tell me, Roly, has he pulled you back into his life for a spot of blackmail?'

What a sledgehammer to take to a man on the verge of collapse. 'Nobody else could ever understand how uplifting our relationship was. Nothing mercenary about it, at all.' The drink is talking now.

'Right. And now that you're together again, how is it working out?'

'Keith, you have to understand that I'm undergoing a kind of thawing-out process, and Piers has of course changed a lot.'

'You mean, he no longer wants the sort of things that I'm ready to offer?'

He isn't a whore like you, which is why he will last much longer in my heart than you ever could. I am here to use you as a convenience, and useful source of intelligence, but Piers is different. I wish we weren't talking about him like this, but I don't know how to stop it.

'Perhaps our mysterious Morri isn't really one of us at all,' Keith went on. 'Not everyone who enjoys an early gay dabble goes on with it in later life, do they? I knew *I* was going to be that way as soon as I realised *I was a boy*. No need for me to wait till puberty, to find *that* out!'

Young man, my whole life has been that kind of quest. I don't think I shall ever find the answer.

'How is it with you, then? You needn't wrestle with yourself. I'm very discreet and, as one well-known don puts it, quite therapeutic!'

The wine takes the cue. 'I've had a succession of males in my life, but I don't love just anyone, because I happen to go with them.' In one short phrase, I betray Barry, Jonathan, Fiona, just as I shall betray you, Keith Fillingham!

He nods, as if what I have just said is the most natural thing in the world. 'Piers is special to you, though, isn't he? I haven't ever spoken to him about the past, on the odd occasion when we've met since, and I think he'd cold-shoulder me if I tried to. But enough of him. Try a drop of this. It's pretty good for the old libido.'

Libido? The chemistry has already begun working away inside my body. My dose of sedative (before the taxi brought me here) has been making an unlikely cocktail with the wine I've just drunk. And now this boy is urging vodka on me. It's an odd sensation to feel oneself levitating, as it were, in a room which has begun to rotate slowly but inexorably. I should be resisting this madness.

But what is this? A flurry of movement somewhere in the gyrating space in front of me, and here is a young male form, undressed, except for a pure white mini-slip and some bauble shining on his left wrist. My mind strains to take all this in, while the lovely youth kneels before me, unbuttons my shirt, puts a warm hand to my chest and gently, - and so expertly – fingers around my nipples, making electric impulses course through my body.

Afire now, I see the bracelet near my face, bearing the initials "KF" in bold letters. Was that there before? Once I was given a ring with two names engraved inside it: "Piers and Roland".

And now this delectable boy is using his tongue, so soft and wet, to make first one of my nipples, and then the other, rise into a hard dark button, like a nut.

My hand strays forward, the back of it questing over the smooth expanses of the young chest, moving into an armpit, then up behind the strong neck, to join my other hand coming round the other way, in the beginnings of an embrace. Forgive me, Piers, I have passed the point of no return.

Sensing that he genuinely wants this kind of tenderness, I bend forward and kiss his fragrant hair.

'You know, Roly, I think I really rather like you!'

The moment of truth arrives. He pulls me to my feet, undresses me with hands well skilled, then sheds his briefs and stands naked, looking at me through his lashes. It isn't his lovely face that dominates the room, though, but the delightful red tip of his exquisite uncircumcised member, while his pubic hair, a delicate auburn shade and as soft as a woman's, invites me to bend over and bury my face in its fragrance.

We move into his bathroom, he gets me to stand in the tub with him, turns on the shower, and we plaster each other with shampoo, transforming the scene into one which an Aubrey Beardsley would have been glad to sketch. We dry each other off with large fluffy towels and go into his bedroom, which, for me, becomes the scene of humiliation and disappointment. No matter what Keith does to rouse me, my equipment refuses to stand. All that my mind can serve up is Mr James's voice, for ever repeating: 'Will you godfather him?'

I am awoken by a stirring in the unusually capacious bed. Did I dream that someone, warm, unclothed, was lying next to me? Piers? No, not Piers, nor a dream either: soft, strong arms grip then caress me, manoeuvre me, still in the dark, into position over the inviting young form beneath me and, this time, I thrust home with a force that makes him catch his breath.

He switches on his bedside lamp, sits up and, propped on one arm, looks down at me. 'Did you get that far with Piers? I heard you say his name just now.'

Piers shielded me from inquisitive people at Wharnley, and now it is time to return the compliment, by speaking the truth: we never did *that*. I beg Keith not to reveal anything of all this. The sheet has slipped off his shoulder, giving him a decidedly Caravaggio air, and I know that I have plumbed the delicious depths of the forbidden, tasted the infinite pleasures of degradation. And I am not ashamed of myself. Piers, you would not make love with me, so this is my answer to you.

*

We kneel side by side in the gloom of this funny little back-street church, my head still throbbing from last night's orgy. And next to me now, amid the sweet, pervasive odour of ancient polished wood and church candles, is the ghost of a dark-haired one. We are oblivious to the half dozen or so other souls who have turned out at this early hour. I know that Piers is humouring me again. He's given up on everything to do with sanctity, but, bless him, he's prepared to do even this for me, before I set off home.

I used to watch him go out to where the priests performed their slow ballet in the sunbeams at the altar rails, would see him take Communion a thousand miles away, as if in another world. Now, our voices blend in the confession of our sins: *The remembrance of them is grievous unto us, the burden of them is intolerable...* And what are his sins? I know what mine are. Could this hole-in-the-corner service uplift him at all, strike a few chords, as it does for me? When we both found, at Wharnley, that we had gone off religion, he called us pagans.

If he found out what I had been getting up to behind his back, he'd drop me like a hot brick. For my part, I seem to share with Keith the faculty of not knowing what shame is. Repentance would even be a luxury...

Fragments of my past, which I had thought lost for ever, come back now, shred by shred, clotting together to form a mosaic picture of myself, like flesh healing over a wound. But there is a danger in it, as my waywardness demonstrates, for I am a bubble, easily destroyed.

Piers gives me a nudge, (the one and only physical contact between us, since we shook hands on my arrival?) Time to get up, and follow him to the altar steps, to kneel just close enough to him without seeming importunate. There are certain proprieties to be observed now: so much has been made clear. Indeed, ever since I arrived in Cambridge, I haven't known how much I might dare to hope for.

Cupping my hands, I am only too well aware that, just to my right, Piers' long pale fingers curl into each other likewise, to receive the wafer. *My communion is with you, and no-one else.*

Breakfast, in his rooms afterwards, is very painful for me. On the one hand, I fear that Mr James might appear at any moment, to conduct a neat little inquisition before I leave. On the other, I still desperately seek a formula to soothe the great, but, as yet, unspoken distress which Piers and I must still be sharing, deep down. You cannot ask a person 'Did I really cause you to have a breakdown?' Not so baldly as that. It's like a great sheet of lead: impossible to find a corner by which to pick it up. And anyway, if Piers was traumatised by me, we wouldn't be enjoying one another's company as we do. He is bound to be much more resilient in these things than I am.

The subject of my thoughts now breaks into them with so innocent a query that I could laugh out loud. 'Can you see Mont Blanc from Geneva?'

So simple, but so apt, and my problem is neatly shelved! 'Yes, if the air is clear.'

'And is it really so that Geneva has a frontier all round it?'

He's been doing his homework, he has taken the bait, and he gives me exactly the opening I have been too timid to come out with, myself. 'Perhaps the best thing would be for you to come and find out.' Do I say that out of a sense of duty? Mr James would no doubt approve of godfather issuing such an invitation to godson. The only way I could get Piers to myself, before, was to isolate him from his school. If I can transfer him to a more exotic setting, it would be a huge step for me, a massive concession from a mind that used to keep a tight control on life. Not *duty* at all, then.

'If only it weren't so far away.'

'Not exactly at the end of the world. If you're keen to come out, I'll stump up the return rail fare - second-class, mind!' Call it conscience money, if you like, after all we have been through. Perhaps I haven't lost my old knack with him, after all.

*

It seems disloyal to be feeling relief that Roland's gone. Inevitably, we were seen around together, and one or two other men made comments, which meant I had to concoct something about him being a former colleague of Father's. At least James took to him, despite that funny do in Hall. He's a very good judge of men, and I'd be intrigued to know what he makes of Roland and me. If I tell him about the invite to Geneva, fare paid, I might get an interesting response.

It's a pity we never found a way of getting round to the important questions. For instance, while I was slogging away at O's and A's, who was Roland with? A man doesn't have to live like a monk, he surely hasn't been simply waiting, as if in some enchanted castle? By any standards, he's well-off enough to go where he likes when it pleases him.

We've met at last in person, but that doesn't mean I know him yet. I was beginning to, at Wharnley, but then it went badly wrong. A bit like Father's death, really.

'You've been seeing a man from the congregation? What about, exactly?' Canon Byatt-Woods got me alone, up in the Minster library. I did my best to parry, but a thirteen-year-old is badly equipped to convey delicate things, the way he wants to. I didn't understand, till that moment, that there could be two such different ways of looking at our stay together at the cottage.   I didn't want to drop either of us in it. The priest made it all sound cheap and tawdry. I see why, now... He obviously took my weeping to be remorse, told me that I'd been in considerable peril.

Peril, with Roland? The only peril was that of being torn apart from him, out of the blue, like death. Was that what he'd expected or even wanted for us, when he told me we'd got too ingrown, that I had to go away and talk about us to someone else? I've often wondered if he knew what would happen to me.

They made it plain that, as a senior boy in a position of trust, I had let my sodding school down. Despite the fact that the rest of my time there was like hell on earth, Roland was still around. I peeped at him, during services, and he looked terrible. Didn't he understand the danger he was in?

I don't much care nowadays about what people think of me, though I know there's a little devil which threatens to pop up and sour things, if not kept in check. In Ely cathedral it urged me to test Roland out with my chorister act - and I got the surprise of my life when I hit the mark and unleashed all that emotion.

Because he's always been very generous to me, I want to give him some companionship in return, as long as he no longer expects... I put that to him as plainly as I could, but there was still that yearning look, especially when we said goodbye, as if he wanted to hug and kiss me. He needs protecting. James, too, has noticed that. I've stirred it all up, like the Sorcerer's Apprentice. Why did I call him back? A mixture of things, some of them not yet clear. All I know is that I've started on a journey.

*

He started. The stewardess had picked up his copy of *La Suisse* from the cabin floor. 'Can I get you anything, sir?'

'A large cognac.' Hair of the dog.

I had hoped to draw up a balance sheet of the benefits which the last few days have brought me, but too much of it refuses to come into focus. Of all the people I have had close dealings with in my life, Piers is the only one who has ever met me on the level marked 'soul'. I know all about the unseen dangers involved if one tries to own another person, and our new linking has already taxed my diplomacy as well as my capacity for restraint. He is very much his own man now. Mr James recognises all that, of course, and, in handing the orphan boy over to me (as it were), is also reminding me of the responsibility that goes with privilege. (Would he have been so ready to do that, if he'd known more about me?)

If Piers does come to Geneva, I shall make no concessions in my own domain. He may be curious to see "Orphéon" (just as he once explored every nook and cranny in the cottage), but I shall still be *seigneur* and hopefully more in command of myself than I was in Cambridge. That fool Le Gaillard intimated that I would spend my days drifting in and out of sanity.

If Piers ever finds out about Keith and myself, I have an answer ready-made: we keep on the right side of Fillingham, because he cottoned on to us at Wharnley, and is still showing interest in us. We don't want any gossiping on that score. There's no getting away from it, however, that I did compromise myself hopelessly. *Une descente dans la dégradation humaine.* In fact, I let myself down on just about every count possible.

And suppose Piers discovers that I have also invited that outrageous young man to come and stay at my place, some time? Or did I dream that? No. Freshly added to the list of names and addresses at the back of my diary, is "Keatsie", in neat, boyish handwriting, plus an address in Merton. Oh God! We were both pretty far gone last night. I am not immune to young men. I gave him a generous tip, 'for expenses' of course – sexy clothes, alcohol, perfumes. He would not like to be thought of as a common rent boy from the gutter.

So how did I deserve Piers, in the first place? Why, it was a unique love, man and boy bridging the great chasms of age and sex, the kind that requires belief to be suspended. What would a sardonic man like Fillingham understand about that? What would anyone? Which is why Piers and I are safe, at least for the present.

Society insists that some kinds of love are wrong, (though it tolerates any kind of hatred), and it thrust me into brutal exile. Now we have people in the wings who undoubtedly realise what was going on five years ago, but who, I earnestly hope, are prepared to accept and even acquiesce. Not just Keith, but James, that incredibly acute man.

Why should Piers want me any more, either for what I was then or am now? I'm sure he doesn't really know why he called me back (any more than I do). All I know is that there exists a deep and precious residue from our previous affair - and this will come to the surface in ways that neither of us can yet foresee.

I did not destroy him, it is clear, even if our former love almost destroyed me. I still love and desire him. The dragon is at large again.

After the cognac, he slept.

*

That evening, he bumped into Filly in the street, who immediately invited him into the nearest pub. 'Haven't seen you in yearsie, Piers!'

Over a lager, they chatted about neutral things, then Keith said, 'My people seem hell bent on coming to visit me here. I don't think I'll be able to stave them off much longer. Do you get plagued in that way - visitors, I mean?'

Piers looked at him sharply, but, behind his long eyelashes, Filly was all innocence. 'Not yet. I expect my mother will want to come and take a look at the place, after Easter or so.' A nasty little suspicion was at work inside him. Roland and Filly had never met, but Roland once asked about the other kid at Wharnley, showed an interest. And I gave him a nice little potted character, told him what he was like - the exhibitionism, and all that.

'I've managed to wangle myself a visit to France,' the other was saying, 'from a chap who's prepared to pay all, in return for the usual little favours, of course.'

'Who is it? What's his name? Whereabouts in France?'

'Back off, Morri,' said Fillingham acidly. 'Just calm it, will you? It's only my History beak, Jeremy, who's got a farm-house in Provence or somewhere deep south.'

A scenario was building up in his mind: despite what he said about his lack of activity these past five years, Roland *must* have been looking up an odd acquaintance or two. Suppose he came to Cambridge to fulfil something he and Filly had previously plotted between them? He didn't approach me in that way this time, he was absolutely polite and correct, but that could be just an elaborate cover, so he could have it off with Filly (whose gayness is so obvious now), and then invite him over for a return match. Why should *I* be the only one who gets to Geneva?

I should have kept a closer eye on Roland all the time. He once told me that I was the only one for him, but how many people does a faithless man say that to, in his life? If he wanted, he had a townful here of desirable males - and a flat conveniently at his disposal!

But then he decided that it was better to take a more cautious line, until he had something resembling proof. If he asked outright, 'Do you know Roland Millan?', Filly, who was sharper, would deflect it, without in the least allaying the suspicion.

'You're looking a bit tired,' said the other, as they parted. 'Hope it isn't because you're working too hard. Only scientists do that, round here. Look, there's a wee party some of us are putting on at Pounters next week. Fancy coming along?'

*

He wandered around his gardens, taking pleasure in the trees in bud and the mildness of the morning. The grass would have to be cut, certainly before Piers arrived. The room where his guest was to sleep was a picture of spartan French shabbiness, brass bedstead and sagging mattress. Never having had a guest before, it was in desperate need of fresh paint, a new bed, covers and curtains, - something male in style, though not too sober. And he would get the railings of the balcony painted, too. Having designed for other people all through his career, he had never yet lavished so much money and attention on a young man. I hope he won't find it overwhelming.

He could not remember when he had last felt so lighthearted. On an impulse, he dashed back to the house, fetched a half-bottle of champagne out of the fridge in the cellar, and continued his stroll round the garden, glass in hand.

It shocks me that I can see Keith so clearly in my mind, but have almost forgotten what Piers looks like. I have no photograph of him *as he is*. Oh, I can see his grey eyes, the dark hair, gelled now, but the face is longer, the skin not so pure and boyish. The details are easy, it is the whole that remains elusive. Shut away in my desk drawer, away from prying eyes, is one of the black and white photos I took of him when he was still just thirteen. Unclothed, pristine, the sexuality beginning to surface... The picture he gave me, of himself as Ariel, taken two years ago, is something to dwell on with special pleasure, but the three images of this boy, present, past and deep past, have no area of overlap at all, as though he were, outwardly at least, three quite different people.

I have Mr James to thank that my thoughts regularly turn to the question of *role*. Of course it cannot be 'godfather'. Will it ever be *lover,* again? For the time being, I must do the boy's bidding and be content with *friend,* but on what terms and whose terms? How do we get round to discussing them? Whatever happens, the old structures can no longer be taken for granted. If James asked me to take him under my wing, does that mean he senses that this one of his students isn't going to stay the course? Piers made it quite plain that he finds Cambridge, and his studies, a real let-down. He's there because his careers master told him to apply – though he does possess unusual intelligence, which I immediately detected all those years ago.

He began his thank-you letter several times in his mind. Did your having me to stay at Cambridge mean that our mutual attraction at Wharnley was acceptable, whatever the painful outcome? The tea-shop, the Minster, the solemn worshippers at services - all that *Englishness* to be overcome! I plucked you out, broadened your view of the trite, stuffy world you were being brought up in.

> *Dear Piers,*
> *Just a couple of lines to thank you for making my stay*
> *at Cambridge so pleasant and interesting. I also enjoyed*

meeting Mr James, and enclose a note of thanks. Please pass it on to him.

Do by all means come out here, so that I can repay the compliment, and show you the sights of Geneva, and perhaps the Alps beyond.

Let me know how things are going, and if you can still come, so I can make the necessary arrangements. I leave it to you to suggest a date. A fortnight would be the minimum, to do this area justice.

Amitiés,
Roland.

*

Dear Roland,

Thanks for your letter. It was really great that you could come and sample Alma Mater (doesn't that sound just too American?) Of course, it gets better as the Spring wears on. But I'm quite forgetting to answer your invite. Of course it's Yes Please. I've been asked to sing an alto solo from Vivaldi's "Gloria" on Easter Day, so am mugging up with a tape I got of Alf doing it. It's pretty hard!

If it's OK, I'll arrive on the 26th (March, of course), Friday, leaving again on the 9th April (another Friday), to be back in Camb in time for the Viv.

Better stop now, as Mother wants me to do some shopping, and I can get this to the post.

Love from Piers.

P.S. James says thanks to you for your letter, you didn't write your address, but I've given it to him. Hope you don't mind.

He went down into St. Julien to post his answer. Factual again, with train times, and a cheque. Even a touch of humour, to mask the combination of alarm and delight he had felt at the "love from Piers".

And what is he doing now, this boy who some day could be a world-class singer? Where is he? Does he think about me, a millionth part of the time that I devote to him? But then he is busy. I have no-one else to occupy me. "Love from Piers..."

His heart bleeding, he walked in his gardens when the moon was almost full. Something was giving off its nocturnal fragrance, and he paused, looking at the silvery light above the silhouette of the Mont Salève. He will come here, but not on my terms at all. He is only seventeen, in some ways quite grown up, but surely impressionable still, so that I must tread with care. The important thing is, never to lose him again.

This was, for him, a ritual time and, in the furthest and darkest corner of his park, he was in a ritual place. He had lived according to Nietzsche's precept of seeking total experience, which had sometimes made him behave unwisely. Barry, Jonathan (even Fiona and Piers) were acquired on the spur of the moment, to be shaken off with varying degrees of difficulty.

He had lived away from the mainstream, a loner resorting to his own devices, tiring quickly of other people, fleeing from things he could not take or control. An oddball, but not utterly devoid of principle.

Even his private addiction - *son rite de faire jaillir de la semence* - was harmless. No-one saw it, it concerned nobody but himself: the earth - his earth - received the secret libation from his loins. There was a time when he would have been shocked at letting himself go like that, but now... In her way, Mother had understood him best, and still she could love him. Piers knew some of the things about him - and he was back on the scene.

How much do I really know about *him*? As little as we know about Christ's boyhood. In those early days, there were aspects I thought I understood: he presented me with so many facets, in his artless way. I was charmed - I still am - but that does not amount to *knowing*. Isn't that what almost destroyed it? I felt only anguish for Piers, after we had finally been torn from each other. He once remarked how much we seemed to have in common, before a word was yet spoken. Even as an adolescent, he was responsive, thoughtful, not pitiful nor weak. I am both pitiful and weak. In finding me again, he has presented me with a quest, perhaps the one great thing left for me to achieve in life.

*

An envelope arrived, bearing the St Neville's crest.

> *My dear Millan,*
>
> *I was sorry not to have the chance to bid you goodbye before your departure, but I trust you had a safe homecoming. Thank you for your nice letter.*
>
> *Piers tells me that you have invited him to visit you. A great believer in foreign travel myself, I am sure he will derive great benefit from it. I shall expect him to report when he returns.*
>
> *I sincerely hope that you found your brief stay congenial. Cambridge is reputed to be a place which, once discovered, one feels the need to return to - and I very much hope you will. In any case, let us remain in touch. I greatly value our acquaintance.*
>
> > *With every good wish,*
> > *Yours,*
> > *Oliver James.*

*

The new paintwork was dry, the lawns had been cut, Madame Bouillot had put in double her usual time on cleaning and generally primping the place up, and "Orphéon" was now ready to receive its visitor.

Coming out of a shop in the centre of St Julien, he was almost run down by an Italian-looking youngster on a bike. He shouted, the boy managed to brake in time, turning a pair of dark eyes full of momentary alarm upon him. Then he muttered something and made off quickly, on his blue and white racer.

When Roland reached the top of the hill, a gang of boys darted past on bikes, shouting and shrieking. And, again, two very black eyes pierced him. The police had issued a warning about burglaries. These were only kids, but...

II.

"After our largely monosyllabic evening meal, over a coffee in the salon, P fell asleep on the settee, like a puppy. I decided against waking him and getting him upstairs again, but eased off his shoes, swung his feet up and put a cushion under his head. I cannot describe how <u>warm</u> that made me feel. I am so unused to any sort of physical closeness.

It was more like dread in my heart when he showed up at the Gare de Cornavin, tousled, grubby and almost too tired to speak - so pale, the choirboy again, like a Caravaggio painting. But he livened up at the first sight of Orphéon. Before anything else, I wanted him to see the newly refurbished room - his room. He looked round it (with evident approval), and then went over to the window, opened both wings and stepped on to the balcony, as if an actor going on stage. 'It's mountains wherever you look.' So like his first visit to the cottage, wanting to explore it all, as soon as he arrived. He slept there, too...

I write this, sitting opposite him, thinking of a past whose mosaic pieces return with a clarity both wonderful and alarming - but obstinately refusing to fit together. Can this young man on my settee really be P as I knew him, in some past millennium? And is it possible that we could edge back towards that special state after such a long period of neglect? Can he be my boy again?"

Closing his diary and putting it and the pen back in his pocket, he went into the *salon,* catching sight of his own reflection in one of the many mirrors which, shaped like windows rounded at the top, lined the walls. As if he too was in here for the very first time, his eye strayed over the tiled floor, the beamed ceiling and the heavy French furniture. And, amid all this, the recumbent figure, watched over by a man with a half-tense, half-amused expression on his face. I am aware of another face looking, as it were, over my shoulder. Mr James, like a ghost, comes to see if I'm matching up to his expectations.

Before I take myself off to bed, I must fetch a blanket to put over the boy. No, not boy. This stranger is a young man now, a fact which I dare not allow myself to forget.

*

Something woke him with a jolt, and he reached out for the light. It was after three in the morning, and he was no longer alone under his own roof. Seizing his dressing-gown, he went out on to the landing.

'Piers, are you all right?'

A sleepy grunt came from below. Roland snapped on the lights on landing and stairs and hurried down. Piers was standing in the hall, like a zombie. He had cannoned into a small table.

'Couldn't find the light. Wanted the loo. Sorry.'

Half an hour later, after a bath, he was in his proper bed, sipping from a mug of hot chocolate, just like the child of old.

I sit on the chair in the corner, though I would have much preferred the end of the bed. I never took unfair advantage of you, in those days. We only went as far as you were prepared to...

'I like your house, though it's rather grand.'

'You must treat it as your own home, Piers.' You'll have forgotten that one day it really will be yours. Now we are away from England, Wharnley, Cambridge, and all their associations, there's a chance that we will get closer to each other. Or am I just a fool?

*

When he opened his curtains, the sun was already up. Turning the catch, he pulled the French doors open, and the cold morning air swept in. An immense grey bluff, streaked with bars of vegetation, blocked the distant view. In the foreground stretched the gardens, whose main lawn was dominated by a magnificent great copper beech. There was a wealth of smaller trees, various leafless bushes and even the occasional yew, all extending into an atmospheric distance.

Droplets of water clung to the ironwork of the balcony. He put his hand on the cold wet metal, to see if it was real. The enchanted castle... All this great house, just for one man. As he stood there, he found himself shivering. Perhaps it was wrong to come here. In a sense, it puts me in his power. As he descended the staircase, his host came out of the kitchen. 'I'll make some coffee, Piers.' He sounded as awkward as he felt.

There were cornflakes and English marmalade, which Roland did not touch. 'I have to pop into Geneva this morning. Join me, if you like, but feel free to come and go as you please while you're here.'

After calling at the accommodation address for mail and messages, they strolled together along the Promenade du Lac, skirting the Jardin Anglais. The sunlight was soft on the enormous inland sea whose shores receded into the far distance. Roller-skaters had set up lines of empty cans on the promenade, and were executing high-speed slalom movements, much to Piers' amuse-ment. His eye was then caught by the high jet of the fountain across the little bay, its spray carrying on the breeze.

'They must have turned it on just for you. It generally only works in the summer.'

'Can you get right out there?'

'Almost.' Taking that as a cue, he dashes off like a schoolboy, while I find a bench to sit on. This increasing awareness of the age-gap depresses me rather, in a way that it never did at Wharnley. He's easily young enough to be my son, perhaps the one whom the psychiatrist said I should have, and certainly the godson Mr James would saddle me with.

Now I have lost him among the tiny anonymous dots of people strung out along the jetty. When I turn round, there's the Mont Salève, daring me to take him up there, for the view. Isn't that the sort of thing one does with a favourite nephew?

Out on the breakwater, you're doubtless being saluted by the immense white plume of spray, as once the surf foamed over your young body, on my piece of shore. With you near, that warmth is growing inside me again. We're no longer just the undergrad and his awkward visitor, but something akin to our deeper past is in the air: a oneness, a communion of souls. Did you not give me a ring with our two names engraved inside it? Whatever torments and buffetings I have had to endure, that is a fact which no event can ever wipe away.

Oblivious to the soaking he'd got from the jet, he stared back to where Roland must still be waiting for him. I need to prove two things to him: firstly, we really are finished in that regard, and secondly, that I have a lot more dimensions in me than he has. I have progressed since Wharnley, whereas he doesn't seem to have moved an inch. I think he still needs me, but much more than I need him. We are going to have to find our levels, and quickly.

Sitting here by the water which usually offers me comfort, I allow it all to unfold like a prayer of thanksgiving for benefits received, even if I am not yet proof against tribulation, not yet quite secure. And now my heart misses a beat in exactly the manner that Aschenbach's did, on seeing Tadzio, for here is my boy, jogging back with an earnest expression that breaks into a grin when he sees me. 'Just look at this. As I was getting near it, the bloody wind changed.' His jeans have gone dark, and droplets sparkle on his navy blue sweater. Now that he has stopped moving, he begins to tremble with the cold. I had better not show my amusement. 'I'll take you home.'

'No need. If we just went for a coffee somewhere, I could dry out. Honest.'

And so, after a brisk walk back along the *quai*, we make for a favourite café of mine, where the proprietress, shaking her head, feels Piers' sweater and the bottoms of his trousers. <You aren't the first to do that!> She sits him down almost on top of a radiator, plying him with steaming coffee and a cognac, and returning now and again to check the progress of the drying-out.

I am not the only one to relish this comic interlude: Piers, pink-faced, clearly enjoys being cossetted - and in French, too. The cognac makes him rather merry. 'Can we go and see the bear-pit? It's here, isn't it?'

I promise him that we shall go to Berne. I shall humour him in every way I can.

'I got wet because I was trying to spot Mont Blanc. You did say it was visible from here, didn't you?'

When he rather shamefacedly admits to being ravenous, I spirit him away to Le Lyrique. Lunch is already being served, and though the restaurant is full, the head waiter finds us a table.

'Do you like fish?'

'Anything, really.'

Having dried out completely, his hair has gone fluffy, as it used to be. I attend to the menu. '*Fera* is rather good - a speciality of these lakes.'

When the waiter returns, he orders in his best French. 'Pour moi, fera aux amandes, s'il vous plaît.'

'Très bien, monsieur. Et pour vous, Monsieur Millan?'

When the waiter has gone, he tells me that this must be the most swish place he's ever been in, but he doesn't feel properly dressed for it.

'Don't worry. They tend to be less formal than you are in England.'

'That's funny.'

'What is?'

'You said, "than *you* are in England", not "*we*".'

I try not to pull a face. 'I've rather got out of the way of thinking myself English. I hardly even speak the language any more.'

As we eat, some people come in and loudly demand a table. The head waiter is apologetic but firm. One of the newcomers shouts something, and they all go out again, slamming the door.

'Germans.' I should be more careful. It is, after all, one of his subjects.

'You don't care for them?' He has picked up the trace of scorn in my voice.

'I don't care for anyone who barges in and thinks he owns the place. And, well... its a bit trite, really, but...'

'No, go on.'

'You see, our house in London got blitzed in the war. Mother and I were lucky to be pulled out of the ruins.' Our faces were white with dust, we were gibbering and screaming. Blood. Broken bones. 'You don't forget something like that.'

He puts down his fork with astonishment in his face. 'Wasn't your father there, too?'

'No. His ship went down.' God, all that is mere history now...

'Roland, you never told me all this before. So we're both *sans père*.'

This gives me pause! I take a sip from my wine glass. 'You now see why I feel more at ease out here. Besides, there are too many things I dislike about present-day Britain.'

'Such as?' A hint of truculence. The young Socialist ready to defend his homeland?

'Government support for the arts is so pathetic, and the problems of crime just never get solved.'

'What do you think we ought to do?' Spoken with genuine interest.

'Change the government, maybe.'

'Hey, not the blinking Tories in again? They'd turn us into a right mess.'

'Isn't that one step higher, perhaps, than a Left mess?'

He looks about to weigh in, but, seeing the humour in my face, leaves it alone.

In the pause between the main course and the dessert, he claps a hand to his head. 'Christ, here you are, feeding me like a lord, and I haven't given you the present I brought. Mother would murder me.'

This is the old Piers, earnest and lively in turn. One never quite knew which he would be next, and I like him for that, - though there's something that bothers me. In Cambridge, I knew the exercise was to be short, with limited or even nil objectives. Here, I've taken him into my home, and for much longer. How will we cope, without destroying one another?

Look how his hands are trembling, as he fumbles in his French handbag for his money. He must be a bundle of nerves inside. *What makes him shake like that?*

Roland looked at his watch, and then at him. 'If you want to see Mont Blanc, it's a good time now.'

With the afternoon sun shining warmly through the windscreen, they drove back to St Julien, took the Annecy road, and made for the ridge of the Salève. From there they could stare south-east across a broad valley to a wooded landscape, out of which rose grey massifs. In the far distance was a cluster of immense peaks, all white.

'That's it, isn't it?' Piers' voice was full of awe, as he pointed to the horizon.

'That's what you came to see.'

'The highest mountain in Europe. Looks like Everest.'

'About sixteen thousand feet.'

'God. Do people climb it?'

'I almost made it to the summit once, with a guide of course.' And Guy Bannerot, but I shan't bring him into it. He'll surface soon enough, anyway.

'I'm full of admiration. What was it like?'

'A bit of a trudge, to be honest. It's the effect of the altitude, you see. I wouldn't really recommend it. We didn't manage to get to the top because the path had been blocked by an avalanche.'

At Petit-Pommier, they got out again.

'There's St Julien. Where's "Orphéon"?'

Roland handed over the binoculars and pointed. 'There, on that small ridge. See the tower among the trees?'

'I can see my balcony.' He swept the glasses round to the right. 'Oh, and there's the jet again. To think I stood under that, this morning.'

I suddenly see the edge of my premonition, like the curve of the crescent moon - sharp, well-delineated: the *quai*, down there, is destined to be the theatre for an event which I as yet cannot guess at, but which will certainly affect us both, even thrust us apart again.

The house was warm when they arrived. Roland switched on lights in the *salon*. 'When I got up in the night,' said Piers, 'I caught sight of myself, dimly, in one of these mirrors. Quite terrified me, at first.'

'French taste, I'm afraid, but I have to confess I rather like it, in a house of this style. I hope you don't mind eating simply. There's soup, bread and cheese, apples.'

But Piers dashed off, shouting 'Your present!', and returned with a packet containing something soft. 'Mother helped me choose it. In a craft shop.'

A long table-runner, russet with red and orange flowers on it. I unfold it slowly, well aware of the anxious eyes on me. 'Thank you. It shall have a place of honour in my study.' In my embarrassment, I fold it up again and resume preparing the supper.

'I haven't been in there yet? Will you show me?'

When we finish eating, we go up, past the black-and-white photos on the wall, which I thought he might comment on. They are of him, after all. 'I have one or two designs which might interest you.' Here he is, entering my most private place, poking around, asking me questions, and yet I do not mind at all, just like the first time he came to see the cottage and some of its precious contents.

'Is that Tadzio?' He picks up a drawing of a youth in an old-fashioned swimming-costume.

'It is.' I take a book down from one of my shelves, and hand it to him. 'This might intrigue you. I can't read it, of course.'

He takes it reverently, opens it and whistles. 'The Luxusausgabe of *Der Tod in Venedig*, from the Hyperion Press, 1912. Limited edition. Did you know it was signed by Thomas Mann?'

'That's why I bought it.'

'And do you understand this handwritten dedication: "Einem gewidmet, dessen Bild mir niemals verbleichen wird"?'

'I was hoping you might help me out.'

'It means "Dedicated to one whose image will never grow pale for me".'

'Ah, I didn't know he had a mistress.'

'No. "Einem" and "dessen" are masculine. Who could it have been?'

Now this gives me a definite *frisson*. Is he teasing?

'Did you actually go to Venice, to get inspiration for your designs?'

I'm not sure if I ever told him about the fiasco of a honeymoon and my intention never to return to that godforsaken hole.

"Now that we seem to be melting some more of the ice-

wall, will I <u>ever</u> be able to talk everything out with him, or shall we soon reach the point beyond which no further exploration of each other will be possible? Perhaps my house is not the place in which to foster closeness. We should lock up and take off for a few days into the mountains, which evidently intrigue him. Why not a voyage of discovery together, with Switzerland the ocean? No charts, no beacon lights, merely a frail cockle-shell bearing two souls along, just as it once was."

*

Waiting for sleep to come, he pondered how much Roland Millan had changed. He's so withdrawn, apparently devoid of any pleasure, as if life in the intervening time has become some kind of penance. For what? Looking back on how we were then, I go hot and cold. I can't really believe it happened, and he acts as if it didn't. I was still only a kid, impulsive. I led him on, that's for sure, but I didn't understand, not properly. Will he accept that I'm grown-up now, that I've changed? In our funny ways, I think we're still fond of each other...

*

Tucking into the cornflakes, he asked what the programme for the day was. It was wet and grey outside.

'How would you like to see mountains from really close range? I think I can allow myself a few days off.' When had he ever said that of himself, to anyone else?

'Gosh, today?'

'Not quite. I must sort out a few details in town, so that we can go first thing tomorrow. Come along, if you want to.'

Almost the same awkward formula, as if he feels he has to earn my company. 'I'll pass on that one, if you don't mind. Better write to Mother.'

At that moment, they heard the back-door open, and a middle-aged woman in an apron and head-scarf arrived shortly afterwards. Roland introduced her (in French) as Madame Bouillot, who came twice a week to clean, do the washing and ironing and, occasionally, cook. She nodded briefly at Piers, then immediately began to discuss with Roland what had to be done that day.

When he had driven off to Geneva, and the rain had stopped, Piers took a pencil and pad and went out into the garden to make a sketch of the house for his mother. As he drew the steep pyramidal slate roof surmounting the corner tower, he became aware of a pale face looking out at him from one of the downstairs windows. It gave him a slight start, until he remembered that the cleaning woman was still on the premises.

When he went indoors again to make a start on his letter, a banging noise from the direction of the kitchen indicated that the floor of the passage was being polished. Instead of going up to his room, he stuck his head round the corner, and smiled.

Madame Bouillot stopped swinging the heavy bumper to and fro, apparently relieved to have an excuse to pause.

<You have a hard job there, madame.> That went down well!
'Il y a des invités toujours?'

Oh no, she said. Never any visitors to speak of. M. Millan never had people to stay.

'Des réunions, alors?' Somehow or other they found themselves at the kitchen table. Madame put some coffee on. Parties? No, nothing like that.

She complimented him on his good French, asked for his dirty washing, and he knew that he was in. He asked her a lot about "Orphéon". It had stood empty for some time before M. Millan bought it, nearly five years ago. It belonged to an old lady who had become demented. When she died, her heirs spent a lot of time quarrelling, because she hadn't made a proper Will. In the end, they cut their losses and sold up. He got it with every stick of furniture for a song.

The shrill ringing of the front-door bell made Piers jump, but Madame Bouillot merely pulled a face and said, <It'll be him, I expect.>

At first, he thought she meant Roland, but then realised that the master of the house would hardly be ringing at his own front door. He told madame not to worry, he would answer it. Even as he walked the length of the hall, he could see a silhouette through the frosted glass panes. It was curious. He had just been told that "Orphéon" had no visitors, and yet one had arrived, as if on cue.

A shortish, rather plump man was on the step. He had curly black hair and looked younger than Roland. Seeing Piers, he lifted his hands in mock surprise. There was a car on the drive behind him.

<Oh. Is Monsieur Millan not in?> He pronounced the name French fashion.

<He's gone out. I am his guest. Would you like to come in, monsieur?>

Piers took the newcomer into the *salon*, offered him a seat and introduced himself.

'From Cambridge?' said the man, with a passable English accent. 'How interesting. I did not know. I am Guy Bannerot.' He shook hands, and then there was a moment of awkward silence. 'Millan receives usually in the kitchen. And what do you study?'

Piers explained.

'German?' said the man, in evident disapproval. 'Ah, but then you are here to perfect your French. Excellent!'

Somewhere upstairs, Madame was crashing about in evident disapproval. Piers began to wish that Roland would come back. What did this man want, anyhow?

'Was there a message for Roland - I mean, Mr. Millan?' He realised, as he spoke, that it sounded as if he was trying to get rid of the visitor.

Guy Bannerot smiled, took out a blue cigarette packet and offered it to Piers, who refused. In a few moments, the acrid smoke had filled the room. It seemed like an affront. 'If you are not occupied for the moment, I am content to talk. I am a musician, by the way. I play violin in the Suisse Romande.'

Not to be outdone, Piers explained a little about his singing. He antipathy to this man beginning to melt away.

'*Magnifique*, then we are fellow musicians. Please, call me Guy. Perhaps you permit me to do the same?'

This unleashed a surprising monologue: in a mixture of English and French, Guy Bannerot described his origins, his parents, his musical training in Paris. It would have been difficult not to be charmed. Somewhere in the middle of it all, Madame Bouillot stuck her head round the door to say, with an audible sniff, that she was going. Her expression left Piers in no doubt about her opinion of people who filled the house with the stink of Gitanes.

'I would like to be *premier violon* soon, then even conductor. It is *frustrant* to play for a man who does not understand how to get the best from his *orchestre*. Nearly fifteen years I am doing this. But you, what will you do about your singing? You could have a very good career here.'

'I don't know about that. Perhaps I'll come and sing abroad, but it could be hard to find work as a counter-tenor, don't you think?'

'But no. The early music comes into the *mode* now. Groups are everywhere on ancient instruments. Monteverdi in the opera houses... To increase your repertoire, study in Europe. England is a good country to perform, but - pardon me - not to study music. You come to Paris or Vienna.'

'The problem is money,' said Piers, feeling ashamed.

Guy threw up his arms. 'But, Piers, *mon cher collègue*, look at this house. Millan can help. If he is your true friend he will do it.'

There was the sound of the front door being opened and then Roland came into the room, looking from one to the other.

'Ah, Millan, I have made friends with Piers, and he is telling me the problem of money for study. I say he must go to *conservatoire*, and Millan will pay. But now you are both silent, both so English!' He lit another Gitane.

'I've made all the arrangements, Piers,' said Roland, as though nothing had happened. 'We can leave tomorrow.'

'Leave? To where?' Guy was not prepared to be ignored for long.

'We're going to the Bernese Oberland for a few days.'

'*Comique, ça*, Millan, how you speak in English. So *inaccoutumé pour moi*. And to be invited into the *salon*! But listen, it is still March. You will not get through. Snow is everywhere, and it is so cold. Why renounce to this *confort*, at dear "Orphéon", in exchange for such *misère*? Just as I make the *connaissance* of Piers, you fly him away. And I am really disappointed. I'd have invited you both to my place.'

'Plenty of time for that later,' said Roland. 'We shan't be away for long. He's really keen to see some mountains, aren't you, Piers?'

It was pointed, and it scored its mark. Piers did not notice the irony, and Guy was put out in any case. He stood up. 'I have a ticket for you, Millan, for the concert tomorrow. I do not give it to you. I send you instead two tickets *gratis* for the next. You must come. Au revoir, Piers. I hope to see you soon.'

He knew his own annoyance was hardly rational. Just like *him* to come and pry around, especially when I'm out and Piers is in. There he was, bold as brass in the *salon*, calling Piers by his first name, planning his musical future at my expense!

He excused himself after lunch, saying he had to work in his study. There was still an atmosphere of disapproval in the place.

'Then I'll go for a walk to stretch my legs,' said Piers. He could not get the Guy Bannerot episode out of his head. Here was a potential ally, but Roland had been so icy. And why did Guy refer to him as Millan, even calling him that to his face? If they were friends, why were they so formal? They're both unmarried men, I suppose. So is there anything in it? Is the surname thing just a joke, to try and conceal something else? Do I really imagine I've some sort of stake in Roland, after all this time? I like Guy. He's very open, he's musical. It's hard not to be disloyal to Roland, but there's a difficult side to him I haven't seen before. I suppose it's kind of him to offer to take me so see mountains, so I'd better play along with it. A fortnight's going to be a bloody long time…

The evening began mournfully. Piers avoided mentioning his new-found ally in Madame Bouillot. That might not meet with approval, either. Better be more careful, here. Not answer the door, nor (if it rings when he's out) the phone. A low profile is safer.

But there were things which he could no longer bottle up: the wicked little demon was awake inside him, urging him into a session of straight questions, requiring straight answers: 'So tell me how you actually spent the last five years here, Roland.'

'You know very well. I worked. I travelled a bit.' Anything to change the subject.

'No, you don't understand. Who did you have for company and what did you do?'

How will he believe the honest truth, when his face says *Who were your lovers?* 'Look, I did absolutely nothing. Nothing, not with anybody. *Voilà!*'

'And you've been happy, living like that?'

Such an innocent question, to unleash such a violent storm. *Happy?* It was too much for him. A vast, deep groan rose up from his diaphragm, seized hold of his vocal chords and gathered into an immense cry of anguish, of the torment and pain locked away over those years.

The younger Piers would doubtless have cuddled and comforted him, but this young man stayed aloof, terribly embarrassed by what he had done, only able to stammer 'Sorry, I didn't mean to hurt you.'

'Perhaps you now believe me,' he managed to say.

'Yes, of course. Look. Would it be better if I went?'

Roland took one of the boy's hands in both of his, and Piers let it happen. 'You mustn't go. You really must stay. I want you to.' Uttered in a hoarse whisper, the face wet with tears, which he did not attempt to wipe away, the expression taut, beseeching.

And, with that, the clouds cleared. They produced *moussaka* with much hilarity. Candlelight and red wine with the meal.

"We faced each other across the table, and clinked glasses. Bless him, he can't bear an upset, either. He obviously realises that, although back at home, I am still by no means problem-free.

When, a little later, we said goodnight, he looked almost ready to hug me, but then slipped shyly away, pausing in the doorway to look back - like Tadzio. My funny turns only really began when I first met him again. The pain is at its worst when a chasm opens and I look directly down *into our past time at the cottage. Is there ever a cure for the longing that one dare not have, for the guilt that one can never wash away? Am I to be for ever condemned to perdition for a love - yes, a <u>love</u> - which the world would see as shameful? It was not shameful, but the odds are stacked up against me.*

How transitory the physical is. As we age, it must be more and more the spiritual that unites us, if anything at all. I wanted him physically, at Wharnley, more than anything else. The challenge which we now face is in being able to cope with each other on an entirely different plane: less tense, freer, unconstrained by the shortness of the time we have, yet still able to rejoice in one another, and wanting each other in different ways. Is this possible for me? Can I make that tremendous leap?"

*

Piers opened his French windows and heard the rain pelting down outside in the gardens, now invisible in the dark. A damp, cold smell came up at him; he slammed the windows shut again, and pulled on the curtain cord. Beyond the fresh paint there was a sweet aroma of polish in his room, as though someone had placed flowers there. Madame Bouillot, of course.

I wondered if he would have any outbursts here, and I'm answered. And it was my fault, (just like at Ely), when I let my little fiend probe him too deeply. Is it better to give him the chance to clear the air, emotionally, like that, or is it better to be silent, so that he has to keep the dampers on everything? Not at all sure about this trip he's planned. I so much wanted to come here, but it seems to be going all wrong. I can't be with Roland for ever – wouldn't want to be - but he seems to need me around. Maybe it'll help to get him sorted out a bit.

*

This morning is a revelation: after the rain, the brilliant sunshine sets every leaf, twig and blade in my garden glittering and trembling, the sky is cloudless. And here he comes out to the car with the bag I've lent him. 'Passport?'

He taps his anorak pocket. 'Do I need anything else?'

'Just yourself.'

The shutters are closed, the house carefully locked up, I slam the gates behind us and drive off, with some trepidation in my heart, not only on my account, but also his. I don't think he meant to upset me like that, yesterday. He hasn't yet grasped how defenceless a creature is when it comes out of its shell after so long in protective captivity.

'Where exactly are we heading?' He's got the atlas on his knees.

'I thought the south shore would be quieter, and the views across the lake are good. We'll be following up the Rhone valley for quite a while.'

Being in close proximity to each other in my car evidently brings back memories to him of how we once drove away together like this. 'Roland, I don't quite know how to put this. When I saw that film with you in, it reminded me of how we'd been made to break up, and the effect it must have had on you.'

It comes out of the blue and I am startled. At last, we are getting near the target. Proof positive that you didn't forget me in those five years, as I thought I'd succeeded in forgetting you.

'I couldn't just leave it like that. That's why I contacted you.'

'How was it for you, then, Piers, when we... broke up..?' Daring, this, because I know the answer, but I want to hear it from him. He mustn't guess I've been talking to Keith.

'Pretty shattering. They gave me a bad time, tried like hell to find out who you were and turn me against you, but I always believed I'd find you again, somehow. And I did! It *was* all right to go looking for you?'

'If you hadn't, we wouldn't be here, now!' As good friends...

With that, our mood lightens. The road at last rewards us with a view of the vast blue expanse of Léman ahead, the occasional white steamer and little boats out fishing - a tranquil sea stretching over to a shore so remote as to be in a different world.

We stop down on the quay at Meillerie, where Piers is anxious to take some photos. I then suggest we have a light lunch in the hotel. Our waitress is blonde, with beautiful wild eyes, and lo! his attention is captured. So, young man, so you are not exactly immune in that direction. This is the first time I have seen you eye a girl. Perhaps you don't know what strange chemistry is working on you, that makes you watch her trim little bottom departing towards the kitchen - but *I* know! How will I ever manage this boy? But then he isn't mine to manage, is he?

The little blue flame licks the base of the pot, the cheese is bubbling already, and, to demonstrate to the young Englishman, she takes up his fork, impales a piece of bread, pops it in the molten cheese, twirls it round, then offers it to his open mouth. Whatever would Freud have made of that? They giggle, Piers says 'merci' with his mouth full, and the siren retires, laughing, clearly assuming that I'm his indulgent father.

He's burnt his tongue, of course. Serve him right, for allowing her to trespass on the bowl of *fondue* meant just for us to share. The intimacy of the occasion is ruined.

'What d'you think of Aimée, Roland?'

'I'm sorry?' Play stupid.

'She's wearing a badge with her name on.'

'Oh! Well, yes, very attentive.'

'Um. I think she's what the lower orders would call a bit of all right.'

The female returns from time to time, ostensibly to check the flame of the burner, but really to exchange a special smile with the boy. Finally, with much ceremony, she scrapes the circle of burnt cheese from the bottom of the pot, and offers it to him as a great delicacy, a pagan sacrifice. 'The best bit,' she says in English, and he eats it to please her.

Their passports were checked at St Gingolph, and they were in Switzerland. The further they advanced up the long, straight road, the more the sides of the valley closed in upon them. The sun was gone, now.

'Where did you say we're heading?'

'Ultimately Interlaken, to the north, the other side of this lot.'

'Does that mean going over a pass?'

'You'll see.'

Suddenly, the dim mountains crowded Piers in, he felt tiny and vulnerable, even within the safety of the car. When I asked where we're heading, I meant it literally, but Roland has probably taken it to mean it's about us. My fault, for coming out with that bit earlier on, about us missing each other after Wharnley. It seems we're on two wavelengths here, and words have double meanings. Could be tricky. I've got to keep on testing him out, even at the risk of hurting him again. He took a deep breath and came out with one of those deceptively innocent-sounding gambits. 'That waitress... Well, I did find her attractive. There aren't too many of those among the blue stockings at Cantab. Hope you don't mind me saying, but I do sometimes think of girls, and even feel something when I look at pictures of them - not porno, or anything, but...'

'Of course, Piers. You are your own man, after all.' There is a bitter taste in my mouth. It's not the kind of confidence I want to hear from him.

A white flurry caught in the headlamps. 'Is that snow?'

'Don't worry, it won't come to anything.'

They turned off and up a road that climbed, endlessly, between banks already covered in it. When they reached Goppenstein it was quite dark, and the falling snow was thickening in the headlights.

'What happens now?' Piers was trying to see beyond the arc lights in front of them. 'Hey, it's a train.'

'It's a car-transporter. It goes through a tunnel under the Alps.'

'Clever stuff! Do we stay in the car, then?'

Roland bought a ticket and an official motioned him to drive on to a line of covered flat wagons, like a metal road. There were already some stationary cars in front, and others drove up behind them. 'There we are. The train does the rest.'

In moments, they accelerated and entered a tunnel, the locomotive filling it with blue electric sparks. Piers shouted something, but it was lost in the roaring and rushing. Eventually they began to slow, lights appeared ahead, and the train came to rest.   Piers read out the name of the station. 'Kandersteg.' He sounded more in his element in German.

'You'll have to do the talking now. It's not my language at all.'

'Kein Problem! Look, Roland, it's not snowing here.'

The boy's exhilarated, it's a treat for him, just like a ride at the fair. This is the level I must try to pitch it at. We'll be fine, as long as it's fun to him, for fun is mostly harmless.

They drove off down the Kandertal to Spiez, and soon reached Interlaken, where Roland stopped opposite the station. 'Will you go and ask someone where the Hotel Metropol is?'

Piers got out, approached a bystander, spoke to him, then came back. 'Straight on. He said you can't miss it. It's a skyscraper. Got its own parking down the side. He had an accent you could cut with a knife.'

Roland followed the instructions and in a few minutes they were parked next to the hotel. They took their bags and approached the front doors, which snapped smartly open. 'I say...' He had evidently never been in such a place before.

The woman at Reception checked their details and a porter came to pick up their bags and escort them to the lift.

'Floor twelve?' said Piers. 'It *is* a skyscraper!'

The porter smiled at him and said, 'Here, sirs, you have the best views in all Switzerland.'

They were shown into adjacent rooms, both with a balcony. Piers went to look out of his window, then came and sat on one of Roland's easy chairs. 'How did you know about this place if you haven't been here before?'

'It's quite well-known. I got the phone number and fixed it up. And now you must forgive me. The drive has rather tired me out. I'll leave you to unpack, or whatever, then I'll knock on your door in an hour, and we'll go down to eat.' If that *fondue* hasn't ruined your appetite.

After Piers had gone out, he went through to the bedroom and lay down in the dark. It's a paradox. At Cambridge, I was hoping we'd talk openly, so I could gauge his feelings and he mine. Here, on my own home territory, I am being cautious. The genii is out of the bottle, for sure, but what havoc might it cause? We remain friends, yes. He has made that plain. I don't know whether that will ever lead to anything else. I'm investing a small fortune in this young man, but I do not want it to seem like trying to buy his favours. In the early stages of our affair, when I summoned up the courage to invite him, the choirboy, out for tea, he played his part impeccably, with a discretion I wouldn't have dared to hope for. Words did not need to bear out the extraordinary *rapport* growing between us. My tentative approaches were blithely seized and developed by the boy himself. What a curious combination of innocence and experience he turned out to be.

Now I'm flummoxed. I don't know where we go from here. Better to sit back and let Fate do its stuff.

Half-way through the veal dish, Piers, who had opted for a crumpled Harris tweed jacket and navy roll-neck sweater, muttered an apology about feeling hot, and slipped off the jacket, whereupon a waiter appeared from nowhere, ready to whisk it up and take it to the *garderobe.* 'Ach nein, lassen Sie's bitte hier, an der Stuhllehne, ja?'

He pushes his sleeves up above his elbows, runs a hand through his hair, every little action a work of art. My God, do other people realise how attractive he is, or am I the only one possessed of magic vision? And how assured he is, with his German. He shows off a little in front of me, but that only adds to the charm!

When we are upstairs again, he asks me in to look at the view. From the high balcony, the lights of cars pass by far below in each direction like orderly strings of fireflies. Opposite the hotel stretches a huge, dark expanse of park with lights on the far side of it. The innumerable stars are like dots of frost set in a black curtain. Enough to make any man giddy.

'If we're going up a mountain, will I need boots?'

'We'll get you kitted out in the morning.' As I turn round, there is the boy struggling to get his sweater off, midriff bare, like Michelangelo's slave. I tell him that breakfast will be brought up at eight and hope he sleeps well. Then I flee, my whole body beginning to shake.

*

He lost control over the wheel, skidded over the verge - the brakes were useless - and down into the lake, falling, tipping into the water with an echoing screech. The passenger side of the car was already submerged: vile green water was pouring in. He fought with his door, struggled out, scrambled up the bank. Even as he looked back, the car's roof was just disappearing below the surface. He saw his own mouth open, but heard nothing. Two bare feet and legs protruded out of the side of the dune. The boy had been tunnelling, and was buried alive by the sand. He must have been dead for hours... The cry finally broke free, came to the surface, and he was conscious, sitting up in bed, damp with the sweat of terror, no idea, at first, where he was.

As he fumbled for a light switch, there was a knock at the door. He put his dressing-gown on, and went to open it.

'I heard you calling out.' Piers was in the bath-robe supplied by the hotel. His hair was tousled.

'Sorry, Piers. Come in. What's the time?'

'Just after two. Was it..?'

'One of my silly nightmares.' I can't take my eyes off him. Opening the mini-bar, I discover a miniature of whisky. 'Want some?'

'No thanks.'

'I seem to spend a lot of time apologising to you for my various little outbursts.'

He flushes. 'Look, don't worry about it. I don't mind checking if you're OK.'

'Thanks anyway. Now you get back to bed. We've quite a day ahead of us.'

He left his light on this time: it had momentarily upskittled him to wake so suddenly in total darkness. The whisky calmed and warmed him. We are sparring, Piers, in this new relationship, which is most certainly not just the old one picked up again where we left off.

This time, his sleep was undisturbed.

*

As they left the hotel, Roland asked at Reception if they could recommend a shop selling mountain boots. They were directed to one just five minutes walk away, and were even given a voucher for ten per cent off. Piers tried on several pairs and finished up with Austrian ones. The car was already packed and they set off in good time.

'Where to?'

'Lauterbrunnen. Not far.'

The drive took them through a pretty village full of old chalets, then up a winding road between a rock face and a river. The morning sun had not yet penetrated into this narrow valley. At Lauterbrunnen, Roland turned off to the multi-storey car-park, where they put on boots and fleeces. 'We need to take our bags with us.'

'Why? Aren't we going back to Interlaken tonight?'

'No.' At the station kiosk he thrust some Swiss notes into Piers' hand. 'Get us two returns to Jungfraujoch.'

'Blimey. Is that the one up high?'

The train up to Wengen was crowded, so that they had to occupy separate seats. As they began the steep climb, Roland could not resist looking back to see Piers chatting away animatedly to a man sitting next to him. He doesn't need me as much as I need him. Perhaps my nightmare has scared him off. But no. After he'd finished his breakfast, he was out on the balcony in his bathrobe, like a young aristocrat on the Grand Tour, admiring the morning sunlight catching the tops of the peaks at the end of the valley.

He thought I was joking when I told him that we needed to be properly kitted out because we would be rubbing shoulders with some real mountaineers today. I had almost forgotten that he is still an untried youth with a cloistered life spent between Wharnley, his family home, and, more recently, Cambridge. Maybe that's why he's put a block in the way of our getting close again - he's really just as vulnerable as I am.

When their train rounded the shoulder of the Wengner Alp, the sun struck them full in the face. The immense rock-walls and snowfields rose beyond the ability of man to comprehend their scale.

At Kleine Scheidegg, the train disgorged all its passengers. More busy station staff, but the mood was relaxed up here.

'Now that's what I call mountains!' said Piers. 'And the air – it's just like breathing in wine.'

'Let's have a cuppa.' He pointed out the Observatory up on the Sphinx, almost touchable from here. 'Our next train will take us up to just below that.'

'Bloody hell! How does it get there?'

He's gone a bit giddy already. Wants to know if the tunnel up inside the Eiger is anything like the Underground.

As they sat with cups of steaming coffee on the terrace next to the station, a man in Swiss costume set up an Alpenhorn and played a tune on it. Don't tell me, we're in for a theatrical moment: Piers, with an abashed little look at me, gets up, exchanges a couple of words with the Swiss, and, the next moment, is holding the end of the enormous instrument and blowing hard. A few rude noises at first, then a long, pure, magical note, which echoes back from the nearest rockface, making a gaggle of Japanese grin, clap and film him.

Piers, the performer. I too point my camera.

'Oh come on, Roland, I haven't taken one of you yet. Over there, look, with that patch of snow behind you.'

Just at that moment there was an announcement in German through the loudspeakers.

'What's up?'

Piers was frowning. 'Had you intended us to stay at the hotel up there?'

'Yes, I booked it.'

'They're saying there's been an electrical fault, so they can't take guests. The cafeteria and shop are OK. So I'm afraid we have to report to that one instead.' He pointed over to the Hôtel des Alpes.

The announcement was repeated in French and, finally in English, at which point a large crowd of Japanese, toting suitcases, also converged on the hotel.

Roland was clearly cross. There was a long queue at reception, but when their turn eventually came, they were assured that a room would be waiting when they came back down. They could leave their bags.

The same crowd, mainly Asian, was boarding the Jungfraujoch train, but Piers found them seats in an unreserved carriage on each side of the centre aisle. 'How long does it take?'

'Just under an hour. We stop twice.'

'In the tunnel?'

'Yes, but there are windows to see out of.' It's bizarre: he spent last night in the kind of room one would choose for a mistress. I bought him boots as though he were my son. Still I cannot tell what I am supposed to be to him. The concept *friends* is as far as the world would permit us to go. With the nonchalance of youth, he copes with it all, while I spend every second analysing, examining my feelings, gauging what best to say next, and pulling to pieces his every word, in case there is something hidden inside.

After the halt at Eigergletscher, they plunged into the tunnel with a loud grinding of wheels, the rock walls inches from the sides of the carriage. Piers' face had gone taut.

'Are you all right?'

'Just a bit dizzy. I expect it's the pressure in the tunnel, or something. This is a heck of a gradient, isn't it?'

I needn't have worried: Swiss accordion music begins to play through the speakers and his face relaxes into a grin. When the *falsetto* yodelling starts, he pretends to mime to the music.

Why on earth did I choose this crazy jaunt? Being sardine-tight in this uncomfortable, noisy train is diametrically opposed to a quiet, idyllic scene where each of us could pour out his heart if he chose.

The train stopped, everyone barged off down a rocky passage and into a space lit by daylight. 'Gosh, Roland, we must be half-way up the North Face.' He edged forward to one of the inspection windows, his breath misting it up. 'Two eight six five metres. Why the heck don't they convert it to feet?'

'Nearly nine and a half thousand.'

'I've never been as high up as this.'

'Not even in a plane?'

'I've not been in a plane. I'm just a simple country boy, remember? Look at that tiny place down there.'

'Grindelwald.'

The second stop, as I predicted, takes his breath clean away: Eismeer, with its huge expanses of tumbled ice, snow and gaping crevasses. Camera in hand, he darts about, looking for the best viewpoint, and I am comforted that there are still vestiges of the eager young boy I once knew.

At long last, the track levelled out, the tunnel widened, strip-lights appeared, and they were at Jungfraujoch. 'Don't rush on ahead. Take it easy, for a few minutes. And you'll need your dark glasses, Piers, when we get outside.'

'Why? I'm OK.' But he soon found himself gasping for breath.

They clambered up some steps and were looking out of a window into sunshine. A giant sheet of ice, arched and rutted, with dark streaks down each side, stretched away far below them, mile upon mile, until it curved out of sight.

His eyes are watering. Perhaps it's just the brilliance of the light. *Or are you moved by all this, Piers?*

They found themselves slithering along a snowy path outside, which ended at a little knoll.

'Over eleven thousand,' said Piers. 'More than a third as high as Everest. What's that glacier called, Roland?'

'The Aletsch. And look the other way. See that blue smudge on the skyline over there? That's the Black Forest.'

A Japanese came up to them, all gold teeth and cameras. Would they take his picture? And then Piers insisted: 'Now its our turn - with the glacier behind us.' He put an arm round Roland's shoulder - man to man, brotherly. 'Like Hillary and Tensing!'

The rarified air is making both of us giddy now. The other tourists seem to melt away. Piers is looking at me with his solemn face. 'There's really no need for you to get upset about us any more. We're together again, and that's all that matters.'

'I know. Thanks.' We have to give it time. You intimated that we can't put the clock back, but that falls a long way short of what I now want for us.

'Had you really had enough of me, by the time you sent me off to talk to that priest?'

The astuteness of the question takes me by surprise. 'I was terribly torn between what I wanted, and what seemed to be the best thing for you. The two things just wouldn't reconcile. You were only a boy, after all. The whole business was bound to have its limitations, wasn't it?'

'So you had to send me away, but live on with that pain?' He knew that his little devil was goading him to stick the knife in ever more deeply.

Today, however, Roland had evidently found the strength to handle such tricky questions. 'I still live with it, but it's easier when we're together like this.'

'I know that you were... worried about us, sometimes.'

'I was afraid that you might have been harmed.'

You were clearly the harmed one, Roland. I wasn't. 'I hope I didn't ever... disgust you.'

'No, never, but you frightened me a good deal at times, Piers. You were so very intense about it.' I hope it doesn't sound as if I'm blaming you, but the right formula eludes me. The keen air surrounds us like a halo of blessing and encouragement. 'Not that I reject what we were, then. You live your life, and you can't unlive it, whether you want to or not.' The slate is marked. I knew, from the very first moment I saw you in the Minster, that you are sensitive. The trouble with this world is that the vulnerable always take the knocks.

Piers aims his camera at the glacier with its patches of sunlight and shadow. There are real mountaineers, where the *Firn* solidifies into the nascent glacier, and, as tiny black specks, they make their way across the rutted ice, roped together. We are neither trippers nor climbers, you and I, but two beings who seem to have come up here with some very important things to iron out.

His attention is drawn by laughter and shouts in the distance.

'Look, Roland, huskie dogs!'

Below the horizon of snow, a line of dots is pulling a larger one. Queueing at the huskie circuit, we watch the dog-team race round with the sledge bumping behind. Then it's our turn, we are muffled up in blankets, the driver shouts at the dogs, the runners of the sledge begin to hiss beneath us, and, faster and faster, we are speeding along through the strange white world of snow and ice. 'It must be like this at the North

Pole!' he shouts.

The giants rise up, thrusting their grey-black jagged flanks through dazzling snowfields, the shadows blue and mysterious: mountains stacked up in haphazard confusion, but making a composition to delight the eye. With their almost vertical profiles, they don't invite us men to approach their glory. Glacial, superb, clear enough to touch from here, they recede into the distance, blotting out vast tracts of blue sky, claiming their kingdom. I'm glad, Piers, that you've had the chance to see this.

We move off across the snow to find a quieter spot. After a while, he says he wants to take more pictures. I linger behind. He is talking animatedly, his face alight, his hands and arms working in support of his words, of which I hear but one in ten, seeing only the vigour, the youthfulness. Piers, how I ache!

This is not the first time I have been subject to forces which I could not properly recognise nor control, but I am now in the grip of a strange sensation, where daring mixes with danger, and joy wrestles with fear. I can no longer play this game by safe, slow steps, for my time is going to run out. As I get older, my chances decrease, my value curves downwards.

It is either the brightness of the light or the altitude which we so rapidly attained, that causes my mind to play one of its silly tricks. I open my mouth and shout, 'Piers, I love you!' But then I reel, as if struck by some external object. Did I say that aloud? And if so, did he hear it?

A hundred paces away, he turns his head, pointing at something, still mouthing words which I cannot hear. He's happy, whatever. *But it matters to me, to know.*

They trudged back to their starting point, Roland still fearful of what he might have just blurted out. As if to mock him, though, a small dark cloud came sidling up, and blotted out Schynige Platte far below. And, with it, a shadow crossed his heart, akin to that little *frisson* of doom which he had felt when looking down on the quays of Geneva from above, but still could not discern what it meant.

As the temperature up here grows chill, Piers' cheeks and ears glow red. I cannot entirely share his joy, but I can be pleased at it for his sake. *"If all the world were gone, and only we two were left"*. So what would happen, what could I possibly hope for, what is left for me? Up in the snow, *he* is as if in paradise, but it is still only a kind of hell for me. If Paradise be like Hell, then how be Hell itself?

Inside the building, they descended again. Did not Tadzio share the lift with Aschenbach, and back away politely when the doors opened to release him to his floor, where his lover found himself one evening? *"By his beloved's chamber door, he leaned his head against the panel, powerless to tear himself away."* Yes, Piers, I broke through that pre-Raphaelite prettiness, I passed on through that door, and the Summoner was there to receive me...

They ate in the cafeteria, Roland with a ham roll, Piers wolfing his sausages and Rösti down as if he had not eaten for days. The light outside was becoming bluer by the minute, the windows steaming up. They were in a lost world on a mountain-top.

Which sea are we charting now, in our cockleshell boat? Which new code are we having to fashion, to provide contact again, but also to conceal that which must not be mentioned? I discovered, in our early days, that to woo a boy is both dangerous and delectable. And you were one who was sloughing off his innocence like a skin being shed. You wanted knowledge, you sought the adventure I was able to give you. Was that so wrong?

My mind, locked up for so long, contains things which have turned into the miasma of the plague, things I could wish unsaid and undone, things to be exorcised. But that is the craven view! Have I not always striven to be myself, to stand by my principles (however at variance they might be with everyone else's), to give myself up to my fate, like Mann's writer on his balcony, singling out the boy on the beach? Oh lord, am I about to succumb again, to let myself drop into the ancient whirlpool?

He found tears in his eyes. Fortunately, Piers had already wandered off somewhere, probably to the gift shop. It was never *that*, I would never have gone to that: *une descente dans la dégradation humaine*, with Keith maybe, but never with you.

We had some sublime moments at the cottage, you and I, because we were in love. Now we are picking up the pieces, trying to fit them together again. A vain enterprise? If you alarmed me sometimes, then, I pray that you may never do so again. And yet there is something better and warmer than the fear and pain inside me: a new light, kindled by you. Surely I must allow myself some hope, some small escape from black despair?

'Are you OK, Roland?'

He started. 'Yes, of course. Why?

How can I tell him that I saw him muttering to himself, from the opposite end of the room?

The sun was already beginning to dip towards the west, and would soon be lost behind the mountains. Straight ahead, lights were appearing in the distance.

'That will be Interlaken,' said Roland.

The train down to Kleine Scheidegg was packed, and, feeling a headache coming on, he shut his eyes and remained thus until they emerged from the deafening tunnel into the sere gloom of the encroaching evening.

Piers was keyed up by this momentous day, on which they had talked, up there in the thin, heady air. I was right about Roland being wounded, when we parted. Adults usually seem so good at handling crises. You don't imagine them ever buckling under, but he did. Said I frightened him sometimes. Me, a twelve-thirteen-year-old! I came over here on the defensive, planning to put him to the test (impossible in Cambridge), to find out what had changed in him and what had not. Now I find I've been putting myself to the test, and I don't see how to explain that to him without compromising the distance that I've moved away from him. On the threshold of teenagedom, I was all too eager to try out that sort of awakening pleasure, ecstasy, all that stuff - and needing someone older to show me the way. But five years on... Maybe we need to find a dispassionate way of talking all this through.

With the steady loss of altitude, they were both overcome by a cosy torpor, but this was rapidly dispelled when they reached Kleine Scheidegg, only to find that the promise of a room in the hotel had mysteriously vanished. Japanese tourists were thronging the vestibule, shouting at the staff. There was nothing for it but to recover their bags and catch the next train back down to Lauterbrunnen.

'Now what?' Piers was exhausted too. 'Back to Interlaken?'

Roland shook his head. 'I'm done in. It must be possible to find a room here.' They went into a hotel near the station, but the reception area was teeming with an English coach party. They fled.

A few doors up the road was another hotel, which looked quieter.

'Can you wait a moment? I need to fetch something from the car,' said Roland. His pills, to calm him down.

'Don't worry. I'll go in and fix us up.'

When he got back to the hotel he found Piers in the vestibule, wearing a nervous grin.

'Have they got a room, then?'

'Oh yes, but you'd better come and see it.' He already had the key, and led the way upstairs, unlocked a door and let Roland go in first. It was not a large room. It had an easy chair, a wardrobe, a double bed, and a shower room leading off.

Roland whipped round. 'This is no good. You'll have to tell them. Just won't do at all. Sorry'. Amid the turmoil of my emotions, I adopt the world's mask in this situation. I went to bed with Keith, but that was different. Piers, you once came slipping into my bed, at the cottage, and that was different, too, a fact which goes on ringing, like a bell. But this is impossible.

'There's nothing else. They're full up with skiers, you see. The receptionist phoned around, but everywhere's chokka. Can't we manage?' Oh God, he's started shaking again.

'There isn't even room for an extra single bed.'

'Look, Roland, if you don't care for it, I'll pay. And it's only for one night...'

'Don't be silly. You're my guest.'

'You aren't annoyed with me, are you?'

What am I supposed to answer to that?

After a strained and largely silent supper, he began to sense the dread an inexperienced bride must feel, on the first night. As the seed grows inside the mind, takes charge, and disconnects one's rationality, one heads for the abyss, so cleverly charted by Mann. He was sweating.

Back in their room, Piers fiddled about in his bag, aware that he had handled this badly. Without looking at Roland, he quickly slipped into his pyjamas, put his clothes in the wardrobe, and sat on the bed. Then a practical thought nearly made him shout with laughter. 'Which side do you want to sleep?'

Roland dropped into the arm-chair. 'It's all right. You have the bed.'

'But what will you do? You can't sit there all night.'

'No, really, I'd much rather.'

'Roland, this is potty. Look, I promise not to kick, and I'll try not to snore.' While the boy was in the shower, he stood staring out at the street. *With my recent track record, I know I'm not worthy of him...*

Piers came back, his hair still wet, putting his pyjama top back on. 'Well, have you chosen?' Miraculously, he fell asleep as soon as his head touched the pillow.

Roland spent a few moments of private nostalgia looking at him, but then his tiredness forced him to capitulate. He got undressed and washed and, like a thief, sneaked into the other side of the bed. Piers stirred a little, then resumed his even breathing.

I am aware of his warmth next to me, although we do not touch. Oh Lord, only a short span ago, it was a different body, but the same kind of warmth. After so long in the cold, I cannot cope with it.

He woke with a start, to find an arm clutching him, a strange breath in his face. At first, in the total darkness, he had no idea where he was nor who it was. And then he knew: Piers. *Is he asleep, or just pretending to be?*

His heart was beating furiously. *Surely the boy must hear it? If only I could see his face, but there is no light at all. Has it been decreed that we may act out our passions in a dark, derelict place, with only our hands and ears to tell us the way?*

Something had begun to struggle within him, like a bubble far below the surface, striving up towards the light. His body was aflame. Here was the only and ultimate truth of truths: *I desire, therefore I am!* And, in this bed, you clasp me, as if we are married again, and my carefully-built defences are already crumbling to dust. I dare not move, dare not stay where I am.

A sudden cough shook him, like an act of mercy, and the arm was lazily withdrawn. Piers rolled over the other way, turned his back and slept on. So my panic is over, just like that. But will a time ever come, when..?

When he woke for the second time, the bed was cold and empty, and it was growing light outside. 'Piers?' He leapt out, put on a light, looked in the shower. There was his flannel, his soap, his hair gel. Some of the clothes had gone, but his bag was still there. Gone jogging! His face smiled bleakly back at him from the mirror on the wardrobe door.

*

'I want to give you this, as a thank-you for – well, not just yesterday, which was so marvellous – but for everything.' From his trouser pocket he takes a neat round box and hands it over.

'Piers, you needn't have.' Once it was a ring, inscribed with our two names. I still have it, somewhere. I open it: a miniature crystal paperweight, with a picture of the Jungfrau. Tasteful, and not cheap. 'It's really lovely. And I got you this.'

When he wasn't looking, I picked up the book about the Jungfrau railway, German version. He is delighted, I am seized in a powerful hug, his breath blowing in my ear. Like a nephew making an affectionate gesture to an uncle, and no more than that?

'Would you be one of the bears of Berne, by any chance?' Unable to react normally to that hug, I try to turn it into a joke.

'Is it possible to go and see them?'

'I don't see why not.' We pack up and go down to breakfast.

*

'Are all Swiss lakes this beautiful?'

We have stopped off for coffee by thelake at Thun.

'This one's a winner. Look at the light on it, and the Jungfrau and co.

up behind. It may still be early Spring, but it could almost be one of the Italian lakes.'

'Do you think I ought to learn Italian?'

He is looking at me over his cup. I am chary about giving advice, not wanting to risk sending him down a wrong path. 'Look how much of the counter-tenor repertoire is in it.'

'I'm not sure about singing as a job. It's not very lucrative. Now if I'd been a lung-busting tenor...'

'In the end, Piers, it boils down to doing what you most like. I've been very lucky to have chosen a line which I enjoy, I'm reasonably successful in, and which brings in a handsome return. If your heart is really set on becoming a professional...'

'Can't imagine I'd ever get up among the best.'

'If you work at it. Luck plays a big part, of course, as does knowing the right people.'

'I don't know any people.'

You know me, and Guy. Won't we do, for starters? 'You'll meet some at Cambridge.'

He shrugs, takes another gulp of coffee and changes the subject. 'Look how beautiful the light is, on the water. You ought to do a painting of that. The Impressionists were great at portraying light, weren't they?'

'It's the key to all good painting, in my opinion. But science sometimes comes creeping into art as well.'

'How?'

'Let me give you a rather mundane example. Light can throw a shadow twice, from the same source. Take this cup: the sunlight falls obliquely across it. The first lip sends a shadow into the cup itself, while the whole cup projects a second one on to the table. This suggests that light is weaker than darkness, because it's restricted in what it can do to combat the darkness it produces. Darkness has to win in the end, because there's so much more of it than there is of light.'

'That's because you are looking at it from the earthling's point of view,' said Piers. 'If you were in the sun, you would never see any shadows at all, since the things lit by the sun perfectly mask their shadows. That's why God cannot see evil.'

We are now on a metaphysical plane! I am as pleased with that as he is, but cannot resist taking up his point. 'Ingenious, but aren't you casting doubts upon God's almightiness? Or are you mistaken in placing God in the sun?' I wonder if you would understand, if I told you that, after hiding my inner light away for so long, I have it again.

*

They left Lake Thun and the high mountains behind and were soon in Berne, where they strolled down the ancient arcaded street and across the bridge, to reach the spot Piers most wanted to see. He is his old, light-hearted self today, which gladdens me. And there he is, round the other side of the pit, leaning over the wall, raising the camera, shooting off frame after frame. This is the boy who gets soaked in the water jet, plays on the alpine horn and then ends up in bed with me. (I am sure he engineered that, just to see my reaction). Piers, I want you so much, I'm jealous of these silly bears! I know you want to be up and away, getting on with your young life, leaving me behind. Perhaps one day, if I am lucky, I shall see you step on to the concert platform or even the stage.

And now here he is, asking if we can eat before we go on. I would give you a banquet if I could, for you are my boy again, my favourite, who lures the dragon out of his lair and gives him such hope.

'I rather fancy some of that Rösti again.'

*

As the car sped down the motorway towards Lausanne, he closed his eyes, letting the light shine pinkly through the lids. That sharing of the bed last night could have been dodgy, but it worked out all right. When I got up, there he was, fast asleep with his mouth open - a picture of innocence! Funny, but I look on him as having grown up in these five years, yet he's been a man all the time I've known him. It's my perspective of it all that's changed, rather than his. We've tried to talk, and there's a hell of a lot more in the pipeline, still to be said, but he seems limited in the extent he can come forward to me.

'Monsieur Bannerot was a bit pessimistic about us driving out here, wasn't he?'

Roland did an exaggerated sigh. 'He doesn't come from the mountains. I doubt if they ever see snow in the Loire valley.'

'Have you been to any of his concerts?'

'I quite often go.'

'Is he good?'

'Must be. A funny chap, though, in some ways.'

'How do you mean?' People surely say the same about you.

'A bit thick-skinned, for a musician. Doesn't think twice about barging in. You see, he'll be on the doorstep when we get home.'

'Not literally? He does live somewhere, doesn't he?'

'He's got a flat at Annecy.'

'Not as grand as "Orphéon", then?'

'I think he rather envies me what he calls my *vie de grand seigneur*.'

'Do you... like him?' There, I've lit that little squib!

'He can be quite amusing. He has this rather blind admiration for the Royal Family. Shook hands once with Prince Charles, and has never been the same since. He even refers to him as the Dauphin! I believe he's currently trying to pursue some woman distantly related to the Comte de Paris.'

'How did you meet?'

'Through rambling. We joined forces on a few guided walks, and found we had music in common as well.'

So *he's* your fellow mountaineer! 'You regard him as a friend, then?'

'He's more of an irritation.' Guy Bannerot might have been working out some inconvenient things about them. Not to have told him about Piers' visit had been a mistake.

They then passed on to the safer topic of how Roland first knew he wanted to study art.

'Funnily enough, I suppose it started with the cinema. My mother was quite addicted to it and she took me regularly, often to ones that weren't really suitable for me. Sometimes I'd get upset or frightened by what I saw. She always tried to comfort me by saying "It's not real", but it was, to me, or it wouldn't have touched me like that. Of course, I was too young then to know about creative talent, and it was a long time before I realised how deep and important art was. Good painting, good music, good literature - those are my realities.' That must sound terribly dated to him.

'So all that began in you when you were quite small?'

'What people call imagination and sensitivity, yes, I suppose so. But naturally I had to be trained how to bring them out. You find your own style, if you're lucky. My chief influence was Cézanne, when I was younger, but I've shifted my ground quite a bit since then.'

'Yes, I remember you saying that on the TV programme. Do you ever exhibit any of your paintings?'

'People often try to twist my arm, but the last thing I would want is them beating a trail to my door.'

This must be why the outside world finds Roland so intriguing – he's cultivated a rarity value! But then, as an artist and a self-made man, he doesn't have the discipline of ordinary people responsible to others. Without ties, like a wife or family, he can please himself, kick over the traces. Perhaps that's why he regards life as a sham, whereas it's maybe art that's the sham. Make-believe is too dangerous in the long run; you lose your grip on the world. He could be going mad, which would explain these emotional outbursts. And wasn't his most violent one when I asked him if he was happy? It all points to his not being happy at all. I wish I could discuss him with someone else. But who? James? Guy?

Lausanne. As we run along by the lakeshore, with elegant villas much in evidence, he, despite his alleged leftist principles, can't help being impressed.

'What's that place over there, on the far side?'

'Évian. We went through it the other day.' It seems like centuries ago...

'Where the mineral water comes from?'

'And where the Route des Grandes Alpes begins.'

'I suppose that goes to Mont Blanc.'

'It touches it, on the way to Nice.'

'Nice? My mother's always talking about wanting to go back there. It's where I was conceived, as she blurted out once, after too much sherry!' He felt silent for a moment, and then was off again: 'Isn't it strange how you can discover a person you were related to, all along, but never really knew? Father bunged me into the Choir School when I was seven, and went off with Mother to do his archaeology and stuff abroad. And then, that summer, when I finished there, he was sort of around again, taking an interest. Oh, it was only for a few days, between places, as you might say, but he talked to me, he looked *at* me instead of *past* me. I don't know the things we said, any more, but that didn't seem to matter. When you're close to someone, you don't have to put everything into words, do you?'

And if he had not died, you would never have sought me out again. I didn't realise until this moment how grateful I am to Mr Moriston for falling off his scaffolding and propelling his orphan back to me.

'Look, Roland, people swimming. Isn't that incredible, for only March?'

'It's going to be April tomorrow!'

In another hour "Orphéon" received them back with what felt to Roland like distant cordiality. Madame Bouillot had opened windows and aired beds, and was bustling about in the kitchen. There was no sign of Guy, nor had he left a message.

After supper, Roland made his apologies: he wanted to take an early bath, then get to bed. Now that we're back, I feel as if we've been weighed, judged... and, despite that persistent little doubt inside me, we have not been found wanting. I examine the last few days, and, in the cautious political parlance of Geneva, we've made some positive progress, our ship is still on course, and Piers, on a deeper level, knows, remembers and loves me still. But there is one thing I still desperately need to know: whether I uttered my avowal out loud up in the snow, those precious, sacred words, not to be cheapened or dirtied by being made public, on the wind. *I love you*, but did I *say* it, and does he *know* it?

III.

When he entered the kitchen, the coffee pot was steaming gently on the breakfast table, but there was no sign of Piers, nor of Madame Bouillot, who should have been there. With a frown he poured himself a cupful, added milk from the jug and two spoonsful of sugar.

Immediately, the mixture in his cup began to curdle and effervesce. 'What the..?'

Laughter rang out from the dining-room next door. In came Piers, followed by Mme Bouillot, both with mischief in their faces. They stood in the kitchen doorway and chanted in unison <April fool!>

He looked from one to the other, and again at his fizzing coffee, then his face crinkled and he joined in the mirth.

'Pardon, monsieur,' said his housekeeper.

<Ah, Piers put you up to that, I'm sure. I know him!> Or do I?

'It was Alka Seltzer crushed up,' said Piers, of the sugar. <I hope, monsieur, I haven't ruined your breakfast.>

Madame, shaking her head in amusement, brought a fresh cup of coffee, and then went to begin her chores.

'What else are you planning for today, Piers, if one is allowed to ask?'

'You mean tricks?'

'I do not,' said Roland drily.

'Thought of going for a swim in the lake.'

'You mean, in one of the pools?'

'Non, *dans le lac*. Like people were doing yesterday.'

'It might be colder than you think. Have you got the necessary gear?'

'Shorts'll be OK. May I take a towel?' He met Madame Bouillot on the stairs, who quietly complimented him on having brought some rare laughter to this house.

While he was changing into shorts and track-suit bottoms, the doorbell rang downstairs. Men's voices. The door shut again. As he seized a towel and began to descend the stairs, the acrid smell of a Gitane stopped him. Guy. Do I go on or back?

But Roland was calling him, in his 'we-have-an-unwelcome-visitor' tone.

They gathered in the *salon,* Piers wondering if this formality was for his benefit. Guy advanced towards him and proffered a hand. 'Bonjour, Piers. C'était bien, l'Oberland Bernois?'

'Magnifique.' He was conscious of Roland standing nearby, but not offering anyone a seat.

Guy had brought the promised tickets. Rossini, Saint-Saëns, Stravinsky. At Lausanne, with an acclaimed young British conductor. The concert was to be on Saturday. Today was Thursday. Would Piers still be here? Excellent.

Roland turned to stare outside, leaving Piers to cope. The gardens were radiant in the morning sunlight. When the cigarette smoke seemed to fill the *salon,* he thrust open the French window, stepped out and looked back. <What if we take a turn round my park?> said with heavy sarcasm. It seemed to him as if the gardens had lost their vegetable innocence, and become a stage set for a possible drama. But whence would it come?

The phone rang indoors and, while he returned to answer it, Guy steered Piers along the paths in a purposeful manner. 'Millan, you know, is a good man but not an easy man. He has his caprices, but I think he esteems you.'

'Pardon?' He was thrown momentarily by the idiom.

'He likes you very much, *n'est-ce pas'*?

He didn't know how to answer this, felt his face going hot.

Guy seemed to understand. 'He is a man with love to give, but it is not so simple because he does not know properly how. I try to talk, try to help him. Do you talk?'

'What,' stammered Piers, 'what about?'

'About his living, the way he... He needs a *confidant*. I think he tries to avoid me, but I always arrive, for the best I can do. Perhaps he talks to you what is in his heart.' This time, he did not stop to see if there was a reaction. 'For you, pardon, it is *difficile*. You have the half of his age, you have your own life. I do not think that what he has in his heart is for you.'

It might have been less clumsily put, but I understand every word. A warning is being spelt out here, by a disinterested party, for the very first time since the Canon delivered his broadside at me and ruined everything. At least Guy can't do that.

Roland, intrigued to find them on the other side of his gardens by now, followed after, only to find that they were deep in argument (mainly English) about the virtues and vices of Saint-Saëns. This apparent take-over irritated him beyond measure. The privacy of "Orphéon" was being abused, Guy's fault, of course. Now, they were engrossed in the *repertoire* of the counter-tenor!

'This voice, I must hear it!' Guy was exclaiming. 'You must not hide art away.'

Piers laughed, self-consciously. He couldn't just strike up here, out in the open, on his own.

'Come, Millan, let us go to your piano. You will play and Piers will sing. You must make my little trip this morning double worthy!'

And so we find ourselves in my sanctum where Bannerot fusses about, looking for suitable music in the cabinet, and I try not to draw comparisons with that session in the practice room at St Neville's.

<Look, this is exactly what I have in mind. A lovely piece by Bach. Piers, *try it*, s'il vous plaît. Et, Millan, ça va, oui? *Not too* difficile *for you*?>

We're both sight-reading from the "Christmas Oratorio" - in April! Oh God, I didn't even know I had any German stuff. Will he manage? Will I?

Piers' smooth cadences hovered in the room, tentative at first, but, as his inhibitions vanished, he gave himself utterly to the music. Roland, on the periphery of it all, was aware of ripples on a pond, of Guy's rapt concentration, of his mouth shaping silent words of astonishment. He made an ugly mistake on the keyboard, shook his head in annoyance, and stopped playing as soon as Piers finished singing, though there were still a few bars left.

Neither notices my act of desecration, they are both on a wavelength which excludes me: professional performers, not fumbling amateurs. He got up briskly, interrupting Bannerot's flow of praise. 'Now we have to be getting into town. Piers has set his heart on a dip in the lake.' I always seem to be bundling Guy out of the house. I cannot blame Piers: he has to be courteous, he does not know Guy as I do, does not feel the harm of it, the harsh light suddenly cast upon the two of us, as never before.

*

After calling in at the office, he found a parking-space in one of the streets leading down to the lake. Piers, uncertain whether to wear his towel draped around his neck, opted instead to carry it rolled up under his arm.

The sun's heat was unwelcome even to Roland, today. Everything that was white glared at him: the lake steamers, the gleaming stone-work of the quays, even people's clothing. The lake was oily, receding into a haze more fitting in August, than now.

In a waterside park, enclosed by trees and a hedge, people were sitting or lying on the grass. A small gate bore the sign "Children not admitted." Hardly surprising, thought Piers. Half the women are topless!

Sensing the boy's sudden interest in this little scene, I try a diversionary remark, but he's engrossed in a young female not far away, lying on her stomach on a towel, her parents beside her. Brilliant turqoise bikini. She's about his age, breasts bare (though this shows only now, as she eases herself up on her elbows a little, saying something to *mère*.) Dark hair, page-boy effect, and, even from here, I can see that she has mischievous eyes.

Piers was feeling in his pocket and screwing up his eyes. 'Damn, I've left my sunglasses in the car.'

How stagey can you get? If it were not so calculated, it would be comic. *So this is it, then.*

'Shall I fetch them, Roland?'

'No, the car alarm's set. I'll go. Stay here, won't you, so I don't miss you?' No fear of that, though, he's glued to the spot.

Piers stood awkwardly by the little gate, aware that she was looking his way. Was that smile meant for him? He put his hands in his pockets, turned round, and began to saunter back along the promenade towards a kiosk he had noticed. A handful of people were buying ice-cream, but of course he hadn't brought any money! Disconsolately, he stopped and faced the lake, watching the constant white surging plume of the jet.

Then something made him turn his head towards the kiosk. There, at the end of the queue, was the girl. She had put her bra back on, and in her hand was a purse.

Before he knew, he was walking back, though he knew it ought to be played more subtly. The sales assistant must be a quick worker, for *she* was nearly at the front already. Roland, don't get back too soon...

Now she was approaching, with two cones in one hand and one in the other. Like a tree taken root, he stood there, right in her path. She looked up, directly into his face. Her lower eyelids were straight, her upper ones made semicircles, which gave her a constantly cheeky look.

And then, as she was almost level with him, one of the two cornets in her right hand dropped and splatted on the path.

She exclaimed. He stepped forward. <Can I help you?>

She smiles at me. Green eyes and a marvellous mouth – she's lovely! <You can hardly pick that up.>

<Hang on, I'll get you another.> But you can't, you fool, you haven't a *sou!*

<Don't bother. Thanks all the same. Would you like one?> She held out one of the two surviving ices to him.

<Yes, but… It's for your parents.>

It didn't matter, she assured him. They wouldn't mind. Her father could buy some more, if they still wanted ices.

They found themselves strolling side by side, licking the ice-cream as it ran down the side of the cones.

<Are you here with your father?> she wanted to know.

She noticed us together. <Oh no. That is, we're together, but he isn't my father.>

He kept talking, anxious to indicate that he was perfectly free to walk along with her like this, if he wished. <Are you French or Swiss?>

<French, of course. Can't you tell the difference?> She wrinkled her nose.

<Not when you're in your bikini,> he ventured to say.

She let out a shout of laughter. By the accent, she meant.

Well, no, he wasn't that good at accents.

<You aren't French,> she said, gravely, looking at him.

<English.>

She stopped in her tracks. <English? But the English are usually so bad at French, and you are so good!>

He knew he was blushing now.

<I'm Adèle, Adèle Calivet. Et toi? Oh, pardon - *vous!*>

How quickly - and purposefully? - she had dropped into the familiar form. He told her his name and, for the first time in his life, felt proud of it.

<Piers Moriston... I like that. And how old are you, Piers?>

She clearly means business. Well, attack is the best form of defence! <Seventeen, and you?>

She put an arm through his, as if they had known one another for years. <The same. Where do you live?>

<A town near London. And you?> Am I in some kind of dream?

<Near Annecy. Do you know Annecy?>

<Not yet, no.> Fishing for an invite now!

<Are you spending your holidays here in Geneva?>

<Nearby. St. Julien.>

This exchange took them back to the expanse of grass where Adèle's parents were waiting. She explained the loss of the ice-cream, the gift of another to <my new friends Piers,> and introductions were made. Monsieur Calivet, in impeccable designer shirt and well-pressed shorts, stood up and shook Piers solemnly by the hand. He was quite short and balding, but he had Adèle's twinkle in his eye. Madame remained stretched out, and held up a languid hand for the newcomer to press. Adèle asked if they could continue their walk together.

Piers remembered that Roland would be returning, but Monsieur

Calivet promised to intercept him.

Linking arms again, they headed, by tacit agreement, for the mole leading out to the *jet d'eau*, the morning sunshine giving them every encouragement.

<Do you have a job?> she wanted to know.

No, he was studying at university. French and German.

Just as Guy had done, she pulled a face at the mention of 'allemand', which made him smile. <And do you work?>

She was doing a domestic science course in Annecy.

<D'you like it?>

She wrinkled her nose again. It was all right.

<And you come to Geneva, to swim, when you have your own lake?>

<Papa likes to say he's been abroad for the day.>

<You regard Switzerland as foreign, then?>

<Of course. Almost more foreign than England.>

<Have you ever been to England?>

A language course in Kent, when she was fourteen, but she'd forgotten most of her English.

'I shall teach you some, then,' said Piers, reverting to his own language.

'You will be teacher after university?'

'No, I don't think so'.

'What? *Interprète*?'

'Perhaps a singer.'

She stopped and looked at him. <In a *night club*?>

That made him laugh.

<What then? In the opéra?>

<Maybe.>

<Are you a tenor or a bass?>

<Neither. I'm counter-tenor.>

She let go of his arm and put her face close to his. <Piers, you must tell me the truth. You are perfectly normal, aren't you? You know...> There was mock solemnity in her voice, but wicked humour in her eyes.

He affected not to understand what she was on about, but when she tapped him lightly on the trousers, *right there*, adding, <That's working, is it?>, he felt himself go scarlet. She began to laugh, put her arms up and round his neck, and he could only laugh too. The spray from the jet made her bare shoulders glisten. She put her cheek to his.

<Of course I'm normal.> He tried not to sound annoyed. Just because he sang *falsetto* didn't mean *that*.

<Then that's fine by me, Piers,> she said, and gave him a quick peck on the cheek. He walked as though on air.

*

Approaching the gate in the hedge, he saw the small Frenchman waiting for him. <My daughter and the young man, Piers, have gone for a walk.> He was invited to meet Madame and introductions were made.

So Eve walked in the garden, and Adam fell. They asked him to join them, which was the last thing he wanted. He was still holding Piers' sunglasses.

<Alors, he is a relative?> Monsieur wanted to know.

<No, a language student. He is here to practise his French.>

<A student where?> Madame wanted to know.

<At Cambridge University. It's - >

He got no further. The name Cambridge worked like a charm on the Calivets, as though minor royalty were being discussed.

And now here they come, arm in arm, very much caught up in each other, *he* moving with the proud grace of a dancer, *she* lithe and boldly close to him - and I feel suddenly as if I've been rammed into a pigeonhole marked "Parent".

<We are very anglophile, monsieur,> her father was saying, with a beam. <As for me, I'm delighted to see my daughter out for a walk with a young gentleman.>

I bet you're pleased. But this is too ridiculous, to have him spirited away from me by a nymph in a skimpy bikini. There's a new look in his eyes, a self-conscious regard for this female. Infatuation already? Courtesy and deference force me into the sidelines. In a few days they'll be parted for ever and, in a few weeks, they'll have forgotten one another. Oh my God, Monsieur is proposing we all lunch together.

'Look, Piers, I met one of my theatre contacts just now. Something rather urgent's cropped up. So I'll leave you to it, and pick you up later. Shall we say here, at four?' Telling lies never did come easily to me.

But Monsieur Calivet had understood enough to interpose: no, he would bring Piers back home afterwards. St Julien was on their road to Annecy. *Pas de problème!*

'Is that all right, Roland? We might get that swim in, after lunch.' Where there should have been anxious concern on Piers' face, there was simply a fatuous expression.

Roland held out his hand, in which he had crumpled up a couple of banknotes. 'Here, so you can pay your share.'

<No, no no.> Monsieur was standing like a rather fussy bird, his arms stuck out slightly behind him, his head forward. <It's an honour for us to do a small service for the English.> Such a pity that Monsieur Millan could not come now, but he would of course be invited to their house, later on.

Roland made a quick departure.

<Your host's a bit funny, isn't he?> said Adèle, but her father hushed her to silence. <What a thing to say about him, when he is so correct! And did this *jeune monsieur* say you could use *tu* to him?>

She pouted: it had simply happened.

Piers wanted to say it didn't matter, that he was only too pleased to be *tutoyé*, but he was in awe of Madame Calivet who, as she levered herself up off her towel, threatened to be as tall as her husband, if not a few millimetres more.

Adèle went to get dressed in their car nearby, her parents followed suit, and then they all made for a restaurant with tables on a terrace overlooking the lake. The linen was dazzling in the sunlight, Piers put on his dark glasses, and realised how much he was enjoying all this.

*

Fighting the tears, he drove home. How could he do that before my very eyes? Doesn't he see how wounding it is? They made their stage entrance, linked up, their every gesture a language that anyone could understand. For them, the brain is switched off and instinct takes over. She's a fast worker, that girl, but she'll turn out to be spoilt and no good for you at all. You'll find yourself caught in a trap, as once happened to me.

And is it somehow my fault, that this has happened? Did I unleash it? Surely not, for I have as little power over others as I have over myself. Why, we returned only yesterday from our trip to the mountains. We were beginning to know each other more deeply, once again, until that little cloud appeared inside me, which has finally taken on definition and blotted out my entire sky, my heaven. I knew something bad would happen just there, by the quay. April Fool, indeed!

I feel robbed: I'd hoped to see him stripped for swimming, just as we once splashed in the sea by the cottage, our bodies like two pieces of pale green plastic under the water. If people only knew the effect of what they did. And that French family - you can see they think they're quite something. That stupid little man with his stiff formality, his idle ugly wife. And the boy goes off for polite lunch in his none-too-clean T-shirt and track-suit trousers. Oh, Piers!

I dread returning to the house which he has been sharing with me, merely to re-enter the dark shell of that existence between his two comings. We were in bed together, at Lauterbrunnen, at "Stella Maris".

The sky in front had begun to darken, and, as he turned up his drive, the first heavy drops began to fall. Leaving his gates open, he made a dash for the house. Upstairs, Piers' French window was open and there were blobs of water already just inside, on his tiled floor. Closing the window, he turned to look at the room, but *his* things were not much in evidence: a small digital clock by the bed that said 14:49, a sweater hanging over the back of a chair, and a vocal score on top of the chest of drawers. Vivaldi's *Gloria*. With a small but delicious feeling of guilt, he opened the cupboard. On the shelves inside, Piers had put his T-shirts, socks, briefs. His best jacket and trousers (which he should be wearing now) were hanging up. Next to the new walking boots on the floor of the cupboard was a pair of sandals, as if a saint had passed that way. Solid curtains of rain made the light more unworldly than any stage designer could have done. The room was a cold bluish-grey now. He hastily retreated downstairs to the kitchen, to get himself something to eat and drink.

Back in his own house, he began to feel better. Why get so worked up? Piers wouldn't want me to, wouldn't understand why I should do. Mustn't get this thing out of proportion. It won't last - that sort of relationship (too grand a word?) is still-born. The storm outside was mocking his weeping. Ever the fond man, trying to distort the world into his own image... But, as he sat there, a new sensation worked its way through to his brain: relief. Yes, relief, such as one is able to feel when told the name of the disease one will die of. I felt that, as well as anguish, when Mother died. Cowardly relief, for I had inherited all, and was totally free at last. Then I found that I had merely exchanged one sort of slavery for another.

There was a loud knocking at the back door. Guy? Never. It must be Piers, back because the storm had stopped their swim or whatever. The French people have cut it short, brought him to me. I'll invite them in, I'll - .

He unlocked the door and opened it, knowing, as he did so, that they would have come to the front. A bedraggled, dripping creature confronted him, in vest and jeans so sodden as to be almost unrecognisable for what they were. Pale skin, sopping strands of dark hair falling over it. So who is this? A child come to beg, in such weather? A shepherd boy from the Auvergne? But two dark and liquid eyes were staring at him, and his mind gave up its rational functions. Stepping back to let the boy in, he glimpsed the blue-and-white jumble of bicycle on the ground behind.

Gently, he closed the door, as if he had admitted something fragile and precious, like a butterfly which might disintegrate if subjected to any shock or noise. The boy just stood there, in silence, visibly trembling, while a small pool of water collected around his trainers.

Of course, bare feet would have better suited the image, but no matter. About twelve, I should think. Smaller than Piers was, even then. His lips began to work, his voice at last broke the silence. <But you're drenched. You're shivering>

I lead the way through to the kitchen, the boy padding wordlessly after me.

<You had best get out of those wet things.> A suspicion of hair on the upper lip. Good torso; the arms almost plump, which he crosses in front of his waist, catching hold of the vest at the bottom and dragging it upwards, the material wilfully sticking to him.

From my cupboard I take out a huge, rough-textured towel. The boy has got the vest over his head now. The chest is well-moulded, the nipples dark in the glistening white flesh, the armpits still quite smooth, as if this were a cherub sculpted by Michelangelo. He wrenches the vest off and hands it to me. I receive the soggy bundle like a sacrament, deposit it reverently, and stand there, as he undoes his waistband, fighting the denim as if it were stiff, soaked sail-canvas. The jeans cling to his legs, but the top is open now. His hands struggle, his eyes never leaving mine. We exchange no word yet. He could have asked me for shelter, but it wasn't necessary.

The boy kicks off his trainers, bends down, forcing the hard wet material to the floor, and I am charmed by this spectacle, this lovely statue, this given treasure. He wears a red mini-slip, dark with the damp. His legs are also white, smooth, soft, just as *his* were that day, when the choristers came through the cloisters in white shorts and shoes.

There is a look of expectancy in those dark eyes now, an expression which finds its mark in me. I hold the towel out to him, but he goes on standing there, dog-like, shaking - with what? With cold, wetness, fear, desire? Or a mixture of all those?

He stepped forward at last, flung the heavy towel round the boy's shoulders and over his head, and began to rub him vigorously. The child's body was firm but pliant in his hands. He could not help an immense surge of affection for this scrap of humanity, for here was his young Piers again, returned, reincarnated.

The boy fought with the towel, to get his face free. His hair was fluffed up now, and Roland passed a hand through it. <What's your name?>

<Raoul, m'sieu.>

<And where do you live?>

<Les Amandaies, m'sieu.> A hamlet up off the Annecy road.

A moist, fragrant smell emanated from Raoul's hair, and his body gave off a human flavour that was not displeasing.

And so they stood for seconds that seemed like delightful hours, while Roland battled with himself, and lost. <That's wet, too,> he gasped, pointing at the briefs.

There is a new look in the boy's eyes, which I know of old. So, for the second time in one day, I am faced with a decisive moment. I am about to drop the towel and help him with the last stage, when something prompts me to ask, <How old are you, then?>

<Already fifteen, m'sieu.>

Fifteen? It couldn't be possible! Then he nearly jumped out of his skin, for there, in the doorway of the kitchen, stood Madame Bouillot in a dark blue raincoat with the hood up, a bulging shopping bag in her hand.

For a second, the three of them were as though transfixed. She looked from one to the other, then, with a few resolute steps forward, seized the boy by the arm and began to drag him along. He tripped over his jeans, which were still round his ankles, and fell to the floor with a bump and a squeal. Then, with surprising alacrity, he picked himself up, pulled up his trousers as best he could, scooped his shoes off the floor and tried to bolt. But she was more than a match for him. Standing between him and the door, the only escape route, she signalled to him to pick up his pathetic vest. Then he was hustled out. Roland, still rooted to the spot, heard her hiss <Get out and don't ever come back here. D'you understand?>

She returned, set-faced. <Pardon, monsieur, but that was a real little tyke. He'd have robbed us. I've sent him packing. He won't be back.>

I think I can read her mind at this moment. What could Monsieur have been thinking of, to take in such an urchin, even in that storm? Is it possible that he was planning to have his way with the child, and in his own kitchen? She doubtless finds me strange, as I stand here, dumb. But no, haven't I always been so very careful at all times? Not a speck of impropriety showing, even if I am unmarried. And I pay her well.

She asks, in all innocence, if Monsieur Piers has gone out, but her face says: 'It would not please him to know of this. He is such a nice young man.'

<He went into town with some friends.> See, I'm lying again.

<How many should I be cooking for?>

He sent her home, surprised to find himself unusually jubilant, as though what was begun here had been seen through to a glorious finish. He marvelled at what Fate had sent him, at the daring of it.

Fetching some wine, he poured a glass and sat down. So what does this make me? My reservoir of frustration very nearly overflowed. Yes, if she hadn't arrived then, we would have already taken to the back stairs and... Why did he say fifteen, when he was nowhere near? His voice was husky, but not broken. Ah, fifteen is the age of consent in France. *Voilà*. Now we have it.

He swilled the wine around. It's as if I've knocked you for six, Piers, you and your new-found girl. Les Amandaies, is it? You may not be coming back here, *petit Raoul*, but I shall come and sniff you out, before long.

In the corner near the door, the towel lay in a crumpled blue heap, proof if needed, that the boy had not been one of his figments. He picked it up, held it against his cheek, but let it drop again: this is identical to the one which Piers took to go swimming. Are they bathing in the lake after the storm and is it worth going to spy on them? No, the day is beginning to shorten in, and I shall sit here and wait for him, however late he arrives.

Every minute that you stay away, the bitterness goes on spreading like a poison in me, while my mind serves up any number of unwelcome scenarios. How can I repay you for hurting me? I hope I am incapable of dreaming up petty sanctions... How many times have I ever said those words to you which my mind formed, up at Jungfraujoch, but which were probably never uttered? (It all seems immaterial now). How cruel Fate can be.

It took a while to recover from this one. He used the towel – Raoul's towel - to mop his face. In a juggling act, something crashes to the floor sooner or later. I'm too old to be playing these games. Piers, Fillingham, and now this child who calls on me, drenched to the delightful skin.

Even if I wanted it, there can be no going back into the shell. I've come so far out, in this short time. I'm just going to have to rationalise and give way a bit, over this girl business. He doesn't love her, it's not possible. That much I take to my comfort.

Only one truth remains constant: I cannot afford to risk losing him. I must stomach the poison, while finding ways and means to keep him. And, if his affection for this girl should grow, then he will want to come back here, if only to see her. His room at "Orphéon" shall be his base, and I shall have to play the indulgent host.

What, though, if he doesn't stay here but is invited there? Suppose he accepts patronage from me but does not want me any more, for myself? He isn't a boy now, seeking adventure. He's grown up and away from all that. Did he come back out of some vestigial fondness for me? Oh Piers, am I wrong to want just one small physical sign of your affection, Lauterbrunnen become conscious?

And how does he put himself across to *them?* Goes down like a house on fire, I'll be sure: playing to the gallery, encouraged by her gaze. And *she'll* have taken him by the hand, asked if he was happy. And, of course, like a moon-calf, he'll have assured her he was happier than he could remember.

*

Tyres crunched on the gravel outside. He ran back down the stairs, and switched on the lights in the hall, not caring about the impetuosity displayed for those outside to see.

Piers, on the doorstep, flushed and happy. Monsieur behind him, a question forming on his lips: <Would it be all right if Piers came over to us tomorrow, for a few days? We would like to show him some of Savoy.>

Just as I feared. But I can hardly say no, can I?

'You're sure you don't mind, Roland? After all, you *have* had an awful lot of me so far. And... I don't have much time left.'

Time you could have spent with me. But it's all about *her*, now, isn't it, while I am relegated to being the complaisant but distant admirer. At least, the girl is not in evidence.

The car roars away into the darkness, I shut the door, and Piers, suddenly become a stranger, is here again, fresh, jubilant and full of it. 'I've had a marvellous time.' After lunch, they went back to the lake and he and Adèle had swum. Then the storm broke. 'Did you have it here, too?'

Oh yes, and a delightful scrap of humanity was washed up with it, but that is not a story I shall be sharing with you.

They'd gone back to the car still wrapped up in towels, Monsieur had driven to Annecy, and by the time they'd got down to the lake at Talloires, the sun had been shining again and they were able to sit out. 'They've got this fantastic house, with gardens right down to the water.'

I'm out of the contest, tired by all this, but I know my duty is to drum up some diplomatic restraint; above all, to remain clearheaded enough to see where it leaves you, Piers. Head over heels, after only one day, or still in the early stages? And (I keep returning to the key question), *where does it leave me?* Am I really banished back to outer darkness?

After they had said goodnight to one another, and retired to bed, Roland lay for a long time, trying to find an angle from which this business would look less threatening, less ugly. But ramifications kept appearing. I don't want you to be spoilt by these people, don't want them to make you selfish, narrow-minded. They represent an affluence and snobbishness which you aren't used to, and which is not going to do you any good. And when you indulge yourself in treacly talk about that girl, I really cannot help wondering whether, consciously or unconsciously, deliberately or not, you will find yourself using me. You never breathed a word of apology about being so late back - which could have eased some of my *pique.* And you allow yourself to be swept away by them tomorrow, so that my nose will be well and truly rubbed in it. You leave me exactly a week today. Perhaps you have left me already...

His bare feet froze on the wet grass. His gardens were silent, the trees dim black shapes set among an expanse of lawn that was hardly lighter. He did not know how he had come to be here, he was shivering in his pyjamas. Behind, the house was dark and dead, as if it had just expelled a miscreant for whom there was never to be any forgiveness.

By the far margin of the garden, he stopped, trying to discern the place where the path ran along outside. *Raoul, are you there?* From somewhere in the invisible town below, a dog barked. An owl answered, it seemed, from closer at hand. And an inspiration came to him, rising from the opaque depths of his mind: do I really want Piers physically any more? If I did, then the Lauterbrunnen episode would have turned into a frenzied approach by me. No, I want Raoul. I am an artist whose job it is to freeze things in their reality, not to follow evolutions, trends, growings-up.

Surely, though my love for Piers is deeper now. If it wasn't, the Adèle thing would not affect me so. And all he is doing is following my advice. I once made him promise to take a wife, and how could he do that without getting to know a girl? Somewhen or other, I urged him to be his own man. Well, now I reap the harvest, while trying to kid myself that that sort of evolution is good.

The sound of a car in the distance made the warmth die in his heart. Piers... They will collect you and whisk you away, and I shall be alone again with my private grief, and my even more private guilt.

*

As he eats his breakfast, he can talk of nothing but this Adèle. It might have intrigued me to see her, passed, as it were, through the filter of his perception (incredibly distorted in her favour, of course), if I were not so racked with the consciousness of my rivalry. I let him prattle on, and have to admit to myself a feeling of relief when, at last, the doorbell rings.

He let Piers answer it, and show the visitors into the *salon,* where he joined them. Monsieur was his usual formal self. The girl perched on one of the heavy chairs, dressed in jeans and T-shirt, and looking rather boyish today. Of Madame there was no sign.

If my face shows my distaste, both at the situation and at her sitting there, then that's just too bad. *He* dashes off upstairs to pack his bag, and I have no option but to walk them round the garden, keeping the conversation bland and safe. Monsieur does most of the talking - she is silent, looking back at the house from time to time, because she cannot bear to be separated from Piers for a minute. That much we do have in common, young woman!

Later, when they had driven away, he drifted into the guest bedroom yet again, to find everything gone: the wardrobe was plundered, not even the clock was there. Just a discarded white tissue on the floor by the bed. The room, as he looked around it, was hostile now: the *décor* had been chosen for Piers, but he was no longer there. It is not my colour-scheme. I could not live in here.

He went to his study and sat down, looking out of the window as he had done on that winter's afternoon when the phone rang. But it was no use. "Orphéon" had become an alien place, no longer the home he had made for himself. It had been the same with the cottage after he lost Piers, the first time; and he had had no option but to slink back home.

Do I have to leave again? If so, to where? The Flying Dutchman, with the curse upon him. Why should I be accursed? Is it because..?

He tried to frame a perspective, to persuade himself that he was exaggerating things, being just plain silly. And selfish: I cannot expect to hoard him up for myself. It's only right to accept that his qualities are not to be kept within narrow confines, but made available to others, as if he were a holy man with special powers. Of course the Calivets approve of him. He is an attractive young man, he speaks their language. And there's always the Cambridge *cachet.*

But it caused him pain to realise how his own role had shifted after all from erstwhile lover to what Mr James had proposed: surrogate father or godfather. On the one hand I am to encourage that which I most fear, while, on the other, I am still for ever juggling with my own curious feelings.

It's the freshness of youth that attracts: Piers at twelve, Raoul... If this theory is right, then any goodlooking young boy would do, and I should be irrevocably stamped with the word I refuse to apply to myself. I have never liked labels, always regarding it as a restriction of personal freedom to slap a word upon a person which might be true of one facet, but totally false for others. There must be a way to soften this pain that is growing like a cancer inside me...

Only now, with him back again, do I begin to recognise a glimmer of what should have happened inside me when we had to part, five years ago: my grief should have been talked out, just as the grieving need to talk about the departed. But I had no-one to turn to, never had a proper chance, not even with the psychiatrist. The poison remained locked up inside me, for I had gone past the stage where tears could any longer bring relief. The emptiness in me now turns to anger. How can anyone be so fickle? One moment we are rediscovering each other up in the snows, the next he has let himself be dragged away by a worthless siren with whom I cannot possibly compete. We can't even discuss it, for, at best, he would be amused, at worst derisive.

I tried so hard not to cram you into a mould which suited me, but might not suit you. I understood (because you taught me) how sensitive a boy on the threshold of manhood can be, how easily ruined. I did not want to hurt you then, nor do I wish to now. I must not stand in your way, nor shall I spend the rest of my life agonising over what we are, what we were, what we might have been. Didn't I tell you, only a day or so ago, to seize the moment when it comes? Well, you've done that, but will you ever live to experience even half of what I'm going through?

So many images of him are coming back now: a boy in cassock and surplice, hurrying over the uneven pavement beneath the Crossing at the Minster; the young god on horseback, splashing through the sea near the cottage; the candles of his birthday cake reflected in his eyes; that furtive look at me between the rails of the choir stalls, after we had been forbidden to communicate any more; the tears coursing down his face when I drove him back for the last time from the cottage to a banishment we could both foresee, but could not bring ourselves to admit.

How can he cope with this new relationship, a boy who only five years ago was in the Choir School, like a novice in a nunnery? Piers is an only child. He doesn't even have any cousins of similar age. How can he know about what the world would call the normalities of life?

I wonder about everything imaginable, now: whether his earlier involvement with me touched him at all, whether I left some hallmark on him for life, whether this girl can obliterate me so quickly and utterly. Which is worse, the desire to possess or to be possessed? Fiona tried to possess me. In any case, will it make a scrap of difference, one way or the other, to sit tight here? If I rage at him, won't it leave me wretched and him unscathed? In the end, he will become just another love-lorn youth, indistinguishable (even for me) from a thousand others.

He opened a bottle of red, and settled down in his study, running through everything he could recall, from the moment he first entered Wharnley Minster, right down to to the present, marvelling at the fineness of the detail that was coming back now. He weighed it all, searching for what there could be, or could have been, between them, to have turned it all so sour now. Sour for me, for Piers in his oblivion isn't bitter.

On his thirteenth birthday, the gold cuff-links made him feel he was being treated almost like another man. But the great surprise was inside the tiny box which he gave me. I shall never know how he, a child still, managed that: a ring, with our two names engraved on the inside. Where is it now? He made me swear on it, but he has broken the oath. With her.

The wine had begun to make his head swim. There were less joyous occasions for us too, when he would sob, and I would clasp him to me, run my hand through his hair and plant kisses on his face until he was comforted.

Now, *she* will comfort him.

He made it to his feet, tottering, clutching at a shelf of books, sweeping half of them to the floor. One particularly heavy one caught him on the ankle and he cried out with the pain. Piers, you were Tadzio, did you know that? Your face, your form, still hold some very deep part of me in thrall.

He was frenzied now, questing for some harm to do. He plucked the perspex cover from the miniature theatre, with its stage model so carefully and intricately constructed, picked it up and smashed it down on the corner of his grand piano, little pieces of card and wood dropping on to the carpet, where he stamped on them in his fury. I'll show you, you little bugger, I'll show you!

The piano strings sang out in alarm. His wine bottle, knocked over, emptied its rich red stain into the carpet and, not for the first time, his voice rose to a note of frustration and despair. Amid all the chaos, he sank down on the floor, his face pressed into the wet carpet, one part of him unrepentant still, the other full of shame and remorse. When did I last get into such a state? This would not have happened if I'd gone on living my safe, hermetic little life.

Once, I lay like this on the beach, totally bereft. It was summer still, but the sea taunted me with little cold droplets. Within the hour, I had packed my things, for he had gone, and there was no reason to stay any more.

He has gone, again. So - do I put this great house up for sale, and continue my pointless roaming through the world? Even if I could somehow keep Piers, it would no longer be the same. I suppose there is no way that she would ever find out that I was ahead of her in one or two respects, as regards her beloved boy. I have shared beds with him, which you haven't! But *will* you? I don't know, nor do I think I want to.

*

With a thief's daring, he drove rapidly, well aware of the risk that they might see him, the wretched *voyeur,* come to prowl and sniff about. And, even as he waited at a traffic light in Annecy *ville*, the white Citroën swung round, passing very close to him. He saw it in perfect slow motion: Monsieur at the wheel, in deep concentration; his wife, slumped beside him, staring round towards a fashion shop; and, behind them, the young couple, as though being driven away already from their civil wedding at the Hôtel de Ville, *she*, behind her father, throwing back her head to laugh at something (which Piers had probably said); and, less clearly defined, in the far corner of the car, there *he* was, his face alive, his eyes shining even from here. My worst fear is confirmed: *I* cannot bring that fire and light to his features. Offer him a toy, a sweet, and off he runs.

*

Sunlight, brilliant on the snow, the air keen and crisp. Monsieur helped him to get his goggles adjusted. This was marvellous: instead of merely watching in envy, as he'd done before, he could now join in, feel himself sliding gently forwards down the slope. Bend your knees, lean into it, concentrate. But then the nearer horizon lifted abruptly at one end, his skis clashed, he tilted over, and was flat on his front, blinded! The stuff was cold on his face, it stuck to his goggles, and he was plastered with it, from head to foot. From nearby came Adèle's laughter, though he couldn't see her. She's killing herself, and although it's at my expense, I just don't mind. He laughed himself, as he fought to get his goggles off, tears mingling with the powdered snow on his face.

<Look at him. Arse over tit!> She went off into more peals. <You'd better take my arm, *vieillard*! Don't you ever have snow in England?>

Yes, but not like this, with the massive bulk of Mont Blanc towering above, and innumerable ants dotted all over the place, being towed up on the hoists, shooting back down or, like me, taking the first baby steps on the safe slopes - and getting it all wrong.

<Viens.> Adèle held him tightly. <You are going to try again. I won't let you fall over this time. Did you hurt yourself just a bit, *chéri*?> She was outrageous!

Her father stood by, his head inclined forward, a smile on his lips. <Never mind, young man. She's right. You just have to try again.>

It worked this time. He thrust the sticks into the snow, keeping his skis parallel, getting the feel of it, like a novice on the heaving deck of a ship. Adèle let go of him.

'Bravo!' Monsieur was all encouragement, and she kept pace with him. <Papa is taking us on film, you must smile!>

<Dressed like we are, it'll be difficult to see which of us is which!>

<Have you a girl friend in England?>

<No.>

<Why not? Don't English boys have girl friends?>

<Mostly. I haven't had much chance.>

<Aren't there any girls like me, then?> Her eyes were merry.

<No. They're too snobbish.>

She roared with laughter. <Piers, d'you like me just a little?>

<You know very well. I adore you.>

<You're teasing. You boys are all the same.>

*

The sound of a car made him rush to the window in the alcove formed by the tower, whence it was possible to see the drive and front steps. But, of course, there was no reason why it should be Piers, unless something was wrong.

Leaden-hearted, he opened the door to Guy. They went into the kitchen, and Roland turned on the coffee machine. <We can't come to your concert. Piers has unexpectedly gone to visit friends.>

<He has made some friends already?>

<A girl from Annecy, and her people.>

<Oh, oh, oh,> said Guy. <A nice girl from Annecy, I hope.>

<Very nice,> said Roland drily. <Very nice people.>

<What is their name? Perhaps I know them. Are they from the *ville*?>

<The Calivets live at Talloires,> he said, barely concealing his impatience. <I don't think you can possibly - >

<Ah, Talloires,> said Guy, lighting a Gitane. <That's up in the world,> as though it were something to which neither of them would ever aspire. <This young Englishman has fallen on his feet. So, Millan, why don't you come yourself to my concert?>

Roland hedged, unable to say that he would not leave the place for too long in case Piers should need him. The blue cigarette smoke filled the kitchen. There, between them, was the expanse of tiled floor where Raoul had stood, light years ago.

<That voice,> Bannerot was saying, <is a marketable asset. A very rare counter-tenor, believe me. You owe it to him to help him..>

The car went off down the drive, leaving Roland in a furious mood. If I had ever entertained the idea of subsidising Piers, the sight of him in that car with *them* has put paid to it. I was living the safe life of the recluse, but then "Orphéon" came under attack, not once but several times. All right, I can always shoo Guy away, but Piers is a different matter, a love-hate affair, and that's something new.

*

There were Sunday boat-trippers everywhere, wind-surfers, water-skiers. In the sky above, hang-gliders, brilliantly-coloured, swooped to and fro. The water lapped against the shore in a self-satisfied way. The Calivets had come out into the garden for the liqueurs and coffee. And then, into this scene of familial closeness there arrived an unexpected visitor. The maid came with a card, which she gave to Monsieur.

<"Bannerot, Guy". Member of the Suisse Romande? Some kind of a joke? Send him away.>

But Piers had heard, he uttered an involuntary 'Oh,' and, in a trice, Guy had been invited in, given a garden chair, and plied with cognac and coffee.

'J'étais désolé,' he said, as he offered Madame a cigarette. So sorry that Piers and Millan had to forgo yesterday's concert.

Adèle, sitting right next to Piers, whispered, <Who is this man, and how does he know you?>

<He may be useful to me in my musical career, if - .>

<Ah, an impresario?>

<Well, not quite. But he knows people.>

<And your Monsieur Millan, does he know people?>

<Yes, in the world of art and design.>

She shrugged. <Papa knows politicians, bankers, people like that.>

Turning to hear what Guy was saying, he was taken aback to find himself the topic of conversation: this *jeune homme* needs to go to a *conservatoire*, he needs funds, he is an orphan. It was just too embarrassing.

After Guy had gone, Piers blurted out a clumsy apology: he didn't understand how M. Bannerot could have known where he was. (Did Roland send him to spy on me?)

Adèle now had a new theme, which she was not going to relinquish so easily. <You really are an orphan, Pierrot? You don't have any parents?>

<I still have a mother.>

<I thought,> said Madame, cutting into this exchange, <that we were going to invite Monsieur Millan for tomorrow. If we don't phone, he will have made other arrangements. If he comes for the *goûter*, he can take Piers back.>

<Oh,> protested her daughter, <he can't go back yet. He's only just come.>

The beginnings of an argument were gently but firmly stifled by her father: it was not fair to M. Millan if they detained his guest for so long.

<Then let me ring him,> said Adèle. <I'll fix it up, you'll see. He's got to share Piers with me.>

*

Madame shovels her food in, keeping her mouth open as she chews it, like a garbage lorry devouring rubbish. Piers is of course too engrossed with the girl to notice anyone else. Oh yes, he greeted me when I arrived, but it was just an act of politeness, consigning me to the periphery.

But Monsieur, ever correct, seats me next to him as if I were the guest of honour. The table is laid for a dozen, though we do not amount to half that number.

Just then there was a sudden influx of other guests, and the room was full of people kissing each other. Adèle's uncle was a gross, balding man with an uninfectious laugh. His wife was a quiet little thing, but their three daughters and their female friends (two rather lesbian-looking girls, thought Roland, with a *frisson* of amusement) made up a lively group, to which Piers and Adèle instantly related.

He comes in for a lot of attention, and obviously enjoys it. But what is this? One of the lesbies is paying me court. Good Lord, she's been to the Grand Théâtre, seen *Death in Venice*. Someone has been doing some expert briefing behind the scenes.

In a way, he was flattered. The girl was barely older than Adèle, but she did not let youth stand in her way. After the *goûter*, when they were all replete, and Monsieur suggested a little promenade in the garden,

Ninette (the name of Roland's latest acquisition, as Piers later put it) hooked her arm through his and strolled along at his side. Piers, his arm round Adèle's waist, looked round at him with an expression which clearly said, 'Now who isn't exactly immune?' Stupid child, don't you understand that I'm taking part in this absurd comedy only out of politeness to you?

The gaiety was not to last: on the way back to St Julien, Piers was gloomy and bereft, as only a youngster can be, who has had to wrench himself away from the girl of his dreams. I need to do some probing into this thing they have set up against me, but the bitterness within threatens to blow it all sky-high. 'You seem to have taken to this girl rather suddenly.'

As I intended, he takes that the wrong way, responds in a truculent tone, on the defensive of course. 'I love her, and she loves me, and that's all that matters.'

'But you're going back to England, the day after tomorrow.' I hope that means you may never see her again.

'Look, Roland, we've talked about having to part, but we intend to stay in contact all the time till... I can get back again. We know it will put our love to the test'

Ah, you have just used the word "love". You cannot begin to understand this chemistry which threatens to tear you away from me again.

His wanting to be with the French lot implies that it is unnatural for him to be with me. I could of course come out with a public avowal about what happened at Wharnley. But then that would fracture not just the link between him and the girl, but the vital filament between him and me.

Supposing he has time to stop and think, what comparisons will he draw between that episode and this? If the Adèle thing really is love (as he claims), was *ours* love, as we both once believed it to be? Or will he have submerged it all (more efficiently than I did) beneath layers, like the slow settlement of a new city of Troy upon its predecessors, till the original events are ground to forgotten dust, and me with them? He won't blurt anything out - he has too much to lose.

'Piers, this may be none of my business, but you must allow me to show some interest in your welfare and happiness. You've known her for a very short time. How can you be so sure?' I believe Mr James would be pleased with that.

'It just clicked, the very first moment, when she dropped the ice-cream. Oh, sorry, you weren't there to see that.'

No, but it rings so truly of manipulation on her part: you and she, walking back together from that jetty, (about which I'd already had a premonition). How do I make you see, without pushing my way into this new equation, that we're getting hot under the collar because this is something new to both of us? Triangles don't work.

*

Back in the safe confines of "Orphéon", and in a more relaxed atmosphere, he brings out photos to show me: sun and snow at Chamonix, himself anonymous in goggles on hired skis, clasping another ski-suited creature to him. His *récit* of all that they packed into their short time smacks of the need to justify it, make it somehow acceptable to me - while, if I were minded, I could so easily blow him out of the water with an account of *my* experiences in his absence!

Was that what went wrong at Wharnley, I wonder - that I began to find him boring, in the end, and had to send him packing? I shall just have to simulate interest in these people, or he will accuse me of heartlessness and I know not what. Maybe that's right, and I *am* dead to everyone else. If he should come to despise me now, I'm finished. If I could only see over the palisades which have been of my own building, I might be able to control things better. Will my corpse be left outside the walls for the stray dogs to devour?

All this talk of his life *chez* Calivet saps his enthusiasm and brings back his leaden mood. Making the excuse that he wants an early night, he goes off like an old man, and I am suddenly lightened, as though my little cloud has blown away, deciding, like a fly, to choose someone else to settle on. It will be all right: he's not going to see her again before he leaves. He's going to see me instead. I shall godfather him for the day, pack him gently off on the train on Wednesday, and revert to my calm haven here. We shall exchange letters, make tentative plans, and the Spring days will lengthen into summer. I might even spoil myself a little, and take a small break, somewhere nice. Not all the way to the tigers...

I was most warmed by the sight of her face as she clung to him: sodden with weeping, and really quite unattractive, unlike little Raoul, who came to my door dripping wet! Love can uglify as well as beautify. Perhaps it will have taught him a lesson. You're not ready yet, and, when you are, and if you must, choose a nice harmless English rose who will bear you beautiful children, to whom I may be a real godfather!

He's probably having a private howl all on his own, up there. I shall forbear looking in to see if he needs comfort. Let him stew in it for a bit.

*

At my breakfast table, on his very last day, he is still full of yesterday's gloom, and I, unable to bear it, fling him a grain of comfort. 'Why don't you ring her?'

The day is bright, scented with sunshine; I cannot let him depart tomorrow like this, leaving only a picture of sorrow in my mind, his face sallow, his eyes dark with pain. At least I'm back in his field of vision, as though he were an infant hoping to be spoilt by an indulgent adult. 'Look, even better - I think I owe the Calivets a spot of hospitality, so why don't you invite them all over for dinner here tonight?' A proper send-off, and not an anti-climax. It's worth it, just to see the transformation in his face.

He comes back from the hall, his eyes shining. 'They want to know what time.'

'Say five o' clock or so. Nice and formal, mind. We'll lead into it gradually. That'll give you time during the day to get packed, and so on.' And what did *she* say, to this piece of news?

'Roland... would you mind if we invited Guy, as well? He's been very kind about me and my music...'

'Why not? Go ahead. It's your show.'

His show it may be, but it will require some speedy stage-management. The *traiteur* at the foot of the hill will produce all that I require, even at such short notice. To hell with the cost: Piers is leaving tomorrow, and he shall have a last evening to surpass even our odyssey in the mountains. It shall almost resemble a wedding breakfast, not for him and her, but for him and me - to remind him, in case he's forgotten, that I still possess that ring with both our names on.

As he packed, Piers was anxious to talk. 'I don't want you to get the wrong idea, Roland. We didn't end up in bed' (here he blushed) 'or anything of that sort. I mean, we're very serious and very close, and able to talk about it. Well, I talked and she listened - I think she's a bit shy about that sort of thing.'

If you believe that, she really must have blinded you.

'And, in any case, we've a whole future in front of us. And we shall see each other again soon.'

'Is she going over to England, then?' I know this will put him on the spot.

'She's doing this domestic science course and can't really get away. You... did say, didn't you, that it'd be all right if I came here again?'

'Yes, of course. You know you're always welcome here, Piers.' My malice ebbs away; I haven't ruined everything, after all.

People began to arrive with flowers, which they set up on stands everywhere. The *salon* had been chosen as the fitting place for the meal, instead of the musty dining-room. Then another army came to replace the furniture with a huge collapsible table, which was soon covered with brilliant white linen and gleaming gold cutlery. Crystal knife-rests and silver candelabra twinkled in the sunlight. Cartons of glasses, stacks of the most tasteful porcelain appeared, and, around midday, the first of the food.

Roland and Piers were able to sit down and sample *pâté de foie gras* and a magnificent red wine for their snack lunch. Then they went all round the gardens, fixing candles in strategic spots. 'Like the last act of *Figaro*, said Piers, 'except that we haven't any fireworks.'

Intuitive youth! *The Marriage of Figaro*, don't forget - with the frustrated Count presiding over all.

"Orphéon" was finally ready, and appetising smells were coming from the kitchen, now in charge of a chef. A bar with an array of bottles had been set up in a corner of the salon, where a lady in a black dress was walking about, checking details and talking quietly to staff, as though the house had suddenly been turned into an exclusive hotel.

They went off to get bathed and changed before their guests arrived, just a few minutes after five.

Piers has chosen a black roll-neck sweater, just like the one he wore when he escaped from school to come to me. It goes well with his dark trousers. Madame comes in a glaring orange dress that does nothing for her whatsoever. I note, as she presses a huge box of chocolates into my hand, that she's forgotten the green shadow on one eyelid. Monsieur is in an immaculate dinner jacket, his daughter in a sky-blue ball gown with short puffy sleeves. The elegant gold necklace cannot quite divert one's attention from her rather pudgy arms. Strange that I didn't notice that before. Piers is, of course, over the moon. And, look, she gives him a present too - not cuff-links, I hope? No, a tiny gold chain for his neck, with a cross on it. He's dumbfounded, because he has nothing to give her in return. Aren't you sufficient recompense, Piers, just being yourself to this girl whom, you tell me, you haven't yet bedded?

As they entered, Monsieur let out a little cry of appreciation. <Mais, Monsieur Millan, c'est exquis. You really go in for style!>

Who could remain obdurate in the face of such flattery? I play the *grand seigneur,* smiling, bowing a little, and taking Madame over to the bar to help her choose an *apéritif.*

Piers was hand-in-hand with Adèle, and so they all carried their glasses out into the garden like old friends, chatting about the usual inconsequential things. She had brought a camera, so that various group permutations could be snapped.

A slight breeze sprang up, causing Madame to shiver. Everyone immediately went indoors again, where the glasses were replenished, and sat down on chairs round the edge of the *salon*. Roland tried to engage Adèle in conversation, but did not get far: she was for Piers, and him alone.

Monsieur delivered a humorous *récit* of their various experiences on the ski slopes at Chamonix. His wife listened with one ear, but her nostrils were all a-twitch, trying to analyse the cooking smells, her eyes straining to see the two neat typewritten menus in their silver stands on the big table.

Having failed with the daughter, I turn my attentions upon her father. <Piers tells me your business is in Paris, monsieur. Do you go there very often?>

<Once or twice a week. Do you know Paris?>

<I studied art there for a while.>

<The Parisians are another race entirely,> said Madame Calivet suddenly. <They suck the blood of the rest of France. They would not care if we were destitute, as long as they can stuff themselves silly.>

Roland had to contain a laugh at the irony of this.

<Talking about stuffing,> said Adèle, <when's it going to start? It smells good.>

Piers looked round, then his expression relaxed: Roland was actually smiling!

<The major-domo has been told seven, but if the *potage* is hot, I don't see why we shouldn't...>

In a trice, they were pulling out chairs and sitting down at the table. Roland's previous private worries about *placement* were easily resolved: Piers sat at the head next to Adèle, he himself was to her left, opposite Madame, and Monsieur was next to him, opposite the empty chair that would be occupied by Guy.

Adèle's mother had already seized one of the menu cards and was reciting a slow litany of approval: <Vegetable soup (that's good), then pâté, hors d'oeuvres, salmon, veal (ô, magnifique!), a green salad, cheese, la meringue glacée and, to complete the banquet, la crêpe flambée. Ô là là, Monsieur Millan, you are feasting us like gods!>

Coming from your mouth, Madame, all my chosen delicacies sound as appetising as sawdust! Her husband echoes his praise more quietly. Piers' mouth drops open, as though he cannot really take it all in.

Waitresses now arrived with steaming tureens, from which the *potage aux légumes* was ladled, each portion with a dollop of sour cream and a sprinkling of *croûtons*.

Monsieur has tucked the corner of his napkin inside the front of his collar, and is spooning up the soup as though he has never eaten before in his life. His wife affects to be more delicate, holding her spoon with her little finger crooked, rather reminiscent of something by Hogarth. The two lovers being bound up in each other, as always, it is up to me to make the running. I ask the Calivets where they are going to spend the summer, but my question seems to surprise them. 'Mais, en Savoie, bien sûr.'

<Let others go to Yugoslavia or Greece,> said Madame. <We are satisfied with our apricot orchard!>

As the first wine was served, shapes were moving on the walls all around them, like figures in halls of mirrors at fair-grounds. The Calivets were surely grotesque enough, without need of further distortion?

The arrival of a newcomer was positively welcome for once. Guy excused his lateness, sat down next to Madame, put her hand to his lips and nodded benignly at everyone else. <A terrible rehearsal. You know, the first bars of *Don Juan*. There is no conductor in the world who can bring the orchestra in together. We try fifty times, and get worse and worse. How very nice to exchange that torment for your delightful ambiance. Millan, I salute you, dear guests I greet you.>

He helped himself to some hors d'oeuvre, which he tucked into with gusto. Then, realising that his glass was full, he turned slightly to his left, raised it and said solemnly, 'J'ai l'honneur de trinquer avec Monsieur Piers et Mademoiselle Adèle'; and he got up, went to the end of the table, and wished them health and happiness.

He too has caught the mood of the wedding breakfast, thought Roland sardonically.

The conversation became more animated, with Guy acting as a kind of catalyst. When the little salmon steaks appeared, it was Calivet's turn to raise his glass and, in the name of his wife and daughter (and, indeed, Piers and Monsieur Bannerot), to thank Monsieur Millan for the warmth of his *acceuil*, and the excellence of his table.

Now the worst moment had come: all eyes were fixed on him again, more intently, it seemed, than before. 'Allez, monsieur, il faut répondre,' said Madame Calivet, and everyone nodded vigorously.

Feeling like a cross between the bride's father and the best man, he got slowly to his feet. To begin 'Dear friends' would sound as hackneyed and insincere as it largely was. A more formal address (*Messieurs, mesdames* and so on) would be pompous in such a small gathering as this.

Waves lapped idly on the shore. The sun was just about to set. He came cantering on horseback across the wet sands, splashing in water that was as pink as the *rosé* wine which is now being poured for us. His body, in its godlike beauty, already tanned by the sun, exuded an elemental purity and mystery. As its hooves churned the sea-water to white foam, the boy reined in the horse, turning it, and both of them, dripping and triumphant, raced back to me, glorious in the light of the departing sun.

<My dear guests. This is, for me in particular, a very special evening. I first knew Piers five years ago, when we were given the good fortune to share some time together and, as I tried to help him to broaden his horizons - his love of music, and so on, - I found myself being given, in return, the fresh and charming companionship of this young man.>

Piers eyes are wide in... can it be horror? Guy has a minatory glint - watch out, Millan, do not put a foot wrong. But this is my house and my evening and, before these Savoyards, I say what I choose.

<Now that he has begun his studies at Cambridge, I am delighted that he has chosen to come here *pour pratiquer son français*, and to get to know our delightful corner where *la jolie Suisse* meets *la belle France*.> (Applause from the Calivets, a nod from Guy). <I trust that, when he leaves us tomorrow for England, he will take with him some fond memories of his stay - and I raise my glass to you all, but especially to Piers, wishing him *bon retour*, and reminding him that we look forward to his next visit to "Orphéon".>

The company says 'Bravo' loudly and clinks glasses, apparently oblivious that the girl has been so carefully excluded from my words. But Piers will have noticed. And the next move can only be his.

The serving staff were respectfully waiting to replace the fish plates with the main course, but Piers was not to be outdone. He now rose, nearly falling back into Adèle's lap, and, with a sweeping gesture of his right hand, commanded the silence which, in fact, he already had.

'Ladies and gentlemen...'

But both the Frenchmen shouted to him to do it in their language.

He swallowed hard and started again. <*Messieurs, madame et Adèle. I don't want to call you* mademoiselle, *its so silly. I would like to thank Roland for his hospitality to me during the past weeks. We have climbed up snowy summits together - we even, at one point (because we forgot to book a room beforehand), had to share the same bed!*>

Roland choked and went red, while laughter rippled round the table, though Guy Bannerot raised his eyebrows.

<He is my best friend in the world. If he hadn't invited me here, I should never have met Adèle - whom I love very much.>

Chorus of 'ah!', and muted applause, the servants dutifully joining in.

His body responds to my urgent prayer by reverting to its seated position, and the confusion is masked by the arrival of the veal and trimmings.

<Oh, I nearly forgot,> Piers shouted from his chair. <To Roland!> And the glasses of *rosé*, sparkling in the light of the newly-lit candelabra, were raised and dipped in salute. More polite applause, and then the busy sound of cutlery attacking meat.

Adèle had clasped Piers to her and was feeding him gobbets of food from her own plate.

My face has gone rigid, like that of someone who has laughed far too long, except that laughter is the last thing I would be capable of here. He nearly brought me down with that mention of what happened at Lauterbrunnen, that moment so sacred to me, dragged out in front of these unspeakable peasants.

It was almost dark now, the dots of candlelight reflected everywhere in the mirror-lined walls, and he found himself listening to a political argument which, in true French fashion, had sprung up between Calivet and Bannerot. After a few minutes of this, he let himself dip back into a dream he'd had a million years ago, in which he had made a speech at Piers' wedding reception. I complimented you on your choice of bride, while indicating quite clearly how close you and I were, and always would be. Afterwards, you came to me distraught, saying exactly what I wanted to hear: I married her because you made me promise to, but nothing between *us* will be any different.

How could I believe that now, sitting so close to them both, and yet light-years away? Her perfume isn't cheap stuff, but she somehow manages to cheapen it and make it poison the whole room.

The bowls of lettuce were served and then the cheeses with a red wine that sent Guy Bannerot into raptures. A 1947 *Château Labique*, to serve with *cheese?* He and Calivet tenderly picked up the bottle in turn, examined the label, sniffed the neck. <How on earth did you get hold of such a noble vintage, Millan? Forty-seven? You weren't even born in forty-seven.>

<Pardon me, but I was at school.>

<Much too young to appreciate a vintage like this,> roared Calivet, <which not even the French themselves ever see, let alone taste.>

He had not noticed that, to his right, Piers' and Adèle's chairs were empty. He looked out of the window and there, in the darkened garden, little flickering lights began to appear. Madame Calivet exclaimed, and pressed her hands together. 'Oh, mais cest joli, ça.'

They all got up and went over to the window, but Roland did not open it. By this time tomorrow he will have gone... He turned back to look at the table. Piers had dropped his napkin on his chair, his wine glasses shone in the candlelight. There might have been a time when I would have thought to acquire as a trophy the glass from which he had drunk. But not any more. Perhaps it should be hurled to the floor, like the Russians did, so that no-one would ever drink from it again.

The young couple came in, flushed and happy. Did everyone like the candles? Again, a little patter of applause, and a wink for Roland from Piers, as if to say 'that was really our hard work, this afternoon.'

Guy Bannerot, who had lit a cigarette during the diversion, stubbed it out and sat down as the first dessert was served, with a glass of sweet Sauternes. <I think that it is high time we all heard this young man's extraordinary singing voice - and I mean that in the best possible way. Millan, you cannot refuse such a request. You must permit us to *monter l'escalier* and give him a proper piano accompaniment.>

But Roland was resolute. No, really, that room was not suitable for receiving guests.

<Come now,> Guy insisted, <this is such a special occasion. Piers, persuade him. You will sing for us, won't you?>

<I should so like to hear you,> cried Madame Calivet, clasping Piers to her. <You would do it for me, *n'est-ce pas?*>

Clearly torn, he looked at Roland, who nearly yielded to a strong urge to take them all up and show them the havoc.

Sanity prevailed, however. <We will compromise in true British fashion. I have an old violin here, in the sideboard. It belonged to a former owner of this house. Piers will sing and Bannerot will provide accompaniment.>

There was laughter at this, and he pressed the instrument into Guy's hands.

'Un moment!' exclaimed Piers. He dashed out of the room with Adèle on his heels, and returned shortly with his score. It was agreed that they should do just one piece, with Bannerot putting in sufficient supporting notes.

'Eh bien, voilà. Allez-y, Piers. Un, deux, trois.'

The acoustic of the huge room amplified Piers' voice without making it sound strident. The violin, so expertly played, caressed the voice, urged it on, turned a piece of house music into something exquisite. "Orphéon" was suddenly a place where Vivaldi's mannered phrases were seized and tossed around, bouncing like the candlelight from the walls. It was a performance, a triumph, and, at the end, the ovation was warm and prolonged. Adèle, who at first had gaped in utter astonishment, was in tears. <Pierrot, c'est magnifique. That voice – I'd never have guessed.>

<I see what you mean,> Calivet was saying to Guy. <This young man needs to be promoted. With a voice like that, he could conquer the world. And I say that as one who has no note of music in his head!>

Roland thought it time to intervene. <For the moment he is committed to a four-year course at our most prestigious university, and it would be tragic if he were persuaded to break it off.> Mr James would approve of that!

Like a dog, Piers looks mournfully at Adèle and then back at me. I think I have scored a very necessary point, and cut off Guy's line of advance. Luckily, their attention is riveted on the *crêpe flambée*. Piers, who has had much too much to drink, is showing off now. There is a wickedness in his face which I have seen before. Yes, see, he staggers to his feet for what I pray will be the final toast of the evening. Ye gods, it is 'To Socialism'. The atmosphere threatens to turn frosty, but then Calivet slaps his thigh and lets out a hoot of laughter which everyone else, including myself, can join in. We're saved, and the silly boy collapses in confusion on his chair.

As we drink coffee, the children slip away once more, and I am tempted to think good riddance. Let them go and savour their last few moments together in the garden while I, the stage-manager, play host to these people, tickle their vanities and wish heartily that, before long, someone will have the good sense to look at his watch. It should be you and I walking out there, not you and she. A wedding without a honeymoon...

At last, Bannerot exclaimed at the lateness of the hour, and got up. <Mille mercis, Millan – for a truly splendid dinner.>

<You won't have to do the washing-up,> said Calivet, with a twinkle.

The lovers reappeared briefly, locked in mourning, then cars drove off, the major-domo and his staff miraculously spirited everything away and restored the *salon* to its normal state of genteel shabbiness.

Roland wrote a huge cheque, and then silence descended over "Orphéon" again. He opened the French window and stepped into his garden, where the occasional candle-end was still guttering out.

There is no light at Piers' window: he's sleeping it off already, then. I must not let myself be bitter: it was a superb evening, in which we all surpassed ourselves, me included. A wedding breakfast, *comme il faut!*

He locked up and went to bed, where his mind would not stop offering up absurd scenarios. 'You have such a nice house,' said Madame Calivet, 'though you have no wife to run it for you.' And Piers, holding his elbow and looking into his eyes, repeated: 'You are my best friend in the world.'

Even in his sleep, he heard the soughing of the wind in the trees outside, like an early lamentation.

*

The drive to the station having taken less time than expected, they found themselves loitering awkwardly on the platform with twenty minutes to spare.

'It's all right, don't wait,' said Piers, and Roland suddenly discovered a grief all of his own, staring him in the face. This was it: like one facing execution, Piers was poised to go. What the hell did you do, in those last, precious moments? He tried to talk to him, to touch upon things they'd done together during the fortnight, but the boy was bleak-faced, his attention elsewhere, obviously wondering if *she* would make a last-minute appearance.

At last, after what seemed like a leaden hour, the train rolled in.

'You will write, won't you?' Christ, that sounds like the queers' goodbye.

Piers stands in the carriage doorway, looking down, and the difference this makes to our heights is intimidating to me.

'You have got everything? Passport? Ticket?' The maiden aunt stunt, now.

He fiddles with the zip of his bag, and nods. 'Roland, it's been a wonderful holiday. Thank you so much.'

The polite formula. A handshake and, as the train begins to move off in its unfussy Swiss way, a wave. It's the end of a piece of theatre, but there is no applause. I am inside a very old body which has been anaesthetised, and is now coming round.

At breakfast, he brought up that perceptive comment again: that I didn't really like Adèle. 'Stuck out a mile. You kept calling her "vous" and "mademoiselle". It would've been funny, if...'

'Piers, if that were true, I would hardly have put on a dinner party, would I? You have to understand that one observes these French formalities quite naturally, but it doesn't mean anything.' I knew all that wouldn't convince him, but then I didn't want it to.

As he walked slowly back through the station building, a thought almost made his heart stop beating. Did he say 'Will you be all right?' before the train drew out, or did I dream it? Did I really call out 'I love you' up at Jungfraujoch? If I didn't, does he know, anyway?

In the crowded place outside the station, he suddenly found a new meaning of agoraphobia: the dragon, roused from slumber, was vulnerable, exposed, having exchanged a frozen darkness for the unprotected place in the sun.

He's gone. It's all wrong: there's so much I wanted to say to him, to ask him. It's as if we are parted in death. Still, he will now be safe from her. When he came downstairs with his luggage, he said, with mock brightness, 'It's not really very long before I come back, is it?' But the length of even a short Cambridge term will be an eternity without her. He was fighting the tears, and I could not help a feeling of triumph. I would have put an arm round his shoulder once...

How can I reasonably mind his falling in love, (if that is what it really is)? One morning, at the cottage, he woke me to see the sunrise, and we stood together at the window, arms clasping each other. He had an agenda to go through, asking me about the other people I had loved, in the depths of my past life, before he came into it. I told him I'd briefly been married to Fiona, who was Scottish, like him. And then, at different times, there were two friends - Jonathan and Barry. It sounded so trivial and loveless, though it hadn't been like that, at the time.

He wanted to know if these men were my lovers, and immediately made it clear that he feared I'd forget all about him soon, because he was only a boy, and find someone else. Even at his tender and inexperienced age, he knew about casual relationships - and he was really upset. His father had told him that such males were lonely and miserable. 'And it gets worse in old age. I can't bear to think of you ending up like that. I won't let you. I'll always be with you.'

I recall having to fight off the grief that was rising inside me. Perhaps he was right, in his vision of the future, but wrong that we could do anything about it. The red splash of sunlight on the wall had grown, and we were both caught in it.

*

It was a mistake to go into his room, to open his cupboard and find his walking boots with the socks stuffed into them still. I am a fool, a lover is a fool, ready to go to any lengths to compromise, no, to give. I made all the running here, and he got all the benefit. He brings me nothing but pain whether he is here or not; but I cannot just push him away.

Am I to be relegated to the role of *voyeur?* I stare at the bath he lay in, even the toilet seat he sat on. It's all so morbid, like embracing a corpse. I tried to make him fit my fantasy, wanted to believe that he might have grown up on a homo-erotic foundation (of my building), that he was somehow available and desirable. I made the mental error of not wanting him to be his own person. To hug someone too tightly is a surer way to lose them than to ignore them altogether. This business with the girl can only be a defence mechanism on his part, to get me to back away a little. If it were truly genuine between them, I'd drop him there and then, as the best and only thing for us both.

My wayward memory serves up the surprisingly intact details of those last moments at Wharnley: I had bathed, shaved and dressed, slowly and carefully, chosen the same light grey suit which I had been wearing when he first looked at me, and, as the early sunlight played on my reflection in the mirror, I was almost elated. The man before me was not one who had suffered a loss, but one about to set out for a joyous occasion. The sun's heat made my clothes stick to my body as I stared across at the door of the Choir School through which he must come. It would be so simple for him to cross the road to me, and safety. The flower in my buttonhole seemed to have become a large chrysanthemum, so urgent was its signalling redness below my chin: you have lost him already, he has left you no forwarding address. And moments later a taxi spirited him away, before my very eyes.

*

"My dear Piers,

> *It's very hard to tell you what I feel at this moment. Having had you to stay made me realise how I have been living in a desert since Wharnley - but all kinds of memories have been surfacing again, thanks to you.*
>
>   *Your stay was short but eventful, and I am glad that it will not be long before we meet once more. I do accept that your life is yours to lead as you will, and with whom you choose. My heart is very full now of the memory of what we once were, and of the warmth left by your visit.*
>
>   *Look after yourself,*
>   *Amitiés*
>   *R."*

How does madness begin? I wait by the phone, my letter to him locked away in the drawer of my desk. I'm well and truly out in the open again, naked, not so much frightened as unsure. Inroads have been made into my prison, - Piers, Raoul, - bringing back the old ecstasy (in the mind, at least), and all the old pain, the scars ripped open. Will I bleed to death?

Two evenings later the phone rang. He was taken aback to hear Mr James's voice. 'Hullo, Millan, I hope you will permit a call, even if the purpose of it is not entirely social. From what I gather, you have been entertaining Piers in lavish style indeed. His progress through Savoy and Switzerland sounds akin to a young lord enjoying the benefits of the Grand Tour. Anyway, I felt it incumbent on me to offer you my own thanks for keeping an eye on him.'

He was frozen almost to silence. Piers has talked to James, but he has not written to me. 'Did he also tell you about - ?'

'About – hum - his romance with this French girl? Oh yes. Showed me a photo of her and her people on your very impressive front steps!'

'He seems rather smitten.'

'Indeed. He became quite emotional, the other evening. Wanted to know how one goes about marrying a foreigner in a hurry.'

'Oh, my God.'

'Well yes, though I managed not to show my reactions, at least till I'd got him calmed down again.'

'I never had the chance for a proper talk with him. He got very touchy when I asked how they knew they loved each other after such a brief contact.'

'Presumably you met her.'

'Oh yes, and her parents, but only superficially. Hard to say how deep it really lies. If he's talking marriage at this stage, then either he's desperate, or she's got her claws well and truly into him. The family's very well off, of course.'

'So he wouldn't want for anything material?'

'He'd certainly want for the deeper things. I don't see how they would be remotely compatible, once the infatuation had worn off. Give it a few months, and it'll be all over.'

'You would welcome that?'

'I don't like to see him throwing himself away so blindly.'

'I ventured to make a suggestion about the May Ball. You see, Millan, he was so clearly expecting me to wave a wand, that I took the liberty of floating the idea that he invite this girl up in June, to coincide with his eighteenth birthday. He didn't need to be asked twice, commandeered my phone, got on to France, and it was fixed there and then: she and her father will be coming over. Don't think I'm matchmaking. I see it rather as an exercise in match-*un*making.'

Roland sighed. 'In the end, they'll do as they damn well please.'

'Do I gather that that makes you unhappy?'

'It doesn't take account of anything that you or I have ever managed to do for him. He's only too ready to accept all that he's given.'

'Why don't you come over too, and make a surprise visit on his birthday?'

It would be a waste of time and money. He wouldn't be interested to see me, if *she* was there. Now, Mr James, if your acute mind has been harbouring suspicions about a possible previous entanglement between Piers and myself, your nagging question receives an answer. The boy has slammed that particular door firmly shut, and I am desolate.

*

Lost in a vacuum of pointlessness, he constantly returned to his current opera project, only to abandon it moments later. The door of "Orphéon" was barred again to visitors, and he had given his housekeeper a week's paid holiday. At long last, or so it seemed, a letter arrived, bearing an English stamp.

> *"Dear Roland,*
>
> *Thank you again <u>mille fois</u> for having me to stay. It really was a superb holiday, and you won't mind, I'm sure, if I say that a high point was meeting Adèle and our falling in love with one another.*
>
> *I miss her very much, though I've been able to phone her once. <u>Would</u> it really be all right for me to come and stay again with you? The Calivets wanted to invite me there, but I said I should ask you about it. They seem to regard you as my guardian, I think!"*

That brought a rare, sardonic smile to his lips. The letter finished with some harmless chatter about music and studying.

> *"Mr. James sends you his best wishes,*
> > *Love,*
> > > *Piers.*
>
> *P.S. I'll be free from the end of June, if that's OK. I'll just be <u>of age</u>!!"*

Eighteen, yes, and in charge of your destiny at last. Touching, that you're still prepared to come here to me. If you had accepted the invitation to Talloires, my defeat would have been total. "Love, Piers" puts me firmly in the pigeon-hole marked "Father", and you play the role for all it's worth, trying to cheer me up on the one hand, and milk me on the other.

Reading the words "falling in love" had only intensified his dark mood. If I'm being punished, what was my sin? We're all of us shackled to our sexuality: if Man didn't have to live by his instincts, he'd be able to rise above all that, and be halfway to Heaven in this life already, instead of halfway to the other place - which is my present predicament. And what's the point of all this breeding, begetting, whelping? Why ensure that a stupid, terrible world goes on existing for ever? An infinity of space is bad enough, but an infinity of time? He found a crumb or two of comfort in pouring it all out in his diary.

> *"I most dread the loss of desire, the waning of my drive, making me into a dry, sapless husk. Surely I can't be your true paederast, because I don't go around chasing boys all the time. Am I really hom? I know I'm not het - if Fiona did nothing else for me, she certainly proved that. So I'm a sort of figure in a vacuum, which P briefly once filled. We came together in the way we did because, at that time, it was the only route that suited us both.*
>
> *But don't hang a label round my neck. I want to be <u>me</u>, and I want him to know that. Then, maybe, we can respect one another and be together again, without inhibitions.*
>
> *Others wouldn't understand (you can't <u>explain</u> it) that sex, for me, is something secret and sacred, not just cheap and everyday. My fool of an analyst would doubtless say: You equate sex with art. For you, sex is self-indulgence, therefore art is also."*

Is it possible, Piers, to go on loving the first person, even after you have fallen in love with a new one? Surely our relationship was valid, and still is, or am I just deluding myself again? Does he, can he, be thinking or even *feeling* things about me, the way I am doing about him? Are we each waiting, like boxers in the ring, for the other to strike first? Natural reticence and good manners. Englishness?

He kept on recalling things that had passed between them, both at Wharnley and here, but all their words of closeness had, as it were, blown up like Krakatoa, and were now descending like a magic dust that conferred impossible desires on him who was powdered over with it.

Hell, he supposed, was when one was no longer allowed any control, when things started to go wrong. Perhaps the only defence for the hypersensitive soul was aggression: Sallowburn taught its sons that, if nothing else. Be brash, make the world notice you. But he'd always resisted that, kicked against it.

In his gardens, the flowers were in blossom, but their fragrance, in the mild evening, along with the fluttering of birds on the wing, only made him feel restless. Maybe it was the memory of bare female flesh by Lake Geneva that set him off.

Back in his study, he began to make some notes but, after a short while, exhaustion caught him out, and his head slumped down on his desk. When he awoke, his house was dark and hostile. He flung a window open, but the perfume rising from the gardens did nothing to dispel his loneliness, the utter pointlessness of living on here, when Piers was gone. He did not want anyone else's company.

*

His flesh glistening, the boy pressed down his briefs with both hands, and stepped out of them. The man continued his towelling. The pubis was like the boy's upper lip: soft down, but no more. He put his hands on the clammy hips, to turn him round and dry the buttocks, and was delighted to find them so full and round. Then he put an arm round the boy's shoulders. 'Are you still cold, Raoul?'

'No, I'm warm.' And he was wrapped up in the towel and tenderly led upstairs, their breaths fusing together.

He woke, drenched with perspiration, his heart pounding in alarm. The grey rectangle in the blackness betrayed the approach of dawn. He fumbled for the switch of his bedside lamp, and light wiped out the nothingness.

Raoul. Would it, *could* it have been like that? He turned on the radio.

"Pendant le matin, quelques averses."

How old were you, really?

"Déviations sur la route nationale, numéro..."

Piers was much the same age, then. Did we do *that*? No, we never did *that*. I never could have, not with him. But Raoul? A boy for pleasure…

A ravaged face looks at me from my mirror. I know my house is empty, apart from me, but I see shadows moving on the stairs, hear footsteps in the night.

Fearful for his sanity, he decided to give himself a break from all this. It amused him that he should be setting off on the day attributed, by a land generously over-sainted, to Ste Rolande, of all people. Madame Bouillot was alerted, to keep an eye on the house in his absence.

I drive away on an impulse, but perhaps I am really a free spirit after all, like the migrating bird which knows, in a level far below consciousness, precisely where it is going, and why.

IV.

In the austere Gothic twilight of the cathedral, where old women pray and light candles, images of the young Piers come filtering back. He doesn't seem to want me any more. He is aiming to marry someone else… Well, at least I'm geographically closer to him here, even if the idea brings me little comfort. There are supposed to be vibrations in this area, ancient lines of Celtic magnetism. Could these have somehow lured me to such a place, away from the lake and its mountains, from "Orphéon" with its bitter-sweet memories? In the main street of Dol de Bretagne I came across a property agency, with photos in the window of restorable grey stone houses and barns, mostly going for a song, and a seed was sown in my mind.

Driving eastwards along a minor road which he had found on the map, he soon made out his objective, hovering above a line of distant poplars, misty blue, like a crown rising to a point, which the eye, once fixed upon, could not let go: the Mont St Michel, mysterious, beckoning. His lane crossed the little river, and joined the main road which, after leaving the hotels behind, ran northwards along on the *digue*. The tide was out, the mudflats glistened in the sunlight. At close quarters, the Mont was golden now, its stone buildings smiling a welcome, from the lowliest cottage within the ramparts at the bottom, to the abbey at the peak.

Leaving his car below the walls, he entered the postern gate and, making his way through a throng of tourists and schoolchildren, began the narrow ascent between gift shops and inns, pausing at the top, to look down over the marshes with their snaking channels. I cannot understand the movements going on inside me, but they seem akin to the conflicting currents of water that fill and empty this bay. Of course, there was no sea at the foot of the hill on which the Minster stood, but entering it on that Spring day gave me this same electric sensation - Wharnley, where I learnt for the first time that disbelief could be suspended and the impossible could happen. And here, in the abbey church, there is that same rich intensity coming out of the stone.

He found a seat in the gardens on the north side, where the shadow of the delectable pyramid thrust out before him across the endless sands. This place, where I detect something of that tranquillity of the soul which men yearn for, possesses its own rhythm of seasons and tides. I like the sea, I always did react to water. And now I have begun another of my crazy exercises, quite unable to see where it might lead.

He knew, as soon as the agent's car pulled up, that he wanted this child's drawing of a house: local stone, four-square, with its centre door and five windows, three above two, and a little *lucarne* in the roof. Neglected, to be sure, (the description had warned of the need for some modernisation) but he was not expecting what he found when the man, having inserted the ancient key, pushed the door open and led the way into an empty hall.

<Where are the stairs, then?>

The agent looked sheepish. It seemed that they had been so worm-eaten that the owner had removed them. One could of course approach him, negotiate a better price.

They found a ladder in the yard at the back, brought it in and climbed up to the landing, whose arched window framed a perfect view of the Mont in the middle distance.

<Splendid, that view, isn't it?> The only property for sale in the whole area, with such a prospect.

Shaking his head, Roland examined the two bedrooms, one of which had a grimy, cracked shower-basin in a corner, to make up for the lack of bathroom. There was an overpowering stench of mould. Downstairs were two good rooms with a scullery tacked on at the back. Some crumbling outbuildings completed the property, before the sandy-white fields took over, undulating away towards a fringe of trees. For a brief moment, he was back in "Stella Maris".

But this place was filthy and tumbledown. It must have been derelict for years, because no Frenchman in his right mind would touch it. A new roof would doubtless be needed, and the inside would have to be totally redone. The agent was looking at him. <Well, sir, what do you think?> The accent was so different from Savoy.

While they debated what would be a realistic offer, the agent drove him back to the office at Pontorson, where he had left his car, promising to contact the vendor's solicitor and ring him at his hotel in Dol, tomorrow morning.

What am I doing? Is this just a mad impulse? How would this flat land look in the rain, instead of under a sun that makes its every colour brighter than life? How would I cope, when the teeming hordes come in the high season, and the Mont threatens to burst?

He drove back to Bas Courtils, walked down a track that led out over the marshes, and sat down, soaking up the heat, the fragrance of the sea herbs, the salty peacefulness of it all. Even as he watched, silver tongues came licking in across the sand, shining, sly, seeking out the fastnesses of the place and filling them rapidly with water. For it was full moon time again, and he had read the warnings about the tides. Opposite, the Mont was reverting to its true island identity, only the *digue* remaining intact, like an umbilical cord. *They say the tide can come in with the speed of a galloping horse, and woe to any man who is caught on the sands! The place moves me in ways that Geneva cannot. And, in the end, it's nearer home, if 'home' still has any meaning.*

He sat till he was famished, the sun already inching into the west, softening the silhouette of the new island (reflected in the now brimming bay) and the coast behind it. When the floodlighting was switched on, the Mont mutated into something so ethereal that his final doubts vanished. *Look at that church on the rock. It must have spiral staircases everywhere. Why, that would be the solution to my problem of getting upstairs in the house, saving space and allowing a proper bathroom. It would be unusual, chic, even. But for whose benefit? Who would be my guests here?*

Just before the *digue* began, he found a hotel with a promising menu, and chose a table to one side of the restaurant, discreetly shielded by an open screen with plants on it. As he sat and ate his *hors d'oeuvre*, a family entered the dining-room: a couple with three children (two adolescent girls and a boy, somewhat younger). Sipping his *Muscadet* in a state of heightened tension, he knew exactly what was happening: this is not the Grand Hôtel des Bains and they are not Poles, but that boy, with his flowing fair hair and, yes, ineffably sweet face, would look quite ravishing in a sailor suit, instead of the dark sweater and white shorts. The father (who has lit a cigarette) has a little dog on a lead under the table. I cannot properly see the mother from here. I am hugely intrigued.

The boy is eating mussels. Looking up, his gaze passes through the screen and catches mine! Oh yes, that is exactly how it began once before, with a converse of looks, growing ever bolder on both sides, till - . I do believe that my therapy has already begun. Enjoy your mussels, boy, but do not forget that you have a brand-new admirer here, in the wings.

My own plate arrives, a king's banquet of mussels, oysters, crayfish, shrimps, crab and pieces of anonymous fish. In honour of my young discovery, a few tables away, I eat a mussel.

As the waiter passes by, I take courage: 'Dites-moi - la famille là-bas, elle est anglaise?' Though I know they cannot possibly be English.

'Ah mais non, monsieur. C'est la famille Duclos, de Tours.'

I have to hand it to this head waiter for being a model of decorum on the one hand and confidentiality on the other: they are holidaying here for two weeks, and looking for a *résidence secondaire* in the area. Very well-to-do people: Monsieur in the Government, the children privately educated. The boy, André, was recovering from a spell in clinic.

Ah, so now we have it. André Duclos. André... Yes, I like that. Did not Mann say that young Tadzio looked sickly, that he would not live long, and that Aschenbach took pleasure at the thought? What is wrong with this boy, I wonder? But the waiter has already moved on. It intrigues me to hear that these people are also house-hunting in the area. I cannot take my eyes off that boy's face. The skin is pure and creamy, like Piers' complexion at that age. There's a sweet solemnity in André's expression. He eats his mussels delicately, aware by now, I'm sure, that the eyes of a certain *monsieur* are on him, and feeling it incumbent upon himself to display perfect manners. I simply have to abandon my meal, because it is impossible to concentrate on it and keep an eye on the boy - and I prefer the latter pursuit.

Prefer? Ever since Piers opened my eyes to what boys are capable of, when it comes to responding to attention, affection even, that flame must have been burning on, deep inside me.

His psychiatrist once gave him a book to read, in which the subject had been clinically dissected: statistics, case studies. The pre-pubertal male child seemed to be the most attractive to susceptible men, while the skin was still smooth and white, and hair had not yet grown on the body, to mar it. Boys who were willing, who enjoyed the attentions of someone older and experienced... He'd read past the clinical data, and found himself there - and Piers.

That must have been the point where my guilt crystallised: reading about us as if it were a murder that had been committed, or any other vile and violent act. Why will the rest of them never, never understand? But I well know that there's another side to it, otherwise I would not be so at odds with myself. No smoke without fire, and no need for guilt if there has been no sin.

The eye can surely enjoy, though. I can admire a boy as he swings past, not always oblivious to the fact he's under observation. And André over there knows very well I'm watching him, but does not give me away. Perhaps a certain sort of boy likes to court attention, and a certain sort of man likes to bestow it. I wonder if he has a room to himself.

The waiter emptied the last of the wine into his glass. Did Monsieur want another bottle? But he waved the notion aside, and ordered coffee instead.

How old is he? Certainly younger than Piers when I first knew him, but, like Piers, imbued with an indefinable quality that makes him seem older and more knowing than his appearance suggests.

When his coffee arrived, he asked if any rooms were free. The waiter went to inquire at Reception. There was, alas, nothing for tonight, but from tomorrow they could offer a very good single room with shower and wc. on the first floor, at the back.

So, young André, I shall soon be under the same roof as you. What folly! And all this, just to pay you back, Piers Moriston, oh, and you, Keith Fillingham, for being grown-up, or inaccessible or downright difficult with me. When Aschenbach chose Tadzio, he knew very well what he was doing.

*

While he stood on the balcony in his bath-robe, enjoying the view of the floodlit Mont, a a young voice cleared its throat behind him. He spun round, and there, on the adjoining balcony and separated only by a low glass screen, was the boy himself in light-blue pyjamas like a track suit.

Our eyes meet. The child, his fair hair caught in the light pouring from his room, simpers. I mustn't assume anything, I don't know him. He is just a little boy still. But no. I'm wrong there: he's holding the rail of the balcony with one hand, but the other is stuck down the front of his trousers. He swings from side to side, stares hard at me, and I'm sweating already. I rush back into my room and slam the French window shut, my whole body aflame. He must be only ten or eleven, yet he has just offered himself in the most unmistakeable fashion. Satyrs are getting younger by the minute. A little tap at my door, I go across, and there he is, taller now, older. <Do you usually visit total strangers like this?>

<Only if I see someone I like. I chat to people who are *sympa*.>
<Always men?>

The boy laughs, showing white teeth, then crosses his arms, seizes the bottom of his pyjama top, pulls it up over his head, and drops it carelessly on the floor. Then, without taking his eyes off me, he takes hold of his waistband pushes down the trousers, kicking them off on the the floor also.

The chest is pale in contrast to his tanned face, the nipples two little dark buds perfectly placed, the skin smooth. He is breathing fast, now, like me.

What a transformation before my eyes - he isn't hairless at all, he's quite well developed, and already excited. He must be fifteen or sixteen.

A curdling and surging sensation takes over my entire body, I pass out...

*

He sat up in bed with a start, panting still. The room looked oddly small, the double bed with its dark wood and brass fittings could have been taken from a museum. He put out a hand to feel the covers. He was alone, but the debauch continued to vibrate in his mind, like bell-notes.

Is the sun up, yet, on the Mont? Will the boy be out on his balcony already? He staggered over to the shuttered window, wrestled with the metal things which folded back with a clang, and there, opposite, was a woman washing down the pavement outside one of the shops in the fresh morning air. Stalls were being erected in the square. Market day in Dol de Bretagne. I don't understand. It's all just a muddle. He began to laugh, then turned away from the window, shaking. How teasing and cruel this dream had been, about a little chap who was doubtless innocence incarnate. He would forget the boy, go home again. There were some mysteries better left unravelled.

What happened? He must have had one of his turns. He could cope perfectly well one day, then, on the very next, find himself back in the whirlpool of doubt. The problem was that he now needed this dangerous stimulus, like a drug.

He checked all his belongings: nothing missing. His *agenda* had a note for today: "Estate agent will ring a.m." What estate agent? Was there nothing that made sense any more?

Downstairs, he ordered a pot of very strong coffee. While he was toying with a *croissant*, the call came through. The vendor had accepted his offer.

<Pardon?> He played stupid.

<The house at Courtils, monsieur. You offered...>

The agent's assistant would be out in that area with various keys in the early afternoon, and would be told to *rendezvous* with him at the house. Was there no end to this madness?

Paying his bill, he set off shortly afterwards for the *digue* and its hotel, anxious to see if his dream had been some kind of portent.

<I dined here, yesterday evening,> he said to the proprietress, at Reception. <And then I inquired about a room.>

He moved up his things immediately, opened the French window and stepped cautiously out on to the balcony, like a man who had nearly departed for ever, but now sees the error of his ways, and comes hastening back. It was not quite the Venice Lido that confronted him, but acre upon acre of saltings, interspersed with trees and occasional farms. Behind a dyke on the other side of the lane, the tamed river flowed sluggishly past, beyond which rose the Mont St Michel, spirit made stone, stone made spirit, waiting like a Valhalla in the sunshine for him to take possession of it.

> *"On the Mont, I caught sight of them outside a tacky gift-shop halfway up, the girls choosing coffee bowls with their names painted on, the parents studying menus nearby, and A, in his sweater and immaculate white shorts, crouching, talking to the dog in a low, coaxing voice. Médor…*
>
> *I walked slowly past, and he looked up at me with what I realised was a flicker of recognition. Oh, the temptation to touch this small child, to whom Fate had carried me back, to see if there was any trace whatever of last night's apparition! Over a coffee, I tried to fit the pieces of the jigsaw together. Something new seems to have begun, and I can no more flee this place now, than return to the shell from which Piers plucked me. Those things in my dream are the sort that can lead to trouble.*
>
> *A little later on, I discovered them up in the Abbey, standing by a model of the Mont. He was pointing eagerly at the tiny street winding up round the hill, his bright voice echoing in the stone room. His father was clearly anxious to keep moving on, and so, for a few brief seconds, A and I were alone on stage in the huge vaulted space. He walked all round the glass case, muttering to himself, craning to look at the minuscule golden angel up on the spire. (I was willing him to turn round and ask me a question.) As he bent down*

to inspect some detail, the white shorts tightened over his buttocks, his little soft brown calves protruding beneath, until they disappeared into his white socks. I was rooted to the spot.

In the heat of the day he had shed his sweater, and was wearing a vest. Bare arms and shoulders deliciously brown, but the crowning feature was undoubtedly the head, with that pure face and shock of golden hair down his neck, giving him a farouche aspect. Then he straightened up, his eye caught mine and he gave me the most wonderful smile, before turning shyly away to hurry, like a lithe young animal, in the direction his family went.

I shadowed them through the gardens, though progress was slow: monsieur for ever stopping to relight his cigar, madame constantly putting the dog down and picking it up again, and the children looking for lizards. A stared round in my direction a few times, and I knew that he knew.

When their mother gave birth to her children, she unwittingly kept the best of herself till last. I have seen that fair hair and those dark eyes somewhere before. His smile is beguiling. Could it mean 'I know, but I shall not betray you'?

We all ended up in Mère Poulard, where I got a table almost next to theirs. A chose to rebel, refusing the omelette. Those eyes were superb, the tears turning them into magnifying lenses, - the pupils huge, the irises almost black. His lower lip trembled very convincingly and he got his way: a fish crêpe!

Monsieur was studying a sheaf of papers, and I wondered what they were chasing after. Just a simple second home, doubtless, for even the most prosperous French don't mind slumming a bit, as long as they can get at the sea.

When it came to dessert, A got a lump of cream on the end of his nose and, with a wicked look in his eye and a *glance straight at me, tried to lick it off. My heart surged. How easy, to enter into a tacit conspiracy with a boy like this. I, the ogling suitor, risked committing an appalling faux pas. It's not a question of <u>loving</u> this child, but I know that there is a bedrock in my being that simply loves responsive boys, full-stop. Why else would I have let Raoul into my house? It was almost a relief when the D's got up and left."*

By the time he had paid his bill and hurried out through the postern gate to the car-park, there was no sign of the French family, and he felt deflated at the loss of his fellow-conspirator. The marshes, drenched in light, stretched joyfully into every distance, but there was a heavy feeling in the air and, as he reached Courtils and drove up to the house, the sky was already beginning to darken in the west. A Mercedes was standing outside. As he walked up to the front door, it opened, and, of all people, Madame Duclos came out, then the two girls, one holding a costumed doll. Ignoring the collection of females, he resolutely continued and stepped inside. Another trio of faces turned to look at him: a young man whom he did not know, and André with his father. The estate agent looked surprised, Monsieur Duclos' eyebrows rose, but clear delight was written all over the boy's face.

Roland explained who he was and that the vendor had already accepted his offer. It was almost as blunt as saying 'This is my house, now. Go, the rest of you.'

M. Duclos' jaw dropped, the agent began to stammer something about a misunderstanding, and André dashed out, shouting, <Maman, maman, the house is already sold!> His father rounded on the agent. Surely he must be aware that he did not care to be made a fool of, that he and his family were looking seriously at properties (implying that Roland might be an idle speculator), and that they had specially set their hearts on this one.

At that moment, the wife and three children came rushing back in: the cloud had burst and it was raining in torrents outside. Papa had, of course, locked the car!

Duclos communicated his disgruntlement to his wife in as low a voice as the rain beating on the roof would permit. When drops began to thud on the bare floor-boards above, André tried to climb the ladder to see what was going on, but the agent stepped forward. 'Non, c'est dangereux.'

Roland, not blind to the potential of this situation, made a conciliatory gesture: he had noticed that the family was staying at the same hotel as he was himself, so why not return there, and discuss the matter round a table?

Remembering his good manners, Monsieur solemnly introduced himself (Armand Duclos, member of the Conseil des Ministres at Paris), his wife Fabienne and his children: <Marie-Louise, who is twelve, Aimée, thirteen, and our little André, who is ten.> Ah ha! So the boy really was only ten. Roland was careful to explain that, though he might be English, he was very much a fixture in the Savoy scene. If only Calivet could hear that!

<Papa, he's English!> shouted the boy in wonder.

The rain stopped as quickly as it had begun, and everyone was ready to move on. Duclos said he would take the estate agent to the Pontorson office, if Monsieur Millan would be so kind as to give the rest of the family a lift back to the hotel. An impractical suggestion but, oh, what comfort it brought him, to be able to cram the mother and two girls into the back of his Renault, and help André, with Médor on his lap, to strap himself in in front.

The Mercedes roared off, *madame* fussed over her daughters, and Roland, checking that his carload was settled, made off cautiously into the sunshine in the opposite direction, like one charged with conveying a holy relic.

As soon as we arrive, Madame whisks her children upstairs to wash and do their hair. Although this cannot be anything more than a fragile relationship straining into life, I feel as if I have begun to conquer a continent. When I first met Piers face to face, I could have destroyed the Temple. Fond man, what do you think you're about, this time?

Shortly after there was a respectful knock at his door, and there, with pride written all over his face, was André, who had been sent to invite Monsieur up to their room. This was large and lavish, and the boy was anxious to show it off to the new guest, but his mother made him sit quietly with his sisters. He pulled a face.

She then explained that her son was rather delicate, and tutored privately at their home in Tours. They were looking for *une petite maison* in this area because they thought the sea air would improve their children's health. Roland found himself nodding sagely, and wondering how Aschenbach would have dealt with Tadzio's mother, had the occasion ever arisen. She opened the minibar, and he chose mineral water, suspecting that a clear head would be needed soon. So amazed am I to be in their midst like this, with this bright-eyed child hanging upon my every word, that I hardly know what our conversation touches upon. It was much the same when Piers and I finally met and spoke, outside the gift shop. His family was far away, though. André is swamped by all these females.

Duclos returned with a glum expression. He shook hands with Roland, admitted he had received confirmation that the house was indeed M. Millan's, and that he therefore renounced any claim to it. Any intention on his part to look for other properties would now be shelved. Despite this, the mood lightened, and when they sat down André insisted on coming over to squat at the feet of his new *monsieur*. Roland, relieved that he had not let himself in for discussions after all, felt able to show a little magnanimity: he was *désolé* that they had missed out on their purchase but, when it had been restored, they would be welcome to call on him there, if they wished.

The boy whipped round and seized one of Rolands knee's, causing his mother to exclaim <Just behave yourself, now.>

His father said: <You must try to be a *gentleman* too.>

The girls were not interested in social graces, having been promised a zoo for that afternoon. But André moved rapidly from scorn to outright defiance: he did not want to go to a zoo. His parents protested. It had been agreed that, if they were good about viewing the house, they should have a treat. Now he was trying to spoil it all by being selfish to his sisters.

The boy beat the floor with both hands in a veritable storm of anger and sorrow. <I don't want to,> he screamed. <I won't!>

Roland would have taken his leave there and then, and let the family sort out its troubles, but André straightened, turned a tear-soaked face up at him and gave him the very cue he needed. <Might I suggest, if this *jeune homme* isn't so keen on the zoo, that he comes on a little outing with me instead?> The menhir at Dol was supposed to be quite *amusant*.

It transpired that the child had been clamouring to see a menhir ever since they had arrived. His father objected, however. It would be a burden to Monsieur to take him on, when he was being so awkward. But André got up, gripped Roland's hand and started to drag him away. His father shrugged and capitulated. <If you are quite sure, monsieur.> His mother handed over his sweater, in case a breeze should spring up. *Et voilà!* Before Roland knew what was happening, they were off down the stairs, the boy hand-in-hand with him and skipping joyfully at his side.

They can have no inkling of the great gladness in my heart, that this sweet child so readily accepts me. Nor do they seem to recognise the potential risk, when an innocent is handed into the care of a perfect stranger (and a foreigner), who might do some irreparable harm. I am humbled, though, for this child is not the satyr I dreamed of, but a dear little scrap who looks appealingly up at me with those dark eyes, silent, waiting upon my every word of command. The irony is that I have to thank Piers, and that girl, for this. Why should I sit at home and brood, when I have a right to live, also?

We get into the car, André flings his sweater on the back seat, carefully attaches his seat-belt, and looks at me. 'OK, chief, less go.'

He's made me laugh! 'Where did you learn that?'

'Huh?'

'Où as-tu appris ça?'

<Oh, on the telly. Maman watches a lot of American films. Sometimes she lets me see one.>

<Which French films do you like best?>

'J'adore Jacques Tati. Vous connaissez *Les Vacances de Monsieur Hulot?* Fantastique.'

We are speeding up the road to Pontorson in the sunshine, the Mont receding behind us, just as the Minster used to do. <I   love   that   bit

where his boat folds up with him inside.> Now it's his turn to roar with laughter. He really is fun, away from his parents. Or do I merely imagine I have some kind of magic influence? If so, it's bound to wear off, and then I too shall be on the receiving end of the tantrums.

At Pontorson, he asks me to stop outside a stationer's for some Astérix stickers. I persuade him that the shops in Dol are much nicer, and he takes the suggestion like a lamb.

<Will we be in Brittany there?>

Yes, like crossing an invisible frontier to freedom.

'Et le Mont St. Michel, c'est en Bretagne aussi?'

<It's really still in Normandy.>

'Tu l'aimes bien, le Mont? C'est sensass.' How easily he slips into the 'tu', the familiar form which I heard on the lips of Piers and Adèle within minutes of that first meeting by the lake. *Tu, toi...* The language of affection.

<Your car does nearly two kilometres a minute,> he says, checking his watch against the white and red markers by the road. It's a weakness of mine, to put my foot down when I'm nervous. We are soon at Dol, which reminds me of that stupid dream and my ensuing panic. Now, as if sent to exorcise it, the child is here at my side.

The stationers do not have the particular Astérix sticker which he most cherishes. I brace myself, but he merely looks up at me, his expression softening. <Never mind, I'll find it one day.>

We could be making some progress!

We drive to the south side of the town, André runs over to the standing stone, which totally dwarfs him, and I take my camera out of the glove compartment.

'Mais, c'est chouette, ça!' (His favourite term of approval). <Even Obélix couldn't lift that one.>

<But he brought it here himself!>

His eyes open wide. <You're joking.>

'Tu blagues, hein?' sounds a bit gangsterish. Would his mother approve, and is it all right for him to run around like this, if he's supposed to be frail? <It's absolutely true, I'm telling you. Obélix carried it here one very dark night, and - >

<That's not true, you rotter!> For all his vehemence, his face is a picture of incredulity suffused with mirth. I'm not sure if he should be calling me names, and I'm certain he shouldn't shove me like that. To stop any further assault, I seize him round the torso with both arms, and lift him off the ground. The little boy is almost weeping with frustration, but then, suddenly, he stops weaving and wriggling, and looks me straight in the face. Our joint laughter is explosive, I feel his saliva on my cheek, his hot breath in my face. My arms encompass the warm body whose bare brown shoulders are so close. I could hold him like this for ever.

At last, André broke free and dropped the short distance to the ground. He took Roland's hand once more, and, as they solemnly walked all round the menhir, asked if he had seen the film *Mon Oncle*.

<Yes.>

<What did you like best?>

<The way Hulot took his nephew away from his stuffy parents, to look for adventure.>

<Like us?>

<I suppose so.>

<Roland, will you be my uncle?>

Is he a mind-reader?

<I've got other uncles, but none of them is as nice as you. Is it all right, or must you be somebody else's uncle?>

Piers would surely have said much the same thing at his age. <No, André, I don't have any relatives.>

He's astonished. <None at all? What happened to them?>

<I was an only child, so I didn't have sisters as you have.>

<Pouah, lucky dog!>

<Nor any brothers.>

<Would you have liked one?>

<Yes, very much.>

<Well then, I'll be your brother and your nephew, then you can have two relatives just in me.> He puts an arm round my waist and stretches his face upwards. 'OK, chef?'

<OK.> I bend down a little and he brushes my cheek with his lips.

And, only this morning, he was screwing up his eyes to look at me, a stranger still!

<Roland, there's a tear in your eye.>

I wipe my face and blame it on a non-existent small fly.

<Can we go to St. Malo as well? I've always wanted to go there. It's got walls round it.>

I am putty in his hands, it seems! We return to the car and consult the map. <It's about the same distance as we've already come from our hotel. *Vingt-cinq kilomètres.*>

<Roland, what's *vingt-cinq* in English?> And so the next leg of the journey is whiled away teaching him some numbers. He picks up the pronunciation very quickly.

We park by the quays, and despite the bright sunshine I make him put on his sweater. We enter the old town by the Grande Porte, and we must make a touching couple, the boy clutching his uncle's hand tightly.

He is fascinated by everything he sees: the live shell-fish for sale, the toyshops, the bookshops, even the fashion *boutiques* and bars. It's as if he never gets out of his own house. <Don't you ever go to Paris?>

<Sometimes, but nearly always they leave me at home with Mademoiselle Prinet.>

<Who's she? Your teacher?>

<She's more like a dragon.>

<Does she breathe fire, then?>

<Usually.>

<How long has she looked after you?>

<Since I was seven. I try to tell Maman I'm old enough now not to have Prinet any more. I'm going to be eleven in August.> Then he stopped and looked up. <I wish you would look after me instead. You are so nice. And you could teach me everything in English.>

<But, André, that wouldn't be right.>

<Why not?>

<Because we've only just met. You don't even know me properly.>

<But you wanted to know us, didn't you? You were everywhere that we were, on the Mont this morning: in the street, the Abbey, and the gardens too. Oh yes, and that stupid omelette place!>

Oh, my little conspirator, how sharp you are!

<And that ruined house that Papa wanted to buy. Then you wanted it, and you won. I think you're so clever, Roland, because nobody ever won over my Papa, but you did!>

This boy, who calls me Roland in the French way, is well versed in the art of manipulation. <Have you no friends your own age?>

<I had Henri, but his family moved away last year. Papa and Maman don't like me meeting other children in case I catch their diseases.>

So you are a prisoner locked up inside their wealth, and I am already locked up in my affection for you. An odd combination.

<Roland, why did you ask about friends?>

<Perhaps I'm a bit old to be your friend.>

<But you're my uncle, so that's all right. Anyway, how old are you?>

Ouch! But I must be utterly truthful with a child like this.

<That's only Maman's age. Papa is ancient, he's centuries older than she is. Roland, look...>

We are on the ramparts, and a party of loud schoolchildren in bright clothing is coming towards us. <Look, they're English. Oh, do say something to them.>

To keep the peace, I say to one of the teachers 'I hope you are enjoying your trip.' It sounds silly. The man stops, looks from André to me and back again, says 'Yes, thank you, yes indeed,' and hurries on.

To my embarrassment, André keeps imitating the man's answer, while the rest of the party files past. 'Yiss, sink you, yiss indid.' We get some funny looks.

If I'm not very careful, I shall begin to take to this child, or is it something subconscious, which will come to the surface like an exploding bubble, to confound me and make me what I never could be: someone else's slave? Is that how it began with us, Piers? I am so keyed up, fearful yet glad to have found another creature who is ready to show affection to a crusty old dragon roused from its slumbers.

A clock strikes, down in the town, reminding me that we must be getting back. We cover the distance to our hotel in under three-quarters of an hour, with André spurring me on.

<Maman, papa, *oncle Roland* took me to St. Malo!>

The two girls exchange a private look, then glance round at André and me. Oh God, do I have to woo them as well? Surely we're all above board?

Madame quietly scolds her son for saying 'tu' so soon to Monsieur Millan, calling him uncle and using his first name: it was not polite, and Monsieur might not like it.

'Aw shucks,' replies her son, in his best American. <You don't mind, do you, Roland?>

This could be tricky: a line has been overstepped, and the parents might be wondering, as the girls evidently are. But no, Duclos *père* seems unaware that a rival has popped up in the affections of his own son - and his wife is concerned only that I might be finding André burdensome: no more than that.

When, at their invitation, he went down to the restaurant later on and joined them at their table, the girls were talking animatedly about their visit to the zoo. André sat scowling, waiting for a gap. He was in a navy-blue sweater with a red and white motif on the front, and long fawn trousers. His face brightened when Roland arrived. 'Viens, je t'ai réservé cette place, ici.'

And so he was received, as it were, into the family, with Duclos remarkably relaxed and forthcoming. <It was good of you, monsieur, to look after the boy for the afternoon.> And then the talk turned, in the discreetest manner, to the little house at Courtils. A charming location, with great possibilities. He knew an excellent surveyor, if Monsieur needed one. A man in Paris, not cheap, of course, but thorough.

André was bursting to show off his English numbers, his parents exchanged a quick look, and Madame complimented Roland on his prowess as a teacher. André could be so *difficile*. At this, the boy gave Roland a little dig in the ribs, pursed his lips together, narrowed his eyes, and said <Prinet gets up my nose, maman. I want Uncle Roland to be my teacher. *In Ingleesh.*>

Madame Duclos brushed this aside, but her expression suggested that the subject was by no means dead. After the meal, Duclos cornered Roland on the pretext of taking a constitutional along the lane behind the hotel.

<We have to look after our boy very carefully. He is asthmatic, and the least thing sets him off. To tell the truth, he is a disappointment. After the girls, I desperately wanted a son, and I wanted him fit and strong, so that he could be a sportsman. You like sport? *Moi, j'adore le tennis.* I fear that a boy who does not partake in sport can become effeminate. What do you think?>

Where could I possibly begin? And, if I did, would you understand one word in fifty? So, coward, I re-invent the shrug. Curious, how different from his father this boy is. From the very first moment, André and I were on a kind of signal wavelength. And this shell of a man, this cigar-smoking husk, this is his progenitor?

Their walk mercifully lasted only half an hour and, when they returned, André was still up, having struck a bargain with his mother: no tantrums, in exchange for a chance to see his new friend once more before bed. His father was already engrossed in the newspaper, which gave him the chance to sidle up and whisper 'Tu viens me baigner, Roland?' But his mother heard this and was quite adamant: it was preposterous to ask Monsieur to bath him.

Roland got up, said goodbye, and was about to turn away when André escaped from his mother and came over to clasp him round the waist. <Roland, please say good night to me.>

He bent down, the boy put his arms up and round his uncle's neck, and pulled till their faces nearly touched. 'Embrasse-moi!' It was the tiniest movement of the lips. Roland gave him a quick kiss on the cheek, ruffled the golden hair and tried to break free.

There was a marvellous light in the boy's eyes. With surprising strength he pulled Roland to him again, gave him a hot, wet kiss right on the lips, and reluctantly let him go. <André, stop that!> His mother sounded shocked.

That surely seals our bond. Two boys in a million seem to be initiated into the Great Secret. Piers. André. Raoul also? I don't know yet about him, and perhaps I don't want to. Maybe this little animal is all I shall ever really need. He doesn't require anything of me materially; it's his emotional need which attracts me so much.

I'm so immensely happy, so fulfilled, so at peace with myself. I dare not analyse this, nor wonder how long it may last. As we drove back from St. Malo, he came out with something that was obviously uppermost in his mind: 'I don't want to go back to them, I want to stay with you.' *Toi et moi!*

He hardly slept at all that night. A dozen times or more, he was out on his own balcony, craning up to where he could just make out André's, against the night sky. How enmeshed am I? I could leave suddenly, with an excuse, rule a neat line beneath the episode. I'm not beholden to these people. It would be one of those chance encounters which take fire for a while, and then die out. The mayfly effect... I'd get over it and so would he.

Deep inside, he was more susceptible than he cared to admit. It is possible to cross the frontiers of age, sex and disposition, but these, more than any others, are beset with hazards. So am I just a man who lets his destiny take him through a minefield, persuaded that it is a bed of flowers?

*

He sat over a coffee, looking at the cold rain on the windows of the breakfast room and pondering the two events which had so coloured his life here in the last twenty-four hours: the boy and the house. It was as if he was being put to the test again, having failed the Cambridge one miserably. There was however the disturbingly attractive retinal image of *that boy,* and the deep conviction that his life was once again subject to forces he simply did not understand. But his thoughts were interrupted by the unexpected arrival of André's father. 'Vous permettez, Monsieur Millan?'

Sitting down at my table, he drops into a confidential tone, which makes me uneasy. His office has called him to Paris on an important matter, which involves taking the car. Since his children absolutely refuse to abandon their holiday, he has no choice but to leave Fabienne with them for a short while. Although he stops short of sounding me out about my own plans, I see what he is moving towards. When I tell him, in my best formal French, that I have to stay around for a while to finalise my house purchase, and suggest that I am happy to continue seeing his charming family, there is sheer relief on his face, followed by the half-amused man-to-man expression which says 'I know you'll keep an eye on them for me.' <Doubtless they will fill up their time with excursions. Please, join them as and when you wish.> He doesn't realise how he is playing into my hands.

With the departure of the Mercedes into the rain half an hour later, a calm seemed to descend over the hotel. As Roland was finishing a letter, there came the awaited knock at his door. It was the first time he had really looked at her. She was wearing a dark-blue trouser-suit with white facings on the tunic, and she exuded a very expensive perfume. Her skin and complexion were still good, the eyes very dark, like André's, and the face quite narrow, the chin almost pre-Raphaelite, the hair short and slightly tinted, reddish-brown. She was quite *petite* (her son came up to her shoulder already). He waved her over to his armchair.

<My husband has gone away.> She clasped and unclasped her hands.

I make the slightest of nods.

<You are so English, monsieur, so unsurprised.>

Her obvious embarrassment and chagrin rouse a naughty kind of warmth inside me, and I mumble something about people of his rank being liable to get summoned back from their holiday now and then.

But she gives me an intense look. <Forgive me, but I cannot expect you to know what I have to put up with.>

I quite expected her to cry <My husband is a monster,> but she is evidently holding herself in check.

<Armand has no inkling of the effect upon the children of what he says and does - André especially, who really isn't strong.>

This time, a tear comes, and I am faintly alarmed that it will be followed by a tempest. So, here we have it: their marriage is in a state. She had suggested buying the holiday home in the hope of giving them a base away from Paris and Tours and all their temptations. <He pretended to be annoyed at losing it to you, monsieur, but in fact he was delighted. And he has not gone away on government business. Oh no. Far from it. After his obligatory few days with me and the children, he is off elsewhere in pursuit of pleasures that I cannot bring myself to give

him. *Il est totalement pervers.* Once I had him followed, but I could not get enough proof to cite him.>

She weeps, and I could almost begin to feel sorry for her, if this were not like some pre-war black-and-white film. Anything I am able to do now is done solely for André's sake.

<Monsieur, forgive me. I am sure your own life must be so calm, so free from all this kind of thing.>

You do not know the half of it, but I shall tell neither a lie nor the truth.

<I have to protect my children, you see. They are my dearest possessions. What is to become of André when Armand and I part? His father treats him like dirt. If a boy has no father, he goes wrong, doesn't he? I know, I have seen it. They become dishonest. I don't want my baby to go that way.>

If this is an act, it's convincingly done.

<Why does he treat me so? I was never unfaithful to him.>

This puts me on my guard. Is she angling for a protector, a lover even, to score over her husband? In my best rational tone I suggest that we go to the children, and plan something for the day. It would do them good to get out.

She takes both my hands in hers. <I do not think I would have coped very well on my own, not just yet. And André wants you. I hope he is not being a nuisance.>

Amazing, to find myself playing the role of ally, and so soon. I did well to mention the children: she will stay off the tricky subjects in front of them.

He should have known better. Madame Duclos hired a large chauffeur-driven car from a firm in Coutances and, when they were all comfortably installed (he and she on the back seat with André and Médor between them, the girls facing them), she opened up on her ideas for her son's future.

<He is delicate, as you know. With his asthma, the air in Tours is not good for him. And his nerves... I'd like him to spend some time in a healthier environment.>

<Had you considered somewhere up in the mountains? It's frankly

much better for the lungs.> It's as if she's playing to a script of my writing!

<I thought the sea air... but perhaps you are right.>

<My own experience is limited to Savoie. But a lot of people go there for their health.>

<The Alps? Armand would argue it's too far. If you knew what a charade I had, just to get him here. And he is so mean. He will hit the roof when he finds I've charged this car to him. But what did he expect me to do, sit in the hotel and twiddle my thumbs all day?>

<Maman,> said André, <I'm sure I would like Savoie, if uncle Roland lives there.>

His mother sighed. <Maybe I could arrange for him to have an extended holiday down there, through the winter. Armand intends to spend Christmas in India, but of course that would not be suitable for the children.>

<Do they have grandparents?>

<We have nothing to do with his side. My mother lives on her own in Amboise, quite close to us. She is fond of André, but he cannot stay there. He is too much of a handful.>

<I'm not a handful, am I, Roland?>

She pouted. <You see, he for ever plays one off against the other.>

The child is natural enough with me. It's this neurotic woman who gets him all on edge. I've seen it so many times: mothers as destroyers, using the maternal cloak to stifle their menfolk. And those two little girls sitting opposite clutch their dolls, as if none of this is of any concern to them.

<Well then,> he heard himself say in a very mock bright English sort of tone, <a period down in our mountains> (*nos montagnes*, to underline the fact that, though he was foreign, he was *seigneur* at "Orphéon") <might well do him some good. There are agencies, I'm sure.>

Madame would not be satisfied with anything as vague as that. <Monsieur, you live on the spot. I am sure that it would not be too difficult to find somewhere suitable for him. I would pay your expenses, of course.>

The boy's eyes are on me, a hand clutches mine in expectation.

<I don't mean an *internat* of any kind, and certainly not a Catholic-run home. He doesn't need to be in with a lot of rough boys, you understand. He needs calm, he needs affection.>

All the things *they* cannot give him.

One of the girls asks where we are going, and their mother replies <To the pink granite coast,> with a surprising decisiveness. I am not to be consulted, it seems, which sorely tempts me to break out of this absurd arrangement – until I catch the boy looking at me.

The rain was perpetually starting and stopping, the landscape was shrouded in a dull mist, the sea quite invisible. At last, the driver dropped them off in the square at Tréguier, promising to return in one hour. Near the cathedral they found a crowded little street with a market in it, and, on the corner, a *crêperie,* which André absolutely insisted on entering. <Maman, Roland, I could eat a horse!> His sisters come to life, and start squabbling over the menu, while Madame sits back and closes her eyes. I would dearly go and sit alone in the cathedral, to try to gather my wits.

<I shall have two *crêpes,*> said André. <A fish one and a jam one. And cider to drink.>

His mother opened her eyes. <You will have lemonade. And one *crêpe.*>

It looks as though we shall spend the rest of this hideous day with rebellion not very cleverly contained. I shall be uncle to André and, I suppose, ogre to his sisters. Madame will continue to confide her dire revelations to me, and perhaps I shall even be regarded as her new companion.

Near Trégastel, we walk in the rain along a sad, deserted beach dotted with lumps of absurd pink rock. The girls seek out minute shells in the sand, and whoop with glee. André pads over the soaking sand, hand-in-hand with me, both of us trying to ignore the others. The tide is out, there's nobody else around at all: Brittany on the ebb.

On the way back, as we pass an elaborate graveyard, I look round at his face. Suppose he were to die young, say at fifteen? Would they allow him one of those ornate tombstones in shiny dark marble, with a photo in an oval frame and bright gilt lettering: "André Duclos, notre fils bien aimé..."?

When we were walking across the sand to the water's edge, he stopped, put his arms round my waist and said: <I want you to be my papa.> He is quite unmoved by his father's withdrawal; there's no love lost between them. Useless to answer 'But you already have one.' He'd only start to attack Duclos. I think I said <But I'm only just your uncle, since yesterday.>

<I mean it, Roland. I wouldn't say something so important if I didn't mean it: I want to be your boy, not his.>

The womenfolk were coming back. I had to shut him up, promising to discuss it again at a more opportune moment.

That came at bathtime, of course. Madame is busy elsewhere, seeing to the girls, so it is the most natural thing in the world that I should fall in with her son's urgent wish and take him off to the tub.

> *"The bath and bed routine provides a delightful interlude in which we can both say whatever we please. It's not until you look closely at someone else's bare flesh, with droplets of water on it, that you realise what a work of art it is. Sitting on the floor, my head level with his, and in constant danger of being splashed, I don't mind how incongruous all this is. The spectacle of the nude body always did appeal to the painterly nature, especially as here, with all those tantalisingly suggestive bubbles positioning themselves in the <u>modest regions</u>. If the good Lord didn't want us to fall in love with boys, why did he make them so comely?*
>
> *The light brings out the three-dimensionality of every curve, the darker places under the arms and, when he stands up, the pelvis, and again (when he turns) the crevice between the buttocks. He is Puck, he is a water-imp, he makes funny noises at me, pretends to puff and blow, and turns his head to see what effect it has. I'm sure my face must give everything away.*
>
> *He said 'I'll come and live with you. Is there room'? I said he could come and visit, so he demanded to know <u>when</u>.*

With a boy like this (P̲ was the same), you can't just say 'soon'. They're too used to the parental 'we'll see', that never comes to anything.

He knows his mother has asked me to find him somewhere at or around Annecy. I ought not to have him under my own roof, because I don't think I could bear the responsibility. Too many broken pieces to be picked up, on both sides. I really should be taking stock of all that has been happening in this remarkably short time, but the dust will have to settle, first."

*

The next morning, his mother comes down to the breakfast room for another of her conversations. <He loves counting in English, he quickly picks up new things from someone he really gets on with. Could you possibly help him a little? Armand cannot speak a word (nor can I), but he sets such store by it.>

I ask her if I may take André with me to the cottage today, where I have arranged to talk to a surveyor. <He must wear old clothes.> This throws her, she is all ready to go into Pontorson to purchase some jeans and a T-shirt, but I assure her that, as it was my suggestion, I will take him and kit him out. She opens her purse, but I refuse, just like a good uncle! <I have to go there, anyway, to pick up my surveyor.>

There was still some mist hanging about on the saltings, out of which the Mont rose, resplendent in the morning sunlight. <Roland, just look at that!>

He seems to have a good visual faculty, and his memory is superb. Without being prompted, he reels off all the English he has heard: not only the numerals from me, but also the phrases used by that English teacher at St.Malo.

We locate a clothing shop. André chooses the most expensive jeans he can find, and goes behind the curtain to change into them. 'Alors, Roland?'

He looks just like any other small boy in those. A T-shirt with a picture of Donald Duck, a soft peaked cap and some rubber boots complete the outfit. His mother will be horrified when she sees him.

Lefebvre, whom he had used when putting "Orphéon" to rights, was waiting for them at the estate agent's office.

<You mean, he's flown all the way from Geneva to Paris?> said André, in amazement.

They drove out to Courtils, the boy in the back, his discarded shorts and sweater beside him on the seat. Once or twice he made as if to say something, but thought better of it.

When they got out, and Roland was walking over to unlock the front door, he asked if he could take Médor with him to Annecy (if he was going).

'Ça dépend.'

<Depends on what? I couldn't bear to be parted from him.>

But Roland was not to be drawn.

Lefebvre got to work, with André in eager attendance, finding tools from the bag he had brought and dashing out into the garden to report to Roland, who was studying the outhouses. <He says it's very bad that there's no staircase, but he let me go up the ladder. He's got a gadget to find damp walls. He's been chipping off bits of wood here and he got me to help him lift a drain cover in the kitchen, and he's got this really powerful torch...> The child was already grimy and obviously in his seventh heaven.

Even if it all has to be torn down, I will rebuild it as a monument to what is already becoming a very happy period of my life. Hell, I'm getting it for next to nothing!

There was a crash and a shriek of delight from the scullery. Roland rushed in to find that the surveyor, in trying to open the window, had dislodged the entire frame, which had fallen out and smashed in the yard. <It was never properly fixed, monsieur. Regardez ça!>

André, in hoots of laughter, was rubbing his hands.

<Are you mocking me in my distress?> said Roland to him. <And who's the *salaud* now?> Just look at him!

Eventually, they returned to the hotel, where Roland, afraid that Madame might catch sight of her filthy son, let André use his shower.

The hotel would launder his clothes. However, the receptionist said that Madame Duclos had gone off with the girls again in a hired car, and was not expected back until dinner that evening.

He sat down with Lefebvre. As he had expected, the roof timbers were rotten, but the walls were sound enough, apart from some damp spots. The floors upstairs would have to be entirely renewed, along with their joists. A staircase would have to be specially made, the place needed rewiring, the water mains and gulleys needed attention. <I should do all this as soon as possible, before the wet weather sets in. One of the outbuildings could be demolished to make way for a garage. The other can go on being a store.>

André reappeared, draped only in a towel, having eavesdropped on most of this.

<Go and get dressed,> said Roland.

<He's a personable young man,> said Lefebvre, when the boy had gone.

Roland quietly explained the situation. The boy needed mountain air, a good family to live with, and so on.

<I have a sister in Annecy,> said the surveyor. <She and her husband have no children, but they love them. I am sure that she could help him.>

<He has temperament, monsieur.>

<So I have noticed, but she would be able to cope. Kids are usually different when they're away from their parents, aren't they? I'll give you her details, in case you don't find anywhere else.> He was given lunch and then driven back to Pontorson to get his train to Paris. He promised to send his written report very shortly.

Since I don't have to produce the money for a few days, when all the legal details will be attended to, my shrimp and I are free. <It's a hot day, so what do you want to do?>

<Let's go to the seaside, like Monsieur Hulot did. We can swim. It'll be nice and cool.>

<Fetch your things, then. We'll go to Carolles-Plage. It's only just up the coast. Don't forget a big towel.>

<Have you got a *maillot de bain*?>

He hadn't anticipated the need for trunks. He'd locate some when they got there. He left a message at Reception to say where they had gone.

They spent the broiling afternoon lying on the sandy beach or frolicking about in the sea. André was his cub, his puppy. They splashed and ducked each other (just as he used to do with Piers), wrestled in the water until they were both exhausted, and retreated to the beach, to flop down in the shade of the umbrella which Roland had hired.

He never has a chance to do this, to be just himself. There are a thousand things I'd like to offer him, camping, for instance, but I am afraid that he would take everything as a promise to be strictly fulfilled. And I'm afraid of myself...

Suddenly, screams and shouting came from further along the beach, a knot of people by the water. Someone was being carried: a little girl, her body quite limp, her head hanging down, pale, her long hair straggling. A crowd formed.

<What's happened? Has she drowned?> asked André, in awe.

The siren of an ambulance sounded, then blue lights were flashing up on the promenade. The rest of the beach had emptied.

<Come on, Roland, let's go and see.>

He was not sure about this, but André was tugging at his hand. The inert body was on the ground by now, the chest being firmly and regularly pressed by an ambulance man kneeling beside it.

<What's he doing?> whispered André.

<He's trying to get her breathing again.>

After what seemed like eternity, the miracle happened: water came spurting out of the girl's mouth, she was making choking noises. A great sigh went round the crowd and someone shouted 'Bravo!' Within seconds, the girl had been wrapped up and carried to the ambulance which tore away, its siren and lights going for all they were worth.

Roland stood there for a moment, frozen in his relief. Their special time together had not been ruined, after all. André took his hand. <She wasn't really dead, was she?>

<She would have been, if that man hadn't known what to do. As I said to you earlier, the sea can be terribly dangerous.>

<But I'm not in danger when I'm with you, Roland, am I?>

I pray God you may not be.

When they got back to the hotel, André delivered the whole story with a few dramatic embellishments. ('Aidez-moi, je me noie!' he claims the girl shouted; and, of course, the *gendarmes* were there in droves).

<Mais André!> said his mother, <Monsieur Millan would never allow you to see anyone he thought might be dead.>

<There was an accident,> said Roland, <but fortunately not fatal.> He heard the absurd formality in his voice, aware that the incident must at all costs be played down.

Madame Duclos hastily changed the subject. The following day they could hire the car again and go further afield. The girls, too, were fond of beaches. They could visit one of the *plages* near Roscoff.

<A big distance for one day, madame.>

<Then what about staying one night in a *logis*? It wouldn't be busy yet.>

<I hate that car,> said Marie-Louise. <I felt sick in it.>

<I fear I cannot presume upon your hospitality any more,> said Roland, as firmly as he could.

But the boy had heard this exchange and began coursing round the room, knocking objects over, cannoning into chairs, roaring with fury mixed with grief. His new friend was set to abandon him.

"Then, out of the blue, he began to pant violently, doubled up, and collapsed on the carpet. I thought he was putting it on, but he looked deathly and his mother said he was having one of his attacks. Between us, we got him on to his bed and calmed him down. He insisted on holding <u>my</u> hand all the time, and, despite his difficult breathing, made it clear how much he wants me to go on this Brittany trip. What could I do, but give in?"

*

After the children had gone to bed, he fetched his *logis* handbook, they chose a place near Roscoff, and got Reception to phone through. Then, intrigued to see her reaction, he reported his inquiries on her son's behalf. She wanted to know more about the surveyor and he gave her the sister's number. She went to phone in her room and, in a few minutes, returned, looking very pleased. <I told Madame Garbet what André needs, and what he is like, and she was helpfulness itself. I said that you have kindly shown an interest in my son, and she hopes it will be possible to meet you.>

<Did you make any arrangement about when André should visit?>

<Only tentatively. My husband will have to agree, of course. The Garbets are going to Corsica in July, so we thought that, if a first visit goes well, on both sides, he could go to them early to mid-August. I should be so happy if you could help him just to settle in. I would come myself, but Armand is so difficult...>

*

The next day dawned bright. Madame Duclos arrived at the breakfast table with her two daughters, to report that all the children were raring to go, then a triumphant André came in, brandishing the morning edition of the local paper. 'Roland, maman, regardez.' He was beside himself with excitement: the story of the nearly-drowned girl had made the front page. <It says she's recovering in hospital. And she's the same age as Marie-Louise. I wish it had happened to her.>

Considering this threat of friction, the day began quite well, but only because each of the children in turn was allowed to sit next to Roland. He took the most direct route, and they reached Roscoff in time for lunch, which was eaten in a huge, sunlit dining-room looking out across the harbour to the Ile de Batz.

André had to have mussels, of course. <Is this our hotel?> he wanted to know. <And when can we go swimming?> He was told they would be staying in a smaller place, and that, if he was good, he should go in the sea with Roland later.

So this is how it might have been, if things had worked out with

Fiona, and I'd become a *paterfamilias*. I see only too well what an *impasse* Duclos has got himself into. The children bicker at each other and constantly vie for supremacy, and the mother's a bag of nerves. To get André away from all this would be to do him a service. He has confidence in me, and, when he is safely installed at Annecy, out of their sight (and probably their minds, too), he will be more under my control and care. All this has been taken out of my hands, and yet it runs like a clock.

The girls wanted to go round the shops with their mother. It was agreed that they would all meet by the church in two hours' time. Roland took André back to the car, having found a good place on the map for bathing.

The tide was rising, lapping almost imperceptibly in between rocky islets and over the flat expanses of sand. They got changed in the car, Roland in the back, where there was more room, André in front, then, moments later, they were running across the wet sand.

<Can one swim at Annecy, Roland?>

<Yes, in the lake.>

<Do you swim there?>

<No.>

<Why not?>

<Because I don't like to go swimming on my own.>

<Haven't you a friend to go with?>

<No, not really.>

André squinted up at him. <If you have no relations and no friends, then I shall be your special friend, and we will always go swimming together when we want to. *D'accord*?>

How can two so ill-assorted people have produced such a sweet child?

He chased André into the water, gave him a piggy-back until the sea was up to his chest, then rolled over into it, so that both of them went right under and came up spluttering.

<Roland, you must rescue me from drowning!> André floated on his back and Roland did likewise, manoeuvring until the boy was just above him, and could be clasped gently round the chest.

<Oh, that's really good. You do it like a real lifeguard.>

Roland made a few languid movements with his legs, and they drifted slowly backwards. <We're floating just above the seaweed, your beloved mussels, and hundreds of crabs.>

André gave a little shriek. <Are there really crabs? Will they get us?> He tried to break free, but Roland held him tightly.

<You're quite safe with me. No need to be frightened.> You are fun, my shrimp, and that's something I thought I could never be allowed to enjoy any more.

<Roland, you're crushing me!>

And so the spell is broken. I relinquish my grip, he turns over and pummels me so that I go under and choke.

We swim back to land, touch bottom and chase each other across the flats. He snatches up a piece of seaweed and tries to hit my legs with it. In the end, we collapse on a bench near the car, panting and laughing. I don't think that he has much fun out of life, either. How pale he is, like a statue near death. I had forgotten the asthma attack. It must affect him badly. <Are you tired, André? Do you want to sleep a little?>

No, he is shivering. He must get dressed. This time, we both climb in the back of the car, I make sure that his top half is dry and get him to put his T-shirt and sweater back on. He wriggles out of his trunks and gives them to me, then rubs his abdomen with the rough towel.

'Oh, Roland, regarde!' The sea-water has left him with an erection!

<Is this the first time that it's happened to you?> I am struggling. The young Piers always knew just what to do, in a case like this.

<No, sometimes it comes up in the bath, or in bed. Why does it do that, Roland?>

<Don't worry, it's quite normal.> And I give him the briefest account of the waywardness of the penis. His father obviously neglects him in every way, and he has no other boy to compare notes with.

> *"P put me in the firing line once or twice, when it came to topics which I certainly regarded as ticklish. And now A, on the outer fringes of adolescence (whoever would have thought it?) produces a real facer. I believe he took my*

respectable <u>oncle</u> explanation, for he said 'My sisters have got those slit things. I've seen them. So <u>that's</u> what they're for. I think it's a bit pathetic.' And after that the subject was dropped. How will bath-time be, now that he knows I know?"

By the time they reached their hotel at Moguériec, he was exhausted, and excused himself until dinner. He scarcely had time to wash, however, and sit down in a chair by the window, to enjoy the sunlight on the boats in the little port, before there was a gentle knock at the door. Madame Duclos.

<André refuses to sleep in the same room as the girls, although there are three beds. There is no space for him to have a bed put in my room, and no other single rooms are free.>

Where have I been in this situation before, and how did it threaten to turn out?

André arrives, furious. <I'm not sleeping with *them*, and that's that!>

He is quick to notice that his uncle's room is bigger than his mother's, and so, to keep the peace, I consent to the mattress from the third bed in the children's room being brought in and placed on my floor. The *patronne* is fortunately understanding, and *mère* allows herself to be overridden.

After the children's light supper, they go to their respective beds. I suspect she might have a scruple about her son sleeping in his adoptive uncle's room, and detains me at the bar, plying me with whisky, and various questions. Was I married? Any children of my own? How long had I been living and working in France? Any thoughts of going back to England?

My brief time with Fiona schooled me in the art of verbal tennis, and Madame seems satisfied about my interest in her boy's welfare. I draw the conversation to a quick close, flee back to my room and turn the key as quietly as I can. André's voice comes at me out of the darkness. 'C'est bien toi?'

<Are you all right?>

<I didn't want to go to sleep till you'd given me my *grosse bise*.>

<You should be fast asleep, *jeune homme*, after your strenuous day.> I switch on a small lamp.

<It was *chouette*. Now, will you come down here by me, and say goodnight?>

I am suddenly so reminded of the young Piers, who was just as affectionate. André puts his arms up, clasps them round my neck and pulls just a bit too hard.

<Hey, that hurts!>

'Bi - bi- bise. Je te commande!' He's curious about the smell on my breath.

<Whisky.> Torn apart inside, I try an avuncular kiss on his cheek.

<No, not there. On my lips!> He wants to taste the whisky, too!

In this painful crouching position, I ruffle his hair and try to get away with a quick peck, but he presses his lips to mine and then begins to whisper in my ear, his breath blowing at me. <Roland, it's happening again. I want you to tell me if it's all right. You needn't look. Just give me your hand.>

So that dream now has its beginnings in a reality where we are both getting involved. His hand takes mine, plunges with it under the bedclothes and, before I know, we are at journey's end. A warm, fleshy little ramrod touches my fingers.

<Hold it. That's good, Roland.>

Faces spin before my inner eye: Piers, Raoul. And I withdraw my hand, backing away.

'Mais q'y a-t-il?' He asks me what's wrong!

<You must never ask me to do that, André. Never.>

<Why not?>

 <Because… Now you go to sleep.>

<What about the big kiss, then?>

<You've already had that.>

<Roland...>

<What?>

<Will Médor be all right, out in your car?>

<He's fine. I looked at him before I came up.>

God, that was close. I lie awake, my mind racing along, only too aware of my young charge on the mattress below, fast asleep, breathing evenly except for a small sigh now and again, and a rustling of the bedclothes as he turns over.

The subject, having been established, will come up again to taunt me. What am I supposed to do, when these things get me excited also? Many more such days, and I shall be a total wreck. André clings to me, but I'm not morally strong enough to fend him off. I escaped from home to find peace and sanctuary here, but it is a hornet's nest.

Weary at last, he fell asleep, only to be wakened by a hammering on his door. It was light already. André shot upright on his mattress, terror in his face.

It was his mother, to say that their hotel at the Mont had rung: Armand was back, and requiring them to return immediately.

Roland looked from the mother to the boy, and back, defiance beginning to seethe inside him. But why? What was the fuss about? They were only on a brief trip.

<Monsieur, you do not know him. He can be so jealous. We must pack at once.> Her voice had taken on a sharp edge.

Not before they had had breakfast, Roland insisted. Amid his scorn, he almost felt sorry for her.

By nine o' clock they were crammed into the car. There was a sea-mist hanging round the little port and, up on the main road, cars had their headlamps on.

<Why did papa have to come back so soon?> asked one of the girls plaintively.

<He's ruined our holiday again,> said André, whose turn it was to sit in front.

<Can we not go a little faster, monsieur?>

When they arrived, Duclos was up in his room. Roland, assuming that the wife would be the best person to calm her ruffled spouse, proposed to go off and unpack.

<But you must come and help me to explain.>

As soon as they entered, Duclos coldly requested Roland to withdraw, but Madame immediately began her operatic approach: <Tell him, monsieur, that I am not unfaithful,> and burst into tears.

The children stood in a line near the door, as if awaiting the firing squad. André was visibly shaking, and breathing noisily.

<There is no need for you, monsieur, to waste your words defending my wife,> said Duclos. <I know her. She is well able to take up with the first man she finds, and - >

<Before you go any further,> said Roland in as steady a voice as he could manage, <you may recall you suggested that I keep an eye on your family in your absence. And that is what I have done, no more, no less. As a change for the children, we chose to spend the night near Roscoff. In fact, André slept on a mattress in my room because the children would not sleep together.>

<It's true, papa, it's true,> said André in a strangled voice.

<And,> said his mother, who had somehow summoned up the courage to return to the fight, <Monsieur Millan has already found us a good family in Annecy for André to board with. I have telephoned the lady, and it only needs him to see her and make the final arrangements. Does that all constitute *taking up*?>

Duclos jaw dropped. <Annecy? André? But whatever for?>

<For his asthma, Armand. We thought the mountains would do him good.>

<We?> stormed her husband. <You mean you and him, behind my back. Am I not approached? Am I not to be involved?>

Roland stepped forward and took him firmly by the arm. <Monsieur, step outside the door for a word, *s'il vous plaît*.>

To his great surprise, Duclos followed him.

<You have completely misinterpreted the situation, and you have wronged both your wife and myself in front of your children. Unless you retract what you said to us, I shall return to Savoie today and consider whether or not a word with my *avocat* might be appropriate. There would of course be no question of my helping your son any further.>

Duclos seemed to shrink while this was being said. From inside the room came the sound of André coughing, and the girls weeping. Roland stared at him in silence, waiting.

<Monsieur,> stammered Duclos, <I realise I have been mistaken. I owe you an apology.>

Roland very nearly forced him inside, to repeat it in the presence of his family. <It would be best if you made your peace with your wife,> he said, and turned on his heel.

<Monsieur Millan...> There was anxiety in the voice now. <You will stay for a while, I hope, and give me - give us - the chance to speak to you again?>

<I shall be at dinner tonight.>

Duclos seized him by the hand. <Thank you, monsieur.>

Like Napoleon retreating from Moscow, thought Roland, as he went back to his own room. The man thinks I'm after his wife!

He was not left undisturbed for long. Madame arrived, falling over herself to express her gratitude.

<So he apologised to you for what he said?>

She looked at him in amazement. <Apologise? My husband would rather go to hell than do that, least of all to us. I came to say that André is having another attack and he wants you, if you could possibly come.>

<Is he in bed?>

<He is sitting in his room. I thought it better if he were somewhere quiet. All this has quite upset him.>

The boy was huddled under a blanket in his arm-chair, his face pale and sweating. He was fighting for breath, and his eyes were huge, brimming.

Roland squatted next to him. <Now, young man, this isn't the André I know, is it?> How clumsy my words are, but they seem to clear the air a little: his expression brightens.

<Roland, put your arm round me. I'm so frightened I shall die.>

<You know that's not true. You've got at least another *soixante ans* to live. Now, what about this violent little *poitrine*?> He pressed the open palm of his hand against the middle of André's clammy chest and, to his great relief, the spasm began to quieten after a few moments.

<Maman, I feel better already. Look, I can breathe now.> The colour began to return to his cheeks.

His mother clasped her hands. <It's a miracle, monsieur. It usually takes ages to get him back to normal. How did you do it?>

He shook his head. He had never believed in faith-healing.

Madame Duclos ran out to fetch her husband.

<André, do you promise me you weren't doing it just for effect?>

At that, the tears overflowed. <Roland, don't you believe me? You cured me.>

Duclos came in. <It seems, monsieur, that my debt of gratitude to you is even greater. How can I repay all your kindness to my dear little son? If you will not be offended, I absolutely insist on paying your hotel bill. No, it is the least I can do. And I am very happy for André to stay at Annecy, if it can be arranged.>

So now the monster turns sentimentalist. "My dear little son". Only a few days ago, it was a very different tune: "He is a disappointment".

As soon as he decently could, he went to Pontorson to have a word with the *notaire* and the agent about the progress of his purchase, then drove to Courtils and spent a couple of pleasant hours poking about, looking out of the landing window at the Mont and generally feeling pleased with himself. If I really did stop André's attack, if I *am* some kind of healer, I could spend the rest of my life laying hands on sick boys' bodies and achieve a kind of voluptuous sanctity!

Things were still moving too quickly: he felt as though, having been trapped for years in a dense forest, paths were opening up to him in all directions. The André business would almost be comic, were it not for the terrible way the boy was treated, which contributed to his asthma. It was simply essential to reduce his hysteria level.

I can do that all right, if I can get him away from his people. But what then? How long will they let him stay? The talk was of his spending the winter there. If so, I'll lose him again in the Spring. I know my problem, but I cannot solve it: I want to freeze Piers and André in a time-warp that gives me perpetual control over them. An artist's function is to encapsulate what he sees, and render it immortal. For me, two particular persons are works of art already. Why, then, must they grow up, become overblown like roses?

The name of my little house shall be "PARR" (standing for Piers, André, Roland and, for good measure, Raoul), testimony enough, at my very front door, to the ways I have trodden and am now treading. Barry and Jonathan were different because they were adult, and my relationships with them did not cross society's lines. But even they were boys once, like me. Where did the transition come? In a part of me, did it ever come? If I am truthful with myself, there is a limit to how far I'm prepared to edge out of my shell.

He arranged for the vendor and his lawyer to meet him in three days' time, to finalise everything. The money was ready, and he could get on with the paperwork for the restoration. During the negotiations, a thought struck him: at the very end of the Wharnley episode, having lost Piers, he was on the point of pulling out of his purchase of "Stella Maris", for why should he ever want it, having lost the one with whom he had spent such a happy time there? But he had once told Piers that he was his heir and one day all these properties would be his. (It was still so. He had not changed his Will). It would have been deceitful to deprive him of the one place which meant so much to them. So he bought "Stella" and allowed the agent to go on letting it – which was still the case, to this day.

First he based some rough notes on Lefebvre's report which had arrived in the meantime. They were both in agreement about basics: the internal walls being sound, there was no question of major alteration to the size or shape of the rooms. The scullery window would have to be replaced at once. He didn't want *forains* getting in and making the place even worse. He took a lot of measurements, and then went back to the room designated as *salon*, where, on a temporary drawing-board, he could rapidly translate his jottings into neat annotated plans which a good builder would be able to work to. He could return to Savoie with an easy mind, knowing that his own supervision of the work need be only minimal.

As he worked, he wondered if he would hear a car drive up outside, - Duclos seeking him out to continue the dialogue of contrition and reconciliation. Of course he won't, he's not that kind of man. One quick, embarrassed encounter, and he steers well clear. The dinner tonight promises to be strained. Perhaps André won't even be there, and I shall have to put up with the rest of them as best I can. Which are worse, I wonder, the Calivets or the Duclos? Are they prototypes for all French families?

When he finally walked out of his door and locked up, his eye was caught by the blue ridge to the east, on which sat the towers of Avranches. Wharnley Minster was up on a hill, just like that. Another subconscious reason for choosing this place?

He dawdled deliberately that evening, but still was first at the table, so ordered an *apéritif* and sat waiting for them to arrive. Duclos came first, of course, cigarette between his fingers, then the two girls and, bringing up the rear, Madame, with her arm round the shoulder of André who, in the Donald Duck T-shirt and jeans, had clearly won the battle over dress.

Duclos suggested champagne. The children had Coke. It was the sort of moment that might have called forth a toast from somebody, or at least a touch of conviviality, but the attempt fell on stony ground.

André sits quietly next to me, as if inside a protective bubble which no-one must pierce, not even I. His trust in me is all-apparent: I now have to learn to deserve it, if I can.

As the menus are brought, the gloom lifts somewhat, Duclos becoming almost animated, as he tries to decide between the *menu gastronomique* and the more enticing areas of the *carte*. His wife is wrapped up in advising the girls, so that leaves André and me to work it out together.

<Roland, how much longer are you going to stay here?>

<A few days. On Monday, I have to meet people about my house, and sign papers and things.>

<Where will you meet them? At the house? But you haven't a table or chairs there. You couldn't sign anything.>

He explained how he would have to shake hands with the man who owned the house, and then pay him money.

<You'll have to tell him there aren't any stairs!>

<I think he already knows that.>

Just then, as the food began to arrive, his father made some show of wishing everyone *bon appétit* and raising his glass to Roland, who felt obliged to do likewise.

<Roland, I want to go swimming with you again. Will you come swimming?>

Oh, those beguiling eyes!

<I think,> said his father brusquely, <that Monsieur Millan has had to put up with quite a lot of your company as it is.>

My turn, now, to save the situation. <Your young man has shown considerable interest in England. That is naturally out of the question for a weekend, but I could offer him the nearest substitute.>

André's eyes were enormous. Even the girls were intrigued.

<With your permission, I shall take him over to Jersey, for an extended English lesson.>

André hugged him.

<It will be a nice way to end your stay here,> said his father, <before we go home on Monday.>

Consternation from his children, but he was adamant.

At bath time, the boy poured out his sorrows. <Papa hates us. He's taking me away from you. I shall be ill again, I know it.>

Fortunately, his mother came in, and heard the last few words. <I too am concerned,> she said. <I have tried to talk to Armand about it but, of course, he is right in a sense and, sooner or later, André has to face the fact. However,> she added rapidly, seeing the expression on her son's face, <there may be a chance to soften it a little.> She beckoned Roland back into the bedroom, and whispered: <Pardon me if I ask when you intend to leave here.>

He tried to sound casual: after the legal transactions had been completed on Monday morning.

<And your route home would take you near Tours?>

<Of course. I broke my journey at Orléans.>

<Then you must break your journey and stay a night with us.>

<And I can ride home in your car!> said André, who, covered only in soap bubbles, had come padding out of the bathroom. <Then I won't mind so much.>

All this resembles the emotional roller-coaster I was on at Wharnley. Look at me: a man makes the acquaintance of a family - total strangers - and, within a week, is virtually accepted as one of them and even encouraged to be in constant and intimate contact with the youngest of its members!

*

As our little ship leaves the shelter of St. Malo harbour, the sea is choppier than expected, and I am afraid that André (resplendent in windcheater and peaked cap) might be seasick, but he revels in it, shouting when the spray comes up over the bows, and pretending to shoot down the seagulls overhead.

<I wish Prinet was here. I'd push her in, and get rid of the old cow!>

<If you come and stay in Savoie, won't Mademoiselle have to come too?> I am being deliberately wicked.

<Pah, she would ruin everything! I told you, I don't need her. I want you to get maman and papa to fire her.>

<I can't do that. It's none of my business.>

There's a moment of reproach in his eyes at this, but then he turns round to look across at the sunlit coast of Normandy slipping past us in the distance, and the moment of potential danger is past. <Roland, do you know the queen of England?>

<What do you mean by *connais-tu*? To speak to?>

<Of course!>

<She does have fifty million other subjects, as well as me.>

<Aren't you important, then?>

<I'm the sort who likes to be very private in his life. I can't stand lots of people, or formal things.>

<What is formal?>

<Oh, going to banquets, dressing up, having to be on one's best behaviour.>

<One day, when I am *Président de la France*, I shall give you a big gold medal, just because you are you...>

He's already thinking into the future, wanting to be a man, desperate to slough off his family, and to become an only child. I do believe that this boy is *wooing* me, that, within this ten-year-old frame, there is a much older emotional being who *understands*. He knows that I have nobody of my own; I believe he wants to model himself on me, get me to fill the vacuum left by his father, whom he despises and rejects – and *that* would place an impossible burden on me.

As we dock at St. Helier, he asks if he'll have to 'speek Eengleesh' all the time. How I love my shrimp! He's fascinated by this absurd Gilbert and Sullivan world of traffic driving on the left, red post-boxes, policemen with helmets and English words and names everywhere, which he tries really hard to read out loud.

'Roland, you like a beer? I like ice cream!'

The accent isn't too bad, and he says Ro-land the English way. He knows that I accept him just as he is. No preconceptions, no expectations, just our joy of being together like this.

<Don't forget we're going to swim.>

We take a bus to a small cove which might have been in Cornwall. Water is his best element. His slim little body emerges, dripping from the sea. His face is a picture. <I'm so happy with you.>

And I am with you. We chase each other through the shallows, I fall down flat and make a huge, loud splash. He leaps on top of me, clasps me, dribbles down my front. And I am full of a guilty kind of delight.

<Roland, you promise that I can ride in your car when we go home on Monday?>

<I've already said you shall.> The little devil knows how to manipulate.

<And you really will stay *chez nous*?>

<If you want me to.> I am already intrigued to see what it is like.

<Will I be able to see *your* house, when I live at Annecy?>

<You shall come for a weekend now and then, if Madame Garbet will allow.>

<She certainly will allow. If papa is paying for me to stay there, she'll have to let me do what I want.>

<André, listen, if I arrange for you to live with another family, you'll be a guest, and you have to behave *comme il faut*. You may be used to getting your way in your own home, but you can't always expect that with other people.> His eyes grow round. He's never heard this kind of talk before, and certainly not from me. I expect the chin to tremble and the tears to come, but he controls it, never taking his eyes off my face.

<Don't worry, I shall do whatever you say.>

Twice now, it seems, I have been awarded the acquaintance of a boy who, when with me, instinctively knows what the rules will and won't permit, and is prepared to play by them. Where do they come from, these fresh, trusting creatures? Am I a kind of candle-flame to them, the moths, and if so, what exactly is the attraction I possess? Piers then, André now, they give me new confidence, help me to step daily a pace or two further out of that grim darkness. Strange: I once assumed that it was God who brought Piers and me together, but I don't feel the same at all about my attachment to this shrimp. Perhaps, on the edge of Brittany, pagan influences are at work on us.

<You're smiling to yourself, Roland. *Pourquoi*?>

<Oh, just a silly thought going through my equally silly head.>

<What thought?>

<It's too complicated to explain.>

<But I insist you tell me the truth: *do you have secrets*?>

<If I had, it wouldn't be any good telling you, because they wouldn't be secrets any more.> This is awkward. The things most important to me are known to Piers, though I can't say how much he may have forgotten or suppressed. I don't want to impart anything to André which he might, with maturity, wish he had never been told. My sort of person needs to be reticent about himself. Who could have been more reticent than Gustav von Aschenbach? All his secrets were committed to the page, sublimated to the world in his art. I made that my goal also, in the years of exile. My refuge became my prison, whence I am now breaking out into dangerous adventures, as a man who has fasted for a long time unwisely falls upon a banquet. These secrets must be kept safe.

<Just one little one,> pleaded André.

<If you really insist, I'll say it in English. *I am fond of you.*>

<And what does that mean?>

Not easy to find a fair French equivalent without erring into the 'I love you' formula, which would require more than the short hop from Jersey to St. Malo to explain. I do my clumsy best.

<But that's not a secret,> he says emphatically. <A secret is something you just have between two people and don't tell anyone else. Everyone knows that you and I like each other, don't they? *Toi idiot,*

give me a real one.>

<Doesn't your papa ever tell you secrets?>

The boy snorted. <He never tells me anything.>

<Don't *you* tell him things?> Haven't you any secrets, then, those precious things that make up the last sanctuary of the only child or, like you, the *quasi* only child? I should know about that. Perhaps, young man, you have hit upon something deep, which will bind us more closely together.

Incredulity in André's eyes. <What sort of thing would I tell papa? He doesn't listen to me, he doesn't want to know. He isn't *fond* of me, the way you are.>

*

Duclos invited him for an *apéritif à deux* that evening. <I hope my boy has not been imposing upon you. He's at the age that tends towards hero-worship. I should not want him to grow up in the idea that other people were put on earth just to be used.>

Hypocrite! And now he takes out his wallet. <I must reimburse you for the trip to Jersey.>

<Please, monsieur, no. The pleasure was mine.>

<The boy is very attached to you, and I can understand that. You are kind to him. What I cannot so easily grasp is why you so like him. He has a charming side, I admit, but he can be a devil when he chooses. He gets all that from his mother, of course. And she does nothing to calm him, but expects me to discipline him, so that he never seems to get the best side of me. Another problem is that my work all too often ties me down.>

He stopped and there was a new and furtive look in his eye. <Under these circumstances, *mon très cher monsieur*, is it surprising if the husband occasionally looks elsewhere?>

My God, even the nudge and wink to go with it. I'm relieved that he's forgotten his probing as to why I like his son.

<If you like,> Duclos was saying in a low voice, <I could give you a contact. In my line of business we have access to some very good little

numbers, with total discretion, of course.>

I thank him gravely, give him my address. It will guarantee that the little fishing trip he's just been on with me produces the catch he's after: Millan is normal, André is safe.

> *"I tried to write to P, but (as so often before), it just would not come right - too fussy, too anxious, too full of self-justification. On Saturday night, when he hugged me and waited for his grosse bise, A said he loved me and would never forget the day he got to know me for the first time. Could an English ten-year-old have put it like that?*
>
> *Final dinner before our departure for Tours. Duclos at his most oily and genial. A apprehensive, maybe because he's going home, and I shall be less available. Postcard to P, as a cowardly compromise, just mentioning buying a small house within sight of the Mont St. Michel. Said I'd show it to him some time. No love, just 'amitiés, R.' It might tickle him, whet his appetite.*
>
> *The Tours house was a shock - so grubby, crumbling and stale, even by French standards. A wrinkled his nose visibly when we first entered. Mme steered me to a guest room which was presentable enough. Thank God it was only for one night. I need never fear that Orphéon isn't up to scratch.*
>
> *A is obviously very much at home here with me, and Mme B. likes to mother my young visitors a bit. He responds, of course!"*

*

<It's raining all over your garden,> he says, bless him, as he dashes up my stairs. <What are you doing, Roland?>

<Just making a sketch.>

<What's that?>

I explain it's a preliminary design for an opera, remembering that one has to be more patient with a younger boy like this. There are so many things which are simply outside his experience.

The drops may be splashing down the study windows, but my heart is light, lighter than it has been for far too long.

<When do we go and see that woman in Annecy?>

<You know very well. And she isn't *that woman*.>

<Must I go back to Tours? You have so many rooms here, just for yourself. Couldn't I creep away into one of them and hide, like a mouse?>

<You can't just choose where you live. You're still too young.>

<Don't you want me, Roland?>

<That's not how it is, as you very well know. You have your life to lead, and I have mine. I travel about a lot. You couldn't come everywhere with me. You mustn't be too demanding. It would turn this house into a prison for both of us.>

<A prison? How could this nice place ever be that? Anyway, if I lived here very quietly, you wouldn't need to know I was here, would you?>

<It would be a very miserable life for you, with no friends to keep you company.>

<I don't need friends, if I've got you.>

<You need people your own age.>

<I don't,> he says, with a scowl. <Other kids – they're rubbish!>

What a tempting prospect, but how impossible and how dangerous.

<Isn't that the Mont?>

Thank goodness my sketching now takes his attention.

<But how can you have *that* in an opera? There wouldn't be space on the stage for it!>

I show him one of my model stages, and explain how scenery can be made and painted to deceive the eye.

<Is it an opera about the Mont, then?>

<It's about a lady imprisoned on Greek island, Naxos, waiting for a man to come and set her free.>

<What's she called?>

<Ariadne.>

<Why can't she just swim away?>

<There wouldn't be any story if she did. But she does get visited by all sorts of people.>

<Are they nice?>

<Rather funny, really. Their job is to cheer her up.>

<And do they?>

<No, she just goes on moping.>

<It sounds a crumby opera to me. What about you, Roland? Do you have a lady - you know, someone to get married to?>

<Would you like me to have?>

<That's not an answer! You're always dodging out of it!>

<I was married once, but it didn't work.> Oh God, I've been along this path with Piers, too.

<Why not?>

<Because we just weren't right for each other, after all.> How could I possibly reduce all that to childish terms?

<What happened? Did you have to kill her? I once heard papa shout at maman that he would kill her. I think it'd be safer for me to live here or Annecy, in case he really does. I wouldn't like to be around.>

<Look, people say things like that when they're cross. They don't necessarily mean them.>

<Papa hit maman once. If he went away, perhaps you could marry her, and then everything would be all right.>

I should be designing *Oedipus*, not *Ariadne*! <Life is never as simple as that.>

<Why not?>

<Other people may not be willing or able to do what you want.>

He looks at my model, and then says slowly, working it out, <If they were all there, on that stage, you would be able to tell them what to do, wouldn't you?> Perceptive lad! However easily our talk runs along, though, I suspect it never quite reaches the conclusion he seems to want. <Will we ever go back to the Mont together?>

<I shall have to visit my little house from time to time.>

<You'll take me with you?>

<If it's convenient to your parents and the Garbets, yes.>

<Do you really own two houses now?>

<That's right.> I shall not tell him about my places in England.

<And when you get tired of one, you can go and live in the other. Why can't you let people live in the one you're not using, while you're away? There are lots of poor, without anywhere to live.>

The child, bless him, has the beginnings of a social conscience.

<What age are boys when they get girl friends?>

This child must be psychic. <Are you wanting a girl friend, then?>

<Later maybe, as long as it wasn't anyone awful, like my sisters.>

<It's usual to be a bit older than you are. I know someone who's just found his first girl friend, and he's eighteen.> It comes out before I can stop it.

<Eighteen? Then he's an old man already.>

What would Piers say to that? <Anyway, it depends. A boy can have a girl just for a friend, without anything romantic in it.>

He gasps. <Romantic? I didn't mean that rubbish.>

Then you could have a girl friend now. It seems to be the custom at "Orphéon" for everyone except me.

<Who's the boy you know who has just got his girl, and is it romantic or not?>

> *"And so I grasped the nettle, and we spent the rest of the wet afternoon with me talking about P (as a platonic kind of friend, liar that I am), and A slipping in questions and comments that ranged from the naive to the perceptive. It warmed me of course, just as did some of those ancient exchanges with P, when he was not much older than my shrimp. Is there just a hint of jealousy in A? If so, I'm in good company.*
>
> *Madame B had done a casserole, but A suddenly wanted to be formal, so we laid the big table in the dining-room with my best napery, cutlery and glass. And, for a few very precious moments I had a delicious vision: they all sat there, the candlelight flickering on their eager young faces, on A's golden hair. Raoul, dark, sitting between him and P, with those huge deep brown eyes. He turned his head to look*

from one to the other, an enigmatic smile on his lips. P, with an earnest expression, reached forward, took up the wine bottle and filled the glasses again. Red droplets splashed on to the white damask. Was his hand shaking? Just as well that it was a warm evening, as none of them had chosen to wear any clothes. Their flesh was like a Caravaggio painting: yellow, dimpled, well-moulded, dark in the crevices, and infinitely desirable."

<What time, tomorrow morning?>

<What's that, sorry?> He brings me back to earth.

<*Notre dame d'Annecy.*>

<Any time between ten and eleven.>

<Can we go on the lake afterwards, in a boat? And then swim?>

He loved the brief trip we made on Léman, to see the *jet d'eau* from close to.

<Roland, that boy in the photo on the stairs. Is that Piers?>

<Yes.> You really don't miss a trick! As if retribution is hot on my heels.

<Did you take it? I want you to take one of me like that, *déshabillé*. Did he mind?>

<Why should he have minded?>

<How old was he in that photo?>

<Thirteen or so.>

<*Ah bon.* I'm going to be eleven soon. Were you fond of him, too, when you took that?>

Now that we've got this far, I must take good care not to get my true feelings for Piers across, or we may all end up in a morass.

<Is he coming here soon?>

<Probably mid-June, when he's finished studying for the year.>

<But won't he study any more before January?>

I explain how the academic year is different.

<I'd like to go to university one day.>

<What would you study?>

<*Eengleesh*! But first you must teach me some more. Perhaps Piers

would help, too. You said he was nice. Will he stay in my room, when he comes?>

I haven't the heart to say that *you* are in *his* room. <And now, *jeune homme*, remember that I promised your *maman* that you would go to bed at a proper time.>

<This Madame Garbet,> he calls, from the bathroom, <what's she like? She won't beat me, will she?>

I stick my head round the door. <If she's like her brother, she'll be all right. You said he was OK, remember?>

But there is that scowl again. <Brothers may be OK, but sisters are always ghastly.>

As I give him his goodnight kiss, I'm all too aware that this is Piers' bed too, and that Piers is no longer kissable. Well, not by me.

<Roland, look at the moonlight.>

The sky has cleared. It's almost full moon. Quite spontaneously, he gets out of bed and takes me by the hand on to the balcony. <The park is so beautiful at night. Médor would love it. Do you think he will ever see it? Can we go for a walk in the park? Please!>

I make him put on his dressing-gown and some shoes, and we go downstairs and out of the back door.

<Can anyone count the stars?>

<Anyone could try. The astronomers probably know how many there are.>

<But what about the ones that are too far away to see?>

<They're too far away to worry about.>

<Roland, are you afraid to die?>

We are walking hand in hand in my garden in the moonlight; the grass smells damp: one of those moments to capture. Do people ever notice when a corner of paradise is lifted for us? <Do you believe in God, André?>

<I don't know. If he is supposed to be good, why does he sometimes make me so ill? Why does he let papa and maman quarrel so much?>

<You asked me if I fear death. I'm a lot nearer to it than you are...>

<No you aren't. My asthma will kill me soon. I know it.>

I stop, and look down at the face that is deathly in the moonlight.

Then I bend down a little, clasp my arms around him and gently lift him up. We must resemble one of those old paintings of St Christopher. <You mustn't talk like that. That's defeatist.>

<Papa says that, sometimes.>

<He's right.>

> *"That really got through to me. A is on the threshold of everything, yet he foretells his own doom, and no amount of comforting on my part seems able to divert his gaze from that."*

*

It was raining, but they had brought their swimming things, in case the weather should cheer up. The drive to Annecy seemed endless. André sat next to him, his chest heaving, his expression mournful, as he stared out at the road and the cars hurtling past, lorries covering them in spray and muck.

But then, just before they got to the outskirts, the rain miraculously stopped, the roads were dry, and the sun came out.

Roland looked at him. <There, you see, it's going to be all right.>

But the boy shook his head. <I don't know why, but I'm scared.>

I can't see why he needs to be.

They found the Garbets' address without difficulty, up out of the old town and overlooking the end of the lake, which the sky and sunlight made a deep blue.

André clung to him, as they opened the gate, passed through a garden full of roses and hydrangeas, and reached a neat, white house with a pantiled roof and window-boxes stocked with red geraniums.

Madame Garbet arrived in her apron, looked quickly from one to the other, and took them into the front room where they could see out over the water. Then she offered them drinks, and sat down next to André, putting some kindly questions to him; and, before long, the boy was answering with confidence, though he still held Roland's hand tightly.

<Now you will want to see your room.> She took them upstairs and into a pleasant, spacious bedroom which also looked out over the lake. Roland had to admit to himself that it was nicer than any of his rooms at "Orphéon", because it showed a woman's touch.

The child is transformed. He opens and shuts drawers and cupboard doors, bounces a little on the bed, hangs out of the window and turns back into the room with a radiant face. He lets her give him a cuddle, and then we all troop downstairs again to see the other rooms, and the garden. Before we leave, I discuss various necessary details with her.

As we get into the car, I ask him if he is still afraid.

<No, of course not. She's nice, like you said.>

<And you'll be happy there?>

<Because it's not far from you, yes.>

Back in Annecy, we park near the quay and are soon sitting in the sun on the deck of a boat, gliding towards the point where the narrow channel broadens out into the lake.

If the Calivets could see us as we sit here, I with an arm round André's shoulder, he with his head resting against me! How stale I had allowed my life to become, before Piers and this shrimp came to people it. We are flesh and blood, and not created to hide ourselves away.

Stepping off at St. Jorioz, we walk along to the p*lage*, where I buy tickets for the changing room. Before we undress, I get us both an ice cream. André's tongue licks the side of the cone like a young calf attacking buds on a tree. His face is a picture. In a sudden panic, I dash off to get changed first, on my own. That moment in my car, after we swam at Roscoff, comes back with alarming clarity. (*He was so desperate to show me.*)

When we are both safely changed, we lie on the soft grass, surrounded by, it seems, the rest of France, with its dogs and babies, then he gets me to chase him into the glittering water. Wind-surfers shoot past, pedalos loiter about, the occasional motor-boat shatters the idyllic scene.

If I compare a lake to the sea, it never seems to contain that intriguing touch of predatory malevolence that always pervades the sea. That little girl at Carolles... Another maiden is over there at Talloires, moping for her swain who is doubtless somewhere on the Backs, mooning over her. How ridiculous that sort of love is, how unproductive. They wait for each other, patient as horses. And yet they know not what they wait for, cannot possibly understand each other, past the few thousandths of a millimetre of skin. They, who want to think that they can be one, are as far apart as planets from different universes. Do I tell Piers that they don't stand a chance, or do I let him find it out? Which is the less cruel? Though I do not really want him to be hurt, I fear that he will be, whatever happens. And, if he is hurt, I probably shall be also - unless, of course, I am the one who hurts him. That would make a difference!

'Roland, viens, viens!' André is off again, he will allow no musing on my part. At last, panting and dripping, we come out of the water and return to our towels. He wipes himself off and lies down flat on his stomach, his head propped up on his elbows, looking at me. We are so close that I can see the tiny fair hairs on his arms, on his upper lip, even. Manhood is in reserve, waiting for the day to start sprouting darkly over this unspoilt body. He is staring back at me, serious now. <What's Piers really like? Is he fun?>

<He can be.>

<I wish I could meet him.>

<Sorry, but you won't be here when he arrives, and...>

<... he'll have gone before I come back?>

<Are you just a little bit *vexé*?>

<Not a little bit, a lot! He'll pinch my room, sleep in my bed, look out into my park.> The tears came. Neither of them had a handkerchief. The boy put the corner of his towel to his nose and blubbed into it.

I knew he'd react like this. I want to have this fragile creature always with me, never letting him return to *them*, but I have a duty to Piers far more binding than any fondness for André can be. There he lies, kicking his legs slowly up and down, to reinforce the vehemence of his words. His face is streaky with dust, where he's rubbed his tears. What a delightful vision, these grubby features, brimming dark eyes, the jaw set defiantly. The trouble is that it strikes deeply inside me as well, like a blowtorch applied to my slowly thawing depths. With the thaw, the pain returns.

The voice fought its way through the strangled sobs that now shook the delicate frame. <I won't leave, I won't. I shall take a knife from the kitchen and stab myself here, in the chest, and then you will have to bury me in your garden, and I shall always be there.> He was yelling now.

Surprised at his own unwonted anger, Roland picked the boy up in his arms and marched back with him to the changing rooms. <When you talk like that, I could shake you, d'you hear? It's stupid, and everyone is looking at us.>

The remarkably heavy body was shivering against his, the arms clasped tightly round his neck, and the grimy little face pressed itself to his. <Oh Roland,> André wailed, beside himself with grief.

Their tears mingled, a great sob broke from Roland's chest, that brought the boy up short.

<Are you crying because of me?>

There was no-one else about in the building. He rocked André in his arms like a baby, then set him gently down and took him back to their cubicle to get dressed.

<Roland, I don't want to leave you, not ever-ever-ever, even if you are cross with me.>

He stands there, quite naked, a frown of intensity on his young face, with another growing erection which the water has caused. I, as moved as he, cannot hold him at arm's length any longer. The door is safely bolted, a wan light comes filtering in. He edges towards me, takes my hand and guides it gently to that little rod which he made me touch before. This time, he knows, I shall not refuse him, nor can I hide my own rising lust. He recognises it, bends over me, clasps me, through my trunks.

I sit him on my knee, and we rub one another in silent ecstasy, but for the sound of our breaths quickening, merging together. He jigs about, wriggling his body, but never lets go of me. <Undress!> he whispers, knowing, as I do, that this is a superb act of conspiracy which nobody outside our cubicle shall even dream of. He gets up, so that I can do as I am bidden and push my trunks down. He squats before me, open-mouthed in astonishment. <Roland, will mine be as big as that, one day?>

I nod. He looks down at himself and back at me, comparing. He raises his hand almost timidly, and touches me. We can only go forward now, and we both know it. He grasps me again, pulls at me (and, with his other hand, himself).

Who else had such a cool, dry, expert little hand, as this? Piers, only Piers, with whom I spent delicious days and nights. *And how does this one know what to do?*

It happens without warning, and he recoils with a sound like an injured animal. I try to play it normal. If only I didn't shake so much! <You wanted a secret, *et voilà!*>

For a moment, he doesn't understand, then a slow smile spreads over his face. He has some of it on his fingers. He sniffs his hand, then wipes it carefully on his own erect little member. <Look, I've got some too.>

Somehow, they got cleaned up and dressed, then André combed his locks in a mirror. <Now I'm a man, just like you.> His initiation complete, the previous upset and its cause were forgotten.

> *"Later on, he was so down-to-earth. I expected him to go on questioning me about it, to find out if I <u>did my secret</u> with <u>P</u>. To him, it seemed merely a thing revealed, a game played. I don't think it could have touched him deeply, as it did me. I kept going hot and cold at the thought of it (still do), wondering if I'd had one of my visitations of the mind, like that dream about him at Dol. But this was no dream. <u>It happened, we did it!</u> The world would say 'No, you cannot, it is all wrong'. Then why do I feel so triumphant, so fulfilled, so charged with glory?*
>
> *He will keep our secret, I know that without needing to ask. It's as personal and private to him as any experience he has ever yet had. To a child, nothing is taboo. A child is always exploring, and everything takes on a legitimacy with him.*
>
> *Did he <u>lead me on</u>, to punish me for saying he'll have to leave, to make me do what he wanted because he was angry with me, just as I had been, with him, a few moments before?*

And then, as the thing progressed, did he forget his anger, and let the voluptuousness of it take him over? He is serene, now: a child enriched, not a child abused. <u>He</u> came to <u>me</u> for this, unencouraged, unenticed, of his own free will (as <u>P</u> once also did). Does that not erase the sin, or at any rate diminish it? If one can live in an <u>ancient</u> Greek basis, in these things, not an English or even French one, then 'tout comprendre, c'est tout pardonner'. <u>P</u> once said 'I'll do anything for you. That sums it up: a deep and very fond link between two people makes things possible (if not rational) that would and could not have otherwise been. Unconsciously, <u>A</u> is fitting himself into the <u>P</u> mould, saying the sort of things <u>P</u> used to, even thinking along his paths of logic. How can this be? They've never even met. Is there some telepathic magnetism between them (for which I am a catalyst), that began with the shepherd boys on the hillsides of Arcady?

<u>P</u>, if he knew, would think I'd become morally flabby...

It's cool tonight, but the windows are all open. <u>A</u> is asleep, none the worse for his day's excitement."

But as he wrote the last words, André's terrible threat came back to him, and he crept downstairs into the kitchen, collected all but one of the sharp knives he could find and, going up the back stairs, locked them away in his special store. You just never know with other people: you think you have them in your palm, but they will slip away, change, become strangers to you.

He went to sleep in his chair and woke to find the dawn filtering through his study windows. He was cold, stiff and full of foreboding.

Breakfast was lightened by André's freshness and humour. They could joke together, even hope a little that things might turn out all right in the end.

The phone rang mid-morning: Madame Duclos, very het-up, to say she would be arriving that afternoon. André took it surprisingly well.

<She's just coming to see I'm all right here, then she'll go and see Mme Garbet, and we'll tell her she can go home again.>

If only I had your assurance! <André, I want to talk to you about yesterday.>

<About visiting Mme Garbet?>

<No, about you and me in the changing cubicle.>

They were walking in the garden. The boy stopped and looked up at him, rather the way he'd done on the Mont, screwing up his eyes against the light. <Why, what's the matter?>

<It's... all about keeping secrets.> He was shaking again, and he knew he'd put that very clumsily.

<I know. You said a secret wasn't a secret any more if you didn't keep it.>

<That's right. So... will you keep it?>

<What do you think I am? Of course I will!>

<Good. And there's something else I have to ask you.>

<What? You're being very strange with me today.>

<If your *maman* said she wanted you to go back with her...>

<I'd refuse!>

<It wouldn't help, if you did that.>

<Roland, I'm not going. Didn't you say it would be all right for me to stay here?>

<In August, yes.>

<But you promised, yesterday.>

<I didn't say it. If you remember, I had to deal with a young man who'd gone berserk.>

The boy's face was dark again. <I don't believe you love me. If you did, you wouldn't tell lies.>

<I'm not lying, and I do love you. But, sometimes, loving someone means you have to part from them a bit.>

<Why can't people who love each other be together? Maman and papa are together, and they don't even love each other.>

<It's a funny world.>

<It's a rotten world. I want you to take me back in, and show me you love me, again.>

<You know I love you very much, without your needing to say that.>

<I won't believe it till you do it again.>

So his apparent matter-of-factness about it all wasn't superficial, after all. He has found a new weapon to bargain with.

<Don't you want to?> André was staring at him, tense, fragile, yet somehow more powerful than his stature suggested.

<It's not a matter of that...>

<I'll tell maman and papa everything.>

<Then you will lose me for ever. Didn't we agree that it's a secret between just us?> Like a game, in which first one player has the advantage, then the other.

The boy took Roland's hand. <I don't want to lose you, ever.>

<Nor do I.>

<Why does it all have to be so hard, Roland?>

<Because we're human beings, and we live on earth.>

<Is it easier for angels?>

<Much easier.>

<How?>

<Oh, I expect they never get cross or jealous.> And they aren't afflicted with these bothersome mortal desires!

At half-past four, a taxi unloaded Madame Duclos and a small suitcase. She was grey-faced and lined.

<My husband has left me,> she announced at once, with no small touch of drama.

She looks as if she expects to stay the night. Does this new development offer me more to hope for, or not?

Madame Bouillot was summoned, to make up André's bed for his mother, and cook a special meal for that evening.

Madame Duclos ordered her son to go and play in the garden. <I hadn't noticed that Armand was taking things surreptitiously - clothes, books, papers - until the day before yesterday, when he confronted me and said he had already decided to go.>

The girls and the dog were at her mother's in Amboise, while she looked desperately for a *logement* for them all. She could not bear the house in Tours any more, with all its associations.

<Incidentally, monsieur, he is only an underling in the legal department. He makes us keep up pretences, but we are not as well-off as we appear. And his extravagances are a constant drain. You saw the house. He hasn't spent a *sou* on it since André was born. It all goes instead on his *maîtresses*.> She could no longer hold back her tears.

<In the circumstances, madame, it would surely be better if André were to stay on. You will have enough to do at home, and he is perfectly happy here.>

But she shook her head. <It is kind of you, but you have already done too much for him. You see, I must have him by me. He has some of his father in him - these sudden rages, for instance - and I'm terrified he will grow up like Armand.>

<What about your plans - our plans - to lodge him with Madame Garbet in August? We visited her only yesterday, and he really took to her.>

<As for that,> she said, in an unusually curt tone, <one will have to see.> She opened her handbag, rummaged in it, and took out a thousand-franc note. <This is a small repayment for all you have done, but I hope you will accept it.>

He firmly declined. <What about his education? You surely cannot afford to employ the governess?>

<I have dismissed the servants. I shall educate him myself, or, if he gets stronger, he can go to school, as the girls do. I have lost my husband, monsieur. I must not lose my son as well.>

> *"While she picked at her food, I spent all my time talking, trying to persuade her, conscious only of <u>A's</u> huge dark eyes supporting me. I tried every ploy: what about his English lessons? But she swept that aside, as one of <u>her husband's</u> notions, managing to imply, in a tight-lipped Gallic way, that English was an acquisition of no consequence to a budding Frenchman like her son. In the end, all my fight deserted me, those eyes haunting me in reproach. She even insisted that he sleep on my camp-bed in her room.*
>
> *And suppose, despite his assurance to me, he blurts out*

something, in an attempt to convince her that I love him better than she does? When she arrived, she did not even kiss him. If he were to tell her of our close moment in the cubicle, what then? Would it really destroy everything, or would she be forced to accept our fondness in all its aspects? No, that is stupid. She belongs to the outside world.

They have gone. I am utterly dejected. I have failed all of us. When the taxi came (I would not have offered, in a thousand years, to take them to the station), and we all went outside, he clung to me. I begged her for an address, a phone number, but she said to wait till they were settled in somewhere. She would be in touch. And that was that. Which was the more painful parting for me, P at Wharnley, and later here, or this?"

He could see it only as a punishment, Fate's vengeance descended upon him, as when Piers was plucked away. Is it because of the physical contact? (I had none, with anyone, in the last five years. It was the truth when I told Piers that.) His tears for André should have been mingled with some sort of joyous anticipation at Piers' imminent arrival, but it all turned to bitterness.

As always, he found some solace in his garden, where everything was in bloom now, surrounded by the heady fragrance, the hum of the town below. Even the Salève had softened its sullen contours. To whom should he raise his glass? To all of them, or none of them? To God, or the Devil? The sounds around him betokened that other people were going about their lives, contributing to the great symphony of which he could never be part. Even as he watched, those very few souls to whom he was able to respond were torn from him, subsumed into the anonymity of the world out there, gone away, to play out their lives on their own levels of consciousness.

There should be some merit in attempting to live a decent life. Those pure ones (they must be innumerable) have no problems: they can pass from cradle to grave without tarnishing their innocence. I have lost mine, so my handicap, in the upward struggle for glory, is crippling.

What comes easily to a sound man is a battle for such as I, who try to kid myself that it's worthwhile, in the cosmic context, to achieve a tiny crumb of integrity, when everything else in me is set against it: my indecision, my dubious sanity, my lack of consistency, my forbidden burning desires, my fatalism, my cowardice, my all-embracing, stifling pre-occupation with myself.

He swung the wine-glass back and then flung it forward in a languid arc. It smashed against the trunk of a tree. I shall survive all this because a coward always puts his own skin first. Besides, I am painfully aware of deeper, ancestral thoughts prowling my depths: stay at home, close the shutters, play it safe!

> *"I had almost forgotten the numb feeling that comes from shouldering a burden of sorrow. It never took a great deal to suggest the pointlessness of life to me, who have a less firm hold on it than most people. Trying to rerun P's visit in my mind, then the encounter with A, was like passing through a mist which allows only the occasional solid object to be glimpsed.*
>
> *I have a recurring dream now: A and P are strolling together in my park, talking animatedly. I see them from a distance, but do not hear them. P throws back his head with a laugh, and puts an arm round A's shoulder. A puts an arm round P's waist, in a very natural and spontaneous way, and they walk on like that. Perhaps they really will meet one day. Will P be as jealous of A as A was of him?*
>
> *I look at photos: P, somewhere in the Rhône valley when (I forget why) I was feeling particularly moved; A on the ramparts at St. Malo, at the menhir, on the beach at Carolles, licking an ice at St. Jorioz. But no pictures of them at Orphéon, as if all fun and pleasure are banned within my domain. There was no time to take that promised picture of A, nu, like the one of P on the wall here. Hardly time to do more than mouth a goodbye.*
>
> *So, if I am not to die another death, I must go out in*

search of what A has brought me. The strange thing about my grief, this time, is that my desire is not stifled but stimulated."

Seeking comfort in music, he put on the record of Tchaikovsky's fourth symphony. While the horns and bassoons of the Fate motif made his windows rattle, he located a book bound in dark red: the miniature scores of the last three symphonies. And there, opposite the first page, were words which could have been written about himself:

"Fate, that ominous power, prevents the craving for happiness from achieving its end. This power is overwhelming and unconquerable; nothing remains but submission, and vain lamentations."

He subsided on to a chair, letting the book fall on the floor, giving himself up to his black bitterness, relishing it, even. The bell rang downstairs. He ignored it. It rang again, insistently. Perhaps Madame had brought André back!

He dashed down, and along the hall. But it was only Guy, who took one look at his ravaged face and stepped back. <Ah, is this a bad moment?>

Roland led him into the kitchen, and poured them both a drink.

Guy sat down, studied his glass for a while, and then looked across. <Do you want to talk? Will it help?>

Regardless of the risk, he poured it all out, his love for Piers, his closeness to André. Raoul's visit he did not divulge.

<I did suspect something of the sort,> said Guy gently, lighting up a cigarette. <Some people say that art is born out of suffering, that the two are inseparable. I hope, for your sake, that you don't go along with such hokum, if it should be applied to what you have just told me. You once said you had had some psychiatric treatment.>

Roland stared away into the garden, wishing everything unsaid. <I must have told you also that it was useless.>

<It's not in a psychiatrist's brief to play the moralist. Without a whiff

of hell-fire, you wouldn't have had a chance. You do see, don't you, that this girl Adèle Calivet (whose nature I was at pains to examine for myself) has exorcised your affection for Piers?>

<But I'm very fond of him still.>

<The deeper aspect is no more, though, is it? So, now you need another boy to return your affection.>

Roland had put his head in his hands. <I really don't know what to do.>

<You will have to exorcise him also.>

<But how, when I don't even want to?>

<Try to see it through the eyes of a child of ten, on the threshold of these things maybe, but still very sensitive, vulnerable, easily - >

<Stop it! How can that possibly help me?>

<Exorcism is not a gentle art,> said Guy, <but you must practise it, metaphorically, for the sake of that boy and your own conscience.>

<Then how,> said Roland weakly, <how is it that I felt so fulfilled, afterwards?>

<That was just blind selfishness. You possibly regarded it as something very special. If you put yourself in the boy's place, you will see that it was merely sordid. Children of that age know instinctively what is right and what is wrong.>

Of course they do. But they also know what is right or wrong for *them*. It's no good. I can't explain to him how André, from the very first moment we saw each other, was leading me on, engineering us into a closeness *à deux*. <Can such a thing never be special?>

<I may be what the world dubs a confirmed bachelor, Millan, but I am prone, as you may know, to the occasional little *aventure* with this woman or that. A very French failing, if you like. My thesis is simply this: if ever I should be careless enough to father a child, I should be less horrified by that than I would be by the thought that it might one day err into the hands of a lustful and irresponsible man. I'm sorry if that shocks you, but it will leave a small therapeutic aftertaste. Oh, I almost forgot why I came. Do you want to go to a concert we're doing at Vevey? To cheer you up, maybe? No? Well, I understand. Do you want to come and stay *chez moi* for a while?>

<No, I'll be all right. Thanks for the medicine!>

<I don't gladly assume the role of doctor,> said Bannerot wryly, as he went out. <When does Piers come back?>

<A fortnight today.>

It was growing dark now. The lights of Guy Bannerot's car receded down the drive, disappeared through the gateway. The world brought its opinion to my door, and now is gone. He followed slowly, shut the gates and then wandered off around his park, trying to collect his thoughts. Did I really tell Guy everything? I've known him for years, but we've never before had such an explicit talk as this. I always maintained a reserve, and he always tolerated me. Now, for the first time, he has seen me as I really am, and he gives it to me straight between the eyes.

But, dispelling all *angst* and gloom, is a new faith now, alongside which everything else pales into insubstantiality: they come to me, they seek me out, because I too must have some special magnetism. With Piers, there was that long conversation of looks, before we ever exchanged a word. I well remember those daring smiles of his at me, before we embarked on our voyage together. And Raoul... He saw me in St. Julien, marked me down and, one wet afternoon, when I was particularly low, homed in on me in a way that surpassed anything that cinema or theatre could serve up.

And my shrimp. How can a ten-year-old manipulate people so? But, my word, he does. How do these boys *know*? There must be some primeval instinct, some distillation going back generations, which is handed on to us, to use as we please: so secret, so precious, that other men are not to know about it, only the initiates. The force transcends all, but it is not bestial, as the world would have us believe. Its more animal qualities are but a physical manifestation of a great spiritual coming together, like a private Day of Judgment, in which we stand naked before one another, are weighed and not found wanting. Our Grail.

Piers and André have a knowledge beyond their years, as if they're mediums for some great external force of love. How do you explain that, in this dead, prosaic world? I am a free spirit. How can I hope to get that across to people who aren't? I cannot fall in with the normality of the rest of them, I am too desperately afraid of boredom.

The short drive to Les Amandaies was rich in self-justification: that woman has taken my André away, and will surely destroy him. That girl has taken my Piers, and will drain him of his blood. I can have no business with the dead.

The Sunday morning sunshine brought out the innocent colour of the landscape, with its brown and white cows, strips of maize, neat houses, their red tiled roofs reaching almost to the ground. Next to the little church, whose white tower was surmounted by an absurd onion dome and spike, was a large old farm building with sets of double doors below, and domestic shuttered windows above. *Is that where he lives?* But nobody was to be seen, and he drove on along a narrow street between farms and houses until, at the far end of the village, he caught sight of lads kicking a ball about on a bit of ground - and his heart leapt. There, unmistakeable in patched old jeans and a navy blue tee-shirt, was a boy with almost black hair. He parked under a tree on the edge of their pitch and pretended to watch, but in fact was searching for a pen and a scrap of paper. "Come back to me again."

But he crumpled this up, found another bit of paper and merely put "This evening?", waited until those distant dark eyes were on him, and flicked it out of the window in such a way as to allow the breeze to carry it a few yards off.

Raoul was not the biggest of the boys, but he had enough skill to get possession of the ball and give it an almighty kick which brought it almost to the car. Shouting <Let me do it,> he came dashing after it, his face full of elation. As he reached the paper, his expression changed. He glanced over, scooped it up and then turned away to kick the ball back into play.

His glance brushed me for a mere moment. Has he read it? Does he understand? Will he ignore what Madame Bouillot said to him, and come back?

The next time the ball came over, it rolled under the car, again with Raoul in hot pursuit. Roland stuck his head out of the window away from the football game, and said <Will you come?>

<Can't,> came a breathless answer. <But my brother Laurent...>

<He's older?>

<Sure. Seventeen, m'sieu. He always asks fifty. I'll tell him.> And he was gone again. Tingling, Roland drove back through the village. Above the blue Jura in the distance were huge white cloud formations, filling him with sudden hope and excitement.

He cancelled Madame Bouillot for that evening and sat down to wait. Suppose this Laurent is a great beefy hetero who will beat me up, for my money? So be it, let's see what he has to offer. I seem to have lost you, Raoul, but this brother of yours, does he look like you, with your dark hair and deep beguiling eyes?

There was no visitor at all, that day. As the hours wore on, he felt himself flagging, becoming disgusted by what he had initiated. Do I really want a rent-boy knocking at my door?

He had noted the Duclos' phone number when at their house. He could hear the long, single note at the other end, then a pause, then the note again, like calm, steady breathing. They must hear it. No, they've dismissed the servants and gone away. I have lost André, lost Piers, lost Raoul. Laurent won't come here, in any case. People don't keep promises any more. Perhaps I would do the world a favour if I jumped into the lake.

> *"What do I, and what should I, understand by the concept BOY? If I am in love with the idea, then I must accept that the bearers of this precious thing will grow up and away, handing on their treasure to the next generations. I can stand by the moving belt and watch its cargo constantly replenished, but always the same age. If I climb on to the belt (as seems to be the case with P), I must admit those changes which I don't want: his relapse into ordinariness, the loss of that attractive freshness. If I stand still, the gap in age grows ever wider. By riding too, I can hold it steady. Then why not stand still with some and ride with others?*
>
> *Tuesday evening, after dusk, there was a tapping at the back door. He surprised me, with his bleached hair and smiling light blue eyes. Medium height and quite solidly put together. A peasant, with a serenity that bowled me over. He*

> *would have made a tolerable matelot, would L̲. Have to say*
> *he was good value for money."*

*

When he had left England, five long years ago, he had abandoned all his hopes as well. Thereafter, even the famous light of Lake Geneva, or that of Venice, (when he was re-creating it for his opera), was only external, never allowed to exist inside him. Indeed, it had forgotten how to do that: light was now something which he, as artist and designer, merely used in his work.

What was I doing all that time, in the dark? Holding myself in readiness for someone, for *him*, for his second coming - was that it? And, when he came, was it so foolish to allow myself a grain or two of optimism, that he might somehow have come back for *me*?

Without a real outlet, I starve, I drown, my existence loses all point. I am taunted at every turn by desirable people, voluptuous thoughts. Not a waking hour passes, without my mind running along this channel: Piers, Raoul, André, and now Laurent. If this were denied me, what else could satisfy me so? Only fools talk about purging desire from one's make-up. Why can't they be honest about it, live with their drives? *I desire, therefore I am!*

I want to hear Piers' voice on the phone, but I can't speak to him without a very good reason. In the house I talk to him, just for the comfort of it. I imagine I see him in rooms, on the stairs, hear him singing - just as people claim to see and hear a recently dead person whose presence is so much a part of them. Sometimes it is André who looms large, even blocking out Piers, doubling my pain. I miss his sweet face, his affectionate way. He will not betray me, but Guy might, Guy who appeared without warning at the Calivets, who sits on his moral throne and sees me as having descended to the lowest level. If he found that girl's house, he could surely locate the Duclos, denounce me to them as a defiler of their son. How can I forestall him?

The return to sanity must be when you can view your own irremediable confusion with lucidity.

Piers has begun - no, had begun - to infuse me with light. I really was crawling back out of the pit, but then that girl came on the scene. My love for him warms me, even so. It must give me more comfort than her fondness for him gives her. I do not need to drive over to Talloires, to spy on the Calivets, nor find out how her deprivation of him measures up to mine.

Two letters the next day, the first from Piers, to thank me for sending him his air-fare for his birthday. He could visualise Mrs Moriston wrathful, blaming her son for gallivanting off to Switzerland when he should have been revising. Then a terse note from Mr. James:

> *"Have met his <u>demoiselle</u>, and tried out my rusty French on her. He was like a dog with two tails."*

There being still no word from Tours, he packed some things and set off for Normandy.

*

Before booking into the hotel by the *digue*, he visited his house, checking that the renovation was well in hand, discussed a few details with the builder, then took himself off over the sands to the north of the Mont, where only the bleating of gulls and the sucking and bubbling of the sand broke the silence. High above and behind him, the spike on the top of the abbey building was thrusting its shadow out over the immense desert.

I am even beginning to feel at home here. Piers and all the rest are right – "Orphéon" is much too big for me. This is an ideal place, gentle and friendly, where all is soft light, lushness, tolerance and sanity. If Savoie is full of hard, cruel rock and long memories, my tiny piece of Normandy is pastoral and unspoilt.

The scent of the sea herbs brings balm to my soul. I can breathe here, not the sultriness of the *sirocco*, nor the cloying disinfectant smell of the plagued city, but ozone from the Atlantic. This is a place where I can exist, and find new inspiration. As I explained to André, one wet afternoon a thousand years ago, Ariadne and the rest will play out the opera on something resembling this island, not in its tourist-ridden, chocolate-box guise, of course, but a mysterious, evocative place. It doesn't do to remove all the wraps. A secret something needs to be left intact, or the art itself is destroyed, as in that model of the Mont which André was looking at up in the museum (not long before we met properly).

Hell, I have pushed the child to the back of my mind. Where is he, how is he, what is he doing? To come to Courtils without him seems wrong. I so much miss his delightful freshness, his street-urchin air. He isn't one of your pure, antiseptic boys. *I must find him.*

The next day he made for Tours with all speed, but the Duclos house was shuttered and hostile, and nobody answered his insistent ringing. He had never before used a private detective, but his time was very short, and he had no idea where to start. There was an agency in the town centre, where he found a man in a creased suit behind a desk. He explained that he was trying to trace an elderly lady living in Amboise, but of course he did not even know André's mother's maiden name. The detective lit a cigarette, noted the Duclos' address and one or two other details, and said, disarmingly, <Do not worry, sir. I have my ways and means.> He then suggested that Roland should go to Amboise, pay his respects to Leonardo's tomb and then visit a *cave* or two. Did Monsieur intend to stay the night? He could recommend the "Lion d'Or".

He drove there as bidden, spent a couple of exhausting hours tramping round the castle, and then, at *apéritif* time, kept the *rendezvous* with the detective, who had checked wedding records in the Mairie in Tours, then, in Amboise, put questions to owners of baker's shops, *librairies, charcuteries,* offered a drink or two at certain bars. <And, monsieur>, he added, with a twinkle, <I have a friend on the computer in the *bureau des impôts,* and another on the police one. Do you want the full story on the *famille* Duclos? It's cheaper if I report verbally.>

<Just give me the address I need.> When I paid the man his fat fee and dismissed him, I realised I hadn't been properly listening to him at all: my mind had begun to question André's very existence. Have I been chasing ghosts? And Piers? What if he never did make contact again, in

January, and everything has been going on inside my head?

It was a neat little house in a quiet side-street near the river. Paving-stones instead of grass in the tiny garden. Ancient, respectable paint on the shutters closed against the burning sun. Madame de Lavallière was a much older and smaller version of her daughter, with the same dyed hair. He immediately noticed the photo on the mantlepiece in the cool dim sitting-room. André and the girls. The excitement which that aroused in him was still no proof that he actually existed.

And then Médor came into the room, wagging his tail and nuzzling against Roland's leg.

Her daughter and grandchildren, Madame was saying, had been cruelly abandoned by her errant son-in-law. <The girls stayed here, while André was with you. It was very kind of you to have him. But now we are all so frightened.>

<Is he ill again?>

<He has had another attack, recently.>

<Where are they, madame? I wish to see them.>

<They are in Paris, but I cannot divulge the address, not even to you. Fabienne is convinced that if her husband finds out where they are, he will try to harm them in some way. He is quite capable of that. I can only give you the telephone number of a near neighbour, who can be trusted.>

He had to be content with that. <If I do not succeed in contacting your daughter, please give her my very sincere regards and tell her that I am still happy to help to get André lodged with Madame Garbet at Annecy. I believe that his health and happiness depend upon it.>

From his hotel, he dialled the number he had just been given, and asked to speak to Madame Fabienne Duclos. After a few minutes, she answered.

He asked her how they all were, and if he could visit.

<Monsieur, I am amazed. How did you find this number?> André was recovering in a Paris clinic, after a bad attack.

<Where? Which clinic? I want to see him.> The urgency of his own voice took him by surprise.

<He returns to me tomorrow.>

<Then let me come and see him. I promise to be discreet. Surely, that can do no harm.>

<I cannot risk it. My husband... You know what he can be like.>

<I thought you said he had left you.> He cajoled her, taunted her even with the fact that he'd employed a detective to locate her mother.

<We do not need to be investigated, monsieur,> she said coldly, and the phone was put down.

André wants me, he's had to endure almost a fortnight without me, like a brain deprived of oxygen. He will urge his mother and even use his trump card: *Oncle Roland loves me best of all...*

While he was eating in the hotel restaurant, he was called to the phone. A contrite Madame Duclos. <I am really sorry. I just spoke to my mother. She told me of your kind concern for André and gave me the name of your hotel. I was so confused when we spoke before. I value the trouble you have gone to, to find us. I see it all now in a different light.>

<And André?>

<Shall I get him to ring you tomorrow, when he gets back here?>

<Let him ring me in the evening, at "Orphéon". Do you have that number still? I shall have got home by then.> He lay back, happy at last.

*

<Is it really you, Roland?> The young voice sounded strained.

<Of course it's me. Are you all right now?>

<When can I come and see you?>

I hesitate. I should have thought this out, with Piers due any minute. André senses my evasiveness, of course. He can't wait two whole months till August. Tears are so impossible to deal with, long distance. <Look, I promise to ring you up once a week, on the same day, at the same time.>

<Every Saturday?>

<Yes, just like today.>

<What time, then?>

<Two o' clock. OK?>'

<You really promise?>

<Of course.>

<If I could just hug you, Roland...>

My hand shakes, as I put the receiver back. Whom am I betraying, in all this? I meant to ask him where he was, and if his sisters were with him.

I'm full of hope and despair at one and the same time. André told me he would be happy to live like a mouse at "Orphéon", but I am the mouse, prey to all the twists and turns of a malevolent fate.

V.

'Her parents will let her take time off college, while I'm here.'

It's high summer, the city swarming, and we had to drive from the airport to St. Julien by back-roads, Piers' ceaseless talk of Adèle erasing all feeling of triumph in me, at having him back. When we reached "Orphéon", he took his things from the car, and jauntily preceded me into the house, asking straightway to use the phone.

'They're coming over in the morning to fetch me. Is that all right?' Eagerness defeats the anxiety in his face.

Is there to be no vestige of protocol? Only here five minutes, and he's proposing to take off. I ought to be grateful that his room is lived in again, that his things are in evidence, but how do I control the seething inside me, how can I ignore the fact that "Orphéon" is a mere springboard to him, where a relationship like that can have its beginnings?

He had so much wanted to talk properly to Piers, but could not break into the monologue about *her* visit to Cambridge, the May Ball, their ever closer fondness for one another; and it disappointed him not to be allowed to play the host celebrating the return of a special guest. When they had finished their light meal in the kitchen, he excused himself, went up to his study and shut the door.

Piers took himself off round the garden, where the vast silhouette of the house showed, reprovingly, it seemed to him, through the trees. Roland's plainly offended. I doubt if he has an inkling of what love really feels like. I'm better out of it, before we start arguing again.

Breakfast was a perfunctory affair. Piers had already brought down a light bag with his night things in it.

'When shall I expect you back, then?' He tried not to let his anger and pain come through.

'You really don't mind, do you, Roland? It's just that - '

It's just the order of priorities, isn't it? My need happens to be poles apart from yours. But then that's bad luck for me.

Tyres on the gravel, Piers ran out and was gone. No question of Roland being invited to step on to his own drive to meet Calivet. He had become an irrelevance.

He made a phone call and then drove to Anthy, to sit by the lake.

Every last detail of what happened between us has now returned, to haunt me. There was a large, electrically operated window in the lounge at the cottage, which Piers loved to activate. We would walk through it, and across the garden and paddock to our beach. There was never anyone else around, to interrupt or disturb us. Unlike now. Why did I have to suppress all that delightfulness during the dark years that followed? Because I was not strong enough to face up to the reality of my terrible loss, which is still not purged.

If I rush into the arms of another boy for consolation, it is because the mosaic which is my life has become hapless, without thrust or direction.

At first, the woman failed to understand his strange request. A man calls at a camp-site on a Sunday morning, with no intention of camping, but of buying, ostensibly for a charity, male *objets trouvés*, clothing abandoned by her departed campers - pyjama bottoms, T-shirts, tracksuits, underpants, towels, swimming trunks.

Returning home, he emptied his booty into a musty-smelling mound in the middle of his study floor. What relieved the mundane activity was the regular discovery of boys' things: they were so careless about their belongings. He picked up a *maillot de bain*, black shiny nylon with a soft lace to tie it at the waist - and rubbed it against his cheek. It seemed to smell of the sea. André would have fitted into it very well.

A tap at the back door at two o'clock, and there was his *matelot* again, with his open, honest smile.

<If you should ever arrive and aren't sure who might be here, use a special knock.> He tapped it out on the kitchen table, and Laurent copied it.

We go upstairs. Our language is physical, it does not involve speech:

I do things to him and with him, some of which I did to and with Piers, five years ago. That was wonderful for both of us, but a lot more hazardous than this. Laurent is at least past the age of consent.

Afterwards, we lie together, side by side. I kiss him on the bare shoulder, in his bleached hair, on his mouth. He tastes good. Still we do not speak: what we have done takes us many stages beyond even the informal 'tu'.

Before he goes, he allows me to photograph him in a selection of my trophies. I sort out some of the bigger things. He models T-shirts, shorts and trunks perfectly, unaware of how he looks, how he stirs me. We do a series of nude ones - serious, not prurient - and he goes home happy with a double fee. I should have liked to ask him whether Raoul would ever call again.

He developed the film in his darkroom off the study, and then produced a good set of black and white enlargements. This young man has his little brother's intensity in the eyes, the languid beauty of Donatello's David, the silent language of Tadzio, hand on hip, in the shallows. Of these pictures, it is not those which rouse me that I would want to keep for ever (like this one, in which he scarcely fits into a white nylon *maillot*), but those which appeal directly through the mind to the soul - they are timeless, absolute, there is a spirit which breathes in them. That is the aspect of BOY which I really love, because it carries no guilt.

And those things we just did together? I was thinking, Piers, this is for you. Only, this time, it's my act of defiance towards you. *I do this to spite you!*

*

Two days later, in the early afternoon, after Calivet and the girl had gone, the two of them went into the *salon*, and sat down, formally. Piers, at first oblivious to the host-guest role-play which Roland was trying to take them through, began by babbling on about what they had done, where they had been.

Roland very soon cut it short: 'I really don't want to hear all this.'

The boy stopped in amazement.

'Piers, you weren't inside my door for thirty seconds before you dashed off again to Talloires, saying nothing about when you were coming back. This isn't a bloody hotel.'

Piers choked. 'I'm sorry, I had no idea that you - '

'No, you wouldn't.' His anger swept him away. 'You're typical of your generation. You don't think and you don't care about anyone apart from yourself.'

'But, Roland, I love Adèle. You know that. It's vital we see each other, when we have to spend so long separated.'

He makes it sound as if they're married already.

'And I'm sorry I didn't manage to contact you. I rang yesterday afternoon, but I got no answer. Look, if I'm a burden to you, I'm sorry again. I try not to be under your feet.'

He's deftly twisting the situation, pointing it back at me, hobbling me with it. 'I wish you were here more, don't you see? I would appreciate a bit more of your company.'

Piers opened his arms in surprise. 'You know I like your company, but haven't you got other friends? There must be loads of people, Guy for instance...'

> *"I cannot get my point across, because he doesn't want to get involved with it. And here am I, all hot and bothered in my own house, and thoroughly irritated by all that he says and does. For two pins, I'd throw all my other indiscretions at him, <u>A</u>, <u>L</u>.*
>
> *Nor can I see the future. Will <u>P</u> be in it, or young <u>A</u>, even? I cannot see even to the end of this month, except that a miracle would have to happen, to make things right, between us. We are slipping off down our separate paths, <u>P</u> and I. He doesn't want to reverse that trend, and I am powerless to do so. Perhaps the age-gap has finally wrecked it all."*

*

Blue cigarette smoke seemed to be everywhere in the *salon*. A glum-looking Piers came in through the French window, his face visibly brightening when he caught sight of Guy. 'Oh, hullo, I've been cutting the grass for Roland.'

'Excellent. And how is *la belle ville de Cambridge*?'

He'd scraped through some of his exams, but others would have to be retaken. Even James had been minatory. Then he looked more cheerful. 'The May Ball was fantastic.'

'May Ball?'

At that moment, their host came in from the kitchen.

'Oh, by the way, Roland, I almost forgot: you're invited to lunch at Talloires on Saturday. They're desperate to have you over.'

<Ah, how wonderfully fresh,> said Guy, as they went into the garden. <I would gladly sit all day here in the shade, and let the orchestra do its tour without me.>

Piers asked him where he was going.

<Scandinavia, which is all very well if you don't mind eating fish until it comes out of your ears.>

<I love fish!>

<Then you must get Millan to take you to his *résidence secondaire* at Mont St. Michel for *les fruits de mer*,> said Guy, giving Roland a sly look. <Is it ready yet for habitation, your *petit cottage?* Why don't you take the young ones to see it?>

Why should I take them to PARR? But Guy's suggestion intrigues me. Piers is looking at me. Did he get my postcard? 'I just happened to take a short trip to Normandy, and fell in love with a ruin that is currently being rebuilt. You may remember I like to be near the sea.' God, that's made him blush! Guy wins himself a point or two for diplomacy. Seeing Piers and Adèle hand-in-hand, he knows I am no longer the threat I once may have been. André is light-years away, safe from my clutches. How wrong, though, to think I could ever have harmed anyone. To force is to harm, but force is not in my armoury, and never was. I win people over by kindness, or not at all, and go a good deal more than halfway, to meet certain of them.

*

As he and Piers drove to Talloires in time for coffee, he was praying that the gaggle of relatives wouldn't be in attendance. *Why can't it just be he and I, a sealed unit, for ever?*

But he was welcomed like a hero, and put at his ease. At least there were no hangers-on today. While Madame Calivet was supervising the hired caterers in her kitchen, her husband engaged him in polite conversation, wanting to know more about the house on the coast.

The loving couple are, as usual, wrapped up in each other, which doesn't bode well for our next few days together. Calivet tries hard to pass me some money. I ward him off with exaggerated correctness: <It was my suggestion that we should go to Courtils, monsieur, and I shall gladly honour it.>

<I fear we shall repay you with a simple little wine today,> said his host. <Nothing to rival your superb *Château Labique*.>

Apéritifs were served. Glasses in hand, they all walked down to the water's edge, defying a stiff breeze which was raising spray on the surface of the lake. Roland tried, as subtly as he could, to sound out Calivet on how far the Piers-Adèle thing had got, but her father passed it off humorously, intimating only that Piers was far from being the first boy in her life.

On the drive home to "Orphéon", with Adèle in front next to him, and Piers behind, leaning forward between them both, Roland's early doubts about the wisdom of the whole exercise began to harden. *I get things wrapped around my silly neck. If the journey to Courtils tomorrow is like this, it will be purgatory all the way.*

"Orphéon", to the astonishment of Piers, who thought he knew the house well, opened up another room to receive him, so that Adèle could have his for the night.

'Sorry to have to put you in the attic,' said Roland, untruthfully. It was a dark little room, bare and unwelcoming, but *he*, proud to offer his own bed to his beloved, seemed not to notice.

Nobody felt like eating anything more that night, so they sat around the kitchen table with a glass of wine.

'Adèle likes this house,' said Piers.

<What's that you just said?> she asked, frowning.

'Let's stick to French, Piers! Alors, mademoiselle, vous - '

But she cut him short. <Monsieur, I wish you would call me by my name and say *tu* to me, as you do to Piers.>

<All right, Adèle, just as you wish. There now!> How false this forced informality sounds! Still, it's worth saying that to her, if only to see the look of immense gratitude on Piers face.

He had intended to close the day with a brisk, almost avuncular exhortation to his young charges to get a good night's sleep before their early start, but they slipped out for a walk in the gardens together, leaving him to wander listlessly upstairs, pack some clothes in a bag and check over a few things.

He had excused himself from the Calivets' lunch table on the dot of two, when the meal was well under way. It sounded a bit odd to be making a vital business call on a Saturday afternoon, but he had ignored the raised eyebrows, and gone out into the hall.

André answered immediately. He had been waiting by the phone in the neighbour's house, and he howled: Piers was at "Orphéon", but he was not. Now it was Roland's turn to get worked up, just as at St. Jorioz that time. When he was almost shouting <Look, for goodness' sake calm down,> and trying to get the vital question through: <Tell me, André, exactly where you are, at this moment,> he realised that Adèle had come out and overheard him. Why, even now, in my garden, she will be telling Piers that I was phoning a woman! <Monsieur Millan has a secret *amour* called Andrée!> He won't know what to say to that, but perhaps it will give him food for thought.

*

The windscreen wiper made its metronome movements. Piers, in the passenger seat, studied the road atlas, not because Roland needed to be told the way, but to mask his own embarrassment at having to explain that, if Adèle was pale and silent and bunched up on the back seat this morning, it was because she'd started a period. Her mother didn't believe in taking anything for it, but did Roland have some pain-killers?

It was a cold day, to be two-thirds of the way through June, and Roland gave her a cushion and a blanket. What a fine start! After a while, she asked if they could stop at a hotel, hurried in, came back and whispered something to Piers.

'Do you mind if she sits in front?' There seemed to be an unspoken law that they should not occupy the back seat together.

She thanked Roland for being *gentil*, and began to talk to him about her course at domestic college, her parents' holidays in Switzerland and Austria, with Piers adding the occasional comment from behind. Then she got on to the subject of the house at Courtils, wanting to know all about each room and how it was decorated, what plans *monsieur* had for changing and improving it. He was both surprised and pleased to find that he could talk to her like this. It made the drive a lot easier.

The rain stopped, they had a snack before Orléans, and then Adèle curled up under her blanket on the back seat again, and went to sleep.

'I do hope you'll get to like her, Roland.'

'Of course.' And I suspect that some of her suggestions about *décor* will be useful. 'After all, a home needs a woman's touch.' Either he doesn't notice my terrible *clichés* or he makes allowances; and she's in no state to make love to anyone at present, so one of my worries has disappeared. Did I dream it, or did Piers once impart a great confidence to me - *that they hadn't done it?* So - at which point along the road do I have to consider myself finally betrayed? How many fondlings, caresses and such-like count towards the ultimate total? *What is the permissible and impermissible quota of love?*

This thought makes my heart sink again. Whatever the answers may be, and wherever you draw the line, I overstepped the mark with him. In that brief time together in my cottage, we went through practically every possible permutation, he and I, until we reached the point where we began to regard it as a marriage of two like souls in two very disparate bodies. I had almost given up feeling guilty, but it remains there, in the background, to be cherished, even, because it proves to me that we *did* something. Without guilt, we would be robbed of existence itself.

At long last, as they approached the coast, the evening sun came out, warm and welcoming. Adèle woke up, and she and Piers, like two children, began to look for the Mont, making a game out of who should see it first.

At the hotel, all three rooms were on the same floor. There was some colour in Adèle's cheeks when he next saw her. She had changed out of her jeans and top into an attractive dark-blue dress with white dots on it. Piers, his hair newly washed, was in grey flannels and a dark green pullover. They both looked very presentable, sitting at the table where the Duclos had eaten when Roland first saw them.

André wept, on the phone. What on earth am I supposed to do? When I can get Piers to myself for a moment, maybe I'll ask his advice. After all, if she is going to tell me which tiles and wallpapers I should choose, surely he, who knows me so very well, could offer my soul some balm, stitch some torn edges together?

The girl wanted only an omelette and some mineral water. Piers, remembering Guy's recommendation, chose the *plateau de fruits de mer*.

<That's really greedy, Pierrot!> she exclaimed, at the sight of the oysters, mussels and everything else piled up on their bed of seaweed and crushed ice. Piers used the long pin to hook a winkle out of its shell, and mischievously offered it to her, but she screwed up her nose.

After the meal, I drive them along the *digue* to see the Mont floodlit. So far, my little trip hasn't worked out so badly. Here I am, walking up to the walls of the Mont St. Michel with her right arm round my waist, her left one round Piers'. (If only I were the one in the middle.) It's her demonstrative nature which attracts him to her. I know he's on cloud nine at this moment, because they think she has so cleverly knitted the three of us together.

The next morning, when they entered the house at Courtils, workmen were still busy inside and out. The spiral staircase was in position, the ancient shower had been torn out, the upstairs floors renewed, and partitions for the new bathroom were already in place. The scullery was rebuilt, the roof had been entirely redone and there was a good smell of fresh paint and plaster. A garage was being built behind the house, the gardens dug over, and new fences erected. Piers and Adèle, not having seen it as it was before, demanded to know all.

After a lively hour or so of this, Roland suggested they drive to the Mont for lunch, and then, if Adèle was up to it, she and Piers could go round the abbey.

'What about you, Roland?' Piers clearly wanted to keep the three of them together.

He had to see the builder about one or two points. Diplomatic withdrawal...

Adèle was all for going to buy tiles with him, but he assured her that the place wasn't ready for that just yet. Despite her bossy tone, he realised he was meant to take all this interest as a compliment, a kind of olive branch, and promised that they would stop somewhere suitable on the way home tomorrow, to get some samples. That seemed to placate her.

'We really do like your house,' said Piers, as they sat in Mère Poulard, having ordered.

He says 'we', as though they're already married. André sat in that chair, over yonder... To get Piers on his own is clearly impossible, and I don't think I could start to broach the topic of André, away from the special force-field which surrounds the Mont.

> *"The girl Adèle shows me deference in all that she says or suggests. She doesn't seem to question my connection with P, but accepts me as a sort of magisterial figure. Putting her arm round my waist was undoubtedly a <u>faux pas</u> on her part, which she has realised, and not repeated. I am 'Roland' and' tu' to P, but 'vous' and 'monsieur' always to her. Thank God for that!*
>
> *Towards him, she is developing a cutting edge, which he doesn't yet seem aware of, but which is all too obvious to me. When we met together, after their tramp round the Mont this afternoon, I sensed a hardness there, a tendency to pooh-pooh some of the things he says. Even her nickname for him,' mon petit Pierrot' (which he loves to hear, as much as I hate to) bears, I think, a trace of scorn. Unless I am very*

much mistaken, there will be a major row between them before long. She expects so much of him, but what can she offer him in return? Have they anything at all in common, apart from their puppy love?"

*

<Do you like this one?> She held out a tile with a large yellow daisy on it.

<Just a shade too Van Gogh for my taste.> I've decided to opt for honesty, or she'll be dictating all the way. She takes down another, and this time she's struck oil: a kitchen tile which we both like - restrained colour, subtle mottling. I could have designed it myself. <What d'you think, Piers?>

Interior decoration wasn't something Piers had ever had to think about: the Choir School had been spartan and tatty, and Mother had chosen her own papers and curtains for her little house in Guildford. He felt upstaged by these two, especially Adèle who was now back on form, picking on things he said, correcting his French, and - worst of all - making comparisons between English and French boys, to his disadvantage, of course. <Pierrot, you are so serious. You like all these old buildings, you drag me up to the top of the Mont just to see an empty church. That's not what I like.> She'd sat him down on a seat in the gardens, had insisted on embracing and kissing him in front of all those people. Usually, it hadn't bothered him so much, but Roland could have popped up at any moment.

She engineered it so that, on the return journey, they were on the back seat of the car together, and I could tell that Piers was embarrassed, muttering curt answers to her questions, trying to involve me. In the restaurant where we stopped for lunch, a baby was screaming in a high chair at the next table. Adèle pulled a face, made it plain that she would never want to go through agonies to give birth, as her *maman* had done. Piers' reaction was interesting: the only child, who used to crave for a brother, would like very much to have children of his own. (And he was asking, but a few weeks ago, how he could go about marrying this girl.)

Taking them to my new home was, an act of faith on my part. I assume that she began by regarding me as a kind of stumbling-block set between her and Piers. She was admittedly very civil to me, but then displayed an unpleasant side to him, which I found very hurtful. He sometimes looked out of his depth - certainly at the end. I'm sure he would have preferred to come back here, with me. That girl has him in her clutches, and, having raised him up so high, is just as likely to drop him all the way down to earth again.

Great drops of water fall off my trees and soak me. Piers' carefully tended lawns are soggy underfoot, the vegetation gives off a mournful smell. As always, I'm not sure when he'll be back – he'll phone. I hope I haven't let him go off to his doom. Hell, he's only just eighteen...

*

He could tell, just by looking at it, that "Orphéon" was locked up. Roland had never seen fit to give him a key. Doubly disconsolate, he wandered round the gardens, unable to understand what had got into her. Since they returned from Normandy, three days ago, she'd become really abrasive. He thought he knew what she was after. They'd gone far enough, as it was.

And today, she really laid into him. Just the two of them, in the house. <You don't want to. Perhaps you can't do it. You're a coward.> How could anyone be so adoring one minute, and a spiteful little bitch the next?

He had tried to reason with her, to explain what his feelings were, but his French wasn't up to it. She'd started to laugh at him, and that made him angry. In a turmoil, he packed his bag and went off down to the steamer landing, where a boat for Annecy was just coming in. She didn't come dashing after him, nor was there any sign of her when the boat, with him on it, passed the end of their garden. It wasn't the first time in his life that he'd known the keen pain of parting, but this was worse than even Wharnley had been, because it had taught him something about himself that he didn't want to know.

One of the outhouses was open. Dropping his bag inside, he fetched out a sunlounger, took it to a shady corner of the gardens, well away from the house, and lay down on it.

How do I explain all this to him? Can it be done in such a way that he'll be sympathetic? He stared gloomily back towards the house that was partly masked by foliage. It was early afternoon, and he was thankful for the coolness under the trees. In the distance, the Salève was a quivering blue mass. From here, he would hear Roland's car returning.

While he was musing over his troubles, his attention was caught by a figure rounding the house from the direction of the front drive. Someone come to make a delivery, doubtless, and Roland was out. He started to get up, but something about the newcomer made him take cover behind a bush.

The youth was fair-haired and stocky, about his own age, also in T-shirt and jeans, but not apparently carrying anything that might be delivered. He moved in a lithe fashion, and, as he went up to the back door, cast a quick glance all around him. Then he raised his hand and, audible even at this distance, tapped on the door with his knuckles. After a moment, it opened, he went in and it was closed again.

This baffled him. He knew that Friday was never one of Madame Bouillot's days here, so who let that youth in? An accomplice? He had to choose now between trying to gain entry himself, to see what was going on, or remaining concealed, to see what would happen next.

Discretion won: hoping he wouldn't be spotted, he moved to another bush much closer to the back door, wondering whether to alert the police. If nothing sinister was going on in there, he'd look a bit of a fool. *But where was Roland?*

The heat made him drowsy, and he lay down under the bush, his head on his arm, his eyes riveted on the back door.

He awoke to the sound of the door shutting, footsteps on the gravel, and sat up. The youth had come out of "Orphéon", but was now heading for the far end of the gardens, where a public footpath ran. His way took him right past Piers, who, holding back the fury that had just taken him over, let the other continue a few paces, then, like a cat, leapt out and surprised him with a tackle from behind. They fell heavily into mud.

The youth let out a yelp and grappled with his attacker. But even his heavy build was no match for Piers, who got him in a strong grip and thumped the back of his head against the ground. They rolled over, locked together, kicking, kneeing. The youth's hot breath was in Piers' face, along with a fresh smell of shower gel. He spat and snarled like an animal. It lasted only a minute or two, without a word spoken on either side. Then Piers managed to kneel up, and would have gladly planted his fist in the other's face, had it not been for the sudden realisation that his anger should be aimed elsewhere. For the first time, he had a proper look at his assailant. Those dark eyes, that fair hair - it could have been a relative of bloody Fillingham! Slowly, he got up and stepped back, gesturing silently to the other to go. They were both scratched and filthy.

With a furious look, the youth got up, made as if to land a parting blow, but then staggered off towards the front drive, nursing his right elbow. On the grass was something light-coloured that had not been there before. Piers bent down, picked it up and unfolded it: a banknote, which could only have come out of the other's pocket.

His initial reaction was alarm at what he had done and found out. Two hammer blows in one day: first Adèle, and then this. How could he face Roland, what could he say? But the crackly note in his right hand was all he needed.

Brushing himself down as best he could, he walked up to the back door of the house and tapped in Morse code, exactly as the youth had done: dot-dash-dot: R. Silence inside. He tried the door, but it was locked. He repeated the knock and, after a few moments, heard a shuffling sound, coming nearer. The door was unlocked and opened, and there, in bathrobe and slippers, his bare legs looking strangely pale, was Roland, an inquiring look on his face, which immediately turned to consternation.

'Yes, it's me, this time,' said Piers, holding out the fifty franc note.

Roland found his voice. 'What's this for?'

'Its yours, isn't it? I picked it up.'

'Now see here,' said Roland, looking quickly past Piers, then edging back, to let him in. 'I think you've got the wrong end of the stick. 'That boy - '

' - was hardly delivering the eggs, was he?' said Piers grimly. 'I did you the favour, if favour it was, of seeing him off. He won't be back.'

Roland had recovered sufficiently to feel a little amused at the sight of Piers, who, by all appearances, had fought for him tooth and nail as his champion. This *peccadillo* was going to take a lot of explaining away. 'I'm sorry, Piers. I didn't know you'd be back so soon.'

'So you had your rent boy round.' His anger finally boiled up. 'You're just a dirty pederast, aren't you? You try to make everyone think you're so proper and respectable, when all that you really want to do is fuck boys. Well, you needn't think that I'm - ' He broke off, seeing a chasm yawning before him.

'Piers, why don't you go up and cool off a bit, in every respect, and we'll talk later on? I think that really would be best.'

An uneasy silence descended on "Orphéon". Piers went into the bathroom to shower, but the room was steamy and hot, reminding him that it had just been used by *them*. Locking his door, he stripped off and had a stand-up wash at the basin. When he had dabbed his various scrapes and scratches, and was dressed in clean clothes, he sat in the chair, not daring to go down.

There was a time when I, idiot that I am, believed that everything he said and did had a sacramental quality to it. Was I ever in moral danger? Perhaps I was, once, but didn't understand, the way I do now. He has this deep and fatal flaw, he must feel miserable and lonely - always hoping and yearning.

Then, as he recalled Adèle to mind, the cause of his own misery, another wave of anger and pain came over him. He suddenly wanted his father, wanted someone he could really trust. My girl has let me down, and so has the man who I thought was my best friend. This house is an accursed place, and I now know exactly why. Roland always protested that he was fond of me, but that was just a front.

He got up, went to the cupboard, fetched his case down and began to pack it. If I can get the first boat out of Talloires, I can get the next train out of Geneva - and balls to the lot of them.

When Roland knocked at his door a little later on, immaculately dressed in flannels, shirt and tie, he was alarmed to find Piers looking at the railway timetable.'

'There's a train just after six. I'll get a bus to Cornavin.' His case was standing ready on the floor.

'You must give me a chance to - '

'You don't deserve any chances,' Piers snapped back at him. 'It's not the first time that boy was here, is it?'

If I thought I'd found a way to punish Piers, it's misfired. Has he forgotten that he came here by plane, that his return flight is booked for the end of July? I must do all I can to obstruct him, keep him here, smooth things over.

'You made me believe you were bisexual,' Piers was saying, 'and I'd managed to come to terms with that, because I thought you respected me, the way I respected you. What happened just now only shows you don't really care for me as I am. You probably don't know how to. For you, I'm just the nude little boy' (he nearly choked on that) 'on the wall there. But I've grown up. So you turn to other boys instead. Isn't that the long and short of it? Have you got any more of them lined up? I find it just cheap, pathetic and squalid.'

'Piers, you can't leave yet.' He had begun to shake.

'I don't want people to think that I'm your kept boy. Christ, those journeys we made must have cost you a bomb. Is *that* what you were leading up to?'

'You've got it all wrong. Where you are concerned, I look upon myself as a kind of patron. That's not unworthy, is it?'

'If "patronage" has the same purpose as your fifty franc notes, then it certainly is unworthy.'

'I wish you would listen, a moment. That boy who came here - I don't love him. To me, you've always been far above people like that. I do respect you, Piers, and I accept the relationship you have with Adèle.'

But this only brought pain to Piers' face. 'What you do in your own house is up to you, Roland, but I have to say it's reckless. You're always so anxious not to trivialise life, but you *are* trivialising it if you do these things. That boy is a prostitute, which proves that you aren't bi-sexual at all. You're *boy*-sexual.'

'Piers, don't let's pursue this any more. If I've injured any affection you ever had for me, I'm ready to make amends. You are the only person in the world I have ever been able to take seriously. I never stopped loving you, never, for a single second. Wharnley was for me the most marvellous thing in my life, and after that I had to bury it all, bury myself here. I was punished, and I still am.' He could not restrain the tears any longer.

'You say you "love" me,' Piers answered with a steady voice, 'but you don't know what it is about me that you love. Even I don't know, and I don't think I want to. Look, I had to dig you out again, after all this time. You never bothered to find out what I might be doing. You can't really say that you care.'

'I was afraid of getting emotionally hurt again. You must accept that I love you for yourself, not as a separate body or soul or mind or whatever. Isn't love the deepest form of respect?'

'If it is, you have a funny way of showing it. You don't know what it's like, in your easy life, to stand up to someone else, fight your corner, be *inconvenienced.*'

Easy life! Is this the moment to tell him about André? No, because in his eyes it would only compound the felony. 'If you pull out now, Piers, what about Adèle? No, please let me finish this. You may despise me - I can quite understand that - but, for your two sakes, I beg you to make "Orphéon" your base for a while longer. Don't ruin your own happiness on account of me. You have so much to live for. She would never understand, if you just went off.'

> *"When he suddenly broke down, I was amazed to find that he'd been bottling up his own troubles. They came pouring out, and eventually we were both calm enough to begin putting down foundations for a fresh start, and I was able to give him some positive advice about his tiff with that girl. I think it's helped me, too. He realises now how desperate I was, to have turned to L, and I'm sure his fury at me was tinged with jealousy. He apologised for things he'd said, I apologised again, and then he said something*

> *which I thought very mature: 'When the storm has blown over, you have to mend your fences and start again.' It's only now that I realise how much I have allowed my judgment to be obliterated by feelings of guilt. He seems to have got me and my odd fixations pretty well summed up, but I believe the homo-erotic scares him, now."*

I once visualised Piers meeting André. I never thought he might meet Laurent. Hard to imagine the two of them fighting like dogs. But he has held up a mirror, to show me my deformities. Guy tries to change me, and now it's Piers' turn. What neither of them understands is that the discrepancy between fantasy and reality excites me. I can live by its energy: it may be dangerous (just as the crime is to the criminal), but it could never be boring. And there's another thing that draws me to Piers: the whiff of anarchy we share, though it causes trouble when it's present in both of us at the same time.

On his own again, he went over the day's events once more. He had even hated Roland, till he saw that, despite everything, the man was still innocent and vulnerable, as he'd been at Cambridge. I need to get through to him to drop these dangerous games - doubtless there *are* other boys... Was it my doing that set him off down this path? He did say: 'You rescued me from oblivion. I'm out in the open now. I have to be something. Can't go on for ever, being nothing at all.'

He seemed for the first time to show some understanding of my feelings for Adèle, suggested I leave it for twenty-four hours and then ring her. He's right: I can't just drop it, like that. There are things we both need to know. Even when I was upset, I didn't tell him every detail about her urging me on. After the sordid business with that youth, I don't know if I should ever be able to talk about sex with him again.

On the phone, Adèle used a soft voice to say she was sorry, begged him to come back to Talloires.

*

Out of the blue, Madame Duclos rang him to say that André had been rushed back to the clinic in Palaiseau. The doctors were really concerned, this time.

<Give me the address. I will come.>

He phoned Talloires, putting Piers off until later in the week, and reached Paris in the early evening. The clinic was a modern building on a hill, among trees. As he entered, his heart was beating hard, his mind full of pictures of Mother during her last illness.

André was in a private room, with a large oxygen cylinder next to his bed, his face so pale as to be scarcely recognisable. His mother rose from her chair, and put out both hands to Roland.

<How is he?>

<He has been sleeping a lot. He is very weak. He cannot keep food down.>

<I would gladly have come earlier,> he said, intending it to sound like a reproach.

André coughed, awoke and, seeing Roland next to his mother, struggled to sit up, the sheet falling off his skinny torso. <Roland, is it really you? Tell me I'm not dead.>

<You are very much alive, and I really am here.>

The boy stretched out two white little arms, and Roland bent over him. The body smelt warm, antiseptic, like that of a new baby. For one supposedly so weak, André had some of the old strength in those arms, as he clasped them round Roland's neck and pulled him down.

<It's all right André. Don't cry. I went to see your grandma and Médor. He's perfectly all right with her.>

The colour was returning to the boy's cheeks, he was breathing quickly but evenly. Despite his tears, he was happy. His mother slipped out. <Quick!> he said, taking Roland's hand.

How do you refuse a patient immobilised in hospital? André was wearing just briefs. <There, you see. I'm already getting better because you're here.>

He pulled his hand back, his head reeling, and placed it gently on the clammy little chest. The breathing was still fast, but stronger and steady now.

<I'm glad you came back, Roland. It was terrible without you, and

it's not the same on the phone. It upsets me, because I want you so much.>

Madame Duclos returned with the doctor, who shook Roland by the hand and then turned to his patient, taking his pulse and listening through his stethoscope. Finally, he faced the two adults. <As I said earlier, madame, his chronic asthma is exacerbated by his bouts of hysteria. At the moment, he is calm. We must do everything possible to keep him like this.>

<Could he grow out of the asthma?> Roland wanted to know.

<It happens,> said the doctor, <but a lot of care and patience are needed, a quiet environment and good air. Madame tells me that you have made an arrangement for him to convalesce at Annecy. How soon can he go?>

<The people are away until the end of July.>

The doctor put his head on one side. <These next few weeks could be quite critical for him. He really cannot afford to have another attack like this last one.>

Roland was tempted to wonder whether the doctor and Mme. Duclos had been conspiring behind his back, but then he caught André's imploring look. <Can we have a word outside, madame?>

She and her husband were still living apart, he now paying for André's medical expenses, and for the girls to attend a boarding school. There had been a violent confrontation. <He does not give *me* a *sou*: I have to manage.>

<And where are you living?>

André and she were sharing a room in a bad part of Paris. There was a lot of racial trouble - the streets were not safe. She had managed to find some part-time secretarial work.

<What about his schooling?>

She shook her head. He'd begun at a school nearby, but his class was full of Algerians and so on, and he simply went under.

<Will your husband pay for him to live near me and, when necessary, the medical attention?>

<I will ask him. But I don't want to let André go.>

<Why don't you try and get a room in Annecy, say, and work down

there? It would be better for you too.> I'm amazed that I could even have suggested this. Her face lights up. Yes, André takes after her - I see it properly when she smiles, which is virtually never.

<Armand would probably be pleased to have us out of the way.>

Roland looked at his watch. <I must book in at a hotel for the night. Can we meet here again, tomorrow morning at ten?>

<You will never never leave me again, I beg you,> André whispered in his ear as they kissed each other goodnight.

I am walking a razor's edge here, picking up responsibilities which I would once never have dreamed of taking on. There are irreconcilable facets to my life: Piers, André, like chalk and cheese. André knows a little about Piers, but there has been no opportunity for me to warn *him*... Imagine, Madame Duclos brings her son to "Orphéon" for lunch: Piers happens to be there and sees this child trying to swamp me with affection. We're already on a potential collision course.

André is almost eleven. Piers was thirteen. Those two years are a lifetime for a child. Piers was a prodigy in all kinds of ways and - in at least one respect - André looks as if he might follow suit. Perhaps my dream of the two of them walking together will come to pass. They may get on famously. One day, they may compare notes...

By the following morning, the doctor had contacted a colleague at a clinic just outside Annecy, who would take André in until he was well. An ambulance-taxi equipped with oxygen would convey the boy from Paris.

But there were hitches. Armand Duclos, whom his wife had telephoned, refused to allow André to go: if it happened against his wishes, then no money would be forthcoming for his treatment and lodging. And André refused utterly to go to Annecy by ambulance: it had to be Roland's car or nothing.

<I propose, madame, that you ignore your husband's threats. I am happy to drive you both to Annecy, if that is feasible and what you wish, and you can find somewhere to live.> My role dances about: today, it's formal adviser.

She was clearly still frightened for herself and her son. Whatever she tried to do to get her children and herself out of the predicament in which Duclos had left them, he sabotaged it all. And why? <André and he are nothing to each other. He isn't really interested in the girls' welfare either. It's all done out of spite. He enjoys himself with his mistresses, and we are left like lepers.>

<How soon can André travel?> Roland wanted to know.

The doctor said immediately, if he had oxygen for the journey, and was kept well wrapped-up.

And so, within a few hours, the patient, who had even eaten a small meal, was with his mother on the back seat of Roland's car, *en route* for Geneva. The oxygen flask, behind them with the luggage, was not needed.

<I am sorry I cannot accommodate you at "Orphéon",> said Roland. <I have a visitor at the moment.>

<Piers,> mumbled André, who was supposed to be trying to sleep.

Although it was Sunday, she had succeeded in phoning her boss to explain her sudden withdrawal from her job. Her mother had offered to take the girls again. Roland assured her that he would cushion any financial problems until she was earning again. Fortunately, she was exhausted and slept for a good deal of the journey.

It's like driving down a cul-de-sac. I have no idea whether or not Annecy will suit her. André will be all right, as long as he can see me. Is that arrogant? I don't know if I shall survive all these conflicting tensions.

André was installed at the clinic above the town, and his mother was delighted to find a pleasant twin-bedded room nearby, at a fraction of the cost of the one in Paris. Roland promised to see the child once a day, until he was released from the clinic, and to remain in touch with his mother. He was privately not a little shocked by what he had just arranged. Piers and André were now living a very short distance apart, and he was going to have to be a kind of pendulum between them, like a man with two... wives would be inappropriate, and so would lovers. He was going to need to live by his wits from now on.

*

It was the first time she'd asked such probing questions about the schools he'd been to, whether he'd had any other girl friends before her. He was thrown off his balance and answered badly, saw a question mark rising suddenly above his head.

<Piers, you're not gay, are you?>

The worst thing she could possibly have said. He protested, she pretended that it had only been a joke, but that rang false. He knew he could have flown to his own defence, but, in his embarrassment, he became fainthearted, despondent. Perhaps she was right. Maybe a girl could tell. Without a word having been said on the subject, she could have built up an intuitive picture of Wharnley and Roland, and all that. Secrets were not safe, and there wasn't anything on earth you could get away with.

<Your monsieur is *sympa*,> she was saying. <I like him.>

He didn't agree too forcefully, afraid of unleashing another *enquête*. It came anyway.

<What sort of school did M. Millan go to?>

The truth, so innocent upon his lips, was instantly seized upon. <All *boys*? From seven to eighteen? Like monks? *O, là là*. You know, we have boarding schools too. My cousin Paul goes to one. The things those boys get up to, when the teachers aren't looking! Oh, but, *mon petit Pierrot*, I've made you blush!>

*

"<u>A</u> is up and about, now, though not allowed to leave the clinic just yet. He has lost his sun-tan, of course, but he's grown a bit taller in the six weeks I've known him, despite his illness - no longer my shrimp, but a young man in the making! It terrifies him that the summer will soon be over, though I keep telling him that we are only at the end of June.

His mother seems to view me the way the Tsarina looked upon Rasputin. I asked her if the arrangement with the Garbets should stand, now that she was settled at Annecy herself, but she thought it best to leave things as they are, for the present.

I wish I could feed him up and get him back to health quickly. But, for this to happen, he'd have to live here with me. I can't juggle with the chalk and the cheese for ever – something's going to have to give.

Courtils will be ready in the early autumn.

<u>P</u> rang - her parents are going away for a few days, so I have given my blessing to a bit of an experiment (I hardly dare contemplate <u>of what kind</u>).

<u>A</u> was allowed out today for the first time. His mother has found a morning job, so he and I went into Annecy, to let him look round toyshops, etc. As we passed a church, he took me inside, steered me over to a rack of candles, solemnly bought one with his own <u>sous</u>, and we <u>both</u> had to hold it while it was lit and put on a spike. I asked him whom he dedicated it to, and he said 'To us, of course'. In his way, he is a great ritualist. Tomorrow, we go swimming."

*

Madame Duclos having agreed that André could spend the night at "Orphéon" after the swimming trip, Roland picked him up just after ten.

He was glum. <Maman lost my trunks when we moved.>

I have a dozen pairs at home, but in any case I can't expect him to don someone else's cast-offs. He wouldn't understand the special significance those things have for me.

And so the boy was taken to a smart sports shop in Annecy where, with impeccable taste, he selected a pair of bright orange mini-trunks with black and white facings. <Like a butterfly.>   When   they approached the changing cubicles at St. Jorioz, all the doors were open. Nobody about - free choice today. Roland made a manful attempt to direct André to a cubicle of his own.

<No I won't. We're staying together!> And he pushed Roland into their old one and closed the door. The same blue light filtered in, there was the same smell of concrete and stale disinfectant. Roland suddenly

sat down on the bench, his heart pounding so hard that he feared he would pass out.

<Are you all right? You've gone very pale.>

<I'll be OK. Get changed. Let's see you in your butterfly trunks, then.>

André crossed his arms at his waist and pulled up his dark-blue sweater. The white T-shirt underneath began to peel up with it.

He isn't the pathetic little wraith I saw in the clinic bed. His chest is already forming, like that of a young brave. He'll be handsome after he's stopped being so pretty.

The shorts were also discarded, and then André paused. He's making it into a bit of theatre just for me. His clothes, which he hands me to fold, are warm from his body. There's a tension in his look which was once in Piers' face. Can I - dare I - defuse it, spoil our rite, threaten our friendship by laughing it away?

André bent down, kissed Roland on the cheek, took one of his hands and placed it firmly on the crutch of his nylon slip.

<When I was in bed in the clinic,> he whispered hoarsely, <I prayed you would come and do it with me again. Do you remember?>

<Of course I do.>

He leans forward again, winds his head and neck round mine, blows his words into my ear.

<And your *semence*. You remember about that?> André pushed down his briefs, and let his sex swing up, pink, pristine, as rigid as a bolt. His dark eyes were fixed on Roland's.

Someone came into the next cubicle, noisily shutting and locking the door. Roland put a finger to his lips and held André's new trunks out to him. His face has dropped a mile, but he understands.

They went down to the *plage* together, Roland battling with his own feelings, and very aware of the skimpiness of the garment he had chosen to wear. We were saved just in time. Didn't I once dream that he was a little satyr?

<You won't forget, will you?> said André, as they swam side by side.

I know what you mean. I don't like evasions, but I don't know what to do. <Look, we're going back to "Orphéon" later. It's safer there, with no-one to disturb us.> Why does it have to be so furtive?

But there was determination in André's eye. <No, it has to be here, like it was before. It matters.>

<Why? What's the difference?>

<Because I shall be cured if we do it here>

<Of your asthma?>

<D'you think I'm stupid, Roland? You think I talk nonsense, but I've worked it out. You'll see. I really do need it.>

<What, exactly?> I've no idea what he's getting at.

<Your sperm. I haven't got any of my own yet. Roland, when does it happen, for a boy? Will it be soon?>

Lost for a reply, I keep an eye on my boy in the water, refusing to allow any horseplay today. <You mustn't get tired or cold.>

<Cold, on a day like this?> André's laughter is silver, like the crinkly bars of sunlight on the surface of the lake.

When we are lying side by side on our towels, he tells me about his terrible life since we last met. <My father can come and kill me if he likes, but I will never go back to Tours, and never never to Paris. I hate Paris, it's like hell.>

I'm relieved that he doesn't blame me for not rescuing him sooner.

<Roland, why didn't Piers come swimming? Did you stop him because you knew we would have our secret today? He doesn't know our secret, does he? How much does he know about me?>

I am doubly stunned. It would hurt this child if I told him the truth, that Piers, just across the lake there, doesn't know *anything* about him. <He's busy today, André.>

<But I'll see him when we go back to your house? He is staying there, isn't he?>

<He's gone away with friends at the moment.>

Just then the boy, having stood up to urge me into the water again, lets out a howl of pain and starts to hop about on one foot, blood dripping from the sole of the other. My fault: I hadn't noticed the fragments of glass on the ground.

I get him to sit down, and examine the cut. <It's not serious. We'll

get a plaster from the *bureau*. You'd better not try to walk on it yet.> I pick him up, and start back. He feels lighter than he was, the last time I did this. <You've lost weight. We must fatten you up!>

But he's whispering at me. <D'you remember? The last time, when you were cross with me, you carried me like this. You aren't cross now?>

<Of course not. It wasn't your fault.>

<And, when we get back to the changing-room, Roland... You know you promised.>

Getting the foot seen to provides a welcome diversion. How long can I stall, in the face of the most persistent person I've ever met? And then, like a *deus ex machina*, a *gendarme* comes round the corner, pauses, looks at us, and then walks away. I put André down. <Did you see that policeman?>

<So what?>

<We'd better get changed in separate cubicles.>

'Mais pourquoi?' He is wide-eyed.

<Because... I think it's a rule and, if the police are about, you don't break rules, do you?>

<What about my cure, then?> He is defiant, his eyes beginning to fill.

<Don't worry, I already told you we'll have plenty of time together before you go back to your *maman*.> When we reach "Orphéon", I hope I shall have got your fevered little brain on to more innocent subjects - or we are lost. I fell once. I dare not fall again, not with you.

He limps with me to the *bureau*, I acquire a plaster, put it on his foot any old how, then bundle him unceremoniously into one cubicle, while I flee into the one next door. <Dry yourself properly. Is your foot all right, now?>

A big sigh from next door. <Some blood's seeping through the plaster.>

<Try to keep your foot up. Be careful how you put your shorts on. Don't get blood on them, or your *maman* won't be pleased.>

A boy can be diverted away from his dangerous path, whereas a man has to go on pursuing his grail. I dress quickly, as never before, and am relieved to find him waiting outside.

<Roland, I haven't got a comb.>

<Here you are. The mirror's over there.>

<I know, I used it last time.>

Words cannot convey the triumphant, desperate feelings in me now, as I drive this child back as if on a superb lap of honour. And yet, there is a hot gnawing feeling at the back of my neck whenever I glance at him, and he looks trustingly back.

By the time they reached "Orphéon", the temperature was oppressive and the tops of the trees in the garden were swaying as if in their death throes.

André went straightway up to the guest room and deposited his little bag. He wanted to know if everything had been left exactly as it was when Piers slept here, but Roland explained that Madame Bouillot had changed the sheets.

<Blow, I've left my trunks in your car.> He dashed out to the car and retrieved the two rolled towels from the back seat. Roland said they could dry their bathing things off in the kitchen. André let his towel unfurl. His *maillot*, now a dark soggy lump, fell on the floor. He seized Roland's towel and let it roll open.

<Oh but where are yours? Have you still got them on?>

In his haste to get out of the cubicle, he'd left his trunks behind.

André was dismayed. <We'll have to go back.>

<It doesn't matter. I've got some other ones.>

"After we'd had something to drink, he took me by the hand, and dragged me upstairs again, to see the study. While he was looking at a pile of photos I had (carelessly) left on the desk, he picked one up and said 'Piers has got dyed hair. And look - he's wearing your maillot!' The amusement mixed with surprise in his face was absolutely wonderful, and I wish I could have snapped it. He then reminded me of my promise to take a picture of him nu, like the one of P, out on the wall.

It would have been too complicated to tell him that the

photo he had in his hand wasn't <u>P</u>. When he asked why <u>P</u> should be wearing <u>my</u> trunks, and hadn't he got any of his own, I passed it off as a magic trick: they'd gone missing after our trip to St. J, and now they'd appeared again on the photo. At first he looked ready to thump me, but he just put down the print, said I could take his picture, and, before my very eyes, stripped right off at top speed! I panicked, said it was too dark because of the storm coming up outside. There was a buffet of wind, then a flash lit up his body."

For a fraction of a second, the light was eery, intense, like the burst of energy which is supposed to cremate people where they stand.

<You can do magic,> said André, <but I'm not afraid. You did some with your *maillot,* and now I want you to do some with me.>

<You'll get cold. Where are your pyjamas?> His control thrown to the winds, he was bitterly regretting having put himself in the hands of Fate.

<I'm not going to bed,> the boy shouted in mirth. <And you can't make me have a bath, because I've been in the lake and I'm beautifully clean!>

To make a joke out of it, Roland lunged out, as if to catch him. Chortling, the boy rushed off, across the landing and into Piers' room. Joining in the spirit of it, Roland followed, saying loudly <Now where has this boy gone?> and walked noisily all round the empty room, going near the cupboard but not opening it. Then he strode to the window and flung it open, calling <André, are you on the balcony?>

The rain beats in on the floor. Piers. Raoul. And André in the cupboard! Quietly, he pushes the door open and comes out, a little grey ghost clad only in Piers' dressing-gown, which is far too big and trails on the floor.

<It's me, Piers!> he cried.

For him, Piers is an infinitely fascinating mystery (in a house which cherishes its secrets). Look at him. The dressing-gown gapes open at the front. I wish I could kiss his knees, so pale now after their long absence from the sun.

They sat down on the bed, André with his arm round Roland's waist, and resting his head against his chest. <I'm so happy here with you.>

It's all right to curl an arm round his shoulder, to feel the warm young body next to mine. André, I love you, but I mustn't say it just yet. It might add some fuel to that young fire.

> *"Looking back, it didn't happen at all the way we'd envisaged. But then life is always different from our preconceptions of it. In one's fevered vision, one sees a torso, carved from living stone, greyish, the hollows where the arms join it still smooth, the navel a mere dimple, the nipples very small, but dark and hard, as though they too have a part to play. The whole is a piece of priceless statuary, laid down flat, the theatre for some great statement by the artist. The world waits, tongue-tied.*
>
> *Outside, the storm is at its height, but all its fury cannot equal the tiniest part of the passion within. At festivals, statues were garlanded, libations poured over them, sacrifices of fire made before them, to placate the deity.*
>
> *Sharp bright strings, like garlands, fall across the torso, like African warpaint, light on a dark body. Which is louder now, the buffeting of the storm, eager to get in through the window again, or the groans of the spasm?*
>
> *Like grey fish-slime, the strings break down, coalesce, spread, filling up the little hollow. A young hand comes up and gently passes over the chest, fashions a glistening relief out of the sculpted flesh. To placate the deity. To heal."*

*

He opened the shutters the next morning. A spider had made the mistake of weaving its web across the gap, and now it dangled, unhoused, bewildered, a droplet in the sunlight, like the bead of saliva in the corner of André's mouth, as he turned over in his sleep.

I took one of his hands, as we sat last night, on Piers' bed. The hand was small, cool, dry. <André, have you made your *première communion* yet?>

'*Oui, monsieur.*' He immediately realised his mistake, and giggled. <I thought, for a moment, that you were the priest.>

<You know we went into that church, you lit a candle, and I asked you who it was for?>

<I already told you - for us.> A hint of truculence, now!

<Yes, but where was God in all that?> Surprised at my own restraint, I pulled the dressing-gown round him, to hide his nakedness, as once, long years ago, I did the same with Piers. <Was he in you, at the moment when you lit the candle?>

He shrugged, so I went straight to the point. <It seems you've got this strange old witch-doctor idea in your head that *seed* is some-how going to cure all your problems.>

He looked at me. <Not all my problems, just my asthma.>

<But how did you get hold of such a notion?>

<For me, sperm is white blood. D'you get it? There's red blood, of course, but white blood is special! And tell me, Roland, do negroes have black sperm?>

Black sperm? What a mind this boy has, so convoluted, as if, at his tender age, he's already dipped into the occult. He believes that semen can be a special curative substance. <André, I've already told you what it's for, what it can do. One day, you'll be old enough to find that out for yourself. It's not something *physical* that you need to help you now, but something spiritual.>

He turned his dark, solemn eyes on me. <What then?>

<You need – and I'll say it in English, - *the peace of God which passeth all understanding.*>

"He made me repeat it, lisping it after me with great concentration. I think that he understood, at last. And then, bless him, he went out like a light, with my arm round him. I kissed him, rubbed my face in his hair, offered up a special vote of thanks, then eased him in under his covers, and

tiptoed away.

I sit here, alone again (but, this time, <u>not</u> bereft), trying to make a proper start to my designs for Ariadne, but, like Aschenbach, inspired only when in the company of someone very special. I cannot be one of those self-contained artists who are both battery <u>and</u> lamp.

The storm has left a legacy of angry-looking clouds today, and, at my desk, I am conscious of a similar wan light, ages ago, when the telephone rang and woke me out of my long fairytale slumber. Providence showers me with riches. I think I have turned a corner with André: we understand and trust one another. I owe it to him to develop a more positive will, more integrity, and not let myself be guided by superstitious follies, nor be carried aloft, like a seed on the wind, accepting all and questioning nothing.

We have left it that, now he's out of the clinic and back with his mother, I'll see them twice a week. <u>He</u> was never in danger, I'm sure, but there were moments when <u>I</u> most certainly was. So, is it time to pull the shutters back down and send them all packing? It was easy at Wharnley, but no longer possible, here. I'm in a fix, my advisers have let me down, gone away, left me to try and sort myself out."

*

The Piers who made a second premature return, late at night and distraught, put me so much in mind of the choirboy in one of his rare moments of outburst with me, that I wondered if time was playing us tricks. Here was a situation which neither could as yet begin to handle: he, in torrents of tears, his body racked with sobs, I at first strangely detached and uninvolved in the jigsaw of his emotions, piecing it together slowly, but in a muddled, unchronological way, like the unwinding of the Dead Sea scrolls. From the many fragments, one saw him mouth a phrase, accompanied by a shudder: 'She called me a eunuch.'

Of course, a man can well understand that: the girl's tone of voice comes through all too strongly. I know about that so well, and the circumstances of it, the final shame, the ultimate humbling... And Piers, on the receiving end of that most bitter and punishing of insults, is shaken to the core, doubting everything about himself - not just that. Eunuch? A cruel word to fling at a boy's self-respect.

> *"He understands now, what betrayal feels like. He has no father to turn to, a mother he cannot talk to. I briefly abandoned him for Laurent, and he has been a dead loss with that girl. I tell him, gently, that he's possibly trying to live too fast, and remind him how far he has come, in five years.*
>
> *At Wharnley, after I made him promise to get married one day, I had a dream which ended in his coming back to me from the honeymoon, wretched, banished, <u>just like this</u>.*
>
> *I'm somewhat relieved to be just a bystander in this storm. I ply him with cognac, I am attentive, diplomatic, but (I cannot deny it) privately <u>triumphant</u>. He returns to me on the rebound, as it were, violently anti-women and anti-self. His body (which, after all, failed the test) now disgusts him. He's angry, frightened and (without knowing it) ineffably sweet in all his grief. He's so very intense. He'd cope much better if he weren't, but then he might not attract me so!"*

When he woke the next morning, it was with the beginnings of a doubt in his mind: if Piers was unable to sustain his erection with that girl, could *I* be in any way to blame for that?

At breakfast, he tried to jolly him along. 'Look, if you come off your bike, you just have to get back on again.'

'You mean, go with some other girl, and get the same result?'

'It's not very likely she's fallen out of love with you over that.'

'Roland, don't you see, that's all she was after? She uses boys.' You, of all people, should know about that!

'If she cares for you at all, she'll get in touch, like she did, the last time you came away.'

Piers shook his head in anguish. 'I don't want to hear her voice - I wouldn't believe her, even if she said sorry, again. I feel such a fool. Tricked. It's just like being robbed of all you have.'

Piers, you are tasting some of the medicine you gave me. As we take a turn round the garden, it is I who must attempt to offer you some therapeutic balm. Mr James looks over my shoulder at moments like these. 'I expect that Adèle wasn't angry with you alone. She was also blaming herself for not... conquering you.' Wasn't there defeat, too, in Fiona's scorn for me?

But he stops suddenly, and there is a savage look on his face. 'You tricked me, too. You made me believe it was all right with you, at Wharnley - all those things... Now I'm bloody well impotent. You've made me turn queer.'

It intrigues me hugely, that we have arrived at the same idea independently. 'You don't really believe that?' The least lame of the answers that come to mind.

'Christ, Roland, I'm not a little kid any more.'

'But surely, you're physically healthy, so it's - '

' - just a psychological bloody hang-up. Precisely.'

'These things can be talked out, you know.'

'Didn't work for you, did it? *You* can't do it with women. If I'd married her earlier, none of this would have happened.'

"In the moments of despair which come over him at ever-lengthening intervals - like all grief - he talks of chucking Cambridge in, says he's no good as a singer either. Sounds suicidal at times. I am keeping a close eye on him.

He's lost his springiness, his elation. He creeps about here like an old man. As the days wear on, and he hears nothing of her, his dejection visibly grows. With the aid of my big dictionary, he wrote a bitter letter, full of hurt and reproach, as well as horrible insults. I persuaded him to tear it up. He wants to phone her, but I somehow manage to overrule this too. I think he's beginning to see the reality of it at last: they just weren't compatible. He was blinded by her.

Apparently, Mme Bouillot discovered him, incoherent and bereft, and took him on as a mother would."

*

They often walked in the gardens, Piers now brooding, now querulous. 'Do you understand?' he kept asking Roland. 'I want you to understand.'

After a few days of this, his view of it all began to appear more dispassionate, without his ever letting go, for a single second. 'Roland, I've got to know this: am I bisexual or homosexual? You of all people should be able to tell. I need to know, if I'm going to live with myself any longer.'

I'm tempted to say that both sides are in everyone, that we spend too much time suppressing bits of ourselves - but it won't help him.

'Women don't understand about male desire, do they? They lure you on, get you all worked up, but then, if it doesn't go right, they pitch into you. I don't think I understand them, either.'

'So she led you on?'

'Her people weren't there, as I think you know, and there was an American film on TV about college boys and their girls. We had a drink, and then sort of got caught up in it.'

'She took the initiative?'

He was crimson.

'There's your clue, Piers. If you'd begun it, it would have ended differently.'

'I was scared of making her pregnant. We didn't take any precaution, you see. I didn't dare let myself go.'

He's relieved at having got all that off his chest! 'So your brain wisely called a halt.' (Faces revolve before my inward eye.)

"Are his inclinations are really manward? If he were to

be fixed up with the right sort of girl? But whatever would Mr James say to that? The boy's obviously still a virgin. I shouldn't want him to rush into another girl's arms when he's only just broken free of this one, and still smarting with the pain of it. I thought I was the only questor with troubles, believing that these teenagers drift in and out of relationships as if it were no more than a game, with nothing to touch the <u>soul</u>. But look at him – it's momentarily destroyed him. I'm glad I'm on hand, to help him through. (I would never have thought myself capable of that). It's a crisis akin to the end of the world to him, whereas I can take the calmer view.

Once in a while, I catch him looking at me with a hint of that grave sweetness of old, which suggests I'm doing him some good. For the very first time, I believe I'm treating him as a <u>person</u>, instead of plaything, chum, idol - I know not what.

And I'm <u>not</u> feeling guilty about the past any more. He's very special. There is no-one else in the world that it could have happened with. I cannot express, even to myself, what we were then - but it was marvellous, wonderful, like paradise. How could any of that have been harmful to him?

Today, he started up on the old tack: her parents liked him, they would put in a good word for him - or I could. 'God, somebody's got to help me!' was how he put it. But it subsided again, as I knew it would, like the moment of false hope that precedes the consumptive's operatic death. The finality of it weighs both of us down, stifling any suggestion as to how he might cope, this time."

*

When the worst was over, he began to regret some of his hastier actions, tearing up every last photo of her, and imploring Roland to take down that one on the landing of himself nude - too ashamed to be paraded in public any longer, like that. Roland called Adèle a pebble on life's path. To me, she was light, fragrant, quite unlike anyone else I'd ever known, but then she turned into an accusing, vindictive harpy. You can never really get to know another person. I know aspects of Roland, but mostly only what he lets me see. I asked him if I ought to get into a profession where a close relationship wasn't necessary. We talked about the priesthood, even about becoming a monk! He asked if I could manage poverty, chastity and silence. Me! (James would have said much the same).

*

'How can I best put it? All great art is flawed, because it is necessarily the fruit of a tortured genius, often inspired by perversion, degradation and despair: the scum on the top of the water.'

Piers cast a look around, hoping that all this wasn't being overheard or understood by the other customers of the wine-bar. He judged it best to pick up the challenge and join in the fencing match. 'Without a negative side to it, art probably wouldn't even exist - it wouldn't need to.'

'Very good,' said Roland. 'How dull a perfect universe would be.' When their talk moved to religion, he readily admitted that he'd only attended all those services because of Piers in his choir-stall opposite. 'Though I did believe that God might be on our side.'

'Don't you believe that any more?' Piers' eyes had regained something of their old brightness.

'Do you?'

'I don't think I know anything, any more... Can there be such a thing as an after-life? I wouldn't want a repeat of some of the things in this one!'

'If sin has to be punished,' said Roland gravely, 'there must be. Sinning down here ought to guarantee one an uncomfortable immortality.'

It's as if this young man and I are walking together in a timeless dimension of ripe cornfields. Another precious moment for me to seize upon!

But his expression has darkened. 'I'm sorry, Roland, but I'm about to spoil our nice evening. I can't stay in Geneva any longer.'

Fool that I am, I should have seen this coming: he hasn't got her now, so his remaining here loses all purpose, and our brave words about art and immortality are so much wasted breath. 'I understand, Piers. "Orphéon" was a kind of base camp to you, and now you don't need it.'

'It's not like that.' He looks embarrassed again.

'You don't like to say you have no further use for me, for fear of hurting my feelings.' I am suddenly on a knife-edge.

But he shakes his head. 'After the business with *her*, I simply can't stand being near where she is. Of course I'm still fond of *you*, despite - . I mean, if I weren't, I wouldn't have come back and got hurt, would I? Think I understand you better than ever, after what we've both just come through, and you seem to know me better than anyone else does. Though I think you're still rather innocent, Roland. I don't think you ever properly understood about boys.'

'No, I don't think I ever did.' I am perched on a cloud. Perhaps I didn't *want* to understand. But, by God, it doesn't stop me loving them!

'And I'm no good with girls.' The wine is bringing on another attack of self-pity. 'It's no good – I've drunk too much again!'

'Piers, there is just one thing which has been nagging at me, though it's nothing to do with recent events. You see, I learnt that you had something approaching a breakdown in the last days at Wharnley, when you were...' I shut up, because his face has gone crimson.

'Who told you that? Ah, I think I can guess. Bloody Fillingham. You must have seen him when you came to Cambridge.'

'I don't deny we bumped into each other. He was wearing the old school tie, and we reminisced.'

'About me?'

'About you and me.' I put it as gently as I can.

'Christ, Roland. You didn't tell him about our times together?'

'No. He'd spotted us, though, and worked out that I took you away for the Whitsun break.'

'And he will have made some nasty guesses about our motives and so on?'

'I don't think you need worry. He promised - '

'Promised not to blab? Has he asked you for money or favours, or whatnot?'

This is the crunch-point, which I have always been dreading. 'Look, Piers, he won't give us away. No-one else will do that. No-one else can possibly know how we were then.'

But he sits there, silently shaking his head. 'Why can't we bury all that, and be as we are now?'

This is the moment I have been waiting for. 'And why not? You talked of leaving Geneva. So… d'you remember my mentioning the Route des Grandes Alpes, the road from Évian to Nice?'

'Believe so.' He is slurring his words.

'Then what about it? The weather's fantastic. We could drive down.'

'But I'd be sponging on you again.'

'Rubbish! If we pack tomorrow, we can leave the next day at dawn.'

'Like two depser - , desperadoes!' There's a soppy grin on his face now.

We return to "Orphéon", where I make some very black coffee.

'There's a crescent moon.' Piers is looking out into the garden.

'Do you know how quickly it grows to full, from that tiny sliver? You can almost stand and watch it happen.'

'Good omen for our journey!'

"I almost told him about my full-moon rite in the garden, but didn't dare. It would almost certainly have shattered the fragile trust growing up again between us. My own clumsiness has wrecked so much in the past, for me and those around me. I fear, in my unstable moments, that I may end up as a totally negative force.

I loved the younger P for his attractive magnetism. We were just two lost souls growing together in mainly physical ways, because neither of us was ready yet for the other things. Now we can approach each other with a different, deeper kind of love.

If I write these words in a state of frenzied affection, I'm sure God will forgive me. After all, he made the miracle happen!"

VI.

Piers stuck his head in at the passenger window. 'Is it serious?'

'Brakes are always serious.' Roland had brought the Renault round to the front door, to begin loading. 'The fluid's been leaking. I'll get someone to come up.'

He'd told Piers to pack every last thing.

'But why? Shan't I be coming back?'

'You'll find out when we get to Nice.'

'But what about my return air ticket? Doesn't it go from here?'

'Too many questions!'

He went off to finish his packing, unable to shoo away the idea that Roland was trying to get rid of him. He hadn't forgotten that boy who called here when he was supposed to be out of the way. A plan began to form in his brain...

The mechanic arrived, fiddled about with the car, shook his head, then loaded it on to his *dépannage* trailer and drove it away.

They sat down with maps and guides. 'Can't begin at Thonon now,' said Roland, 'having lost half a day. Well cut a corner, and - '   'It won't mean we'll have to go through Annecy?'

But Roland reassured him. They had a light lunch, the car was returned, fit for service, and they started to load up.

'Adieu, then "Orphéon".'

Piers' air of wistful finality is more akin to André. 'Not "adieu". I trust you'll be coming here again?'

'Is Madame Bouillot around? I'd have liked to say goodbye to her. She's been very kind to me.'

'Ah yes, I nearly forgot. She's due any moment.'

When Piers came downstairs again, after checking that he had left nothing behind, Madame Bouillot's bicycle was leaning against the wall outside, and she was talking to Roland, as he attended to the car.

<Well, Monsieur Piers, *bonne route*. And do come back soon, won't you?>

He gave her a hug, Roland noticing with private amusement that she didn't mind. Then they drove away, raising the dust.

'How long will it take to get to Nice, now?'

'Probably till about this time on Thursday, if we don't have any more hold-ups.'

They drove towards the mountains through Sallanches and Megève, then began climbing between wooded hills.

'Are you used to mountain roads, Roland?' Piers had the atlas on his knees.

'I got us to the Bernese Oberland and back, didn't I?'

'Those were big. The one up to the Col des Saisies looks like a concertina'd caterpillar.'

This trip will be therapeutic for both of us. He is shot of that girl, and I shall be able, for a few days, to forget André and all his demands. Annecy carefully bypassed!

The sun hits us near the top of the col, and he shades his face with his hand. 'What are all those pylons and buildings for? Electricity?'

'No. Ski-lifts. The whole region comes alive in the winter.'

At the mention of skiing, Piers pulled a face.

Descending gingerly to Beaufort, they threaded through its busy streets. Roland noticed that Piers' hair was wet with perspiration. He grew it differently now, no longer the fluffy choirboy fringe, but a shorter style, rather Italian.

'Another curly little road coming up now, the Col de Méraillet. There's a big lake at the top.'

'Can you bear another col?'

'Of course. I'm fine.'

As they teetered round unprotected hairpin bends with lorries and coaches occasionally coming at them, they were within inches of death. Roland expected him to be more concerned than this. Perhaps the altitude affected one's judgment. At the sight of the Barrage de

Roselend in the late afternoon sunlight, Piers was a young boy again, leaping out with his camera, to snap the blue water of the lake and the huge rock towering over its east end, reducing them, the car, even the little chapel, to insignificance. Amid all this immensity, our own preoccupations and concerns go for virtually nothing. But I don't care any more, as long as he's with me.

'Did you realise, Roland, that the Italian frontier's only about ten miles away? I'll be qualified to write a guidebook to all this!'

'You ought to keep notes, or you won't remember where everything was when you see your photos.' When I am no longer on the scene.

'In my diary?'

'Why not?'

'Do you keep a diary, too?'

'I have been, recently.'

'Oh gosh. Am I in it?'

It's a bit much, expecting me to play verbal tennis and keep an eye on a road which seems hell bent on hurling us to our perdition. 'Well, arrivals, departures, that sort of thing.' What a liar I can be, when I choose!

They made a reasonably sedate descent into Bourg St. Maurice, where they inquired about rooms.

<You will not find anywhere here tonight, monsieur. We have our festival. I would advise you to look for somewhere in Séez. It isn't far.>

And so, as the sun was about to dip below a high ridge, they pulled up outside a hotel in the next village, and were immediately welcomed in. <A nice room, messieurs, with two beds and a shower.>

The dining-room being not quite ready to serve, they took their *apéritif* in the garden, watching the sky overhead darken, and the first stars begin to appear.

'You know, Piers, I think this trip's already doing us good.'

'The driving's hard on you. We did three passes today. If you add their heights together, it must be well up Everest!'

As we sip our drinks, lights start to go on in the hamlet, one of those rare tranquil moments to take and cherish, without any past or future attached. Both of us free, now, untrammelled.

As if their waiter sensed something in the air, the candle was lit on their table. Half-way through the main course, when an excellent red wine was easing their tongues, Piers began to get some things off his chest. 'Friendship isn't so all-consuming, is it? With love, you can't see anything at all. If you're just friends with someone, it allows you to stand back and see them properly.'

He is trying to please me and neutralise me at one and the same time. I am pleased, but I am far from neutralised. How could I be? I just wish I had the courage, here and now, to tell you how I once lived for every moment with you, wanted nobody else in the world but you. Now you can view these things more dispassionately, (a faculty which has always been denied me.) What you need is to be friends with a succession of girls, until the love thing bites you again. You've had your baptism of fire.

'Before I met Adèle, sex just wasn't real at all, but it jolly well became real with her, even if it didn't work out. I understand it better now.' He stopped in confusion. 'Hope you don't mind me saying these things.'

I try to make a suitable face, not knowing what to think or mind, at this moment.

'Roland, what sort of girl do you think would be best for me?'

Quelle question! 'One who could at least give you something in return for your affection, and not just take everything.'

'Oh but - ' he begins, then stops. 'Well, I suppose you're right about her. I misjudged them rather badly. I was blinded by their... opulence, if that's the right word.'

'Their taste was not quite *moi*, I have to say.'

'Roland, they *had* no taste. It was all done to impress.'

I raise a finger. 'But isn't that very French?'

'How can you live among all that?'

'I don't normally mix with such people.'

'Sorry if I made you.'

'Oh, it was quite eye-opening, especially when Calivet favoured me with his advice. On one occasion, he even suggested I might sell some of my drawings in Paris". I imagined myself squatting among the *bouquinistes* by the Seine.'

This makes him choke with mirth, and I reach across and tap him on the back. Will your mother thank me for rescuing you, I wonder? The moon, still an imperfect circle, rises, flooding the street outside with its light. Let me frame this moment for eternity, with the candlelight dancing in a pair of dark, liquid eyes opposite.

'Are you OK, Roland?'

'Surely. Why not?'

'You just wiped your brow. And you've been giving me such an odd look.'

It must be the heat... that rouses passions so readily. 'Piers, I want you to tell me something about that time when we were up in the snow at Jungfraujoch. Did I... call anything out?'

'Such as what?'

My stupidity erases a delicious moment, and I am dumb.

Piers leans forward, looking at me under his brows, half amused, just as he sometimes did from his choir stall. 'Come on. You know you can say anything to me. After all, it wouldn't have been a banality, like "don't slip in the snow".'

I think you know what it was. My forced quietness belies the storm raging inside me. I dare to reach across and take one of his hands in mine.

He doesn't pull it back, but keeps those burning eyes fixed on me, while his lips frame the oft-repeated formula: 'I love you'. The light voice wavers a little, and I know that, in taking the words out of my mouth, Piers is not merely quoting, but reiterating the ancient truth which neither of us has so far dared to utter. To confirm it, he puts his other hand over mine. He's not even qualifying it any more, not adding 'in a purely platonic way, of course.' He, whom I once so desired and won, has found himself at last. My earlier possessive-ness shames me now, but it was, after all, merely an aspect of my love for him. Piers, you are still my sole heir. I never changed my Will, though you urged me to. And we are still both married to each other, but I shall not embarrass you by alluding to that now. A different tack, then: 'I don't think you ever let out the real reason why you came in pursuit of me.'

He looked surprised, but did not take his hand back. 'I think I've finally got that worked out: I wanted to know if our relationship had only been physical on both sides. It mostly was for me, you see.'

'On my side, the whole thing deepened when I realised you were no ordinary pre-adolescent. You do understand that I couldn't have entered into it like that if you'd been just any kid?' My lips are almost too benumbed by the alcohol to utter the words, but my brain is remarkably clear.

The waiter comes to take our plates, we release one another's hands and sit back like two chastened schoolboys.

'You haven't really changed, Roland. You're still the same warm man I knew five years ago. I've changed a lot, though I've still got a long way to go. I really did love her, you know, and I believe I'm capable of that again. Mine for you is different. Sounds inconsistent, perhaps, but you can get a new love without letting go of the old, can't you?'

'Of course.' You are leading me through a garden of delights.

'So…' He's whispering now, just like André. 'Shall we forgo the dessert?'

There, at long last, in Cambridge-type language, is the coded invitation, and we go upstairs together like two club members who, well in their cups, clasp each other for support. Some other guests stare, but nothing is said.

Like a shy girl about to give herself, he slips into the bathroom and comes back, smelling of toothpaste. Piers, that's how it used to be, when you came out of the school in your black polo-neck sweater and climbed into my car. And that morning at the cottage, when you came sliding into my bed. Now, again, adventure is afoot…

It seemed fitting that the one should undress the other and that, in the hot shower, they should soap each other. Roland was praying hard that one (or both) of them would not go out like a light in the middle of it all. Then they rubbed each other down with rough towels and stepped into the bedroom, both panting, red, aroused like stallions ready for the mare. Who did I last share a shower with?

One of the beds was rolled across so that they could lie side by side in comfort. At first, they were tentative, shy. Then Roland took the initiative and planted a gentle kiss on Piers shoulder, another, more boldly, on his chest, a third on his forehead and the fourth squarely on his mouth. Piers flung his arms around him, ground their faces and mouths together, and, buffeting him with an animal ferocity, bit into his shoulder. Hands sought, found, fondled, were anointed with pearly droplets. Their breaths mingled, their hot and heady whispers fused.

It is vital for him to prove he can get it right, sustain it all the way. I am, as before, his mentor: with my legs up over his shoulders, I guide him in. Now, as he makes it amid gasps, I receive the fruits of his lusting into my bowels, a libation indeed, fit for the gods. The moon smiles down on us and our Bacchanalian revels!

He bursts into tears, buries his head in my chest. I feel my heart pounding. What is it? Remorse? Shame?

'Thank you, Roland. Bless you.'

It is his initiation, and I am anxious not to steal any of his thunder. 'It's all right, Piers, old love, you can just finish me off.' Brought to its ferment by his cool, dry hand, the ejaculation is superb, the cabinet of memories now totally unlocked.

'We'll have to shower all over again!' chortled Piers. And they did.

When they were lying on the beds, totally relaxed, Roland said 'Do you remember what you used to call "big game"? When did you first manage it?'

Amazingly, Piers blushed. 'Well, the old wet dream, to start with. Just happened when I was almost fourteen, but... no need to dwell on all that now. It's so much better with two, isn't it?'

'Did you ever do it with anyone else?'

'No, never could do that. Well, I'd already had some dry runs with you... And how about your first time?' It slipped out before he realised, as if they'd been comparing some wholly innocent experiences.

'I was a bit of a prodigy in that regard. It first happened when I was eight.'

'*Eight?*' Piers' face was incredulous.

'During the blitz, when the bomb hit our house and buried us, I was terrified. Thought I'd wet my pyjamas, but it was different. Mother took me to a doctor, and he said it had been brought on by fear, and that I was producing sperm very prematurely anyway. I made the mistake of confiding it to someone at my boarding school, and from then on they regarded me as a bit of a freak.'

'Bloody awful places, public schools,' said Piers.

'But if you hadn't gone to choir school, we would never have met or gone to the cottage together. And we wouldn't be here now, like this.' To my great relief, he hasn't mentioned that boy Fillingham again.

'Roland, thank you for tonight. For the first time in my life I feel truly liberated. It won't have to be another five years before we meet again, will it? Suppose I hadn't rung you?'

I would have been in purgatory for life.

They fell asleep in each others' arms.

*

He woke with a dry mouth. I must be having one of my strange heads: the wallpaper, in true French fashion, marches its spidery flowers up the walls and across the ceiling. Where is this, Dol de Bretagne? And who is this naked youth asleep next to me, with his arm across my equally bare chest?

He nearly shot up into the air. No dream at all. Ye gods, Piers on a plate! He and I, at last, and all my dearest ambitions realised. Well, almost all. I brush his shoulder with my lips. His skin is very cool. I pull a cover over us. It's dawn, and the most wonderful, wonderful moment.

I hope he'll feel at ease about it when he wakes up. I don't want him to be shocked at himself, at us both, or reproach me for getting him drunk and taking advantage of him. After all, it was he who brought me up here, he who took me, as a lover eagerly takes a girl.

How will it be now, between us? Will he merely chalk this up to experience, and go his own way? Will we not even allude to it, when we sit at the breakfast table over *croissants* and coffee? Will English reserve put the dampers on the whole business?

I need never lose him, not while both of us are walking this earth. I need to be able to set beacons of hope across our future, to know that we shan't ever be spiritually apart, that we shall keep regular contact, even if not under the same roof, nor in the same bed.

I didn't think I had any claim upon you, but I can adapt that now, Piers. Last night you gave me proof that our relationship is two-sided and very, very special. What would Mr James say to all this? *Would you godfather him?*

So my boy had to find out something vital about himself and me, and he has, here in a French hotel bedroom, as well as *chez* Calivet. He has discovered what I always wanted for him, always suspected: he is stamped, and was so, even before we ever met. Oh, how easy it is to know, but how hard to admit it, come to terms with it. You, lying there, are not the young boy I once knew. We can now share all these experiences as man with man.

He drifted back to sleep.

*

When he opened his eyes to find himself naked beneath the bedclothes next to Roland, and the events of last night began to return like fragments falling back out of the sky after an explosion, he could not help a smile of triumph. I'm not impotent, and I've proved it to us both. Does it matter so much that it was with another man? No, its very *modern*, and even accepted. I now know what normal is – it's doing what you think is appropriate, whoever it's with. Roland and I made love, it was splendid, and there's no need for either of us to worry about it. I've made the breakthrough, but I'm no longer shocked or turned off. Might even permit a return match, that is, if I'm around for one. It rather looks as if he's trying to bundle me out again. Did my subconscious tell me to seduce him, so that he would be sure to keep me?

Then he remembered Adèle, and his elation was momentarily punctured. What would she have thought about this? That her worst suspicions were confirmed? She hurt me badly, and, in a way, what I did last night was to pay her back, *and* Roland, for going with that other boy. No, because I do love him, I wanted to show him properly, as a distillation of all I've ever felt for him. It doesn't have to mean that I'm queer. I can well understand why he doesn't care for labels.

When I think how much he wanted us to come together like that. It broke his final seals of reserve, just as it broke mine. Poor old Roland, eating your heart out for me, all that time - and I wouldn't let you within reach, though there were plenty of opportunities. That double bed at Lauterbrunnen: I think that the naughty little devil inside me made me engineer that one - there *were* other rooms free! And he was terrified, I know.

What am I going to tell James? I'm sure he used to think Roland and I were lovers, ex-lovers, I know not what. I still get a funny feeling inside, remembering how much I, a mere choirboy in a surplice and ruff, wanted him. It's stupid to think that life has to be lived in watertight compartments, such as: "I'm hetero, so there - stand back, don't touch me!" Poor old Roland. No wonder he's been adrift with his neuroses. Maybe I was to blame for that. We'll be able to talk about it all, now.

*

'Thought it easier to order breakfast,' said Piers, as the tray was brought in, the young waiter blushing when he saw the two beds pushed together. 'I was afraid that, if we ate downstairs, people might look.'

'Why should they? How could they possibly know?'

'I shouted out, didn't I? You had to put your hand over my mouth!'

'Piers, don't make light of it. It was beautiful. We won't just walk away from it and pretend it didn't happen, will we?' We may be a touch lighthearted now, but that's just to mask the much deeper level behind it. When you woke up just now, the astonishment in your face was swept away by the sort of loving look I remember so well from our time at the cottage. We've had a very long courtship, but it has paid off. And this is exactly how a honeymoon should be: no champagne, just closeness.

'No, Roland, we won't.'

'How about...' I pause, aware of the daring on the end of my tongue. 'How about your coming to live at "Orphéon" later on? Base yourself, and work from there.' So that we can always be together. I'll chase the others away...

He pours me some coffee. 'That's very kind of you, and don't think I'm ducking out, but I must try to make my own way for a bit.' Seeing my face, he clasps me round the shoulder. 'You do understand? Besides, if we went back now, we'd never get this marvellous tour finished, and I so much wanted to see Nice.'

'I meant after you've finished your studies.'

'I know, I know. I was just ribbing you.'

He's as high as a kite this morning. 'Look, Piers, this is important. You mustn't discount girls. Don't forget that I nurture a secret ambition to be godfather to one of your children.'

He stops eating. 'Do you still mean that?'

'Yes, I do.'

'But... is that compatible with...?'

'As far as I'm concerned, it's perfectly compatible with anything you care to mention.' I put my arms out, hugging him to me.

'Roland have you ever let anyone else do that to you?'

Of course he would ask me that, just as he peppered me with searching questions at Wharnley, and I, in my typically complacent way, wasn't prepared. 'Well...'

'The truth!'

'Not much, and it never meant anything. The truth, as I've already told you, is that nobody has ever matched you in my affections.'

'That Laurent cove...'

He really sticks in your gullet! 'Forget him. I sinned, I was punished. You banished him for ever, and a good thing too.'

'And... Filly? Cos he's one, too, and you did meet him.'

Now its my turn to blush. 'Nothing at all to report in that department.' What a liar you are, Millan!

'Then we were both virgins when we came together last night?'

Yes, Piers, if you are in the business of redefining such words.

'And we consummated what we began at Wharnley?'

'That's right.' His seriousness brings me to heel.

'So this is a proper sort of honeymoon?'

Roland heaved a deep sigh. 'Piers, I never dared to hope for this.' He hadn't meant to break down, but the sediment of all the shameful, empty years had been stirred up, and was now being leached out of him. Purification, both joyful and painful at the same time. A process had had its beginnings, but was far from spent.

Now it was Piers who gripped him tightly, rocking him as one would do to comfort an upset child. 'I'll look after you, Roland. We'll look after each other.'

As they packed their things into the car in the brilliant sunshine, a priest walked past and nodded at them. In a trice, Piers had thrust his camera into the man's hands, and put an arm round Roland's shoulder. 'We haven't got one of both of us together, have we?'

The *abbé* clicked the button, handed the camera back without a word, and passed on.

'If he only knew, Roland! Hey, I don't think I ought to become a priest, do you?' There was devilry in his face.

We have changed so much since we arrived here yesterday. Is it just the heady air that makes you fling yourself into my arms? Why are we going on southwards? Because, damn it, I've arranged something at the other end, a commitment to be honoured, which ruins any chance of our going back to St. Julien and building on what we have now rediscovered in each other. I just hope that you will forgive me...

*

He had to concentrate hard on the road up to Val d'Isère, with its tunnels, lorries and roadworks, the dust casting a pall over every-thing. Thirty kilometres of arduous stuff but, in the company of this new, affectionate Piers, hardships were of no consequence. They were within sight of the huge dam in very good time.

'Look at that face they've painted on it! Looks like Elvis. The French put up some pretty strange monuments, don't they?'

'Perhaps they'll put up one to us some day.' There was a time, (only hours ago), when I would never have spoken my thoughts like that.

Over coffee at Val d'Isère, Piers had one of his more serious moments. 'How will it be from now on? Will we be able to see each other quite regularly?'

Virtually the same question as the one he put to me, at the end of our week in the cottage near Wharnley. 'It's what I most want, but I mustn't be an encumbrance to you.'

'And I mustn't keep on taking from you, all the time.'

If you were my son, I'd be supporting you, but you are much, much dearer than family could ever be.

Light of heart, they drove on up the Col de l'Iséran, and found some patches of snow. The road narrowed, became steeper and more twisting.

'Like a fairground ride gone barmy,' said Piers. 'Gosh, it's over nine thousand feet at the top of this. The guide says it's the highest.'

He stopped the car in one of the hairpin bends.

They climbed out, and Piers pulled a sweater from his bag, for the wind was chill even in the brilliant sunshine. Roland took a picture of him. Rollneck sweater - *ça fait beau garçon*!

All around them, vast grey cliff faces towered up, streaked with a snow which coalesced on the tops into the beginnings of glaciers. No trees were visible, just patches of coarse grass amid the rocks.

'So it was worth doing the Route des Grandes Alpes?'

'It's not over yet,' said Piers. 'And besides, I'm looking forward to Nice. Don't forget Nice.'

Oh, I shan't, I assure you. Nor, when you get there, will you.

'Doesn't this remind you of the surface of the moon? Like those pictures they sent back, - you know, with the astronauts kicking up the dust.'

'It's a lot starker than my area,' said Roland, to whom all this seemed like a giddy film unrolling before his consciousness.

'You've got two homes over here now.'

'So I have.'

'May I come and stay at Courtils when its finished?'

'It's nearly finished already. Of course you can. But Piers...'

'What?' There was a sudden alarm in his face as he stood there, the wind tugging at his sweater and jeans as if it was trying to tear them from him.

'I repeat something I said to you earlier on. I have no claim upon you. We are both free spirits. We can - '

'We can be free spirits together, can't we? You aren't going to tire of me, are you?'

'Never, never!'

I suspect you did once, but this is not the time to disinter that. 'D'you know, Roland...?'

Piers' intensity and attack were battering him as much as the wind.

'If we were like Rimbaud and Verlaine, we'd spend all our time having what my French tutor calls "lovers' tiffs", because the one or the other was constantly having partners outside the relationship. But *we* needn't be like that, need we?'

Oh my God, André doesn't count as a *partner*, surely? As we regain the shelter of the car, I admit to him some of the pain I felt about his seeing that girl.

This makes him throw back his head. 'You were incredibly jealous. Some of the things you said. But then I was jealous of that lout I made bite the dust. So we're quits, *n'est-ce pas*?'

I hastily agree, knowing that it is yet another of my precious lies. Anything, to keep the peace.

As they began the perilous descent to the Arc valley, Piers declared he was ravenous. 'D'you suppose it's the altitude or the sex?'

'I expect it's both,' he said, seeing the humour in it.

The squat huddle that was Bonneval came into view far below. At last, they reached the flat-bottomed valley, and stopped by the church. It was soon apparent that there was nowhere they could eat, so they drove on down the valley in broiling heat to Lanslebourg, where they found lunch on a hotel terrace .

'Winter sports place,' said Piers. Did you notice how quickly we left the snow behind? Moments later, he asked where they would be sleeping that night.

'Another room with flowers all over the ceiling, I expect.'

'A double bed, this time? After all, we do have something to finish...' Roland's coloured up!

You once told me, in your piping treble voice, that you'd do anything for me. *Anything.* But, in those days, you didn't really understand what that meant. Now, Piers, we're in business at last.

Outside Modane, a huge stone fortress with red-tiled roofs tumbled down the mountain-side to greet them. 'Piers, are you sure you want to go through with this? If we carry straight on here, the road goes to Albertville and then Annecy in no time.' He knew that there were three or four escape roads on their route.

'Annecy? Stuff that for a lark,' his passenger said vehemently. 'Let's say we've passed the point of no return. OK?'

Their little road to the Col du Télégraphe hoisted them out of the Arc valley, but Roland seemed inured to these sinuous roads and precipices. 'How high's this one?'

'Oh, a mere five thousand feet, but the next is nearly nine thou again. We'll be making for Briançon.'

Between the two cols, they stopped at a hotel opposite the church and drank coffee on a cool terrace.

'Would you be doing all this if you were on your own, Roland?'

'What would be the point?'

In the gloom of the church, they held hands, and, as if an electrical charge passed between them, a recorded snatch of piping treble voice filled the space. Piers gently withdrew his hand and looked at Roland. 'I had to sing that, once.'

'Schubert?'

'Yep. The *Agnus Dei* from the *Mass.*'

'Do you like it?'

'I really can't be doing with that stuff any more, I obviously don't fancy being in a chorus, and I'm not very attracted to consorts. Is there any room in art for a swimmer against the tide?'

'Of course there is. I've always been one, myself. But it would make your career as a soloist very much harder, because, unless you're good enough to state your own terms, the offers would start to dry up if you kept turning down the ones you didn't want.'

'I've toyed with the idea of teaching, but I'm sure it's not me at all.'

'You be and do just what's really you. I can help you over the first few hurdles, if you'll let me.' In fairness, I don't ignore Guy's little proddings.

Snaking up out of the grassy lower slopes, the road scaled the débris-strewn scarp, in all its grey, sere inhospitality. They stopped at the top of the pass, to stand in the icy wind and inspect a hovel selling sheepskins and souvenirs. Roland suddenly staggered and sat down where he stood.

'You OK?' Piers too was short of breath.

'We're not used to this. If we stayed high up in the mountains for long enough, we'd get acclimatised.' *Why do other, delectable faces come crowding in on me? André, that youth Fillingham, even those disreputable brothers, Laurent, Raoul... Have I no proper concept of loyalty and fidelity?*

The road forward involved many hairpins, and views of a glacier to their right. At length, they joined the main road from Grenoble, passed through a tunnel and continued the long descent. In the hamlets, the older chalets had painted tin roofs.

'Look! said Piers, 'there's the citadel.' They were reaching a town bathed in the evening sunlight. To the east hung a perfect moon, which Roland privately registered as an omen.

They left the car outside the old walls and went in through a gate, tired, hot, not wanting to be confronted by any problems. After the second hotel had turned them away, they held a brief council of war in the old main street.

'Bloody puritans,' said Piers. 'They don't want two men in the same room, let alone the same bed!'

In the end, they secured a room each in hotels a couple of hundred yards apart. Though Roland tried to pass it off lightly, the evening was ruined. Indeed, their whole trip suddenly looked like ending in disaster. They ate in a restaurant on neutral ground, as Piers put it glumly, and then went for a stroll.

'We've managed to be devoid of people so far, Roland, and we have to come to a place that's swarming.' He was about to add 'Why don't we just drive off and have a private moment somewhere remote?' But caution stayed his tongue.

Roland went back with him to his hotel room. 'We're both exhausted by all this switchback stuff,' he said gently.

'Do you mean emotionally?'

'Perhaps that as well.' He clasped Piers to him. 'Goodnight, old love.' The sounds of people in the corridor outside inhibited any real closeness.

He went back to his own hotel, feeling sick and punished. Walking the ramparts with Piers, he had seen a van scurry past below, with one name painted in large letters on the side: "André". The walls of St. Malo... What day is it? When did I say I'd phone? Did I promise to phone? In the last twenty-four hours, everything has been turned on its head. My future, if God is good to us, will be centred firmly around Piers, so where does that leave André now? He remembered that he had to let Nice know when they expected to arrive - all being well. How will Piers take it? Do I prepare him for what's going to happen? I daren't, I cannot. He and I both have our streak of cowardice. That's something else which draws us together.

*

'Didn't like being separated from you, last night.' Piers' preoccupation came to the surface as they headed up the Col de l'Izoard.

'Nor did I.'

'Ironic, isn't it, that we're forced apart just when we most want to be together?'

'We'll have plenty of chances in the future, Piers. When we started on this trip, neither of us dreamed how it would turn out.'

'You didn't plan it then?'

'I certainly didn't!'

'I've been a bit mixed up. Thought I was going to spend the rest of my life living by a tribal code, when I should have been looking instead at personalities.'

'So you're not shocked by us?' A very straight question, for such a crooked road!

'Shocked? Why should I be? Hell, no. We are us, and that's special. We express all that in the ways that we can. I couldn't stop thinking about it all, last night - Wharnley too.'

'You were a very passionate boy then.'

'And I still am, even more so,' he laughed. 'Only, this is the last place in the world to be passionate in.'

They had reached the stele at the summit of the col. '2361 metres,' said Piers, as he got out. 'That's... not far off eight thousand feet.'

Roland reached for his anorak, wondering how the boy would survive this in his skimpy shorts.

'That building down there is the Réfuge Napoléon. Looks a bit like a railway station, doesn't it?'

We once had an agonised parting at the Gare de Cornavin...

They stood for a short while admiring the view, until Piers, shaking with cold, dashed back into the car.

'Do you want a rug?'

'Much rather have a h-hug. Hold me t-tight for a moment.' His teeth were chattering so much that he could hardly speak.

But a coach came up and stopped near them. Children's faces peered curiously out of the windows. 'Oh lor, *voici toute la bloody France* again,' said Piers in disgust.

Roland drove away and turned on the heater. 'I don't think there's a single remote place left on this earth.'

Their road wound past oddly-shaped rocks, and then began to drop into a valley with fir-trees growing in it. The morning sun cheered up the stark mountains looking down on them from both sides, as they negotiated the hairpins.

'Good thing you got the brakes seen to.'

Even as he spoke, they both felt a bump behind them, and Roland pulled in. The offside rear tyre was almost flat.

'Got a pump?'

'Of course. Give me a hand.'

Piers pumped vigorously. 'Don't think it's making any difference!'

'We'll have to get it seen to in Guillestre,' said Roland, checking the pressure. 'I'm not into changing wheels.'

With the loss of height, the implacable heat embraced them again. Perhaps his colourful shorts are right, after all.

'Would we have got to Nice today?'

'No, but I've already arranged for us to get there tomorrow.'

'Then where will we spend tonight? Not Guillestre? It's much too soon.'

'Bound to be a hotel somewhere on the way. And I promise you that we shan't be separated this time.'

Piers stared at the atlas and then at him, but said nothing.

Guillestre, a cramped little town with narrow streets, was a welcome sight until they realised that it was midday and most things were shut, including the garage. An old woman dressed in blue and wearing a headscarf told them they would find the owner in the bar opposite.

A few minutes later, having persuaded the man to fix the tyre as soon as he was ready, they were sitting at a table under a huge sunshade outside a restaurant. The terrace was full, but they had managed to get the last table. Most people seemed to be young mixed couples, making a lot of noise and evidently enjoying themselves.

Piers scowled. 'Seeing these so-called civilised people stuffing their faces puts it in context, doesn't it? I mean, it's not just the sense of achievement in chalking up two or three really arduous passes in a day, it's the totally different world up there. It may be bare and unwelcoming, but it's pure. I can begin to understand why people climb mountains. You feel free for the first time. You've done something. And then you come back down, and find the stupid old materialistic rat-race again, all around you.'

I have never heard him so philosophical!

'When you get back home, Roland, will you paint a picture of us, in the mountains?'

It was too hot to eat properly, and they returned to the garage where the owner, true to his word, was repairing the tyre. <Are you going far, *messieurs?*>

'Jusqu'à Nice,' said Piers, with pride.

<But not today, surely?> The mechanic paused to look at his watch. <It's a good stretch from here.>

<I know,> said Roland quietly. <Which route would you recommend?>

<Take the Col de Vars to Barcelonette, then the Col de la Cayolle

and the Gorges de Daluis. *C'est joli, ça.* In this way you avoid the worst road. A man only goes via the Bonette if he is well in with the angels!>

It was past four when they set off again, almost dead with the heat. The road to Vars quickly whisked them up a thousand feet and then, by the time they reached the little settlement, another thousand.

'This is better,' said Roland. 'You can breathe up here.' He suddenly remembered André and his asthma.

'It's the effect of these shady woods. And doesn't it smell different?'

'Southern. You feel you're getting away from the grim northern world of toil...'

'... into the land *"wo die Zitronen blühen".'*

'Let me guess. Have you just quoted Goethe? He came to Switzerland, like Byron.'

'Got it in one. Roland... Was Byron really bisexual?'

'It certainly looked like it.'

'Do you think being that helped him to write his poetry?'

They had passed another Réfuge Napoléon, and had got out at the top of the Col de Vars to admire a panorama of mountain upon mountain.

I have no doubt of it, knowing myself and my art so well, and the way they interact.

'I asked you the other day if you thought I was bisexual, and you parried it. But I sort of am, aren't I? It doesn't matter, does it?'

'No. The important thing is to be honest with yourself. Don't be afraid to live.' My last vestige of guilt vanishes!

'I've come to realise that, when we first got to know each other, it wasn't just physical. There was something else, infinitely better. You once told me that love is much wider than sex. But having sex with someone is like reaffirming vows, isn't it?'

'Is it allowed to be enjoyable, too?'

Piers laughed. 'Of course. Why else would we do it?'

They crawled down the steep and tortuous south side of the col, and by the time they reached the valley of the Ubaye, it was in deep shadow. Barcelonette was a disaster: because of a cycle race, they were told, every last room was booked up. Nor would the nearby mountain resort of Sauze be able to take them. It was sticky and stuffy in the town.

'I think we're best off up on a mountain,' said Roland.

'When we came through that little place before here, there was a sign to Nice off to the left.'

'Well, why not? It's sure to be a more direct road, and we'll manage, Piers. Just leave it to me.'

They doubled back, and began to climb at once up a road which, after the first few miles, shrank almost to nothing, at a clutch of hairpin bends. The sun gilds the peaks to our left, throwing deep shadows everywhere else, and I recall the moment in *Death in Venice* where Aschenbach said: *"If all the world had gone and only we two were left"*. Utter contentment, the two of us all alone here, on the roof of the world.

But Piers was looking at him. 'You do realise there won't be any hotels this way for ages, and it's getting dark all the time? You won't be able to do the next col by night. It's the Bonette, the highest of the lot.'

Roland smiled at his English concern. 'I know. In fact, I wasn't planning to cross it tonight. I thought we could - '

' - camp out?'

'Why not? It's going to be a fine night.'

'But we haven't got sleeping bags or food or anything.' Piers fell into a moody silence, while Roland eased the car on higher, glorying in his new feeling of superiority.

More hairpins, throwing them this way and that, until they suddenly emerged into a great basin, a tranquil little lake set in its floor. No trees, hardly any grass, just grim rocks taunting their human fragility. The road wound on past the tarn, climbing towards the far lip, but Roland drove off it to a flat spot overlooking the expanse of water. 'This will do us fine.'

Piers shook his head, but said nothing. Roland glanced at him with a quick, half-humorous look, got out and went round to the back of the car. 'We have blankets here, and pillows, and a good big groundsheet, and my incomparable housekeeper has packed us a hamper with food and drink.'

At the eastern edge of the mighty bowl, the full moon was just coming up into view.

'I told you not to worry. We shall have some light as well.'

Piers came over and put a strong arm round him. 'Sorry I was such a softy. Look, it's the very picture I asked you to do. Pure magic!'

Roland hugged him tightly and dropped a kiss on his brow. 'You are most definitely psychic and, unless I'm mistaken, your stomach's rumbling. *Mangeons*!'

Madame Bouillot's hamper contained home-made pastries, tinned *pâté*, bread, wine, cheese, beer and fruit. The beer was put in the lake to cool, and they attacked everything else.

'This is great!' shouted Piers, and they were both momentarily alarmed when a distant voice answered identically. He let out some Red Indian calls, and they listened as the sound bounced off the rocks, seeming to reverberate all round their huge amphitheatre. 'I bet the Romans did plays here. Wouldn't it be just right for an opera, Roland? Can you imagine *Aida* up here?'

If this place is the crater of a defunct volcano, then what is boiling inside me would outdistance any seething lava. He's still wearing those brightly-coloured shorts, though it's getting cooler and, apart from the moon, nearly dark now.

They ate in great contentment in their solitude. When they had finished, Piers got up, threw off his clothes and, like a white wraith, stepped down into the lake.

'Is it freezing?'

'Not bad. Why don't you come on in?'

The moonlight had advanced to the floor of the immense arena, and was scattering bright droplets across the surface of the water. Rocks, ghostly in their pallor, threw deep black shadows. Far above, a distant hum and a tiny flashing light betrayed a passing plane, unnecessary token of civilisation left behind. Not even a goat was to be seen or heard here. The bowl was its own desert, secretive, con-spiratorial.

Or was this really a stretch of the Moon's surface, illuminated by the sickly light of the fickle, foolish Earth? What had happened to gravity up here, where one became giddy and unsteady? Why was the air so thin, making one gasp and struggle for breath?

Far off, a pinpoint of light moved slowly down from the top of the crater, as if a shepherd were out still with a torch, looking for his sheep.

Too smooth to be in a man's hand, it dipped down and approached, became two lights at a fixed distance apart. The whine of the engine filled the bowl, rousing echoes in the darkness. Suddenly, the beams picked out two pale bodies writhing together, seemed to hold them for an eternity. But then oblivion returned, the lights swept on their way, and the noise of the car was lost among the rocks.

The lava boils, not under me but in me. It collects like a flood, ready to surge forth and destroy the world. He, beneath my body, moans but will not stop me now. As I thrust myself into him, the other faces reappear, to mock me: Raoul, André, Laurent, Keith... But no: Piers, this is for you. I am fulfilled at last. His face is wet. 'Did I hurt you?'

'No, it's just that I came at the same time. I had no idea it could work like that.' Piers rubbed his hand across his stomach, making it glisten like oil in the moonlight, like fish slime.

They dipped again in the now icy water of the lake, as if performing a sacrifice. Then, trembling, they got into some clothes and huddled together under the blankets.

'I can see you in the moonlight, *mon beau garçon!*'

Piers began to sing an ancient French lullaby, but very softly, so as not to reawaken the echoes (which, at the moment of their climax, had chattered back at them like a swarm of devils.)

Late on in the night, when the moon had crossed almost to the opposite rim, two motorbikes passed by, their echoes rising to a crescendo, and then dying away. That was all.

*

In the tender grey light of morning, Roland raised his head from the pillow. Piers' tousled head is next to mine; I even have the warmth of his body against mine. I want this moment to last for ever.

Bright fingers of light are beginning to flare up from behind the eastern ridge, and still he sleeps. Bless this place called Restefond. It has witnessed an act of true marriage. On a morning like this, you once came leaping into my bed. Never had I known such a welcome bedfellow! I now know that I need never have been ashamed of us, nor of what we were, even then. The love between us obliterates all else, just as the rising sun is chasing the shadows away, filling our great cup as though its light were water from the lake. If I ever believed that darkness could be victorious, here is my proof to the contrary.

But then came a thought to sober him: we get to Nice today, back to the hot, weary world and all its problems. How will that turn out, I wonder?

'Hallo, Roland. I dreamt I was sleeping by a pond, and I jolly well am! Just look at that sunrise.'

Over the remains of the food (they drank water from the lake), Roland, almost paralysed by a sudden shyness, asked Piers if he was all right.

Piers took one of his hands and kissed it. 'I feel like a novice. In the last few days, I've learned things I never thought to experience like this.'

'I'm glad we weren't disturbed here.'

'I wouldn't have cared if Napoleon had come over with all his army and his elephants.'

'The elephants were Hannibal's,' laughed Roland.

'Oops, so they were... I did think there could have been a firework display afterwards, one of those really spectacular ones.'

'I should have brought some.'

'Roland...'

He already feared the question in Piers' face.

'You really won't ever reject me, now that we've..?'

'I swear!'

'By *les pierres de Restefond*!'

Roland picked up two pebbles. 'I swear by these stones that I will always, always be faithful to you.' Even if I do not really understand what that word means. His voice broke at the end, and he handed a pebble to Piers, who solemnly looked at it and put it in his pocket.

'What I like about here is its space. D'you know what I mean? Something I've always desperately wanted, but never had, because I spent my youth being herded around with a lot of other kids.'

'I know exactly what you mean. Perhaps we need to get away from others because we're both only children.'

'That's exactly it, Roland. I was never happier at Cambridge than when I slammed my door shut and wasn't available. I'm glad you and I are on the same wavelength.'

'Piers, about last night. I hope I haven't established a pattern for you.'

'It's your concern for me that makes you so special. Look, I am me. *Je suis moi!* I'm a rational being, and I do what I want. Nobody changes that. Three cheers for free spirits!'

'I was just concerned, after those rather no-nonsense, defensive-sounding hetero pronouncements you made earlier - at Cambridge and so on.'

'My God, you make it sound like heavy artillery! Forget those. I was just buying a bit of time. You see, I had no idea what I might have unleashed in digging you up again.'

'And you can live with what we've both unleashed?'

'What do you think?'

The road lifted them up out of the bowl, looping and rising past the ruins of barrack buildings. Skeletal rocks showed through the brownish earth which, bitter and plantless, covered everything but the road itself. Although it was not long after nine o clock, the sun was already stabbing down at them.

'The book says the Col de la Bonette is the highest in Europe. D'you think we'll need oxygen?'

Suddenly, at the base of the huge pyramid before them, there was a choice of route. 'A droite,' said Piers, and they found themselves on an even narrower road, with immense drops to their right. Roland inched the car along. 'I pray we don't meet a coach coming the other way.'

Piers wanted to get out and take photos. 'Let's go to the top. It's only "une demie-heure à pied, aller-retour."

A moon-walk without a moon. At the top, they were both panting, their lungs fit to burst.

The panorama of mountain ranges was never-ending. 'Look, that's the Pelvoux, over near Briançon. Nearly thirteen thousand feet.' There was no breeze as yet, and they were both perspiring in the sunshine.

'Just the two of us,' said Roland suddenly.

'Not even a priest to take our photo.'

'My camera has a timer release.' He set it up on the viewing table, positioned Piers, pressed the button and darted back. Goaded on by the fact that the boy was wearing the briefest of shorts today, he clasped him tightly and, after a few delicious seconds, heard a distant click.

'I wish I could get a postcard of this, to send to Mother.'

You'd certainly better not give her a copy of what I've just snapped!

The little road crawled all round the cone on which they had just been standing, joined its other arm and then passed a shrine to the Virgin. Piers took a picture of the star-studded image of Notre Dame. 'Typical piece of French bad taste!'

'Don't mock! The man at Guillestre told us that we should only attempt this col if the angels were on our side, and it seems they were.'

'We aren't down, yet!'

The road slipped gently below the ridge for a while, lulling them into false security. The Col des Fourches, with its steep sections and a succession of tight curves, provided the last real hurdle. Fortunately there was no other traffic at all.

'Tour de France country,' remarked Piers, tapping his knees with his hands. 'Shouldn't mind riding *down* it.'

The narrow valley of the Tinée began to acquire trees, and the road finally settled down to behave itself. Even so, Roland did not hurry. Nice lay somewhere in front, but Nice could still wait a while.

Larch trees granted them patches of shade, primitive hamlets showed up along their way. 'How do these people exist?'

Roland was all set to answer 'They eat and drink and make love,' but could not combat the feeling that their return to civilisation would bring down barriers of decorum again. Was our coming together up there what the vulgar world calls a one-off or dare I hope that this closeness might be repeated?

Reaching St. Sauveur at eleven-thirty, they were hungry and thirsty. No hotel, no restaurant, but a shop where they got bread, fruit, chocolate and beer.

'Hey,' said Piers, 'what about that beer we put in the lake to cool? It's still there!'

'If you think I'm going to drive all the way back up that road!'

They pulled off into some shade lower down, and devoured the food as if they had never eaten before. Roland looked at Piers. 'Would you say our relationship has survived?'

'What do you mean? Survived what?'

'Well, in a lot of cases the physical would have killed it stone dead. It only succeeds with one in a million.'

'Then we are the one in a million,' he said, but without defiance. 'We have come through it.'

'But now we return to the world as completely different from what we were when we began this journey.'

'I don't know if we're that different. We had all the makings of this inside us at Wharnley. It just needed something to fuse it together.'

'Do we meet on all possible planes, then, Piers?'

'Yes, I think we do.'

As they continued down the lovely valley, the ferocity of the heat assailed them, but nothing could spoil their shared bliss.

At one o' clock, they joined a main road, and Piers began to get excited. 'If we were Alexander and that lot, we'd shout *"thalatta"* as soon as we caught sight of it.'

The sea, the Mediteranean, lies somewhere just ahead, and I am suddenly in dread of arriving. 'Piers...'

'Yes?'

'No, it's all right.'

The Var valley was charged with lorries and, as it approached Nice, increasingly industrialised. The temperature was devastating, though they drove with their windows right down.

Ahead, an aeroplane was coming in to land. 'There's the airport, and look, Roland, there's the sea!'

They followed signs saying "Côte dAzur", and were suddenly on a broad, tree-lined carriageway running along the sea-front, lined on the landward side with elegant buildings. Roland slackened his speed, and then found a place to park in the shade of a palm-tree.

'Amazing,' shouted Piers. 'Let's go for a swim!'

He's like a small boy, like André even. I'm glad I brought my respectable trunks!

The light over the Mediterranean was soft, the sea frisky in the afternoon breeze. They grabbed their swimming things and got down on to the sand. Swimmers and sunbathers were everywhere. Piers tried to ignore the topless females lying, like seals, on their stomachs. They found a spot to sit on, and got changed.

'I've never swum in the Med before!' Piers called out.

I wish I hadn't had to lock my camera away for safety. His body has begun to get a tan. Look at him, prancing into the water, like the liberated spirit he is. Piers, we have known each other's body and we have not ruined everything, not at all. We have a future together, provided, of course, you don't hate me for what is about to happen.

They swam far out, looking back at the superb curve of the bay with its fine buildings and green hills.

'We made it, we made it!' shouted Piers, and tried to duck Roland. They grappled with each other, both went under, emerged spluttering and laughing, and struck out for the beach.

Aeons ago, we did this in the sea off "Stella Maris". And, on that same beach, all alone, like a stricken god, broken, I clawed in desperation at the sand.

'When we've got dressed, why don't we celebrate with a beer?' God, I need a drink!

'But we've only just arrived. What time are we due at the hotel? Where is it, anyway?'

'I told them mid-afternoon. It's not far.'

When they got back to the car, Roland said 'Best togs,' and took a white suit out of his case.

'Mais c'est très Aschenbach!' exclaimed Piers.

'Do you think so? It's comfortable in this sort of heat.'

'Can't I wear my shorts, then?' He submitted with good grace, and put on a clean T-shirt and a pair of light trousers.

They crossed the road and sat down outside a café.

'How long are we going to be in Nice? When do I actually fly back to England? When will I see you again, Roland?'

His questions, like André's, tear at my heart. I try to parry, pass them off humorously, without actually answering them - allude instead to the imminent surprise.

My heart is beating again, as we drive along the Promenade des Anglais. I've got it wrong, I know I have. It's going to be a *fiasco*.

The avenue became the Quai des États-Unis and, just when it began to swing to the right, round the headland, they turned into the grounds of a hotel tucked in at the foot of the hill. Shady gardens, sunblinds down. Piers knew at once that Roland had picked their classiest place of all.

'Sorry, but it's bags better than Geneva.'

'That's hardly difficult, is it?' He handed the car keys to the porter, who directed a boy in uniform to carry in the luggage. They went into a lobby that was deliciously cool. Marble floors, varnished woodwork, *art nouveau* lamps.

People were sitting about, taking tea or sipping drinks in a big lounge which opened on to a terrace overlooking the sea.

'Can we go out there and look at the view?' said Piers eagerly.

Roland followed him, but then banged into him from behind, because Piers had stopped dead in his tracks. A lady in an elegant blue silk dress, who had been standing by the parapet, turned to look at them.

'Mother!' Piers whipped round and, momentarily, there was anger in his face. But then, as he looked back at Mrs Moriston, who was walking towards them, his expression softened. 'Roland, this is your doing!' There was humour already in his voice. He gave his mother a hug, received a kiss in return, and then recovered his Cambridge manners. 'Mother, this is Roland.'

'I know. We spoke on the telephone, didn't we, Mr Millan? I have a very big "thank you" to say to you.'

Roland solemnly shook hands with her, grateful for the protection afforded by formality, then said 'I'll see about the rooms and the luggage,' and fled, leaving them together.

At first, at the reception desk, his mind seized up. He scarcely knew his own name, let alone what day it was, knew only that their improbable love was secure, after all. The discipline of filling in the *fiche* slowly restored him, and he allowed himself to be shown up to his room, where he stepped out on to the balcony.

The sea was a brilliant strip of light before him. He could hear seagulls, the excited shouts of children on the *plage* and in the water. The breeze blew playfully in his face and he found he was laughing and crying at one and the same time.